About the author

Tony Bryan is working hard on the final edit of *Baltimore. Book 3* and, in discussion with Pegasus, hopes to have the completed trilogy in the market in the spring of this year.

Meanwhile he continues to push for a breakthrough in screen-writing with further success of *The Decline of Daisy de Melker* awarded top five status and achieved an 'Honourable Mention' at the Los Angeles Movie Awards script writing competition earlier this year.

The screenplay for *Baltimore. Book 1* is completed and has been selected for the final top-five in the Autumn Screenplay Awards in Los Angeles. This is the first competition entered for *Baltimore* which bodes well for the prospect of a future movie or TV mini-series.

Next project is *The Tailor Spy*, a novel based on real happenings in Worcester, England, during the final battle of the English Civil War in 1651. Both novel and screenplay will be in the market by the middle of next year.

Tony is busy marketing and networking and has book signings and festival appearances lined-up.

BALTIMORE BOOK 2

Tony Bryan

BALTIMORE BOOK 2

Vanguard Press

VANGUARD PAPERBACK

© Copyright 2020
Tony Bryan

A CIP catalogue record for this title is
available from the British Library.

ISBN 9781784656 82-9

*Vanguard Press is an imprint of
Pegasus Elliot MacKenzie Publishers Ltd.*
www.pegasuspublishers.com

First Published in 2020

**Vanguard Press
Sheraton House Castle Park
Cambridge England**

Printed & Bound in Great Britain

Dedication

I dedicate this book to my wife, Pauline. We have been together a long time and I will always be grateful for her endurance, devotion and support, particularly as mine is such a selfish preoccupation.

Also to my brother John, whose journey was cut short.

Hold your head up to the sky, every flower must live, and die,
but the story will never end!*

* From the song *The World Will be You Friend* by John Bryan

Author's Note

The Sack of Baltimore was an historic incident which actually took place in 1631, when it is recorded that Moroccan raiders, led by a Dutch Sea captain, carried out a substantial raid on the Irish fishing village. Many of the villagers were killed and many more were carried off, destined for the slave markets on the Barbary Coast. The community was largely destroyed.

In the early 2000s, a sunken ship was discovered off the Irish coast which was strongly believed to have been the very ship which used to carry out the raid. It was reading the story of this discovery that inspired me to write my own, completely fictitious account of what might have happened. This became my novel *Baltimore* – the full story told in three parts, books 1, 2 and 3.

I intentionally placed my story in the 1730s, approximately one hundred years after the original event. I was intent of delivering a far-reaching saga which spanned a vivid period of history. Whilst the 1600s were turbulent years, the major events – such as the expansion of the British Empire, the Seven Years War and the establishment of Colonies leading to the American War of Independence – held, for me, a more vivid and identifiable period in which to set my story. I hope the reader, and particularly those of the South- West Cork Region, will forgive my deviation.

Tony Bryan

Chapter 1
Daemon

Sailing from the Niger River into the Atlantic, once losing sight of land, was a new experience way beyond the imagination. The dark blue-black of the heavy ocean different somehow from the expanse of the Mediterranean in texture and resonance.

Although Daemon was aware that hundreds, perhaps thousands had already made the journey during the seventeenth and earlier in the eighteenth century, it still gripped him in awe and wonderment.

The ship was bound for another world, one he had heard only little about. The imagination began and stopped on a scale which was based on familiarity. It could never have grasped the vastness of the seas that lay ahead, the time it took to cross them or the ferocity of the swell when weather impacted every moment of every day upon their existence.

The first days were filled with short bursts of activity, bedding down the cargo of African humanity, feeding and watering them, experiencing the first human frailties of the compacted, humid confinement of their inhuman surroundings.

Daemon had not been comfortable in his own mind with the concept of slavery. Hadn't his own land, his own remote circle of existence in coastal Ireland already been destroyed by the greed and lust for empowerment and profit? Hadn't the love of his life, his beautiful, innocent, fresh-faced young girlfriend been snatched away into enslavement? Now he had pledged himself to his friend and mentor, in this venture to the new world with a prime cargo of — human beings!

His future, as far as he dare consider, was now fated to the life of a slaver, driving the ship and the souls it contained across this vast abyss, to a future of bondage, humility and dependence.

His thoughts were eclipsed by a shrill cry from below decks, where he knew the female negroes were confined. One of the crew, encamped upon the balustrade adjacent to the helmsman, stirred, considered attending the outcry, then slumped back into his position.

This had been a calmer morning. First light had broken only moments earlier and the sun rose laconically upon the eastern horizon. The daylight was barely able to penetrate the shadows of the lifting darkness, and certainly would not have leant any light to the covered enclosures below decks.

Nonetheless, Daemon decided to investigate upon the second, more muted, but equally terror-stricken scream. Then a third, then a rising babble. Others, in the 'male' enclosure, became alarmed and began stifled murmurings.

Removing the hatch and descending the first few steps saw Daemon stop and wait. His eyes had to adjust to the darkness to be of any use to him. After a moment, he ducked his head down further and dropped quietly onto the lower deck. Following the sound of strangled sobbing and new moaning coming from the area to his right, he ducked under a beam and could make out shapes in the gloom. Chains, swinging gently, hanging like abandoned vines, partially blocked his view.

Three women, their simple white rags adorning their upper and lower bodies, gathered around another, more perpendicular shape. They appeared almost as if in prayer, holding their dark arms over their heads as if imploring divinity to intervene.

Close enough now to touch the gathering, having picked his way through other awakened bodies, Daemon could now make out sufficiently to see a young woman, barely post-puberty, hanging from a beam. Her tongue hung limply from one corner of her mouth, her head slumped over, loosely on a long, now flaxen, neck. The chain around her neck dug into her flesh so completely that two or three links were not visible.

Reaching out to touch her face, Daemon realised she was stone dead. The cold, unnatural feel of her skin told him she had been hanging for some hours. He sat motionless on his haunches for some moments, unable to withdraw his hand, or his eyes, from the pathetic, lifeless form.

Turning towards the first, then other pleading eyes, he shook his head sadly and brought fresh cries and anguished denials from the gathering.

A hand touched his shoulder, another his knee. Grasping, pleading hands implored him to do something. All he could do was to shake his head further and quietly mutter, 'No good, no good!'

One after another, the swelling crowd picked up the phrase, 'Ngo goo. Ngo goo!' The shaking of the head, accompanied by these few words, had come to represent anything and everything which signified a problem. The only words of communication thus far exchanged and accepted by both crew and cargo, 'No good' represented all that was not well aboard the *Durham*.

A burial of sorts was arranged, and Daemon contrived with John Standing to provide a short ceremony; defining which of the females were related or in any way connected to the dead girl, they allowed a party of seven on to the deck, said a short prayer and lowered the enshrouded figure over the side.

A strained but tuneful voice chanted out a melodic line. For some moments it hung in the air and the assembly had begun to break up, when another shrill cry interrupted. Several now repeated the chant and then all came to a sort of chorus. The lament was tuneful and rhythmic, and with a calm sea and little noise from the rigging and the deck boards, the 'song' continued, over and over again, but with the slightest alteration with each attempt. Harmonies intruded, demanding the attention of the crew focused now on the gathering.

None aboard the ship had ever heard such a mournful, but beautiful communion of sound. The song penetrated the air and emanated emotions which normally lay well below the surface of the hardened, weather-beaten crew. A chant of pure African origin introduced itself to all of those on board, and a sort of reluctant admiration permeated throughout the ship.

Uninterrupted, the song may have continued for hours, but Standing, aware of the demands of the day that lay ahead, gave out a gruff, throaty sound in the direction of the choir, and the elder of them turned, nodded and gathered up the others with a gentle arm, guiding them towards the hatch.

From that moment, the seed of change had been planted among the masters and crew of the *Durham*.

This would be no routine slave crossing and ejaculation of a human cargo onto the shores of a distant and hostile community. This would be a passage different from those that had gone before and may become a blueprint for others that followed.

It began over the evening meal when Daemon, having sat quietly through the courses and supped little wine, finally spoke out to his friend.

'John, my conscience is ill at ease; you may have not ...' he had been about to say 'noticed', but there had been no need to complete the line. Standing intervened with a hand, held in front of his face as he responded.

'Daemon, my friend! I feel this every bit as much as you! We are dealing with a cargo of human beings, not animals! I know you feel you are not cut-out for such an undertaking — but it is that very fact that tells me it is essential that you remain with us and make this a voyage with a difference.'

'John, please! I thank you for your words, of course. But believe me, I have no intention of abandoning this mission. Quite the opposite: I would not want to be any place on earth other than where I am today. I feel I am in the right place. I have work to do. I want to make changes, to do right by these people. But my loyalty to you is unaltered. I want your interests to be fulfilled in every way. Sorry, that was quite a speech, and I... I thank you for listening...'

'My word! Your passion almost frightens me. I admire you for taking a stand. Believe me, we are not at odds here, my friend. We simply have to find a way to make this journey *matter*. Not only to ourselves, but to them, and the thousands that will follow them. I believe in *you*, Daemon! You have an innocent truth about you that drives you on. You know instinctively what is right and do not worry about how it is to be achieved. Well, let's see if we can make a plan.'

Daemon stood. 'John, if we could... do something! Manage to get these people safely to the New World, see them secure, in places they choose to be, instead of imprisonment or whatever it is they were destined for. I don't want to cause you to lose out, to lose "face", or anything... I want the best for John Standing... but if you just allow me, I think I can make a difference for them below decks... I have to try.'

'My friend, I'm right with you. Don't worry, we will find a way; the crew will go along — they want profit, they will have it! But we will do it your way. Whatever that might be.'

'I think I can talk to them. Not well, properly, not yet. But I think communication is possible.'

Chapter 2
Communication

Daemon considered for a moment what they had thus far achieved. They had set in motion a range of simple tasks which brought the male negroes on to the deck, in rotating groups, to set them to swabbing and swilling down. It had been only partly successful, but better, thought Daemon, than no activities at all!

'We've made a start. Let's keep on with the daily chores. It is our best chance to communicate with them for the moment.'

'We can build from there. We have to get them covered up. Even the males are a distraction for the crew, and the females — my God, not even the Pope in Rome could turn his eyes from them! It takes me an hour to recover every day when they have shown themselves in the mornings! I can't clear my head until I have forced myself up to the crow's nest.'

The two men laughed and agreed that there was a powerful attraction to the women captives that no red-blooded man could resist without a fight. 'We must control those things; we must find a way to make the females feel secure and free from threat.' They agreed again that the task ahead was mountainous, but determined between them to turn the tide, and that the *Durham* would be a slave-ship with a difference.

Days passed, and the routine was resumed: the black females were allowed on deck for hosing and washing their coverings, such as they were, but Daemon rigged up a screen. Behind it, the women were allowed to disrobe and shower each other. Day by day they became accustomed to the ritual, and instead of enduring the formerly shameful and threatening process, began to enjoy the experience. Gradually, their grumbling turned to chatter as girlish laughter filled the air.

The sounds emanating from this daily ritual became a heart-warming and refreshing interlude for Daemon. Even the crew grudgingly acknowledged that this was a sensible and civilised process.

Another word became routinely utilised among the occupants of the *Durham*. Along with 'Ngoo ngoo' for all that was wrong — 'Gnoo Good' — followed by vigorous nodding of the head — became the normal response for all that was acceptable.

Chapter 3
Amerigo de Ville

During the second week into the voyage, sail was spotted on the horizon.

Baptiste, the gruff Frenchman who generally spoke for the crew, had proven a strong and resilient ally when difficulties arose. His willingness to respond to the call for help or need for organisation had led naturally to him being given the description of a 'First Mate', if not actually in name. He brushed off attempts to provide him with a title, but performed all of the tasks normally demanded.

Upon first meeting, this was a man to command grudging respect. He stood only five feet in height, thickset and rangy, a paunch betraying his lusty appetites, but formidable upper body strength evidence of, if not an athletic frame, then power gained by a spell of some repetitive hard labour.

A number of scars, one in particular across his right eye, which reached into his hairline, told of times of conflict or military service. He spoke little of his past, but rumour had it that he had escaped a French penal colony in Africa.

Thick, sandy hair, plaid 'rope-like' and pulled together with a strip of black leather, completed his make-up. He spoke little, but conveyed much in gesture and had demonstrated a level of dependability.

This morning, he burst into the cabin to alert Standing. 'Monsieur — ship on the horizon!' He turned, leading John and Daemon up onto the for'ard deck. Leaping on to the bow rail, Daemon clambered up two rungs of rigging to improve his view. Fixing a glass to one eye, he pointed in the starboard direction, before passing the glass to Standing.

Standing in turn took up a vantage position, before nodding an acknowledgment. 'Three-master. A Barque; might be Spanish. We will fly our French-Moroccan flag and refrain from any aggression. Daemon, man the guns, but keep low until the situation develops. Baptiste! Two or three men to the poop deck — routine swabbing, but keep small arms under canvas, where you may reach them if needed. We will continue our course, which will take us to within a league or two of her larb'd flank. So all other hands to the starb'd guns!'

The two vessels closed on one another for an hour, until a signal came from the east-bound ship. She was certainly intent on contact. Under-manned as they were, those on the *Durham* had to hope and pray for a peaceful encounter.

Standing motioned to Daemon to join him at the wheel. 'I have been thinking about the possibilities of trading with our intruder. We will have to wait and see what she is carrying. I thought maybe some muslin would be of use. The females below deck could fashion some clothing with a bit of guidance from the sailors. If they are coming from the West Indies, perhaps they have on board someone who has learned the dialogue of our Africans?'

'Let's hope we can gain something from the encounter. Perhaps one or two hands willing to sail with the *Durham*?'

'Let's make our approach, but be diligent, above all. Let us signal that we would welcome them alongside.'

The sea calmed, enabling the two ships to close until just a hundred yards separated them. An overdressed captain stood, almost showing a gesture of indifference to the potential difficulties of the encounter. John Standing stood on the deck, both hands on his hips, his white blouse billowing gently on the breeze and his tricorn hat in place, showing respect towards his opposite number.

The bewigged captain made a gesture with his free hand, whilst his other stayed close to a pistol at his hip. 'Your servant, sir. I am Amerigo de Ville Baloroso of Lagos, Portugal! Master of the *Santiago*. Perhaps we have met on another occasion?'

'John Granville Fitzwilliam, Earl of Olney, at your service.' John used his elder brother's title for impact. 'I somehow think I might have remembered had we met on a prior occasion, sir.'

With his right hand, John swept his tricorn from his head down below his left knee and the two men, sufficiently impressed with one another, arranged that a boat would convey the Portuguese across to the *Durham*.

A line was strung out to hold the two vessels in proximity, although they acknowledged that the encounter must be a brief one, that a squall of even low velocity would bring about separation, which could take days to sufficiently re-align.

De Ville dropped easily over the rail and offered a hand in greeting. Daemon was introduced by Standing as my 'partner', and a short, stocky, shaven-headed companion introduced by de Ville as 'Rinaldi, my physician', took their hands in turn. De Ville proposed that any on board suffering an ailment might be treated by Rinaldi, a 'magician' with potions and affectations.

Standing politely declined the offer, considering that leading the 'physician' around their facilities might reveal a little too much about their strength, leaving them vulnerable.

'Come, come, my friend, you have a cargo of slaves, am I right? Surely, they are suffering ailments of all the usual kind? Allow my man to provide some advice, if not medication.'

'Let us talk first. I do have certain needs, for which you may proffer a suitable remedy. Come, let me offer you a glass of port — perhaps you have exhausted your stock on your long voyage! I am sure *Port* is your preference, although you fly the flag of France.'

'A simple diversion. I use it to advantage on occasion! Meanwhile indeed, sirrah, the dignitaries of the Argentine have taken a great liking to our precious libation! I have traded every last bottle in Buenos Aires, for commodities of which they appear to have in abundance.' Waving gold-encrusted fingers in the air, de Ville added, 'I am sure you know to what I refer.'

After two neat helpings from an elegant bottle of Fortified wine, de Ville warmed significantly to the company, becoming quite overt with comments and anecdotes of his adventures. He had transported laces and wines to the developing society of the Argentine and was returning with a substantial collection of old Aztec gold:

ornaments and adornments which would be melted down for the benefit of the Portuguese Crown.

De Ville had correctly assessed that Standing posed no threat to his ship or to his cargo, and in turn he conceded that there was little benefit in taking the slaver, and its hold full of Africans, back to its origins.

He assumed rightly, that, other than provisions for the voyage, there was little else of value aboard the *Durham*; though a fine ship in itself might be worth the fight, he decided against it in favour, perhaps, of an enjoyable diversion.

He was pleased to relax and enjoy their discourse with no other agenda. Indeed, he was quick to extend the hand of friendship, offering assistance of any kind in order to make their passage less arduous.

Standing made his request at this stage for muslin or calico cloth, which was met with fascinated interest from de Ville. 'My friend, you want to adorn your females? Hah! They should be clothed in Barbados before auction, but clothing them during the voyage? Surely it would be a waste of good cloth? The fabrics chafe on their skin, become matted and threadbare with friction. Believe me, it would not work, my friend. Whatever your intention, I would advise strongly against clothing them.'

'I take your point, senor! My friend and I have a struggle with conscience. These are human beings, and we wish to treat them as such. How can we alleviate their suffering? Why, even after a few days, their skin begins to break, and rawness shows on their knees, their elbows and ankles.'

'Yes,' Rinaldi interrupted, 'these are the elements they use to steady themselves when the ship rocks. They would roll around all night if it were not for this. You have to find a way for them to remain upright, or to take such regular exercise that they spend less time in the prone position. Mind you, this is not easy. You have to keep discipline. Besides, their wounds do heal very quickly. The skin, however, grows coarse. The lustre is lost and so their value is diminished. You must give them exercise and allow them to rub in tallow, something to waterproof the skin and yet keep them *supple*.'

'Your advice is well received, although easier said than done! How we achieve these things will truly be a challenge. I do not have the resources. Perhaps, I may enquire as to your strength? Would you consider letting some of your crewmen transfer to the *Durham* and journey on in our company?'

'Hah! I expected this, my friend. I see you are ten or twelve men short of a good crew. I had been giving some thought myself as to which of them I could spare and which of them might accept. But I conclude that two, maybe three at the most, may consider such a proposal, and then only for the right incentive, of course!'

'I am most gratified, senor... I would like to make a deal.'

'Ah, not so fast, my friend! I would, of course, require suitable compensation, ahem, for myself...'

'Naturally... we would pay you for your inconvenience. Indeed, were you to facilitate a crew member with an understanding of the native language, then, even more so, our gratitude would be unbounded.'

'That is also within my compass, but first we must come to terms. Perhaps myself, and the Doctori, could inspect the cargo whilst you consider your end of the bargain?'

Standing was cordial in his response, grasping the opportunity for time to consider his options. 'Daemon, perhaps you would be kind enough to conduct our guests into the hold. I am sure a few moments will be sufficient for me to consider a proposal.'

Daemon held out a hand, gesturing for de Ville and Rinaldi to follow. Down below, with all hatches completely uncovered, allowing both light and air to pass freely, the hold did not present the usual fetid, suffocating atmosphere.

Some of the women sat together, working each other's hair into braided tentacles. The males seemed almost playful in their counting games, resembling 'rock-paper-string', which in truth were actually quite intense games of chance, upon which the promise of high stakes often rode.

The Africans were not displaying any great degree of discomfort, whilst Rinaldi paid particular attention to elbows and knees. The entire focus then turned to the young females. Checking their eyes, teeth and the shapes of the torso in particular, he muttered once or twice into a vacant ear and received recognition on both occasions.

De Ville eyed up the cargo as a cattleman might an auction of calves. He seemed to draw his contemplations to a conclusion, nodding his head, in satisfaction at the quality.

Rinaldi joined him in the nodding ritual and by mutual consent they made for the steps and returned to the upper decks.

Re-joining Standing, Rinaldi exchanged a few words aside to his captain, before turning to Standing.

Bowing slightly, he began, 'Ahem, we are most impressed with the stock you have aboard, sir. Most impressed! Ashanti and, erm, perhaps some Akan...? I know these people.'

'I also have a modicum of understanding of the African tongue. Although it may depend greatly on the regional dialect as to whether I am able to grasp their meaning. In this case, I have managed to ascertain that the tongue used by those east of Sierra Leone appears to achieve recognition.'

'Therefore, I offer my own services,' Rinaldi continued. 'I have no connections awaiting my arrival in Europe and I have a great affection for the Caribbean. Besides, the Marquise has done with me for the time being.

'Two other reliable men, of my choice, will join us and gladly become members of your company! Suitable remuneration will be agreed upon reaching our destination, which I assume is Barbados?'

Standing rose. 'This is a most generous offer, gentlemen! We are indeed heading for the Blue Mountain regions.' He glanced from one to the other. 'May I enquire as to what sort of payment the senor would require in return for the loss of his physician, and two members of his crew? I have to confess, I have been unable to conjure up a suitable proposal. We have little gold on our outward journey.'

Rinaldi continued to speak for de Ville, who had assumed a pose of indifference once again, seeming to wish the negotiation, and the visit, to a hasty conclusion. 'The senor wishes to acquire some of the female stock to return with him to his homeland and enjoy the comforts of his substantial hacienda up in the hills above Lagos. They would serve as housemaids and chambermaids to the household.'

Standing looked in Daemon's direction and caught his friend's instant reaction of disapproval. However, he understood that if there were to be a trade, then perhaps this was inevitably the currency with which they would reach agreement.

'No males? Strong, capable and intelligent males? You wish to take females instead?'

De Ville interjected 'My Friend Rinaldi is correct. I saw Ashanti. These females make very good "housemaids", shall we say! But the males can be quite rebellious at times. I have no need of them.'

'Well if that is your preference, I suppose I could offer the choice of two of my post-pubescent females for your consideration.'

Without turning his gaze from the distant horizon, de Ville held up a hand, displaying all five digits. 'Cinco... five!'

'Five? Why, senor, I feel your request a little unreasonable' Five of my cargo of less than one hundred females represents a heavy price and a serious depletion of profit. I thought two of my prime specimens sufficient, even three, given the unquestionable value which senor Rinaldi brings. But five? I feel the senor is taking advantage of the situation.'

'I am not an unreasonable man, Your Lordship. I am known for my fairness in all dealings, but this is a small price to pay for the benefits I offer. I will make your decision easier and extend to you ten bales of muslin cloth, as a make-weight. Are you not impressed? You will be able to clothe your chattels like Barbary whores on a Saturday night! Make your decision and let's have done with it; I feel the swell and there is weather on the horizon.'

Standing also felt that the tide of their relationship might be on the turn. He thought for a moment longer but, in the end, reached out a hand to de Ville and shook on the deal.

Five prime young women were cut free and, protesting beyond expectation, they were herded into a boat and the line was cast free of the *Durham* and tethered to the launch.

Daemon watched as the boat bobbed on the waves. A second boat was closing on their larb'd side, containing Rinaldi and two bronzed, fair-haired crewmen. They were welcomed aboard and made comfortable as the sun set rapidly on the western horizon.

Daemon's gaze remained fixed on the departing craft as it bumped into the timbers of the *Santiago*, watching as the five females were absorbed in the gloom into the bowels of the strange vessel. He dare not imagine to what fate they had been condemned, but made an effort to console himself that those bound for the New World might arrive in better health and spirits for the sacrifices of their departed friends.

Chapter 4
Vive La Difference

Under full sail, the *Durham* made real headway over the following five or six days. Rinaldi proved an amiable companion and a valuable asset in attending and administering to the natives. He was enabled free access to the cargo hold and spent much time checking and soothing the scrapes and rawness suffered.

He took great care to make sure a daily ration of fresh water was consumed by all and organised a more extensive exercise routine on a twice-daily basis. The hard work involved in the running of the ship was dwarfed by the ritual of caring for the slaves.

Daemon was involved around the clock: he performed every task and took up every shortfall. He was on constant alert to the behaviour of the crew, the well-being of the Africans and the speedy progress of the ship.

He picked up words and sounds of communication from Rinaldi and became 'mother', 'father' and teacher to the slaves.

They loved to sing, or chant, as on most occasions the few variants were dropped progressively until the chosen theme was uttered over and over again. A trance-like state was achieved until tiredness or the rolling of the ship disrupted their energies.

Some of these chants were led by the more passive or, as Daemon considered, prepossessed individuals, who seemed to be respected by others. These were the one's upon which Daemon chose to focus his attentions, trying to help them understand some of the words: 'day' or 'night', 'sun and 'moon', 'light' and 'dark' — he found that their own version was often very different, making it difficult to relate or associate sounds and meanings.

Rinaldi proved very patient, almost caring, once it had been established that they were serious in treating this cargo differently. He gave the natives guidance and instructions when Daemon and the crew were arranging exercise; then the understanding of the terms 'respect' or 'behaviour' required by their captors. It was the prime necessity that order was maintained.

The crew generally accepted this strange process without complaint. As long as their own supplies were plentiful and their 'grog' dutifully administered, they would often stand around listening to the singing, particularly from the females, but their attentions were, in the main, harmless.

Sven and Eric, the two blond, sun-drenched members joining from the *Santiago*, were 'unnatural', as instantly recognised by Baptiste when they hopped on board in Rinaldi's wake. Baptiste approached and put a hand on the neck of the first, as he was introduced.

Athletic and broad at the shoulders, shirt open to the waist, with a tight belt drawing together striped pantaloons, Sven presented a colourful and impressive figure. Eric followed, almost matching him in every way, equally handsome, but with shorter, snatched-back hair. The two invited a string of comments from the crew.

Eric gently removed Baptiste's hands from the neck of his friend, waving a finger in his face, and he made it quite clear that Sven was *his* 'possession' and no other hands would be welcome!

Baptiste laughed loudly and turned to the crew, offering a number of effeminate gestures, which conveyed that these two were easy game and might provide some entertainment during the long days ahead.

Within hardly the blink of an eye, Eric had the blade of a fine and hefty horn-mounted dagger at the Frenchman's throat, leaving him in no doubt that any further reference to their status or future well-being might result in a swift and dynamic response.

Baptiste decided to laugh off the incident, easing the tension, until the dagger was returned to its scabbard at the waist-band resting in the small of Sven's back.

'Vive la difference!' Baptiste uttered almost inaudibly with a shrug of his shoulders.

Immediately, the dagger was at his throat again. In a broken, Scandinavian-influenced English, Eric asked calmly, 'What did you say?'

Baptiste, not taking his eye from his assailant for one second, returned with another less demonstrative shrug, 'Vive la difference!' Repeated this time so that those in the vicinity could hear quite clearly. A moment of deathly silence descended on the gathering, with Standing closing his hand on the pistol at his waist.

'Vive la difference?' Eric repeated the saying, then a second time, copying the Frenchman's accent.

He suddenly nodded and laughed loudly. Sven caught on, quickly joining him, and the two became engulfed in laughter affecting the whole of the assembly, until even Baptiste realised the lighter side of the situation.

31

Eric replaced the dagger. 'Vive la difference! Ha! Vive la difference!' Patting the Frenchman on the back, he proceeded to put an arm around his companion and together offered greetings to the crew like long-lost friends. At first hesitant, the crew returned hand-shakes and back-slapping until all were introduced and the two new members absorbed into the company.

Standing and Daemon exchanged glances which portrayed their own, mildly amused acceptance of this little twist to the situation.

'I think perhaps de Ville knew exactly what he was doing when he chose our Nordic friends as the ones to join us. Indeed, the Old Dog is not without a sense of humour,' Standing laughed, whilst Daemon, again finding himself short of a sensible comment, just shook his head and grinned widely.

Chapter 5
The Wind Doth Blow

Eleven days out to sea and the weather began to turn.

The Africans had great difficulty walking around the deck as the *Durham* bucked and plunged into the heavy swell. Many slipped and slid across the decks, finding it difficult to regain their feet when exercising. Fresh water spilled from the barrels, losing precious quantities into the brine.

The crew struggled to keep them moving along safety lines which their hands were un-used to handling. There was no option but to return them to the hold and to batten down the hatches.

A sinister low chant of protest broke out among the natives, which could be heard only as long, drawn-out droning beneath the sound of the crashing waves.

A long day passed, with the ship making little headway. The North and South Atlantic currents seemed to clash together, creating a stormy cauldron. Night came and the seas were unrelenting.

Vomiting and piteous wailing broke out universally below decks. The Africans had hardly developed 'sea-legs' and were ill-equipped to cope with a storm.

In the hold they huddled together, but the movement of the ship meant that each would have to try to hold onto a beam or rail whilst clinging desperately to each other.

Vomit and urine swilled around the hold, along with sea water, pouring incessantly through every crack and through the gaps around the hatches. Desperate cries, screaming from the females, replaced the low moaning.

No indignity was spared as slop buckets were upturned, grappling limbs clung desperately to the timber benches and all order was lost.

A new substance mingled with the swirling mess around their ankles. Blood! Blood from cuts and grazes. Blood being passed by internal distress among the women, blood being vomited up by raw intestines.

There was suffering and distress in every quarter, which neither Daemon nor John Standing nor the crew could do anything about.

Another day passed with little respite. An attempt at feeding and watering the cargo was abandoned when more and more provisions ended up abandoned and discarded, adding to the disgusting stench that had developed throughout the hold.

Standing battened down everything that could previously have been a moving object. Sail was lashed fast to the rigging and the ship continued to plunge and roll on high-crested waves.

At the end of the fourth day, the edge of the overhanging blackness was clearly visible above the horizon. Almost as a shelf or a lid partly shifted from its place on a container. Beyond was a yellow-tinged blueness that was clear sky, framing a sunset that was already beyond the far horizon.

The blueness grew until it was half of the visible sky, darker now as the light of the day faded. But a clear sky brought an eerie calm which spelled the end of the storm and the opportunity of desperately needed respite.

The movement of the ship eased to a rhythmic roll. A breeze gently ruffled the sail where it had become loose on its moorings. Standing ordered full sail to be set and the ship picked up pace on the breeze and began to follow the glow left by the setting sun deep to the western horizon.

The babble relented below decks, becoming a low drone of exhausted murmurings.

Daemon began preparation for untying the hatches, his intention being to feed and water the Africans. But Standing called to him, motioning that the situation should be left for the moment.

Under sail, the *Durham* resumed its stately progress and made good headway. In the relative quiet after the storm, Standing was able to speak in a normal tone for the first time in days when he called Daemon to his side.

'We should leave them. Let them rest for now. We should spend the next few days recovering the ground we have lost.'

Daemon raised a hand as if to interrupt.

'No, listen to me, my friend. We may have been blown miles from our course. We may even have lost many miles. I will attempt to re-establish our position over the next twenty-four hours. Meanwhile, all hands need to be engaged in righting the ship for the remainder of the voyage, for making up as much time as we possibly can. Allow Rinaldi to administer to the Africans. We must focus on our task.'

Standing was firm, leaving Daemon with little room for protest. With reluctance, they both turned to matters in hand.

The crew were whipped into a frenzy of activity in switching fore and aft to counter shifts in the wind. Experienced hands turned to the skills learned over arduous years on the high seas.

Daemon was glad of the addition to the ship's complement of two agile and adept sailors like Eric and Sven, clambering more swiftly and with greater assurance than almost any of the original members. Only Baptiste could match them, using his strength to haul himself into position, against their greater agility.

Their performance in swinging in the rigging and using one another to move swiftly from transom to transom was a wonder to watch.

One or two of the crew told of east European performers travelling around the land displaying amazing skills of strength and timing in swinging upside down and flying through the air between horizontal poles. They would catch a third member from another's hands and sometimes the other acrobat would spin in the air, before reaching out and holding onto the waiting grasp of a comrade.

This was becoming the sort of entertainment frequently to be found in the rich capital societies of Rome, Vienna, Budapest and Prague. Such skills were developed among the seafarers of the Mediterranean and the Baltic.

Chapter 6
The Flux

Rinaldi brought the whole process to a grizzly halt when he began bringing the dead from the hold on the twentieth day at sea. Some of the younger women were going down with an intestinal complaint which caused bleeding from the bowel. There was anguish among the other females. They blamed the conditions, lack of fresh food; menstruation was always a problem, but this was not linked.

They simply could not hold anything inside and evacuation of the bowel could occur at any time, without warning, creating a terrible reaction in the afflicted and those in the vicinity. The crew withdrew, determined to have no contact with them.

Rinaldi was busy administering his potions, but even he found this difficult to deal with.

He told of dysentery, which made them dysfunctional, which he had experienced on other voyages, and he insisted that they were given porter or rum in boiled water.

Daemon threw himself into the tasks set by Rinaldi and nursed the afflicted around the clock. Despite his best efforts, the toll was heavy and worsening. They would start with bleeding, grow pale and limp, then their eyes would turn yellow and their lips cracked. Rinaldi told him of the effects of dehydration, but simply pumping them full of fresh water was not enough — something had to bind it, hold it in them for longer to be of any effect.

As the death toll mounted beyond twelve over a period of three days, Standing called them together.

'There must be a solution to this; we can't be the first ship affected by this malady, surely? Rinaldi, you have to find a solution.'

'Senor, I have considered everything. I am afraid, unless we can reach dry land and return them to normal functional intake of solid foods — we may lose them all.'

'Senor Rinaldi — tell me what it is exactly they need? I am at my wits' end. The value of our stock is diminishing rapidly, and these are our people. I have grown to... well, we must treat them like people.'

'Senor,' Rinaldi protested, 'if they were my own daughters, I could not do any more for them; I could not find an answer. From the resources at my disposal, I could not save my own self.'

Daemon was sympathetic, but persisted, 'Senor Rinaldi — is it a sickness? A disease? Is it in the very water we give them?'

'I cannot be sure. I have tried different solutions, but I think it is something eating at them internally. I think there is a tiny enzyme, a parasite! We must try to give them only the purest substances that will not feed the parasite.'

Daemon jumped into the discourse. 'What if we boiled everything? My Da' used to boil water and let it cool in a container, with a lid, like a kettle. Then you would know that everything had been purified.'

'Of course, this is good practice; in the European medical colleges, they advocate boiling water. When we produce the finest spirits, the liquids are boiled over and over, distilling the condensed liquids from the steam created.'

'What do we have in sufficient quantities that we could process this way? We could make a mash from grain and feed it to them. We must try something. We could add sugar… it may go down a little easier.'

'Do it, then!' Rinaldi looked towards Standing and awaited his nod of approval. Baptiste and Daemon broke away to begin hauling up sacks of grain and set five native males to the task of grinding it and putting the dust into a cauldron.

When they strapped a lid on the cauldron, a pipe was fed into a hole left after Daemon wrenched off the handle.

The steam produced a constant stream of liquid, which they fed into the flagons vacated by the grog consumed over the course of the voyage; corks were applied to the narrow necks of the flagons and the liquid was preserved.

Everything was washed clean or held over open flame. It was decided — after a few days, they had no choice but to administer the potion.

When the natives were fed this brew, they sipped at it and pulled faces; it seemed to have a soporific effect, and mostly they made their way to their cramped bunks and lay still.

Some singing and chanting could be heard late into the evening long after eight bells, and there grew a temporary calm about the lower deck.

Rinaldi joined Daemon, Baptiste and the Nordic 'twins' at the table in John's quarters. Standing handed each a glass of port and raised his own. 'Let's hope and pray that the spirit works its magic and that the cargo is restored to us.'

They raised their cups in unison. 'Hear, hear!'

'I will be on my knees this evening, to pray for a swift end to this voyage!' Baptiste's deep French tone expressed his feelings more than his words. 'I swear, I will turn back to the Church if God is listening!' He raised his cup again, performing another toast: 'May the Lord help us to help them!' He gestured towards the cargo hold; they all followed his meaning and raised their own in turn.

Tired from both mental and physical endeavour, all six drifted off to sleep as the warm glow of the liquor inhabited their bodies.

Chapter 7
Vasteron

A shattering noise, ringing of the night bell and muffled voices brought them back to the real world.

A sharp rattling of the cabin door, before it sprung open, revealing Aseef, one of the Arab crew, leaning breathlessly into the room.

'Monsieur, monsieur, come quickly! There is a ship; it is heading straight for us! We cannot determine her origin, nor her intentions!'

Standing leapt for the stairway, grabbing his coat and tricorn as he passed the hall stand.

Daemon quickly followed, the others falling into line.

There were no clear markings, but the full rig and the almost confident way the ship sliced through the foam convinced Standing that this was a warship and no merchantman.

Taking the glass from Baptiste, a few moments passed before he announced that, 'She's a Britisher!'

A murmur of relief passed quickly through the ranks and Daemon leapt onto the rigging to take a clearer view, momentarily praying that she was not formerly of Fielding's command!

There was nothing familiar, but Daemon sank into the background whilst the crew clung to the vantage points and watched as she lagged away to starb'd, before coming around and falling in alongside.

Grappling hooks, of peaceful intent, were slung across to willing hands and the two ships barged one another, bobbing on a gentle swell.

Their captain — thankfully, for Daemon, a total stranger — yelled across from the poop-deck.

'Ahoy, Commander! I trust all is well?'

'Indeed.' responded Standing. 'Mostly, the conditions have been very kind to us. We are three weeks out of West Africa.'

'Bound for the Windies?'

'Indeed, sir. We have a cargo of souls for the coffee plantations.'

'You are no more than two weeks from safe harbour, sir. But I must warn you, there may be trouble ahead if you are not at fighting strength.'

'Oh... indeed? What have you to report, Captain? Er... forgive me... I'm John Standing, third son to the Earl of Olney. May I offer you some refreshment, Captain?'

'Delighted, sir. We will tie on and make fast. I and my First Lieutenant shall join you. Although you must allow me to provide the food. We have been well stocked for three months under sail.'

'By all means, Captain. I will prepare a table.'

Within a few moments, Baptiste showed the visitors into the cabin. 'Captain Vasteron and Lieutenant Bartholemew of His Majesty's ship *Elsinore*.'

Standing shook their hands heartily. 'My second in command, Mr Daemon Quirk, and Doctori Rinaldi. Please, make yourselves comfortable.'

Bartholemew produced a basket, removing a colourful cloth as he set it down on the table.

He removed other muslin cloths from a ham and recently-baked bread, grapes and oranges were laid out. Two fine bottles were ceremoniously presented, before he set about uncorking the first.

When cups had been filled and King George toasted, Vasteron sank into his chair in an easy movement.

'I commend you on the orderliness of your vessel, gentlemen. It is clear that you have willing hands and a fastidious regime. You seem to have everything nicely under control.'

'Aye, indeed, Captain, but I must warn you — we have been smitten with the flux recently, having a third of our cargo affected. We have lost twenty Africans already and I am fearful that more will be lost.'

Lieutenant Bartholemew addressed his superior. 'If I may, Captain? You are not alone, sir. Almost every slave landed in the West Indies has suffered this infection.'

'I fear for my cargo. I fear for them as I would for our own men!'

'Sir, you are truly compassionate. I assume the Doctori has tried fresh boiled water? Has he administered a potion of any kind?'

Daemon took the opportunity to explain their theory about distilled water, which appeared to amuse the visitors. 'Hah... you may have a drunken ship on your hands, but if it stops the buggers bleeding, eh?'

Standing put the lighter conversation to one side immediately by requesting Vasteron explain his remark about the danger ahead.

'Piracy, sir! You will not be surprised to learn that the Spanish and French are at large causing mischief to His Majesty's ships at every opportunity. Under Privateer

Flags, they hound our merchant friends all across the Caribbean. We are at full stretch to protect our interests in this part of the world.'

'Judging our position, am I correct in assuming you are returning to England, Captain?'

'On the contrary, we have been engaged in a lengthy pursuit of a Spanish and a Portuguese, and find ourselves drawn from the thick of the action. We have been gone far too long and were under sail bound again for the West Indies when we spotted you on our nor'east side. At first, I thought we had found our prey as we came about, but soon realised it was not the case.'

'We are headed in the same direction, then? Might I dare suggest we come under your protection during the next chapter of our voyage?'

'My pleasure, sir. What are we about if we cannot protect our merchant fleet? We will proceed at one thousand yards off your bow and damn me if we don't spot land around St Lucia or Barbados within ten days.'

Standing raised his glass. 'Captain, I believe the last leg of our voyage will be in the safest hands, and I can't thank you enough for your proposal.'

'Not at all, Sir John, it is my pleasure; but may I offer a little advice? Upon reaching Barbados, which currently remains one of the few territorial gains and therefore a safe harbour, you may only move ten percent of your stock onto the island; but in terms of making acquaintance and establishing your credentials, it is well worth the while in landing. You would do well to continue to Trinidad, where you will find the Dutch and Spanish masters will pay a handsome price to replenish the workforce. For the sugar-cane and Mahogany forest, don't you know.

'The finer Africans in your stock will be most welcome in the "Coffee Mountain" in Barbados.

'You will not be under our protection from Barbados onward. But a week at sea and with Madame Fortune on your side, you could make your trade and commence your return to British territory.'

'I respect your advice, Captain. Do you expect hostilities to continue for long between the English and the Allies?'

'Who can tell? We may find ourselves on the side of the Spanish and at odds with the French by the time we reach the Caribbean! It is a very volatile situation and the *status quo* has a habit of changing with great rapidity.

'Now, if I might offer some further advice? Quarantine your infected stock, keep them away from the healthy — a complete division and a strict regime should be enforced. We have some fresh produce which could prove of value. I wish you good fortune with this damnable affliction. The Flux has to be dealt with or you could lose everything.'

'Very sobering indeed, Captain. I take heed and will review our position daily. Might I suggest we continue with all haste to our destination?'

'Indeed, sir, although I have to warn you once again, I'm afraid. The landowners won't take them with the Flux. You will need to cure it or cover it up. Either way, your investment will be drastically devalued if you cannot conquer the problem.'

'Thank you, Captain, and I bid you farewell. We will shadow you over the coming weeks and hope your estimation is correct. Meanwhile, we will do everything we can to deliver a healthy cargo.'

The two stood and shook hands. Captain Vasteron turned and nodded in Daemon's direction and wished them a good night.

'Captain — one moment, if I may? Your name, sir, surely of Spanish origin...?'

Vasteron laughed heartily. 'Wondered when you might mention it, sir. Ludlow, Shropshire, is the humble abode of my family. Great-great-grandfather drifted inland when his ship floundered on the return from the devastation of the Armada. You see — I have the *sea* in my blood — even though it may have origins in the Iberian Peninsula!' He hopped jauntily over the side to the waiting boat.

Standing and Daemon exchanged a smile and few words, before setting the watch and turning in for the evening.

Both found sleep difficult to come by. Thoughts raced around in each of their heads and solutions, or options, popped up and were dismissed in turn. Eight bells sounded, and the ship felt reasonably calm, but the sound of groaning and other exclamations of discomfort, though in the native tongue, was a constant reminder that all was far from well.

A new day dawned and, fresh from sleep, the two met on deck, with the sun just above the horizon to the rear. A thousand yards off their starboard, the full rig strained against her three masts and propelled the powerful *Elsinore* through the surf.

Their own, lighter vessel cut through equally well, a sleek ship herself, competing for speed with her finely tuned companion.

Chapter 8
Thadeus Vine

Banoldino turned, his highly polished, leather-bound chair creaking lavishly under his bulk. He set a file of papers down on the grand oak desk in front of him. Looking up, his visitor appeared uncomfortable as a pair of hawkish eyes surveyed his attire, though the visitor felt perhaps those eyes bored straight through the outer layers, reaching his very core.

The visitor began to doubt himself. His own story, his own prepared speech, having been lightly dealt with, his report and written presentation had just received an equally unremarkable reaction. He made an attempt to sink into the chair, which he could feel with the backs of his knees, but the attention now weighing upon him made him return swiftly to an upright position.

'I think your proposal has... possibilities.'

'You do?'

'Please, take a seat.'

'Y-y-yes. Thank you.'

'Of course, we would have to change one or two things, but in principle, I like it.'

'You do?'

'When do you propose to start, let's say, given that the funds can be... made available?'

'Er... well... right away, sir! I could begin... erm, erm... right away!'

To open up a store, providing essentials for fishing, trading vessels and all things maritime, was a long-term ambition of Thadeus Vine, having traded in equestrian goods and ironmongery in his home town of Bristol, in South-West England. Thadeus had a decent understanding of stock and re-stocking, trading and developing a customer base.

In the New World, he had taken just three months to assess the situation and come up with an idea.

He watched the timber supplies coming in on a regular basis to the shipyards, and sailmakers and carpenters plying their trade with skill and alacrity. But he also saw the shortcomings, the long periods and the *drama* of waiting for equipment to arrive from Europe. The problems if the wrong materials arrived, or the wrong specification, or simply being held up or pirated away on the high seas.

His dream was to set up a trading post for shipbuilders and ship users. There was a constant demand for replacement parts, raw materials and the paraphernalia that made the job of the merchant sailor easier, or simply more efficient.

It would make a challenging but, *he was convinced*, rewarding business venture. Thadeus needed a partner, so his wife, Mathilda, urged him to make his move. He must 'approach Senor Don Bosco — the hero, the gallante!' The man everyone admired and most of them feared.

It took several weeks for Thadeus to be sufficiently happy with his presentation. He outlined the premises, a store front and a warehouse behind. The preferred location, naturally, alongside the dockyards, but near enough to the major access places, or crossings. He drew up a range of products and proposed stock levels.

He prepared a financial projection: what it would take to set up, stock up and a first-year anticipated turnover.

Then the five-year plan. It would be slow; at first, it would be almost a year in preparation, six months before the stock began to move, but then there would be bulk orders and continuity.

He needed eight hundred pounds. It was a colossal sum, but the returns would be substantial, as Banoldino himself was just now concluding.

There was a future for this business and he would, of course, want fifty percent of the venture for himself. This is how it worked for Banoldino — he wanted trusting partners, he wanted to motivate and encourage industry, but he demanded an equal share; if there were ten partners or just one, his share was fifty percent! He would take all of the financial risk, but the return could be plentiful.

Besides, his instinct was good. He had proven that, in the twenty months since his injury, he had sat behind his desk and let his brain do the work. The only thing not impaired by the terrible explosion which had wrecked the burning barn beneath his feet, had pulverised and broken his body, was his analytical mind.

In fact, he was now aware how events had sharpened his mind, his decision-making, his instinct. He was very rarely proven wrong, and he had launched a dozen enterprises and begun to see the rewards stack up.

He had only recently witnessed the folly of trusting his assets to a third party when 'Beausejour Investment Bank' had folded, or, rather, taken flight, and taken the life savings and hard-won profits of forty-two settlers with it.

So, the *New York Bank of Commerce* had been established by himself, Ranleigh, Berkeley and Fitzroy. There was no safer bank than one you controlled yourself.

Just as Thadeus rose to take his leave, Kirsten arrived, the door swinging open. She bustled in, dragging the multiple skirts of her dress through the opening. Untying her bonnet, she briefly shook her hair and turned her dazzling smile upon Mr Vine.

'Miz... er... ma'am. How do you do?' Vine managed, bowing his head a little too low.

'Good morning, Mr... er. I'm sorry, we have not been introduced.'

'My dearest, please meet our new partner, Mr Thadeus Vine. Mr Vine, my wife, Mrs Don Bosco.'

'Mr Vine.'

'Mrs Don Bosco. Honoured.' Another courteous bow, before returning his attention to Banoldino.

'Mr Vine... could you please return on Thursday I will have my lawyer draw up some papers. That is... of course, if you are happy with our terms.'

Vine bowed low again. 'I am more than... yes! Thursday. I will be ready...'

'And now, my wife and I bid you good day.'

Vine backed away and fumbled with the door, before closing it at the second attempt.

'Partner? Are you sure, darling?'

'Hah! Yes, my dear. Please do not worry. Thadeus Vine will make us lots of money, I assure you. Now, what can I do for you, my sweet? You know I have other meetings, but we have a few moments...'

'Darling, I wanted to talk with you about Allison Smith, and her, well, you know, the captain is her husband.'

'Yes, yes. What of it?' Banoldino grew impatient. Smith had been his Ranking Officer during the frontier campaign, and his role in returning Banoldino from death's door, and his attentions long after, only too clearly came to mind.

'Well, darling, you know the captain is away on duty much of the time? Since her marriage, leaving us and going to the fort, she leads such a lonely life. They have a small homestead out towards the Twilleries. It is very remote, and she is such a nice girl... her child is very similar in age to our own son.'

'Yes, my dear, I know Allison and her child very well, since she was part of our household. What is it you want me to do with her?'

'I would like her to stay in town; perhaps she could return to our *house* and help me with one or two little things?'

'Little things?'

'Well, darling, you know, I have one or two little commitments... there's the Infirmary, and the new arrivals, and the store and the Christian...'

Banoldino laughed. 'All right, all right! Enough! You clearly have a few things to occupy your time... I'm sure Mrs Allison Smith will prove herself a very able companion. Does Lady Evelyn know you are bidding to replace her?'

'Darling, how could you think such a thing? Evelyn is my friend — and constant companion. As you well know... It's just, well... she is getting to the point where she needs a little rest and, well, things can be very taxing, popping about town as we have to, constantly on the move...'

'Popping, you say? What is this "popping"?'

'Er... I think I meant "hopping" ...either way, don't tease me; you know very well I do a lot of, well, "popping" here and there, you might say — from one brief event to the next.'

'And what of the gallant Captain George?'

'I believe he will stay at the fort and visit the family as often as possible!'

Banoldino held out an arm and his wife swept around the desk to come up just behind his right shoulder. He switched position so that his hand could reach up to her neck as she brought her face near to his. Her two hands massaged his shoulder from behind, and momentarily his eyes closed and his face relaxed into a contented smile. Her lips sought his ear and brushed the side of his face.

Suddenly, his eyes opened. He shrugged and patted her on the arm. 'There now, my love, we must do something about your massive itinerary!' His tone, and the pat' on her arm, were dismissive. Kirsten straightened up, gave his shoulder one last bit of attention and returned to the opposite side of the desk.

Banoldino addressed some documents, looking up briefly to smile and bid her good day. 'Dinner?'

'Around eight o'clock — you remember? The Berkeley's are coming.'

'Of course, my dear. Now... off with you.'

Chapter 9
George Smith and Kirsten

Kirsten turned and removed herself, her concealed face a mirror of grim acceptance, her lips thin and whitening under pressure, her head full of misgivings.

The game was being played out on a daily basis. The sham her marriage had become! The wealth that had arrived in a tidal wave of activity. The wonderful trappings of society, the high-born and ambitious friends that filled their evenings and holy days. How long could this go on?

How long before even their friendship palled. The last remnants of the great romance snuffed out like a tired bedside candle.

Since the end of the 'troubles', and Otte's disappearance, Kirsten had led two lives.

Her life, mainly during day-time, had become a whirlwind of activity. She made herself busy, she joined in with every community initiative and threw herself into society. She tired herself out by the end of each day, and that made it so much easier to bear the change in her relationship with Banoldino.

It was remarkable how she had managed to recover and resume normal society after her final encounter with Wolfgang Otte.

On the run from the rope, Otte had been determined to finally force himself upon Kirsten at any cost, even re-capture and death. He had succeeded and left her, surprisingly, in control of herself, even having suffered the ultimate physical degradation.

The encounter had been brief, and the consequences minimal. She let him go; she wanted him dead, but out of her life was just as good, as long as it spared Banoldino a further encounter with this, his personal *tormentor*.

The result of Banoldino's terrible injuries meant the end of the physical side of their marriage. Kirsten enjoyed moments of tenderness for what they were. She almost enjoyed nursing him back to health. Her nights, alone in the dark, however, were hellish. She would toss and turn, sleepless for hour after hour; it was not desperation for the full physical union — she could hardly explain it herself, but it came down to the simplest things in the end, the lack of a compassionate hand on her naked body.

Banoldino withdrew from every encounter; he would retreat into his own private anguish and leave Kirsten to watch the moon, switching positions on her tear-stained pillow.

The physical exertions of his own daily activities were sufficient most nights to see him off into a long, albeit fitful, sleep.

Night became a time of dread and despair. Kirsten moved to her own rooms eventually, where she spent time honing her hair and her skin, whilst every evening enjoying long, luxurious immersion in her Spanish copper bathing closet.

Every night she took a copious linen sheet from her maidservant Matilda and wrapped it around her torso several times, before sitting in front of the looking glass whilst her hair was groomed.

She would be helped into her silken nightgown, before bidding Matilda good night.

Often, she wrapped her own arms about her as tightly as she could, a sort of substitute for Banoldino's powerful embrace. Her frustration would become agonising after she would lean over to douse the bedside candle. She allowed the moon to flood into the room through open drapes and watched the shadows change, before merciful sleep would envelop her.

Captain Smith came as a completely uninvited and unexpected, but life-changing, intrusion.

His concern for his colleague and erstwhile co-commander of the Militia was a credit to him. He had visited often; his attention in bringing only carefully selected information, only occasionally taxing demands, was also a credit to his understanding.

He knew Banoldino would never be the same warrior that had ridden out to join him in 1745. He knew his military days were concluded. The ceremony that had followed, the constant demand for detail, the stories, the trial, the aftermath of what had become a legendary engagement at the frontier outpost had been more than Banoldino could cope with.

Smith had done everything in his power to fend off the attention on Banoldino's behalf, and when it was necessary that they attend a meeting, a briefing or even a funeral, he made sure that as little time as possible was spent before returning a tired, damaged companion to the bosom of his family.

The need of his attentions had become quite rare by this time and his visits less frequent.

On many occasions, he bade a polite 'good night' after Banoldino had been placed back in Kirsten's care. He was respectful of his own duties to family, and the Army, confined to his post as he often was, inside the small Fort that had become the base for the territorial command.

A night came, almost two years after the insurrection, when Smith had dutifully returned a slightly inebriated Banoldino to his home and stood holding his hat and cloak in the hallway as Kirsten and Allison struggled to manoeuvre Banoldino to his room.

Drako arrived, taking the weight once they reached the top of the staircase, and Kirsten returned to offer Smith her thanks and to bid him goodnight as she had done on numerous occasions. Allison appeared from the drawing room and gave her husband a playful slap across his upper arm.

'I hope you will call in and say g'night to your lonely wife before you set off into the night, George Smith!'

'My dear. You know I have to return to the fort... but I can promise I will be here for *two* nights when I return to give my quarterly report to the Assembly.'

He kissed her gently on the cheek and whipped his hat playfully across her rump.

'Ahh me! Such is my life, ma'am... I don't count for anything compared to the Army,' she remarked for Kirsten's benefit, thinking the Lady may have considered their 'banter' in any way disrespectful.

Instead, Kirsten smiled. 'Good night, Allison... Would you look in on John Nathan before you go to bed?'

'Well, as I will find my rooms quite empty and lonely, I will look in and settle down in the nursery for the night. I can take care of everyone from there!'

Shifting from one foot to another gave the captain a sort of school-boyish look. His head bowed slightly, as always for a tall man. It was as if to come down to normal height so that anyone close would hear if he muttered a comment. He watched his wife disappear, before he managed a private word with Kirsten.

'Ma'am, I hope all is well, ahem... with the Colonel?'

Kirsten smiled at him. 'Captain, I think I might ask that question of you! I think maybe you see more of my husb...' Suddenly, she became serious. 'My apologies, Captain. I should not have...'

'Ma'am, please, do not apologise. I shouldn't have...'

'Captain Smith, you know things have been... *difficult*, for my husband, since... You, out of everyone, know how bad his injuries...' A tear filled her eye. 'I have not been able to talk about...' Suddenly, she sobbed, and he was at her side.

Her head pressed into his shoulder as she stifled her emotions. Her tears would not be restrained, drops appearing on his pale leather tunic. Looking up, her mournful face, framed in sumptuous golden hair, her blue eyes wet and blinking back more tears, her beauty astonished him. Her lips seemed irresistible. As his hand held her firmly to him, his own lips gently melded into them.

The embrace was long and intoxicating for both of them, trepidation on his part making the moment all the sweeter; surprise and desperation on hers, making it a moment of heart-stopping intensity.

Her hands went to his chest and eased him gently away, until their lips unlocked. He stood back, his own hands, one still holding his soft leather gloves, held up before him as if in surrender.

They both whispered feverishly.

'Miss... Mistress Don Bos... please forgive me... I...'

'No, Captain, please, don't scold yourself; the fault...' Suddenly, she took a step forward and threw herself into his arms, and that kiss was re-discovered in all its intensity.

His lips found her cheek and he nestled his face in her hair.

'Oh God, Kirsten, I have longed for this moment. For as long as I have known you, since our very first meeting... I have cherished every second, every chance meeting... I have loved you...'

'Hush now, Captain, I have, too! I couldn't help myself. I knew you liked me... I...'

'Liked? I *liked* you... yes, and I worshipped the very ground you walked on... I would hold for a day a handkerchief or a piece of cloth or a harness or strap that you had even for a second held in your hand.' He kissed her again and again.

'Captain. George! I know. You don't have to tell me. I return your feelings. I... am lonely, I am, I need...' She sobbed afresh, and he caressed her face with the palm of his hand, kissing her eyes and savouring the taste of her tears.

He pulled her hard up against him, and their lips met again as he felt her body warm and needy against his. She took his hand and pulled him towards the parlour. Quietly, she eased the doors shut behind her and he stood just inches from her as she leaned back against them, hardly daring to look up into his eyes again.

They tore at each other's clothing, until her blouse and tunic were frothing around her waist. She raised a long limb and it reached up to his own waist, his hand catching her and discovering her soft naked thigh above her stocking. His naked chest, covered with fine, dark hairs, pressed against her upturned nipples.

They sank to the ground. She, momentarily, felt strange as the feel of the thick rug beneath her crystallised for a moment, the reality of this encounter. But his lips on her breast, seeking its throbbing core, completely vanquished all thought from her mind.

The encounter was brief, their desperation and the new-ness meaning all restraint was abandoned. They lay panting and drowning in the warm moistness of each touching part. For long moments his head was on her breast and her hand held it tight and relentlessly in position. She cherished the free hand that gently stroked away at her back and the deep caverns between her legs, reminding her nerve endings of the part they had played, only moments before, in a tumultuous union.

'Kirsten, my love!'

Her finger found his lips. For a moment she quietened him, not wanting to disrupt her delight.

Then she found herself easing him up and making enough space to regain at least a kneeling position. 'Captain! George, we must be careful.' Her hand went to his head, brushing his thick, damp mane of hair back behind his ear. 'I want you, I *need* you! I do not want this to end here.'

'Kirsten... I can't stop saying your name! Kirsten, my love, I want to be near you, always. I will never leave your side. Tell me what to do and...'

His hand unconsciously traced the raised ridge scar on her shoulder, reminding her of the lash, of terrible times, of her saviour, her husband, lying in restless sleep only a staircase away.

'It will be difficult, but... we will find a way... Please, say you will be patient. We have time...'

She had learned to be patient, to wait for the things she secretly wanted. She had learned to deal with pain and frustration.

'I will never leave him while he needs me. You must know that.'

His eyes dropped as a moment passed. 'I know. I do understand... I have the greatest respect for him. I will always envy him *you*! The moments you have together, waking and sleeping.'

'It must be so. I owe him. I still love him dearly, like a father. The flame of our passion has... gone, but we have our child, we have...'

His hand went to her lips. 'My dear, darling Kirsten, I do understand... I, I will be forever grateful for this.... For tonight and for all the other nights... if they ever happen! I am yours... from this moment on.'

They kissed once more. He rose and gathered his things about him. Kirsten straightened her dress, pulling it roughly into position. She took a quick look into the Hall and left the door ajar as he pulled his tunic together and fastened his discarded belt and scabbard.

Opening the door, she ushered him into the night. She watched from a side window as he mounted the horse that had been standing since being tethered almost an hour earlier by Drako. She lost sight of him in the gloom against the backdrop of the forest. Turning, she made for the stairs, biting her lip as she looked towards the corridor which led to the nursery and Allison's rooms.

Her own room lay silent and, for once, welcoming, with the moonlight shafting beams of light across her bed.

As she pulled off her things, she reached for a cloth, dousing it in the bowl near her window seat.

Her thoughts lingered for a moment on the horror of her encounter with Otte, of a so, so different outcome. She squirmed joyously as she slipped, naked, between the cool sheets, and memories of Otte were banished to the remotest corner of her mind.

Chapter 10
The Aristocrat

Approaching Christmas 1749, the bustling township of New York became highly animated. The growth of Philadelphia brought new county boundaries, and the civic authorities grew in power and influence.

Allison, as always, accompanied Kirsten throughout her daily routine. Now much preparation was under way, for the Township called on the great and the good to contribute to the festivities.

Comfortable in the two rooms in the East Wing of the Don Bosco residence with her son, and with a tutor looking after the two children together from the hours of eight in the morning until two in the afternoon, the arrangement suited them well.

Her husband began visiting several evenings each week, but returned to the Fort, where his responsibilities for the moment were focused on training and keeping the men occupied so that the boredom did not lead them to wasteful folly.

Every new arrival in New York had to go before the Council, to be assessed, before they were permitted status in the Township. A new arrival with poor prospects was moved on and encouraged to seek acceptance further down-river.

Those considered acceptable, or with an idea, were encouraged to stay. Those with collateral, or with gold, were elevated immediately into society, introduced and feted wherever they were introduced.

It was an evolutionary process, finding potential, then allowing it to flourish.

Commerce was king. Anything that created wealth or financial gain was immediately elevated towards the bastions of power and status.

Of course, there was the occasional mistake when someone clever enough to outwit or deceive, suddenly found themselves in advantageous positions. It was uncannily predictable, that those who lacked substance, or promoted themselves beyond their ability, were found out, quickly, and ceremoniously dumped by the hierarchy.

Such was the potential for gain that those in power hardly ever missed an opportunity. Those with little or nothing found themselves exploited or ditched. It was a brutal process: you were either 'in' or you were 'out'.

The 'outs' found themselves loading up covered wagons and joining long trains with others seeking free land or undiscovered fortunes. They banded together and, in many cases, found salvation and a future, in making the journey into the unknown. Many did not, finding the journey and all its perils costly and unforgiving.

The wagon trains grew ever longer. They needed protection, or at least a guide, someone who had travelled the same paths and lived to tell the tale — or someone who had enough gumption to bluff it out and take the gamble, taking others along for the ride.

People came and went, were processed with amazing ease and with limited fuss. They either stayed and grew into their new surroundings, or they were processed through and became the homesteaders and pioneers.

Banoldino and Kirsten's rise was extraordinary. They had arrived early and been established quickly. They were able to resist all challenges and to grasp every opportunity.

Banoldino was aggressive, almost greedy, in his lust for power and influence. He was considered a *Great Man*, a true leader — his opportunism knew no boundaries. He was first in the queue when the new arrivals paraded their potential. He was first to spot and take advantage of an opportunity.

For all Ranleigh's influence and stature, Banoldino had long surpassed him in commerce. Together they presented an ideal partnership. The unquestioned trust and benevolence associated with a peer of the realm, and the determined, focused, power of the 'noble' Spaniard.

Together they provided one cornerstone of the new society, one unimpeachable pillar of the community. They could not fail, they could not shrink; their only path was upward and onward. They carried along many others upon whose lifelong gratitude and devotion they were able to count.

Christmas was the time when all commerce was put aside and other matters, spiritual and community, were brought to the fore. The Town 'fathers', Ranleigh and Banoldino amongst them, established the festivities, essentially to generate trade and show off ideas and achievement.

A market was established. The Germans and Dutch in the town were first to appreciate the opportunity to replicate the atmosphere of the typical European 'fayre'. Entertainment was laid on to bring all the settlers from outlying areas into the Township to sample the delights of 'community' but also to generate trading relationships, outlets for goods and equipment and new business partnerships.

Occasionally, a newcomer with power and influence would arrive, be processed, but show sufficient independence to resist the circle of influence cast by Banoldino and his associates. A man who could threaten the *status quo* was rare, but there had to be new and strong players to continue the spread of power.

Such a man was Richard Carstein, a mid-European of aristocratic back-ground. This was a man who needed no help to establish his place among the hierarchy. He was dashing in looks and attitude, bold in his intentions. He staked his claim in position and influence and a rival force developed. Someone to take on the 'establishment' and compete for the opportunities that were presented almost daily.

He was independently wealthy, and his followers showed unbridled respect, which in turn told others that this man was not to be taken lightly.

He rode about the town on a mighty black stallion, 'Bavaria', that would have graced the stables of kings. Carstein surveyed the stores, the shipyards, the fishing harbours, the farms and the great houses and took stock of everything the New World had fostered.

Although the War of the Austrian Succession was still burning in Europe, he declared himself for neither side and left all to ponder on his true background and his intentions. He was respectful towards those that had established the colony, he was charming to the ladies, but he offered no favours and promised no associations.

A plot of land was acquired so that construction of a substantial, stone-built property was able to begin. He paid for materials and labour with gold coin and brought fittings and furniture in what appeared to be his own or a privately commissioned three-masted East Indiaman, *The Ajax*, finely built in the Dutch boatyards.

He simply watched and waited, remaining aloof and irritatingly inactive, whilst his property, his seat of power, was established.

Banoldino called on him one morning, having left a significant time-span since the arrival. He took the carriage, alone and un-announced. The main house had been recently finished and a number of outbuildings, stables and a barn were in various stages of completion.

'Bavaria' pranced about a corral away to the left, near a clearing in the forest. He snorted and reared up as if to make certain the attention of the visitor. Banoldino thought to himself, the horse and owner were much alike.

Flourishing his card, Banoldino waited for a few moments, before the servant returned with an encouraging nod, whilst opening wide the door to the visitors' entrance into the large reception Hall.

Descending a grand, sweeping staircase in front of him was Carstein, dressed in an exotic, velvet-trimmed house-coat.

'Senor Banoldino,' he uttered in a clipped European accent, 'please, allow me.'

With a wave of his hand, Carstein ushered Banoldino into a long gallery, windows all along one side, and paintings, some mounted, others in stages of readiness, leaning against the wall beneath a designated space.

'As you see, I am not completely ready to accept visitors.' An exaggerated shrug. 'But, in your case, senor, I am glad to be able to extend my hospitality, such as it is.'

'Not at all, sir, I apologise for my intrusion. I would gladly retire and await your invitation...'

'No, senor, you have arrived, and I am pleased that you are my first visitor. I am glad of the opportunity to make an acquaintance... indeed, I have met only two individuals with whom I have held conversation in some months — a physician and a lawyer — and I must admit, the dialogue was hardly inspiring.'

'A physician?'

'Indeed, sir. You may be acquainted with Joffrey Mengel? I think that is the correct name.'

'Er, yes, I believe we have met! A very sensitive sort of man. Perhaps the Church would have been a better calling!'

'Perhaps!' Carstein smiled. 'However, he knows the anatomy, and his attentions have been most welcome.'

'You have an affliction...? My own doctor is a *magician*!'

'No, no, I assure you I have been treated very well. An old war wound, you might say. I was a Colonel in the Austrian Army. I served at Weissenburg, a brutal encounter. I was fortunate to escape with my life. But then peace-time can be just as brutal. And yourself? I have heard: your exploits are legendary in these parts. I trust you are fully recovered?'

'Well, let's say I am as good as I will ever be. Enough of old war wounds; we look to the future, no?'

'Yes, we do! Indeed, that is why we are *here*. The future is bright, and we should make the most of our opportunities. May I offer you some libation?'

Some time passed in easy conversation whilst three measures of whisky were comfortably downed by each. Neither attempted to outdo the other, upstage or impress their achievements upon the other. A sort of natural self-effacing dialogue found each revealing almost all of their secrets.

'So, you suffered your injury in a duel?'

Carstein responded 'The weakness in my left knee I owe to the war. I would not normally tell of this, but the truth is, I did have the occasion to engage in a duel. I disarmed him, and I had the right to finish him, but I turned my back on the scoundrel and walked towards my second to surrender my weapon. He thrust at me from behind. The blow pierced my lung and extended fully six inches from my chest. He missed the heart — but some damage was inevitable. I rounded on him with his blade still inside me and slashed his throat with a reverse sweep.'

'He was served just desserts, I suggest! You were indeed fortunate to escape with your life, and *he* died the death of a traitor to his class.'

'There, I knew you would understand. For my part, I bore no ill will beyond that it left me with a hole in my life, so to speak!'

'In your chest, I think?'

'No. Indeed my friend, I mean my life! I had a great affection for the man... we had been — how you say? — inseparable, for many years. Our two families, they were connected, historically; we were like brothers. We quarrelled over another member of the family, our cousin Marie-Anne: she was the light of my life. Unfortunately, Gambon also held great ambition towards her...'

'You did not want this... duel?'

'I did everything possible to avoid it. I offered to leave the country, turn my back on everything. He said he would never be rid of me, that *she* would never be rid of me. I thought to run away with her, but I have too much respect for her family. I could not deprive them of their cherished daughter.

'Gambon persisted. He insulted me in public. He was enraged. I turned my back on him, prepared to forego my honour and the honour of my family. But he challenged me in a salon, whipping my face!' Carstein's hand went to his cheek, where the back of his fingers brushed lightly, as if the slap was still causing pain.

'Finally, I accepted his challenge, though I knew I could not kill him. He had been such a friend, such an honourable and faithful friend. The duel was short. He did not have the strength in his wrist. I disarmed him and turned to walk away from him. Such is life! Such is *passion*! I believe he was out of his mind with this misplaced devotion. She never loved him.'

'Well, my friend, here you are in the New World! You will, I am certain, make an impact on our humble society.'

'Senor, let me tell you, I have been most surprised at how well this "humble society" has blossomed. Indeed, I am more than impressed. I intend to bring my entire fortune here to make my own contribution to the New World.' Rising, he made his way towards Banoldino.

'My friend, I have shared with you my story... I trust this will be held in confidence. I would not normally open my heart to a stranger, but in this case, I sense something. I hope we will become great friends. Who knows, we may even do a little business.' At that, both men laughed and shook hands firmly.

'Please, call on me; indeed, I would like you to join my wife and I for dinner on Friday. Shall we say sunset? If you don't mind, I will invite one or two other guests. Just a few close friends.'

'I accept the invitation, senor, and look forward to meeting your wife and family.'

Chapter 11
Saved by the Still

For seven days, the crew of the *Durham* cleaned and force-fed the natives, allowing them fresh air and time to stretch their legs. And, above all, the opportunity to take distilled water throughout the day. The women continued using the screen to contain their modesty, but, nonetheless, allowed Rinaldi and Daemon freedom to come and go, inspecting and encouraging cleanliness and diligence.

Miraculously, the flux abated; slowly but surely, less and less of the cargo showed the dreaded signs of discomfort. There were lessening numbers in the quarantine. Rinaldi was taking regular walks around the decks, refreshing his clothing, his spirits lifted and his manner eased. The constant questioning and insinuation from the crew had mercifully tailed off, the repetition of which had taxed Rinaldi to the limits.

Now he offered an occasional word of encouragement and more detailed descriptions of the improvements experienced.

Daemon began to believe they had conquered the pestilence, and he also found spirits rising even in the Africans, who appeared becalmed, almost contented, which brought him great relief.

As Standing studied his maps and drew up a charter for the slave auction, his attention lapsed one afternoon.

Many of the natives sat languidly about the decks, having taken in the air, as they had been allowed to slump against the inner rails, with manacles on their wrists, their only restraint. Children were allowed to run free, some even engaging the crew.

Daemon allowed his mind to wander whilst positioned so that he could glance behind the screen, where thirty or more of the females were lined up to show Rinaldi their tongues, whilst demonstrating clean hands and feet after dousing.

Suddenly, there were raised voices, footfalls upon the deck. A musket cracked, followed by a scream, then more aggressive yelling.

Daemon quickly leapt onto the rigging to gain a clear view of the deck, remaining free of the disruption that had broken out on the other side of the canvas screen. Immediately, he realised a rebellion was sweeping through the ship.

John Standing emerged from his quarters, raising his pistol: he intended to secure the wheel and prevent any interference with control of the ship. Two natives leapt from the rail and grappled him to his knees; the pistol went off and a slave yelped as the shot pierced his throat, propelling him backward and overboard.

Standing was immediately overwhelmed as six or seven more natives crudely beat him with rope or palings that had been torn loose.

Two armed men stood at the prow with muskets aimed into the crowd, but clearly were not able to make a decisive intrusion.

The women below Daemon, mostly naked and dripping wet from their afternoon cleansing, bunched together, a sea of glistening ebony.

Two of the rebel natives emerged as if to assume command, shouting and cajoling, pushing crew members into a defensive huddle and yelling orders at the others; but more than twenty males had broken free and were now racing in confusion from one side of the deck to the other.

Their blows were not lethal or indeed causing serious damage, as they appeared to behave just as an unruly mob, lacking any kind of strategy. It reminded Daemon of children hacking and kicking their way towards a makeshift timber goal with a patched-up, inflated bladder.

Daemon had to act quickly, knowing options were limited. Dragging at the lashings, he allowed the large canvas curtain to drop onto the deck, exposing the swarm of terrified females.

Immediately being revealed and witnessing the violence and the ferocity of the two leaders, they began to scatter in all directions. Daemon's ploy was instantly rewarded, as some of the African males were immediately distracted and began to corner and grope the naked females.

For a few moments, chaos reigned, but the emphasis of the attack had shifted. The two leaders became engulfed by the others dashing in all directions, barging and grappling among themselves.

The makeshift weapons were discarded when the women, having experienced weeks of privacy, fought off the attentions of the males with ferocity.

Daemon made his way to the armed sailors at the prow, yelling into their ears above the mêlée to fire over the heads of the rabble. A violent crash rang out as two muskets were discharged, and Daemon immediately had the two re-loading.

Swinging down on a loose rope, he made across the deck towards the downed figure of John Standing, barging into the three remaining rebels who were trying to restrain the captain.

All were thrown off their feet so that, in the mêlée, Standing was able to wriggle free, pistol in hand, and he raced towards the galley, where he knew other armaments were secured. Manhandling the cook and his mate, and pushing them towards the arms cache, he put cutlasses and pistols into their hands and ordered them to follow.

Daemon by now had thrown one of the rebels over the side, and found himself pulling two males away from a screaming female victim. Seeing Standing and his armed men emerge, he raced over to join them.

More pistol shots cracked the air, and the natives collectively recoiled and ran towards the bow of the ship: there was a riot of humanity dashing and leaping around the main deck.

Identifying two of the ring leaders, Standing and Daemon gathered them together, thrusting cutlass blades to their throats, backing them towards the bridge. The ship's bell promised to be the only thing that might pierce the roar of uncontrolled rabble, so Standing thrashed at it with the butt of his pistol.

The bell rang out loud and clear, a new sound, a new influence over the chaos. A moment passed, but gradually the Africans became calmer and showed some restraint. There was still harsh contradictory shouting, and one of them, eyes bulging, attempted to scream instructions towards the others.

Some of the females began to break away and form a separate huddle near the galley.

The two seamen, with re-loaded muskets, at the far end of the ship, raced towards the captain. Daemon took hold of one of the weapons, swapping it for a cutlass. Moving towards the crowd, he held it at shoulder height, pointing towards the most volatile sector of the melee. By slowly scanning across the crowd, he brought stillness and quiet, by conveying his intent to use it at the slightest provocation.

Now, in the midst of them, he showed his anger and brought them wide-eyed to their knees, where they became once more completely under control.

Daemon's entire demeanour showed his disappointment. He let them experience real anger that the mutiny had broken out, despite the lengths he and Standing had gone to, in protecting and nurturing the cargo.

With every glance and movement, he let them see his anger. He felt that in the face of provocation he could have freely brought down two or three of them to truly show how betrayed he felt.

Furious, he now fixed the bayonet to the end of the musket; using this as a pointer, he separated the males from the remaining females and herded them into two separate groups.

Calling at the crew for support, he began directing the males in the direction of the hatches, where they could be taken down and secured. When a gap opened, and he was able to see the hatch covers at the far end, a sight greeted him which turned his blood cold.

Eric staggered towards him with Sven draped across his arms, his face awash with tears, the body streaming blood onto the deck. Sven's throat had been cut. His head drooped unnaturally to one side. Eric laid him down where everyone could see.

Some of the women wailed, shocked and saddened themselves to see the muscular, blood-soaked torso of one who, despite being physically alien to them, had become almost a friend. One whose flashing smile had, in truth, made many of them playfully giggle and swoon.

It occurred to both John Standing and Daemon that the momentum for this insurrection may have grown from the seeds of jealousy.

Some of the black males resented Sven his attentions and the perceived threat to their manhood. That the native males misinterpreted the friendship between the two strange crewmen to the extent that they, or at least one of them, was bent on retribution?

It could have been the case that jealousy had inspired the act of murder, that achieving the ultimate revenge had fired up the belligerence of some of the slaves.

If that were the case, it had tragic consequences for not only Sven, but even as the toll now stood, to three of their own.

Now seeing the murdered body of a good friend and very capable seaman, Standing ranged forward, finding it difficult to restrain his own fury. He raised his pistol towards the heads of the more prominent of the rabble and demanded each in turn, 'Who has done this? Which one of you...? I demand an answer!'

One of the natives lost control and began shuffling away, receding deeper into the throng, but Standing saw his movement. The captain singled him out, firmly beating him across the brow with the butt of the pistol.

The native cowered down onto the deck, yelping in pain. Standing raised the gun again. 'Is this the man?' He raised his voice to a crescendo — 'Is this the man?'

Many heads began shaking in denial. Others began raising their hands, pointing, but many in different directions. It was impossible to pinpoint the culprit in this way.

Suddenly, one of the natives broke away and leapt for the side, and he was in the water, thrashing about, by the time Daemon and Standing reached the rail. The ship eased away from him, but Standing yelled, 'Lower the boats!' Immediately, hands went to the life-boat and it was hurriedly dumped over the side. 'Three men!' yelled Standing.

Within minutes, they were eating up the distance between them and the panicking figure in the water, dragging him into the boat. Standing knelt on his chest, pinning him to the hull. The *Durham* ranged in a wide arc, managing to return to its original course. Half an hour later, they tied the boat on to a line, hauling themselves alongside.

The African had lost all resistance and was now shepherded in silence up the rigging until waiting arms pinned him against the bulkhead.

Wet and windswept, Standing dropped on to the deck, taking Daemon one side. Confirming that order had been restored, the slaves were shackled in their appropriate bays. There had been little protestation, though much weeping and universal misery prevailed. Standing addressed his number two.

'Daemon, I am determined to act decisively and dispassionately to punish the guilty and demonstrate that insurgence of any kind will mean the worst outcome imaginable. I trust you are with me on this.'

'I *am*, John; you know you can count on me. I, like yourself, want this mess cleared up and order restored as soon as it's possible. I am mystified at their actions. I can't help but feel some guilt or some failing on my part. Somehow this should have been prevented.'

'I intend to find out; I am holding a trial. We will bury our dead comrade and hold a trial and retribution. The natives will be present. It must be after first light on the morrow.'

'I agree. I am sickened by this revolt. I will talk with Eric and find out what he knows.'

Just at that moment, a shout from above alerted them to the presence of the *Elsinore*. 'Ship ahoy, off the larb'd.'

Bartholemew was at the rail with a loud hailer. 'Captain, could you report your status?'

'Thank you for your concern. We have had some problems, but order is restored. We had a man overboard, but he is now back in our hands.'

'Are you sure there is nothing we can do to help? Can we not provide you with assistance? We have made quite a detour; there must be something we can offer.'

'Tell your captain we are in good shape, although I would appreciate four men-at-arms. Would that be possible?'

'I will make it so. Please provide a boat and we shall make arrangements.'

Chapter 12
The Pursuit

Another hour passed whilst the day grew a little darker. There was evidence of unsettled weather on the horizon, and they acted with all haste now to make the exchange. Daemon took four crewmen in the boat and they fought through the increasing swell to pull alongside *Elsinore*. Four Redcoats dropped into the boat and took their places in the centre two stoops.

Within a few minutes, they were passing muskets and powder cases to the waiting hands on deck and then grasped the rigging to climb onto the deck.

John Standing awaited their assembly, before taking them to their quarters and giving them a duty roster. He ordered that two, armed men, should be on deck at all times, responding to any command from himself or Daemon Quirk.

They appeared cheerful enough at the assignment and it could not be ignored that the possibility of spending some weeks with native slave girls in their midst may have brought about an unparalleled response to the request for volunteers.

Standing was glad to have them, but was surprised to find that shortly after the return of his own boat, a second vessel thudded into the bow, their friend Vasteron's head appearing over the rail.

Standing, responding with immediate attention, made his way towards the captain. 'Always a pleasure, my dear Captain, in this case unexpected. What may have brought you across such an uncomfortable if mercifully short diversion?'

'Concern, my friend. I have become much interested in seeing you through this perilous exercise undefeated. I am concerned that trouble of an unexpected kind may be brewing beneath the surface.'

'Have no fear. It was indeed unexpected — but perhaps we brought it on ourselves. We had become a little too benevolent towards our stock, allowed them too much freedom. It has cost us the life of a dear friend. Sven was murdered — by a native — and we have had to deal with the consequences. We were driven off course in pursuit of the savage, as he seemed bent on a watery grave — but that would have served no purpose. We must demonstrate trial and retribution, or the entire episode will pass without any lessons learned.

'We will hold the man accountable tomorrow at first light and use his punishment as an example to all. I have no hesitation in taking these actions because the man is guilty beyond doubt of a heinous crime.

'Tomorrow, the natives will understand what this means. For their own good, the punishment will be brutal.'

'My friend, I am sorry to hear of this tragedy. It is most unfortunate. The man was much loved by his companions, this much was obvious. Please accept my condolences.

'Might I beg of you, however, should there be any similar infringements upon our progress, that you would be so kind as to let the man drown! I have one of our former protagonists in sight. A Spaniard was spotted two miles off starb'd this morning and, unbeknownst to yourselves, you have accompanied our intense pursuit of the brigand all through this day!'

Standing made as if to extend a mighty apology, but Vasteron held up a hand. 'No, do not reproach yourself; we will have him tomorrow or I'll be damned! He will not make the same progress under the stars — and night is falling. We will surprise him in the morning.'

'Captain, I hope and pray you will. I would hate to think our lapse had cost you and your men dearly. Please allow me to make amends. How can we help?'

'Stay in contact with us at all times. Close the distance to six hundred yards and await my signal. We will engage him around mid-day. The sight of the *Durham* on our flank will limit his evasive action. He will not be able to make sou'west, because of your presence. I will come on him from nor'east. He will feel it futile to take flight. When we fire some nine-pounders into his rigging, he may raise a white flag. If not, we will close on him. I would insist that the *Durham* stand off, just to collect any escaping crew or cut off latent attempts at retreat.

'Please, I implore you, do not engage. Your own mission will be jeopardised if you come under fire. Besides, it will not be necessary,'

'I will follow your directions to the letter, Captain. Please accept my wishes for a successful encounter.'

The two men shook hands and Vasteron turned away and disappeared over the rail.

Turning to Daemon, Standing nodded an acknowledgement that the days ahead would require focus and skill; following such precise instructions would take all their resources and no mistakes could be contemplated.

Chapter 13
Caught in the Crossfire

Dawn arrived with Daemon taking over from Standing at the helm.

An uneventful night had passed, finding the *Elsinore* within six or seven hundred yards off their bows, and Standing was grateful to be relieved.

'Daemon, we have our work cut out today. Our role will take as much seamanship and concentration as if we were about to fully engage the enemy. I would like to defer the punishment of Sven's murderer until our task is completed.'

'I follow your reasoning, John. He will spend a day longer than he deserves on this Earth, but, for the sake of the mission, I fully support your decision.'

Standing clapped his friend across the shoulders and left him to the watch.

Daemon patrolled up and down for ten minutes before, seeing the arrival of Baptiste to take up the wheel, he relaxed and found a comfortable spot to draw up his knees and rest. After a few exchanges, the pair grew silent, leaving Daemon to contemplate the warm breeze and the potential of a scorching day ahead.

In his mind, he envisaged the coming encounter through to completion, followed by a successful home run into the Caribbean; but, noticing the gradual increase in the depth to which the bow was dipping into the waves, told him that the day may yet have a surprise or two in store. He had learned that nothing is totally predictable when at sea.

Daemon took a ladle of water across to the forecastle where, out of sight of the main deck, the prisoner slumped at its base, arms stretched and wrapped in reverse around the mast, meeting by means of chain and shackles beyond. Two sips were allowed. Daemon could not bear to remain at his side for more than a moment.

As the morning evolved, the crew stretched the sleep from their joints whilst Daemon issued orders that the natives were to be processed swiftly this day. The feeding and sluicing down would be a brief and perfunctory procession, leading to the prompt battening of hatches and a return to the main issues of the day.

This was achieved without much difficulty. Daemon had the four Redcoats, in prominent view at the rail of the poop deck, with muskets at arms, cocked and ready. The Africans, through their naturally extravagant, wide-eyed gestures, made it clear that they had noticed and were paying full respect to the new situation.

The screens were drawn up as usual, which made the process more formal and orderly. The mood of the slaves was sombre, and they kept discipline, demonstrating respect in their familiar ways.

The task of maintaining speed and keeping pace with *Elsinore* was exacting and, by mid-morning, Standing returned from a brief but valuable respite. An hour passed with both men at the prow, watching and guiding the progress of their vessel, even despite the additional swell. The wind blowing from the South Atlantic provided maximum speed, although, quite clearly, this was exactly what the other vessels in this theatre enjoyed. It became almost an enjoyment to watch the steady progress and to wonder how they might be faring in terms of distance from the enemy.

The question was answered sooner than any of them could have expected.

Vasteron had predicted correctly that their prey may have relaxed into a false sense of security in the belief that they had shaken off their pursuer. The Spaniard appeared, full ahead, under less than full sail. By noon, he could not ignore the presence of the British vessel, in the realisation that getting under full sail and fleeing may be pointless, as they had indeed been caught unawares and at a disadvantage.

The Spaniard made a definite turn in a southerly direction and brought an immediate reaction from *Elsinore*. For an hour, the distance closed the angle of pursuit changing as the *Elsinore* sought to cut off the flight of her target. *Durham* kept up, but carefully maintained distance, some six hundred yards off *Elsinore*'s larb'd, and now a similar distance again from the Spaniard.

Quite suddenly, the Spaniard lurched as she was brought about, her circle of turning remarkably small, and her progress through the water increasing as the southerly wind filled her sails. With an act of great seamanship and courage, the Spaniard had turned flight into attack, and came about with guns at the ready.

Passing on the *Elsinore*'s starboard side, he kept the encounter one-on-one, making the *Durham*'s involvement count for nothing.

Within a few minutes, the first broadside was exchanged, both ships lurching away from their opponent with the full weight of recoil as they began their next manoeuvre. The sounds of battle cracked the mid-day air and both drew blood in terms of structural damage, the Spaniard losing her fore-mast, and *Elsinore* losing a couple of guns along her number-one deck and incurring fire in the forecastle as a burning sail dropped heavily onto the bow.

The Spaniard then surprised his pursuer completely by turning in a much wider arc and quite blatantly making towards the *Durham*.

Standing was caught in two minds: should he keep *Elsinore* between them, or manoeuvre away from the battleground completely, leaving the two well-matched professionals to fight it out?

Daemon quickly realised that *Elsinore* had temporarily been wrong-footed herself and was in no position to intervene.

'John, we must do something. *Elsinore* is out-manoeuvred; we must draw fire whilst she recovers.'

'That's precisely against Vasteron's instructions. We must not come under fire.'

'What are your orders, Captain?' Daemon yelled with only a hint of irony.

'We must turn into the wind. We can pass her on her starb'd and risk volleys only from her two bow-cannons. With a bit of luck, we can also draw her attention for a few moments and give Vasteron a chance to show what he's made of.'

'Aye, aye, Captain!' Daemon was swinging up, taking position alongside Baptiste at the wheel.

The two men pulled on her until a half turn saw them heading northerly, across the Spaniard's bow.

Gathering momentum, *The Durham* passed two hundred yards in front of her, taking a flaming ball in her fore-sail and seeing another plunging into the waves right in her path.

A volley of musket-fire was heard, which incredibly saw John Standing suddenly spin round, gasping and tearing at his throat. A fountain of blood spurted in a wide arc from a hole in his neck. He slumped over the rail and landed beneath the bow rail, from where he had seconds earlier directed the action.

Daemon leapt over the rail and raced across the deck, grazing his knees on the deck as he came to Standing's side and thrust his hand into the gaping wound to try to stem the flow. Standing looked at him, eyes wide open with surprise — a one-in-a-thousand chance a musket-ball, fired almost certainly in the direction of *Elsinore*, had brought down his friend.

Standing tried to speak. Daemon shook him violently, but the effort merely produced an increased flow from his jugular vein. There was no way of stopping it. A pool larger than their combined silhouette formed around them, Standing's life-blood gushing away. Rinaldi slumped down beside them, his own hand in the wound and a suture rapidly engulfing Standing's head and shoulders. Daemon gasped, 'Quickly, do something, for Christ's sake, do something!'

Standing gagged, and blood spat across the short distance between them, spraying a vivid pattern onto Daemon's white blouse. 'She's all yours, my friend...' His head immediately slumped to one side, his eyes appearing to stare upwards, until they flickered and closed.

'Oh, Jesus...!' was all Daemon could manage. 'Jesus,

Mary and Joseph...! In God's name!'

Rinaldi continued to wrap Standing's head until the wadding and the lack of pressure stemmed the flow. The eyes of the entire ship's company were drawn to the scene as the two men leaned over the prone figure of their leader. The scene, frozen in time, would be etched into the minds of all those present.

'Come on, lads, let's get the bastards!' Barking the order, the sergeant of the Redcoats turned and began firing into the Spanish rigging. The four men loaded and re-loaded, giving everything they had, until distance made it futile.

To Daemon, it all seemed so unreal; but seeing the guards' determination and professionalism brought him to his feet. His insides lurched, retching up the contents of his stomach, briefly delaying his response, though he soon recovered sufficiently to release a dozen rounds of his own.

Reeling in his own rage and confusion, he reached the water barrel, sluicing cold water into his face and over his head. Regaining his composure, he sprang up to the wheel and screamed an order for the four-gun crews to position themselves for an attack.

He brought the wheel violently around and ordered Baptiste to complete the manoeuvre, whilst he raced towards the gun crew. 'Bring us about, brings us about... We must pass her full to her beam and give her something for John. Go! For Christ's sake, for John's sake, pull her round...!'

The *Durham* lurched and hauled herself into a tight turn. She closed on the beam end of the Spaniard and passed within one hundred and fifty yards. 'Fire, fire, fire,

fire!' In rapid succession, Daemon yelled his instructions, and canon-balls crashed into the Spaniard's castle, raking the quarters and galley areas. A crash and thunderous roar resulted, with fire immediately breaking out widespread across the rear of the galleon. By some miracle, Daemon had scored a hit on the munitions store.

Regaining some composure, Daemon returned to the wheel. 'Now get us the hell away from here!'

He watched as Baptiste hauled on the wheel, pulling her rudder around. With full sail, she put distance between herself and the stricken ship. Daemon now sighted *Elsinore*; having regained her own momentum, she closed on the Spaniard from the south. There were less than five hundred yards between them. The Spaniard appeared to turn slowly, lacking in purpose. The damage appeared to have rendered her helpless.

As the *Durham* put a thousand yards between them, Daemon was able to watch as *Elsinore* closed on her and hit her midships with a full volley. Thirty-six guns, at a range of a hundred yards, sent hot steel thudding into her. A token resistance of five or six cannons was the only fire returned.

There was general mayhem aboard the Spaniard. Fire crews attempted to stifle the flames, and twenty marines took up position to repel boarders; but, as *Elsinore* came alongside, there came a general calm. Arms were raised, and her flag came down. Soon, her crew were seen diving overboard to avoid the thick black smoke and searing heat of the fire.

Daemon signalled *Elsinore* for instruction, unsure as to whether *Durham* had any further part to play.

A boat and makeshift rafts appeared, with individuals

swimming and floundering. Daemon signalled to Baptiste to move in, the intention being to save lives and make prisoners of the fleeing Spanish.

The rescue operation went on for several hours, before the galleon sank slowly beneath the waves, fire having consumed the very bowels of the ship.

A plan was drawn up between Vasteron, Bartholemew and Daemon.

The two vessels, for the moment drawn together, would set sail for the nearest friendly port. Bartholemew would join the *Durham*, lending navigational and sailing experience to Daemon's drive and enthusiasm. Retaining forty prisoners on board promised an exacting and difficult passage, but her crew would also be boosted by a further six marines and two sea-men.

The plan was roundly approved, so the two ships made ready for a newly defined destination; but first, the matter of sending John Standing, third son of the Earl of Olney, to a watery grave.

Vasteron conducted the ceremony as dusk was falling, the sun a red ball on the western horizon. Daemon took his place on the captain's right hand, Bartholemew on the left. A sombre and respectful silence settled on the decks; below, terrified natives sat huddled and silent out of some sixth sense of the mood of those on deck.

Even the Spanish attempted to sit respectfully upright.

'The Lord giveth and the Lord taketh away...' began Vasteron.

Daemon's head sank to his chest and inwardly he chanted, 'Hail Mary, full of grace...' ten or fifteen times in succession.

'... Now and at the hour of our death.' Every time he

reached that point, his heart sank as he contemplated the finality of death. He saw Standing's face, ready smile, ironic raising of an eyebrow, hands always reaching out to encourage and to frame a picture from his own imagination.

His thoughts strayed to Margaret, their parting and the promises made of a life together. How would that be mended? She was a world away.

'We now commend his body into thy hands, to the depth of the oceans created by your Power, and we implore thy mercy and commend John Standing into thy Grace for ever and ever. Amen.'

The words invaded Daemon's thoughts like a pistol crack. There was a rumble as the body of his companion slid along the board, appearing briefly from under the Ensign colours, before disappearing over the side. A simple apologetic 'sploosh' signalled contact with the ocean.

Daemon reflected on the decision to bury John's lovely young sister on solid ground in Algeria, the first opportunity presenting itself following her tragic demise. The simple logic was that, should her family wish to visit her resting place, it may be deemed to be accessible. How that decision changed his own life, eventually bringing him together with Lady Daphne's own brother. Now he was gone, and there was no resting place where it was conceivable for his family to pay tribute.

Seven guns fired a volley, dispelling all thoughts and bringing him back to the moment. Vasteron gave the bible to Daemon and put a hand on his shoulder.

'A great responsibility passes to you, young man. This is a day you will remember for the rest of your life, for many reasons. Work with my officer. Lose your grief in endeavour and application. You will come through, and at the end of this voyage you will become a man of *means*. This is his legacy to you. Grasp it with both hands.'

With that, he held out his hand and shook with Daemon firmly, before turning. 'Bring her safe to port, Mr Bartholemew.' He dropped into the waiting boat and returned to *Elsinore*.

Daemon smiled grimly towards Bartholemew, and together they began to release the knots that bound together the two vessels at a safe fifty yards.

A burst of activity showed that the crew were as keen as ever to see the journey completed, for many of their own reasons. Some simply out of duty. Others thinking of a life in the New World. Some yearning to be back in their homeland. They nonetheless took up their duties with a burst of enthusiasm Daemon recalled from only the first few days on open water.

That night, as Daemon lay exhausted and satisfied that everything had been achieved that could be done, he stared at the tiny cabin space around him, the same view John Standing would have had many a night. The glow from a lone candle, lit areas of the room, leaving corners unpenetrated.

Daemon saw shadows, visions. He believed Standing was in the room. His mind went again to Margaret. Then to the Arab masters and to sharing profit. He thought about the goods they would bring from the West Indies for trade into Bristol and Liverpool, then the return south to Africa.

He could see himself on his knees, explaining John's sad departure. He could see himself in Margaret's arms. He did not feel at all comfortable, despite that she appeared ravishing and grown into a rare beauty in his imaginings.

His thoughts went to Kirsten: he could smell her hair.

He turned irritably and realised that sleep was eluding him, despite his desperate need of it.

Fresh thoughts of their arrival in Barbados — would it be Barbados? What about the onward journey? What about the Africans: would they run riot again? How would he manage to feed and water all of them, amongst forty dissident Spanish prisoners?

Daemon's head shook almost of its own volition. The task was beginning to overwhelm him: how would they manage, how would it all turn out? Dark, restless dream-filled sleep engulfed him.

The following morning provided no respite for Daemon. His first action was to deal with Sven's killer, still bound to the mast and presenting a very sorry sight. Daemon's anger had completely subsided though he knew the right thing to do was to go through a 'trial', find him guilty and hang him from the yard-arms! After a long moment poised over the prisoner, Daemon simply cut him free and charged Eric with the responsibility of shackling the man and returning him to the hold.

Daemon did not see Eric slit the man's throat from ear to ear and drop him over the side.

Chapter 14
A Measured Mile

A game of stud poker was underway. Banoldino sat opposite Carstein, each man resting their chin on a single upturned hand, two fingers pointing skyward.

Banoldino's right hand played with two gold-encrusted discs. Carstein dabbed the butt of his cigar, adding to the small hillock of ash that had grown in the tiny metal dish to his right.

A subdued gathering of fifteen or so had formed around their table; a colourful pile sat at its centre.

Smoke gently wafted into the air above the table, and three empty glasses stood around its edges, whilst two more, half-filled with amber liquid, rested near the two protagonists.

Banoldino suddenly shifted his weight, releasing his left hand to flip over the small fan of cards that had lay in front of him. 'Low flush.' was all he said.

'Hah! Low flush? My friend, you have a nerve! I threw away a low flush... replacing it with this!'

He turned over a full house. 'Jacks and eights!'

'So, you have me again. Your night, I declare, Carstein.'

The gathering rumbled into life, a few of them offering a smattering of applause. Others laughed lightly. One or two murmured condolences. Carstein gathered in his winnings and pushed a disc toward the dealer.

The Mexican, carefully dressed in white blouse and lace necktie, spilling from an embroidered waist-coat, nodded gratitude. 'Senor!'

Carstein stood, bowed respectfully and smiled towards Banoldino. 'Another fine evening in distinguished company. Your turn to win next time, I am sure of it.'

'Ha! Every evening you utter those words. I think "next time" becomes less and less likely! I think you have my measure at the card table, sir. I will have to think of another way to cross swords with the great Carstein.'

'Ha, ha! I hope it never comes to swords, senor. Perhaps a little fishing next time?'

'Anything you wish!' Banoldino edged around the vacated chairs. 'You know, I would take equal pleasure if we rolled dice or bowled a few Boules! But I wish to make a suggestion. Something I have had in mind for some time.' The crowd purred with delight and exchanged looks of intrigue. All were hushed for a moment, awaiting the proposal.

'I have managed to purchase a fine filly recently. Such an animal should not be put into the harness to plough fields. Such an animal, long, slender flanks, proud head, muscular across the chest. I would like to extend a challenge... I would match her with "Bavaria". What do you say to a marked-out mile? I hear horse-racing is all the rage in Europe.'

'Hmmmmh! You intrigue me, my friend. "Bavaria" is a fine specimen, I will admit. He would carry me all day without a sign of fatigue.'

'I have no wish to force the issue. I know my "Morning Star" would maintain a healthy pace over a mile. I did not intend to take advantage. I am happy for you to take time to consider, even perhaps try your stallion over distance and let me know if you think there is a reasonable challenge to be met.'

'Well, I appreciate the gesture. I will consider your challenge. Yes, why not! Given two weeks, I will prepare "Bavaria". If I consider the challenge reasonable, then, my friend, we make a wager!'

Both men laughed and shook hands and a rumble of approval from around them confirmed that the crowd was eager. Already bets were being made and a new, fresh topic invaded their pleasure-seeking lives, where it would fester and grow for many a day to come.

Chapter 15
Kirsten on the Edge

Kirsten rolled away from George Smith. Her pillow felt clean and fresh; the warmth of their bodies had brought a film of sweat to cover them, which felt good at first. But when the ardour cooled, she preferred the feel of clean linen all around her.

Smith felt aggrieved. He reached out for her. His arm slipped under hers and his hand rested on a full breast, by which he eased their two bodies back into close contact.

'George, you must let me go. I have to cool off.'

'Never! I'll never let you go! Come, come back to me, let's...'

She laughed, a throaty depth to her voice, deepened by the encounter. 'You mustn't — we can't lay here much longer... you know what we agreed: "we will cause no pain to anyone". So, we must not be found together, or even raise a suspicion or doubt.'

'I know, my love, but that was all before. Before I truly loved you. Now I need your body... I need all of you... all of the time. There is never a moment when I would not be by your side. I am lost without you.'

'George, don't say that! You know we could lose control and ruin everything, hurt those we love; we would end up hating each other for the damage we have done. No — it's better this way. We have... well, we have love. We make love, and I yearn for you, too. But it is better to have this... than nothing at all.'

Her soft, yielding flesh gently brushed against him as she unintentionally jiggled her hips up and down.

In seconds, he was ready for her again and slipped inside her. Moments later she moaned, low and throaty. Almost sobbing.

He stiffened and threw back his head.

A few minutes passed. Kirsten did sob this time as he pulled away. She bit the pillow to drown her protest. He breathed heavily but dragged himself upright and began to pull on his shirt. Kirsten did not turn. Her tears were private. She hugged her belly; a deep, ticklish sensation made her draw her legs up until she could get both arms locked around them.

Nothing more was said, before he slipped out of the room. The door came silently into position as he retreated down the corridor.

It had been four months since they first lay together. Kirsten constantly surprised herself that she could keep the relationship locked away somewhere so deep where no one would know it was happening. She and Allison were inseparable sometimes. Others Kirsten was able to communicate with Smith when he came up to the house every five or six days. They managed to arrange several rendezvous. Other times he managed to visit Kirsten, secretly, at the house, then appear, as if from a long ride, he would come to Allison's quarters as he would have, just arriving from the Fort.

So far they had been so careful it had worked to perfection. There was not a moment when they thought they might be exposed. This night, Kirsten spent another hour adjusting to these new sensations. She felt an overwhelming sense of possession. She began to fear that one day, this must subside and the energy must become diverted to a more deserving cause. She allowed herself a little smile, feeling mischievous.

Just then, Banoldino pushed on her door and was taken a little by surprise that it gave under his weight. He staggered a little as the door swung, but regained his footing, and waved his hand above his head, then down to one knee, an exaggerated gesture of salute.

'My darling, how are you? I have missed you. Please consent to joining me at the tables now and again. I am sure all our friends would be glad to see you. It's been far too long since we entertained or held a real occasion.'

He slumped down a little heavily beside her and threw an arm across her shoulders, which were well concealed beneath a large eider-down quilt.

Kirsten worried for a moment that the scent of her encounter with Smith had lingered, but Banoldino breathed the heavy aroma of stale brandy and cigars into her face and she knew he would detect nothing. Nonetheless, she blushed strongly, and her guilt brought a physical response which found her sitting upright and straightening out the covers, moving herself from his immediate proximity.

'Darling, please, you smell of tobacco and liquor, for goodness sakes; my bedding will need changing...'

'Oh, don't, my precious, don't chide me. I have had such a time... a very entertaining evening. I hope yours was, also?'

'Don't worry, my love, I have been well entertained, feeding and amusing your son, chasing around after him until we collapsed in a heap. I have been into town, brought the things we need for the entertainment of your friends. My life is never dull, I promise you.'

'In a way I am so glad to hear it. But I want you to be by my side. I see Carstein, and Ranleigh, Van der Mil, Fitzroy and the others, and they are often accompanied.'

'But not by their wives, I am sure!'

'Occasionally, Lady Evelyn comes along, but now Anabelle, she has grown, blossomed into a very fine young lady, she is "in society", you know. She would love to be your friend, I am sure. You could help her, guide her in the right direction.'

'Banolo, darling, I have too much to do than to be chaperoning a headstrong young madam around the cafes and salons of New York.'

'You think her headstrong? I did not realise you didn't like her, my love.'

'Oh, it's not that I don't like her... not at all. She can be a sweet girl, but she is a little old for her age... if you know what I mean. Besides, she remembers me when I used to fetch and carry for them... she never allows me to forget it.'

'Oh, I'm sure she means nothing by it... she is just a girl. I know she loves you like a sister really.'

'Sisters, is it? Well, I can tell you of sisters that fight like cats and dogs and would think nothing of destroying the other if it was to their own good.'

'Well, all the more reason why she should benefit from your friendship! She needs a guiding hand.'

'I hear she will soon get one. A mature hand at that!'

'What's this? You think she has a suitor?'

'Suitor, you may call it — pursuer, I would call it!'

'Who can you mean? Someone from the Township? Philadelphia, perhaps? Do I know him?'

'You know everybody, my love!'

'Then please put me out of my misery. I am at a loss.'

'You see him almost every night. How can this be that you are so blind?'

'Who? Tell me... surely, you cannot mean... Not *Carstein*? I would know, I would have noticed something. Does Ranleigh know?'

'Of course he knows! *She* knows! Lady Eve is most concerned... he is old enough to... well, he could even be her own age.'

'I am sure she is concerned. It concerns me very much, also. I know of his background... He is... honourable. His heritage is noble, in fact, but... I suppose she is flattered? What do you think?'

'Many would say it is a good match. He has everything a woman could want, but his age... well, it's... horrible!'

'Do you really think so, my love? And what about... us? You and me, are we *horrible*, also?'

'Oh, my darling, don't say it! You are my love, my soul. You brought me out of the ocean...'

'I brought you, yes. I found a young girl. I turned her into a wife. I am now damaged. I am not young... Do people look at us and say this is obscene?'

'Darling, I did not use such a word. I merely said "horrible" because we have seen Anabelle grow from a child, into... into... She is still barely seventeen!'

'Darling, don't worry, this is a world of adventure; she may find a beau walking through the door tomorrow, or she may be swept up and taken off into all sorts of danger along the frontier, and even beyond.

'There are many other things you could wish for a young, beautiful girl, blossoming into life, than to have someone with a fortune to look after her...'

Kirsten looked uneasily toward her husband.

'I begin to see a parallel' he said. 'I begin to see us for what we are. I am not liking what I see.'

Banoldino's head slumped onto the pillow and his gaze was lost above in the ornate ceiling decoration. A tear formed at the corner of his eye. Kirsten turned to him and lay her head upon his shoulder.

Nothing else passed between them, his thoughts lost in an uncertain, changing landscape; hers in the face, the look and the embrace of another man much closer to herself in years and in vitality.

Chapter 16
Race for Barbados

Daemon punished himself. Hour after hour, day after day, the ship ploughed on towards the ever-setting sun, the climate growing warm and the smell changing from day to day, one day sweet, the next of heavy, dank forest. He knew land could not be far off, but every day the lookout would call back that the horizon was clear.

The *Elsinore* up ahead, a guiding light! The comfort and security she brought was priceless and much appreciated. That one morning he might awake and find the *Durham* alone, plagued his quiet moments.

Yet Bartholemew had proven a capable and amiable companion, taking Standing's place in many ways: he knew the seas, he knew the stars. The reality was that he was more than capable of guiding the ship to safe harbour. Yet Daemon suffered moments of despair, of fear and loneliness.

He missed John Standing, an older brother, a friend, a mentor, a man. The man who had brought him from less than nothing to a world of possibilities and promise. He could almost sense that the end of the game was in sight.

Stepping carefully over outstretched legs, picking his way across the deck to the bow, he visually checked the bindings, the restraints and shackles of the prisoners on deck. Many proved decent, dedicated sailing men, oblivious to political aims and objectives. They enjoyed the sea, enjoyed the adventure and lived a day at a time.

They were grateful for the rations that were offered, and proved to be easy to deal with and showed restraint. The only moment of concern involved the herding of the forty-plus tethered seamen into a roped-in area, when the Africans came to the decks twice each day. They laughed and joked and threw remarks into the air that, apart from Rinaldi and one or two of *Durham*'s original crew, only they understood.

Their Spanish was guttural and unintelligible, except to the most trained ear. Whilst natural Italian and Spanish dialogue had a familiarity which could be understood if accompanied by the correct gesture, when the prisoners wanted to be understood only by their own kind, the words used were obscure, the dialect exaggerated, and it was impossible from the shapes formed around invariably broken, yellowing teeth, to understand a word.

Such banter began immediately a native emerged from the hatch. Grotesque gestures and mocking laughter accompanied the entire procedure.

The babble reached a crescendo when the women emerged. They retreated as quickly as they could manage behind the makeshift screen, where they were happy to wash down and exercise quickly, perfunctorily and without fuss, before returning to below decks at the earliest signal.

The process took two hours each morning and two hours in late afternoon. Dusk closed in when the hatches had been finally battened down. Then the crew turned to their own rituals of feeding and watering.

The chanting would begin building up to repetitive and inspiring harmonies.

Night's Watch took its place and the ship lunged on, into the deep metal sheen of the ocean.

'A drop of Madeira?'

'Indeed, why not.' Daemon poured two equal measures.

'You miss your friend?' Bartholemew asked him.

'Very much. John was more than a friend, almost like my older brother; he taught me everything.'

'You joined him in England...?'

'No, in Africa... I, er... I was rescued from a damaged ship.'

'One of ours?'

'Er, no... a merchantman. Off the coast, Agadir.'

'Oh, I see. What were you carrying?'

'Er... grain, and beef. Stuff for the English garrisons.'

'Oh... I see...'

'I met Standing in Morocco — we were travelling in the same direction, and he allowed me to join his train.'

'Ahh... Was he a married man?'

'Er... yes, indeed. He married while we were in Port... Margaret... My God... I have to take the news to her and I would rather face a Portuguese man-o-war!'

'I can imagine; the task would not be one I would relish myself.'

'Are you married?' Daemon asked him, to try to ease the conversation away from his own recent history.

'Er, no. I have not had the opportunity. I mean, the time... I have been at sea since I was eleven years of age.'

'My God, eleven?'

'Yes. My father *decided* I would be a Naval Officer. Mother fought him over it; time and again she begged him. The atmosphere was so desperate at home, I was glad to get away in the end! I still remember the morning. Cold, misty, they brought the chaise and Mother stood on the steps, with my sister Emily; they cried and hugged each other. Father stood aloof, at the side. He shook my hand, then stooped and clapped me on the back. Mother turned away and ran back into the house.

'I was miserable and sick on the journey, but mercifully it came to an end around noon. I arrived at London Bridge. Myself and another boy were taken by small boat down to Greenwich.

'London was breathtaking: the tall buildings, ships of every shape and size. The river was the busiest place I have ever seen. There were so many boats, you could almost walk across the river by passing from one to the other.

'All the time I held a roll of parchment in my hand. A small valise contained everything I owned.

'We were deposited on the banks at Greenwich. Four tall, full-masted ships were alongside. Flags flew from every building. I was terrified!'

'Your story is a bit different from mine.' Daemon smiled, the irony in his voice and demeanour obvious.

Bartholemew laughed. 'How so?' But as Daemon smile inwardly, he continued with his own story.

'The Captain looked us both up and down, but stopped to glare down into my eyes. My eyes stared back, but, hard as I resisted, tears formed on my eyelids. It was not crying, but, well, I just couldn't help it; it was like my eyes were stinging — but to all the world, it must have appeared as if I were crying! "Sort yourself out, boy, I'll not have withering infants aboard my ship," he bellowed. "Desist! Desist that whimpering or I'll have you flogged!"'

'Another Midshipman, a little older than us, yelled at us in a broken voice to "follow me or be damned" ...leading us away from the Captain and down into the quarters. I swear I could hear the Captain and the First Mate chuckling above. But it gave me no comfort, I can tell you!'

'I'm sure it didn't! Now, sadly, I must take to my bunk. There may just be a big day ahead of us.' Daemon rose and stretched. 'I bid you good night. Please, help yourself to another tot, if you've a mind.' With that, he turned out of the door and into his own cabin, where he lay down and found the immediate solace of a sound sleep.

The noisy clang of the bell aloft brought him so quickly upright that for a full minute he was disorientated. Was he in a Moroccan gaol? His hammock aboard the *Warrior*? The exotic quarters of Agadir?

With thoughts of Standing's demise doggedly replaying in his mind, he got to his feet and grabbed his tricorn, before mounting the stairs.

The ship's bell rung out incessantly, as Baptiste was determined to *herald* the New World.

'Land... *LAND*! Off the starb'd bow, skipper! Land off the starb'd bow!'

There was a buzz of excitement as the dusky light was cast by a retreating moon and the warm glow of the sun on the eastern horizon. These effects combined to frame the black shape of an elephant's back, away in the distance.

Daemon was in the rigging in seconds. The hum of conversation, a babble of excitement, even the wailing from below, all provided a cacophony of noise, from which only the incessant ringing of the bell could compete.

Land! Undeniably, a half a day's sail away, straight along their current line of latitude.

Signals were exchanged with *Elsinore*, where great preparation had been under way for some time.

There was activity in every direction, a constant rumble of sound, equipment echoing and its own bell continuously clanging.

Below decks, the Africans realised something was happening: they were audibly pulling at their shackles, chain rasping through rings and thudding onto the deck.

The Marines were on their feet in preparation and were first at the ready.

By the time darkness fell, the triangle of light at the rear of *Elsinore* performed its role as a perfect guide, navigating around the island

Soon, more lights appeared through the gloom. *Elsinore* came to anchor and the lights beyond her provided a colourful backdrop. Intoxicating smells, a mixture of spicy food and rotten eggs wafted towards them.

Elsinore had brought them to a safe distance of three hundred feet, and their own anchor plunged into the still waters of the harbour.

A boat made its way across the void between them and clunked into the hull. Vasteron dropped jauntily onto the deck.

With a sweep of his tricorn, he bade them, 'Welcome to the Caribbean!'

Chapter 17
The Plantationers

Within forty-eight hours, the *Durham* was being readied for her onward journey. The time in harbour at Barbados had proven vital in terms of experience for Daemon and his crew, alerting them to the dangers that lurked in every situation.

Captain Vasteron had ferried Daemon and Rinaldi to the wharf, where they were, as usual, beset by every manner of life-form, from errant clergymen to drunken natives, prostitutes and entertainers, cut-throats and fortune-hunters. All saw opportunity when a new ship arrived.

Fighting their way through, the shore party managed to make it to the Governor's residence, where Daemon was introduced to Sir James Deakin of Derbyshire, who had been seconded to this rejuvenating outpost in the bosom of the Spanish Empire as a reward for failure as a Captain in his Majesty's Navy.

An amputated limb had left him without the spirit for adventure. He accepted the Governorship as an alternative to further pain and discomfort as a Junior Commander under Admiral Hope, a man who truly hated him, in return for his own utter loathing of the man.

James Deakin was not an evil man, a coward or a despot, but he had made enemies and preferred to sit in a seat located near to an exit door, with a horse and trap readied for a journey.

He eyed Daemon intensely as Vasteron recounted the previous thirty days in a dramatic narrative. Deakin, although he did not set out with the intention of profiteering from every situation, considered himself a man with an eye for an opportunity. He may have seen Daemon as a man out-of-his-depth by inference, and perhaps open to a proposition or two.

Vasteron kept a fatherly eye over the proceedings, as much as his position would allow, but nonetheless felt that unless he acted with some stealth, he may be feeding his young friend to the wolves.

'So, young man, you have my deepest sympathy; you have lost your leader, your friend, in such tragic circumstances. Such a burden he has left you... We must see how we can assist in your endeavours.'

'Sir, I would be grateful for any guidance; under the circumstances, we need all the help we can get.'

'Please, assemble a sample of your cargo for our inspection, say four or five, representative of the health and vitality of the natives you have brought to our shores. We will do our best with what we find.'

Rinaldi interjected at this point. 'Sir, if I may, the cargo, as you call it, consists of some of the finest specimens ever to reach these shores, I am certain of it.'

'No doubt... er, Senor Doctori. I am filled with expectation, but you must appreciate, we have been well supplied. Why, every slaver that sailed in a westerly direction has found the way to our harbour! We have been the first drop of many a voyager. Our plantations are well stocked.

'Please! Come! Let us not debate the matter when it is in our interests to wait until we have feasted our eyes.'

A pleasant evening passed as Deakin held court and provided a decent repast and fine wines. He continuously goaded Rinaldi over his nationality and his connections.

'I have spent many an evening with your former master... a rogue and a pirate of the first order! Yet a man I could compare with the best for entertainment and bonhomie. What do you say, Young Master Quirk?'

He had taken a liking to the quick-witted and unpretentious young Irishman, but insisted on keeping him in his place, with reference to 'Young Master' or 'My dear boy'. Such was his intention in keeping his forbearance over the situation for his own eventual advantage.

'If, as you insist, your cargo is of the finest African flesh, then surely you have seconded a handmaid for your own... ahem, daily requirements?' The company joined him in raising a glass to 'imagined delights'.

Daemon laughed and chided his host with a friendly denial, following up a little more intently with, 'My conscience and my respect for the value of unsullied cargo would not allow me the merest indulgence, although the temptations were as those of Jesus in the Wilderness! Get thee behind me, Satan!'

They laughed uproariously and topped up their glasses with more copious helpings of wine.

The following day, a gathering of prospective buyers was assembled with due diligence by the Governor, who presided over this exhibition, as would a baron at a joust.

Chairs were set out, a dais and sail-cloth formed a canopy, and palm leaves wafted in unison in a wide arch around both ends and to the rear of the assembled gathering of plantation owners.

One, in particular, was given pride of place. This man held himself particularly highly, and afforded great attention to a comely, bonneted girl, holding herself with a gracious air beneath a parasol. They were introduced as "Willem van Eyck and his lovely daughter Gertrude".

Daemon bowed low upon meeting them and stood back until they had arranged themselves in the most advantageous seating.

Rinaldi had been appointed to orchestrate the presentation.

Daemon carefully selected the stock to be displayed, choosing in turn general health, symmetry of features and skin texture as main criteria. In the case of the two full-grown males, broad shoulders and narrow hips, long legs with thick thigh muscles.

The female 'companion' was a pleasant-looking, tall specimen with skin of darkest ebony, which glowed with health and vitality. A younger male, not fully developed in height and girth, was followed by a pubescent teenage female and a younger, pre-pubescent girl. A beautiful boy of Nubian features, but a shock of black curls framing his angelic face, completed the exhibits.

They were paraded on to the dais, suitably attired in white calico, with their limbs oiled and shining.

Daemon stood proudly to one side as they were organised into a line-up as the gathering murmured its approval and chatted gaily among themselves.

It had been some five months since the last cargo had been produced at the island. A dozen slaves had been purchased, but this arrival was, despite the Governor's protestations, more *timely*.

The crops were full and ripe and awaiting harvest, and some of the better house slaves had been converted to field hands, in order to cope with the demand for manpower.

A shortfall had developed, of house slaves and with field hands, which had only partially been redressed.

There were eight plantation owners assembled, four of them British, two Dutch, one Portuguese and one Spanish.

Their produce consisted of sugar cane and coffee but most also produced wheat or barley as a second string to meet the demand of basic feeds such as bread and ale.

Between them, there was potential for fifty purchases, and Daemon, whilst considering that the pickings should be balanced, determined not to allow only the best of their cargo to be off-loaded here in the British dominion.

He held on to the belief, because he knew that Standing would have, that the best deals would be done in Spanish territory or Saint Domingue, where the French owners were getting fat on the success of their own coffee and cocoa plantations.

Daemon knew he would be sailing unprotected into French and Spanish waters, but recent history held that a deal could be done with the rich owners, and they remained more favourable to their profitability than patriotic allegiance to France. They were enterprising producers and traders; they did not want, nor support, conflict between the European Heads of State.

Were an eighty-gun galleon to sail into the harbour bearing the French flag, they would pay dutiful homage until its sail could be seen tiny on the horizon, when everything would return to normal.

The presentation in Barbados ran its course, with a collection of owners and their associates eyeing the slaves, before designating a member to pay close inspection.

In turn, they would be introduced as 'my Physician' or my 'overseer' or even 'my slave-master'. Each in their finery, well-dressed and respectable, they would conduct a detailed examination with the same ruthless indifference that they might inspect a goat. Mouths were held open, tongues pulled to one side, ears poked, hair combed and examined. Armpits were inspected, buttocks splayed and breasts prodded and rolled.

There was no distinction between the child and the most powerful male. They were treated with equal disdain and equally rough handling.

All the time, the Africans accepted this treatment, and only their eyes betrayed that each was filled with fear and indignation.

Daemon stepped in to save further discomfort upon the exhibits, attempting to dismiss them, so that he could open up the discussion on 'terms'. Just then, Gertrude van Eyck rose and determinedly shouldered her way through to the line-up.

'Hold, please. I haf not carried out my inspection!' She spoke in lightly accented English.

Daemon stood in her way and, with the most dignified bow and sweep of his hat, he attempted to indicate that the moment had passed.

'Ma'am, please forgive me, I thought we had satisfied interest to the point of tedium. Perhaps there is one last thing we may offer before rounding up the display, for today at least.'

'Niet! I haf not concluded... Do you think I am here to mop my father's brow? I am an experienced breeder of animals and livestock of every kind. There is far less value in a field hand or a plough horse, than in a thoroughbred which can produce other thoroughbreds. I am sure you vud acgree!'

Daemon stood aside and allowed the girl to pass, whilst standing erect and allowing himself an overdramatic shrug of the shoulders, at which the Governor smiled and returned the gesture with one of his own, in his case by adding an indulgent twist of the mouth.

Gertrude moved towards the adolescent male and yanked at his wrappings, exposing him to all eyes.

A murmur of approbation rose up, despite the youth's frantic attempt to gather himself. Gertrude removed his hands from their task and proceeded to finger and fondle his unsuspecting genitalia. Then she turned on the pubescent girl and thrust a hand between her legs, probing determinedly until she was ready to pull away.

Daemon moved threateningly towards Ms van Eyck, until a restraining hand from Rinaldi pulled him back. Daemon clamped his mouth closed and turned so that he did not have to watch as the brash, heartless Hollander mauled the testicles and manhood of the male slaves and pushed and probed at the females.

His anger mounted as the group reacted like a family of shamed Hebrews cast out of an Egyptian township, struggling to cover themselves and maintain some semblance of dignity.

'Speak to them,' he said to Rinaldi through gritted teeth. 'Find out the sort of numbers they are considering and let us get out of here. If it were my decision, I swear before I accept a penny of their stinking coin, I would starve myself for a year.'

When it came time for the Van Eycks to withdraw, they asked in a most civilised manner if Daemon and the 'good Doctori' would like to join them for supper.

After declining graciously, due to demands which awaited him back on board, Daemon turned to Rinaldi. 'I would rather eat in the hold with the slaves than sit at the same table as them, God forgive me!'

Rinaldi held a hand in the air. 'Daemon, your heart is too pure for the work ahead! I will try to help all I can. But I must insist: allow *me* to handle the business — I will get the right price, I give my word.' With hands held up as if in prayer, Rinaldi implored Daemon to be calm. A resigned shake of the head was all Daemon could muster in response.

Rinaldi returned to the buyers, whilst Daemon returned to the Governor. 'Young sir, please join me in a glass of fine Madeira. Do you know, they are copying the process in the islands and producing a wine almost as fine as the original?'

Daemon allowed the Governor his indulgence, although he knew well enough that his attention was being drawn from the proceedings, which he all too obviously found unpalatable.

'I have arranged a small reception for the farmers. They have taken a day away from normal routine to attend, and we owe it to them to make their sojourn as pleasant as possible. Come, we will arrange ourselves so that we may greet them as they arrive!'

Daemon allowed himself to be led away towards a marquee, arranged with the Governor's colours flying over the entrance. Inside, tables had been bedecked with white cloth and sashes, chairs arranged around in groups of eight.

The owners and their companions would be welcomed to dine before departing. Deakin assured Daemon that the more wine they consumed, the more generous the bidding would be, and every deal, done on a handshake, would be honoured no matter what.

Each of the owners would want the others to think their purchases had been of superior stock. So even those not perhaps totally enamoured at their final selection, would never admit to having been outdone.

Despite his ill humour, Daemon did enjoy the repartee, confusing at first, as the plantation owners and breeders exchanged insults and goading, whilst every attempt at humour was greatly exaggerated and repeated a number of times until the subject-matter dimmed or was replaced by something equally tired and re-used.

'I tell yea, there are demons at large in my fields. Because every time I weigh a bale, I swear there is a body hiding in there to make it weigh more. Soon as I make the count, the darn things seem to get smaller and lighter.'

'Why, McCormack, you know if you prod 'em, real fierce-like with a pitchfork, you are sure to find a peqininne balled up inside.'

'Heh, heh... Found myself twins one time...!'

'Ha, He, Haw — there was a whole family in one o' ma bales last spring... I was glad to get shot of 'em on account of they wuz eatin' us outa- house-an-home!'

So it went on, until tears of laughter ran tracks down their now dusty faces.

The women fanned themselves and loosened their necklines when the afternoon heat rose to a peak, before wine by the flagon was consumed and the diners spewed out into the hot sun.

Daemon walked among them, politely introducing himself in person until each member of the party had been greeted. The Honourable Judge Edmunds pulled Daemon aside at one point and suggested that he take the first offer made by Van Eyck — he was not apparently used to bargaining and would never allow himself to be out-bid; the others generally allowed him first choice, as they would always have found it difficult to outbid him.

Daemon assumed therefore that the price he offered would be deemed fair and reasonable. He reminded himself that he would allow Rinaldi to conduct matters with Van Eyck, and therefore must be advised as he himself had been.

Thanking the former judge, Daemon set off into the gathering, now standing around under a parasol, whilst the huge form of McAndrew, still sporting a tartan waistcoat, as if anyone needed reminding of his origins. His booming voice commanded everyone's attention.

'So, laddie, tell us of your exploits on the high seas. Was the voyage two steps from hell... or just the one?'

'Indeed, sir, there were times when I would have wished myself elsewhere... indeed many times...!'

'Did you lose much of your stock? Will we see the entire head count... or d'yea only intend us to have the ailing and infirm dumped upon our shores?'

'I assure you, sir, whatever your desires may be, we are only here to serve. I swear you have seen a very fair representation of the quality of our stock. You will be delighted at your purchases and you may determine the numbers.'

Chapter 18
Gertrude

The following morning, Daemon and Baptiste worked tirelessly in preparation of the fifty Africans to be offered at the auction. Baptiste led the way, with a trail of chained humanity stretching back fifty yards or so behind him.

Draped in fresh muslin and with the sunlight caressing the bare shoulders, arms and legs of the naturally handsome negroes, the stock would have been considered prime at any auction yard.

Directed towards a cattle-pen, they were urged to parade around the perimeter so that the gathering could appraise them at close quarters.

The Governor had seen to it that refreshments were provided, as the owners gathered again in increased numbers.

With the arrival of the parade, a hum of expectation rose as the wine-fuelled repartee swelled the atmosphere into something similar to a fair-ground.

When Van Eyck edged towards the rail and helped his daughter into an advantageous position, a hush settled, allowing an air of anticipation to replace the carnival atmosphere.

Gertrude pushed her way into the pen and began slapping a number of them with white labels, by means of some sort of honey-based substance so that the labels clung to the shoulders of the chosen. When she had finished, two 'bucks' and four females, two of which had a child at their side, were edged away from the shuffling parade into the centre.

Van Eyck turned to Daemon, whilst Baptiste continued to press the others in their circuitous route around the corral.

'Seventy-five guineas for the bucks, fifty for the females. I'll allow them to retain their pequininnies... we want them to breed — but they will definitely produce more if they know they will be allowed to nurture dem and watch dem grow.'

'That is entirely your affair, sir; when you own them, you may conduct your business to suit yourself... However, I do believe a fair price for the bucks, as you call them, would be *ninety-five* guineas, and the dams sixty-five. The children will grow true and strong and they are worth fifteen guineas of anyone's money.'

A sharp intake of breath among the gathering focused all the attention on the discourse between these two. Even the negroes stopped and observed, although they may have only been able to guess at the meaning or direction of the discussion.

Mr... er... Captain... I am not used to having my judgement questioned... I have offered you exactly what these negroes are worth to me — or, in fact, to anyone on this island... You may take that as the Gospel truth!'

Daemon looked Van Eyck steadily in the eye and said simply, 'Then I'm afraid we can't do business, sir.'

'Papa!' Suddenly Gertrude was at his side, taking his gloved hand in hers. 'Papa — perhaps you are a little disadvantaged by the light from where you stand... Please accompany me into the ring, where you may see better from there.'

Van Eyck turned, astonished at this outburst from his daughter, and for some moments appeared as though he would strike her; but a gentle pressure being applied to his hands gradually calmed him. Blinking into the sunlight, he allowed himself to be led by his daughter.

Out of earshot from most of the gathering, she whispered something, and he looked at her again, before slowly turning to Daemon.

'Why, young man, I think I may have been mistaken. Your valuation appears to have been correct. I will agree your terms except for the young. I do believe they might fetch thirty guineas at auction and, therefore, I am prepared to match that sum.'

Daemon could hardly have been more surprised. Leaning across, he shook Van Eyck's hand, noticing the beaming smile offered in his direction by Gertrude, and he could hardly have mistaken the message it carried.

With that deal completed, the other owners pressed in and began to raise their arms for attention. One or two also carried markers, but the bids made — raised by the Dutchman's acceptance of Daemon's valuation — all achieved a more than satisfactory level. Rinaldi and Baptiste completed the rest of the business for the day, with all fifty-two souls brought out having been purchased.

Daemon stood with Baptiste as they watched wagons turn and wheel away into the distance, accompanied by the sounds of simpering and sobbing and calling out that echoed across the bay until the last of them disappeared.

This had been business conducted in as humane a manner as had been previously experienced. No whip or baton had been used throughout the entire process. The handling of the natives imbued a respect which the landowners had not previously witnessed.

The slaves were more often handled with such savagery and disdain that the landowners felt almost obliged to treat their purchases cruelly, matching the behaviour of the slavers.

They often sped away so as to be able to ease off and begin at the earliest possible moment to encourage the slaves to believe that they 'belonged' or had been 'saved', thereby owing the masters and owners a debt of gratitude.

The events of the day had left them all with a slight uneasiness at the way things had been done. This may not prevail beyond the first days back. The new purchases would soon be harvesting, chopping, gathering or grinding as part of their normal daily routine. The conditions varied, but generally they would be well treated and fed, so that their productivity was never adversely affected.

Daemon left the auction with a sense of relief that things had not been as bad as he imagined, that perhaps the negroes had been brought to a better life.

Certainly, better than life on the open seas, better than the life enslaved to their own kind, where respect for the life of a neighbour, or inferior, was less than that of a persistent mosquito.

Keen to be back aboard, and to provide the usual washing and feeding routine that the natives had begun to thrive upon, Daemon tried his best to extricate himself from the town and from further engagement.

He had to remind himself this was, after all, a British possession and that he may well need to dock here again, to re-stock or to conduct repairs. He wanted to leave without having burned any bridges.

Just then, he noticed a veiled conversation passing between the Governor and Gertrude van Eyck.

The Governor approached Daemon, again expressing his satisfaction at how the proceedings had been conducted by extending an invitation to Daemon to dine that evening at the behest of the Van Eycks.

Daemon faltered only when Gertrude confirmed that the invitation would include the opportunity to bath and change for dinner, having impressed on her father the need for civility.

Desperate as he was to make his departure, the notion of another good meal, some fine wine and the opportunity to bathe in warmed water, became too good to resist.

Gertrude cast another inviting smile in Daemon's direction, with such a change in her demeanour that he began to appreciate that she was a comely young lady, and not quite the harridan he had first thought.

Baptiste and Rinaldi both accepted Daemon's urgings that they, at least, return to the ship and make her sound for the night.

Satisfied that the natives would be well cared for, Daemon prepared himself for the task ahead.

Chapter 19
A Swift Departure

Before joining the Governor, Daemon had some farewells to complete. Vasteron had confirmed his intention to return to Europe and, in particular, to take his prize from the contents of the Spanish galleon.

Daemon caught up with the Captain in the harbour, boarding *Elsinore* by invitation from the bridge, as his boat pulled alongside. Bartholemew had re-joined the ship's company following the transfer of all seventy Spanish prisoners into the hands of Governor Deakin.

Deakin had complained that he had precious little reserves of food and could not imagine what he would do with seventy Spaniards. However, Vasteron gave him a full assurance that a fleet of British ships was making its way to the Caribbean. Its objective was to take a firm hold in the region and that Trinidad, Jamaica and St Lucia would soon be under the British flag.

A great deal of scope would be found for Spanish prisoners, either in exchange for territorial gains or for British prisoners. The Spaniards would be used, so the problem would not long be the responsibility of Barbados, and major change would soon be evident.

Vasteron bade a fond farewell to Daemon and his crew. He offered to return messages and belongings to the family of John Standing, but Daemon insisted that the task would be his alone and that it would increase his determination to make a speedy return.

The two Captains and Lt Bartholemew clapped one another on the back and agreed that, at some time in the future, they would meet again and share a flagon.

Daemon left them in high spirits, but was soon brought firmly down to the ground when his boat bumped along the hull of the *Durham*, a sharp reminder that two hundred souls still rested in the cramped confines of the hold.

The Governor pointed out the outstanding views and features of the ranch as they passed a good half mile from the dirt road that snaked up from the bay.

They had been on Van Eyck land for at least ten minutes at a steady trot and the house was still not in view. Four outriders, Redcoats from the garrison, ambled ahead of the Governor's carriage, although they were at ease, with minimal expectation of interference with the progress of this popular appointee.

'A very impressive estate! I imagine Mr Van Eyck is a powerful man on this island,' Daemon offered, feeling that the pause in conversation was his responsibility.

'Oh, yes. He was already a wealthy man, but apparently had a calamitous affair with a member of the Dutch Royal family. He arrived with a minimal household, a pregnant wife and one chest containing his treasured possessions. Once he had established the lie of the land, he put his wealth to work. Harnessing the resources of the most capable builders and carpenters, and appointing the best plantation manager in the Caribbean, he set up a profitable sugar plantation in a matter of three seasons.

'His wife gave birth and died in the process. She was not the member of the Dutch Royals, but another he had turned to, apparently in spite of his own family's urgings. He never communicated again with anyone from his own country, except for a very astute lawyer who, to this day, takes care of his trading contracts in Europe.

'The daughter was brought up on the estate, exposed to all the intricacies of keeping and utilising the slave population and maintaining the *status quo*. Van Eyck runs his affairs with a heavy hand, but he has made a great success of business here in the islands — riding one storm after another, seemingly always coming out on top in his dealings.

'The daughter has had a number of suitors and appears to have frightened off most of them. She is a chip off the old block, if you take my meaning!'

'I can understand that. In fact, she terrifies me...' Daemon was joined in a short burst of laughter by the Governor.

'I do believe you handled yourself well this afternoon, even in that respect! I think Gertrude took quite a fancy to you.'

'That's exactly what I mean...!'

'You know, a man like yourself, young, with an engaging way about him, could do very well in these parts. What do you intend to do when you have completed this voyage? Will you return to Europe with a cargo?'

'Oh, yes. I have a debt of honour to keep. I have a duty to my late friend John Standing, which will mean returning to Port Said. I owe it to him to make a success of the return journey and to make a full account over to his wife.'

'Come, come, you may do all you must without returning in person. You may miss the opportunity of a lifetime fulfilling such a sentimental wish.'

'No, sir, believe me. I will return. I must tell her of the man she married. They had only a few days together. I brought them together, and I feel it is my duty…'

'Is there more than just loyalty, or is the lady also of interest now that she is free?'

'Strangely, I do not take offence at your suggestion; rather, it inspires me to consider the very motives which drive me. I do have feelings for Margaret. We were… let's say, we both suffered misfortune. She helped me, and then I was able to return her kindness. But my feelings towards her are something perhaps like that of a brother to a sister. I am fond of her, and I am fiercely loyal. But I have no other intentions. I simply must return.'

'Well, such devotion is uncommon these days, I do declare. With the world opening up and travel abroad so commonplace, a man may disappear for a lifetime — change his nature and his name and survive in a world very different to that of his origins. Wealthy men with great burdens or responsibilities may migrate to another land and become humble farmers or traders, changing the very nature of their upbringings. Poor men, without a hope or prayer, may venture into the unknown and emerge as rich and powerful, "worldly", men of great influence. These things are possible nowadays. In fact, anything is possible. All that is required is the ability to make the right decision almost within a split second of an opportunity presenting itself, and a man can change his destiny.'

'Well, Governor, you might say I have actually achieved that in a minor way. I have experienced such opportunism myself. I must, however, fulfil my duty, before I think again of my own destiny. I once set out on a quest, to rescue a girl. I have not been able to fulfil my obligation in that respect. I believe the lady in that case to have suffered and died. In this case, to the best of my knowledge, the lady is alive and waiting.'

'You are a determined young man! Be careful that you do not wander too far from your course when confronted with other very determined individuals. You have my respect, young man, for what you achieved here at the stockyard and for what you have told me. I wish you well; and, indeed, if there is a service which is within my powers, I would be ready and willing to fulfil any request you may wish to make. Please consider my door open.'

'I thank you, Governor. I hope we may have a chance to meet in the future and that it may always be on these terms.'

Two or three moments passed, with the twilight settling all around, leaving the image, when it appeared, of the stately, columned mansion-house, a stark blue-white against the darkening skies. Lanterns glowed from all of the downstairs and some of the upper rooms.

A number of carriages had already arrived and stood to the side, whilst horses and tenders were at ease on the well-trimmed, grassy slopes beyond.

An over-dressed, black footman showed them into the grand hallway, which was opulently arranged with paintings, tapestries, a huge chandelier and ornate staircase sweeping in an arc towards the upper floors.

Van Eyck, dressed in purple velvet and a fine powdered wig, greeted them just inside the main doors. There were six or seven other guests, most of whom

Daemon had enjoyed a moment or two in conversation with earlier in the day.

Polite, but again extremely formal, Van Eyck performed the ritual welcome and grunted his impatience at the non-arrival of his daughter, making his annoyance plain to everyone, as the servants fluttered around nervously in anticipation of his ill humour.

A string quartet began with some intricate European music, undoubtedly fresh from the Viennese conservatoires but on this occasion performed by well-rehearsed Africans. Meanwhile, Van Eyck waved brusquely towards a waiter with a tray of glasses, which were speedily offered to the guests in turn.

Daemon shuffled along with the gathering forming a small group, wishing to blend in as much as possible. Within moments, they turned as one towards the stairway, where Gertrude had appeared, smiling and gracefully poised in a glittering gown which frothed around her ankles as she elegantly descended.

Her hair was arranged on one side and curled around her bare shoulder, above an ample and very nicely displayed bosom.

Nipped at the waist with a royal blue sash, she looked as if she had stepped from the balcony of a grand opera-house and was about to deliver an aria.

Eventually, she arrived at the bottom step, where she proceeded to extend her hand to the guests in turn, until, finally, Daemon saw that it was no longer possible for him to hold back, so he stepped forward.

She offered her hand and retained her hold on him, closing her gloved hand around his fingers.

Moving in comfortably at his side, she steered him towards the open doors into the dining room and placed him in the seat next to the one she would eventually occupy.

Each took their turn in claiming a seat at the table. Four ladies and five gentlemen taking their places. The first courses arrived and polite conversation was exchanged.

Much of what was said recounted the day's events, commenting on the quality of stock they had claimed at the auction ring and how the natives had been able to settle into their new surroundings, one boasting that he got half a day's work out of one of them before the charge-hand called time to bring the day to a close.

Daemon pushed all thoughts of protestation to the farthest corners of his mind. Remembering the level of hospitality provided, in truth since the moment they had landed on the island, he had acted on the principle that one day he may have to return.

He felt fortunate indeed to have been accepted as a genuine trader, a businessman, albeit a fairly inexperienced one, and they had given him an easy ride.

Opposite sat Jarvis Howard, a man who may also have climbed from the very base of society to forge a place of respectability in the New World. Beside him was his bride, of Spanish origin, as it turned out, having been rescued at sea when pirates attacked the ship bound for her father's homeland, where she was to be married to a distant cousin.

She was brought, instead, to Barbados by English Captain Brandon Cransford, who caught the offender attempting to leave the area with a bounty-laden vessel.

Giullianna had her heart set on her rescuer. To her numbing disappointment, the Captain was recalled to duty. He re-stocked his ship and set off for the North Americas, where support was needed for the British forces occupying the southern territories accessed from Chesapeake Bay.

There was no promise of a reunion, so Giullianna was put ashore, minus a father, and, faced with an interminable wait for a ship which may transport her back to Spanish territory and eventually to Spain, she decided to seek the protection of the first male of substance she could find.

She found in Jarvis a bitter and resentful companion. She clearly did not love him and found it difficult to pretend. He showed her off like a prize pony, but tethered her in every possible way in their failing domestic alliance.

She held her head up in a way only the Spanish aristocracy can, proud and aloof, but hardening her previously attractive features into a stony, hawk-like visage which nonetheless softened when congenial conversation was offered by gentlemen of her own breeding.

Alongside Giullianna, sat low in his chair by dint of a stooped back, was the Reverend Caitlin and his companion in the Protestant mission, Ruth Hebburn. *Grey* in complexion and in every other particular, Ruth portrayed the faithful apostle to the Reverend to perfection. She agreed with his every utterance and insisted on reinforcing all forthcomings by her own repetitious approvals.

The Reverend's humble prayer before the dining commenced. 'May God grant us good spirits and health to enjoy the fruits of our labour', which was enthusiastically followed by 'Amen, amen! We hear you Lord.'

Daemon looked up and the first thing that crossed his mind when the chanting ceased was 'the fruits of who's labour exactly?' as the self-satisfied priest and his companion tucked in to the lavish offerings.

The party was completed by a sickly-looking 'Viscompt', introduced as a 'force to be reckoned with' in the New World. The 'Viscompt', in truth, looked as though he had had quite enough of the New World and would be happier finding a comfortable berth on the way back to the civilised Punch Rooms of European Spa culture.

He was significantly out of sorts; his health and his desire to be elsewhere rendered him a sour and miserable companion. His wife, also pale and jaded, mirrored his own wish to be elsewhere. Nonetheless, she warmed to the occasion when her second goblet of wine had been seen off. She became almost vivacious in her manner and quite engaging in her volatile response to any attempt at humour.

Rickenbach had arrived fourteen years earlier, bought out a failing plantation, re-stocked with capable slave labour and produced ten good harvests in the previous twelve years. His achievement had hardly been bettered, but his demeanour wilted under the strain. He longed to be back in civilisation, and it was this subject which occupied the gathering throughout the second course.

Would Daemon be at all interested in purchasing the plantation and its assets and replacing the 'Viscompt', enabling him to return to his native land?

Daemon provided every possible protestation, but could not deter or deflect the idea which seemed to appeal to everyone around the table except himself.

Daemon had almost run out of polite objections and was becoming desperate, firstly to not offend, and secondly to rule himself unequivocally out of the question.

Fortunately, the Reverend brought up the question of breeding — with the contention that breeding thoroughbred horses was very much akin to breeding native Africans.

This became the next topic of conversation, which also brought in the ladies, in particular Gertrude, who had a great deal to say on the matter. Without fully becoming a battlefield, this lasted through to the moment which saw male and female guests temporarily parting. Havana cigars and Brandy awaited the men. Polite conversation and a pianoforte awaited the women.

Throughout the evening, Daemon had felt the playful nudging and indeed teasing contact which had been conducted by Gertrude since the moment she had taken her seat.

Not simply content with brushing her leg against his own, she proceeded to allow her hand to drop, frequently, onto his thigh and to place her right foot between his two feet in a way that enabled her to run her shoe up and down the inside of his leg.

The evening had progressed to perfection in every other respect as Daemon remained an eager supporter of the Governor in most of his statements and proclamations.

It was not essentially blind acquiescence as much as actually seeing eye-to-eye with the Governor. Daemon tended to agree with everything James Deakin espoused.

Daemon, reluctant to spoil the ambience and out of respect to his host, refrained from taking any evasive action or to expose Gertrude's impropriety. He simply endured the unwelcome attentions inflicted upon him with as much aplomb as he could muster.

Even when Gertrude's hand strayed from his thigh to a more intimate location, as she danced her fingers in little rhythmic patterns on the inside of his leg, he merely smiled and responded as the conversation demanded.

Gertrude was intent on torturing him and pushing the situation to the limits.

Eventually, Daemon stood and declared that the day's activities had 'completely overwhelmed' him, with her hand still holding his leg just above the knee to the extent that when he began to move he almost dislodged her from her chair.

The table was heavily bumped and glasses began to rattle as he attempted to free himself.

'Please excuse me, Mr van Eyck, 'the cloth snagged against my britches.'

'What's come over you, young man? Do you have a fire in your pants?'

'Er... no, no, sir. I just thought it may be polite to bring the festivities to a close...'

'Do sit down, sir. I was just going to call for the Brandy.'

To Daemon's relief, this was the moment they parted company with the ladies.

Over cigars, the 'Viscompt' posed a number of probing questions, pursuing Daemon for more and more information concerning his encounters with the British naval ships, including the *Elsinore*.

Although Daemon attempted to be as helpful as possible, he began to feel a little uneasy about the sustained intensity of the questions. For a man who had previously spoken little during the evening, the 'Viscompt' was quite animated.

Daemon began to tailor his answers, particularly about the strength of the *Elsinore* and the capabilities of her captain. As his responses grew vague, so did the patience of the inquisitor.

Deakin, sensing the tension in the situation, began to divert some of the questions and interjected some of his own insignificant knowledge of the captain and his capabilities.

Soon, the 'Viscompt' tired of the matter and began to release a series of platitudes, which rounded off the conversation.

Re-joining the ladies, Deakin suggested it might be time to close the proceedings.

Addressing Daemon, he pronounced, 'I must say, we are all enthralled by the sequence of events which brought you to Barbados and to our humble gathering. The arrival of a new and promising ally in these regions has captured our hearts and our imagination. I wish you a safe and profitable onward journey, Daemon Quirk, and a speedy return.'

Van Eyck managed a 'Hear, hear.' The 'Viscompt' raised his almost empty glass.

Just then, Gertrude intervened. 'Papa, perhaps we could extend our hospitality a little further in the case of Captain Quirk? And, of course, the Governor. Surely it is a little late for Mr Deakin to travel back to town? Perhaps he may prefer to rest up for the evening and make a fresh departure in the morning. I am sure the Captain must also be in need of a good night's rest…?'

'Er, for my part, no! Perhaps even now I should be preparing for our onward voyage.' Daemon's response had a tinge of panic about it, and he looked despairingly towards Deakin.

Deakin's response surprised him for once, as the Governor rubbed his false leg, before declaring, 'You know, that sounds like a decent suggestion. I thank you, my dear. My old leg has been giving me some discomfort all evening.'

Daemon saw the hopelessness of the situation as the Governor's carriage remained the only plausible means of a return to the ship. 'I could ride back! Perhaps Mr van Eyck could lone me a horse and return to collect it taking my place in the carriage?'

'Not necessary — surely a good start in the morning would be much as though you had returned and awakened late or in ill humour? We must insist!' Gertrude was determined. All resistance seemed futile.

Accepting a guest bedroom on the third floor, Daemon made light of the situation. Taking his leave at the most opportune moment, he slipped quietly away and closed the door firmly behind him, seeking a locking mechanism of some sort. When one was not evident, he realised that he would have to either prop the door or disappear through the window to avoid the fate which appeared to be almost inevitable.

Within moments, his fears had been realised. A click saw the motion of the door knob, turning and releasing. The door quietly opened and a figure in ghostly, flowing gossamer slipped into the room. Daemon could not see the face of this apparition, only the lithe form as it made its way towards the bed through the gloom, a hint of moonlight illuminating the garment around her knees.

Surprisingly slender without the reinforced layers of clothing, her warm, athletic form wrapped around him.

Her kisses were surprisingly sweet, her embrace more sensual than he could have imagined. She moved with ease, reaching, probing, engrossing herself. His mouth was seeking hers, involuntarily, but hungry to recapture the first moments of coming together. It seemed as fresh and stimulating every single time as they repeatedly massaged their lips one on the other, pushing, probing, licking.

Without design or direction, they came together. Daemon felt the incredible intimacy, a deeper sensation than he thought possible. She made herself a perfect receptacle for him as he arched and straightened. Her hips began to move with the same accomplishment he had experienced at the hands of the consummate professional concubines of the Casbah.

This was no shy virgin: this was a beautiful woman using all her physical perfection to meet his needs. Their encounter was perfect, satisfying, engorging, complete.

Thirty minutes had passed in the blink of an eye. Daemon freed himself momentarily to take a breath of air.

Gertrude rolled away, putting distance between them. They lay silent for a moment, before Daemon moved to caress her shoulder. She turned and almost again without perceptible movement, she positioned herself perfectly to receive him. When he was ready, they came together again, as he buried his head in the nape of her neck and the magic began over again.

Her heaving bosom pressing and massaging his chest, the tips puffy and responsive, they proved irresistible to

Daemon, seeking them with the tip of his tongue, his lips, even his ear. The sound, suddenly, of her rampant heartbeat penetrating those soft, luscious pillows of protection, drove him on.

Daemon was lost for words. He did not quite know how to communicate with this *alien* being. Harsh, business-like, domineering and aggressive — compared to this — the perfect sexual partner, a warm, soft, responsive feminine being who understood a man's every need.

'I'm so glad you stayed. Are you? Are you thinking at all about tomorrow?' she uttered. 'Why not stay? You could have everything a man could want!'

'Gertrude, I cannot think about… I have a duty. I must do what I set out to do.'

'You can't mean it! You just have to take a little time. Think again. You could have such a life. Here, with me.'

Daemon did not know what to say. How could he answer? How could he offend this wonderful girl? He knew only one thing, that this had been an apparition. He knew that, come the morrow, this day would have been forgotten.

Their reunion, one day, would surely come. He knew that, physically, she had everything a man could want.

But he knew, once she pulled on her clothes, her *working* clothes, once she picked up the tasks of her daily routine, she would be another woman, a woman engaged in a business he could hardly stomach.

His one thought at that moment was to complete his task and 'free' the slaves. His concept for them, of a life in 'employment', was somewhat different to a life in chains. He wanted to rid himself of the task of keeping these humans alive for the sake of a good price in the sale room.

'Daemon, you know you want me.' Her hands were on the back of his neck. She eased his head towards her bosom and brushed his face with a smooth, soft mound.

'I have deep, deep feelings for you, but I cannot do what you want me to do. Come with me, come away. Leave this life behind and take your chance with me!' When she failed to respond, he pulled away and sat upright.

'You will not turn your back on me! Turn around. Look at me, damn you!'

Daemon did turn, but only after he had stood and pulled on his britches.

Then he shook his head from side to side and his eyes closed. He may have been trying to blot out her image or relay to her his determination.

'You will not make me change my mind; you may wait until hell freezes over! But I will not break my oath to my friend in his dying moment. I will fulfil my promise, even if I have to *walk* away from here tonight. When I have done all I set out to do, I might one day return to see if you still...'

'If I what? If you walk away from me now, after everything we have done, you will rot in hell! But only if my father leaves anything left of you after I tell him what you have done!'

'Gertrude, please do not make a scene; we have to part as friends... I will return...'

'To hell with you!' She was kneeling now and pulling a sheet up to her neck, every sinew twisted as her face turned the colour of the setting sun. 'Don't you dare, don't dare to think you can use me like this and walk away. I'll have you whipped, you dog! Who do you think you are?

You've used me, used me and thrown me away like slops from a table. How dare you?'

Daemon was fully dressed by now, as a jug of water came hurtling towards him, but he managed to duck, and watched it crash into a painting on the far wall.

Gertrude had risen and made towards him, with both hands attempting to grab his hair, but her sheet dropped to the floor, causing her to stumble. Beautiful as she was naked, she fell into an ungainly pile, and with her red hair wildly flying in every direction — this was not the picture by which Daemon wanted to remember their encounter.

Feeling for the door knob without taking his eyes away for a second, he found himself in the hallway and made for the stairs.

He was torn about alerting the Governor to try to make an escape in his carriage. But, realising that dawn had not yet broken, that the Governor may be unfixed from his wooden prosthetic, Daemon decided the only way was to effect a solo escape, and hope that none of the troops from the garrison were awake and on duty through the night; he hoped he might have a clean getaway.

His conscience was telling him to stay and face the situation, but he could not predict how it would turn out. He now knew that Gertrude was capable of anything, that her father, after all, was extremely volatile and that even the Governor might take offence that Daemon had abused his good offices, and the hospitality of an important man.

All he could do was return to the ship by any means and as fast as that means would take him.

Finding the stables, by process of elimination, and the smell of horse, he managed to whisper in the ear of the closest to the doors, affecting some sort of submission, whilst he managed to fix a bridle. He knew a saddle would be asking too much of the situation and threw his leg over its back, managing to hold on for dear life while the horse bolted from the open door and across the corral.

Without another human encounter, Daemon was away and free. Rising the top of a small hillock, he pulled up just before taking a bend in the road. He turned to witness lanterns being lit in several rooms and the warm light of the hallway candles flowing into the courtyard. He knew Gertrude had disturbed the entire household and would by now be screaming retribution.

Turning the now-becalmed animal by a tug on the rein, he forced her into a canter, making good time on the road back to the port.

Reaching the harbour, he used the first boat he could manage to free and rowed out to the *Durham*. Climbing over the side, he found an orderly and shipshape vessel as ready for sea as he had hoped. Calling Baptiste, he explained the need to depart by catching a favourable tide around dawn and making headway into the sea.

In minutes the ship was alive. The men responded. Sail was set and the *Durham* turned keenly towards the harbour opening, and she began to roll in response to a light breeze. They were set fair for Trinidad and the next stage of their journey. Daemon stood at the side, watching for activity along the harbour. Nothing stirred and he was grateful, for fortune had indeed been on his side this day.

Yet a deep twisting in his stomach and a feeling of something akin to sadness engulfed him. In his mind, he saw Gertrude again, not as a flailing harridan, screaming up at him from the floor, but as a shimmering, beautiful apparition with moonlight caressing her bare shoulders as she leaned down to kiss him.

He shook his head, once, then got on with his life.

Chapter 20
A Match for Carstein

Banoldino was in fine form, his health improved, his demeanour that of a man twenty years his junior. He had enjoyed a new lease of life of late.

His thoroughbred horse had beaten Carstein's by twenty lengths at the County Fair. He could not have been *more* proud. Adding a hundred gold coins to his well-filled coffers was a bonus.

Banoldino watched as his wife laughed gaily and her friends drew around her.

Carstein had good-naturedly slapped his back and chided him over his new-found champion. Both men knew it was important for a man like Banoldino to keep his spirits up and keep him striving for the future, even the very future of the community.

Certainly, New York was becoming a citadel to business and opportunism. Many difficulties had been overcome, but a range of Europeans flocked to their shores and the intake brought wealth, commerce, opportunity and benefits of many kinds.

The founders, the Banoldinos of his world, began to reap all they had sown.

Now they had established a new order. There was a group of wealthy, enterprising men who rose out of the chaos to become the 'elite', the decision-makers that were elected to represent and to lead.

Banoldino and Carstein would be among them.

Now, their horse-race, a grand gala of a day and a populace ever willing to laud and applaud, worked to Banoldino's advancement in the community. Even so for Carstein, as gracious in defeat as Banoldino was ebullient in victory.

But the greatest news to the baying crowd was the challenge set down, and accepted, by Carstein to Banoldino — a 'return' match, but this time Carstein knew for what he had to prepare, and he could name the time and place.

This time, the challenge would be met by thoroughbreds of similar breeding and capacity for flat-out racing for the line.

But Carstein had other priorities. His position in society would no longer be blighted by the lack of a partner. He was to take a wife, and there were choices to be made.

He had long considered bringing out a 'cousin' from Europe. A lady who had historical designs upon the Count and would have been a willing partner. However, Carstein knew that her delicate constitution would present too many challenges in the New World. He believed most of the establishment in Europe's fine houses would find the Americas too great a challenge.

So, he turned his sights on the New England society and found, to his slight annoyance, a lack of suitable choices.

There was the sister of a leading merchant, whose greatest assets were undoubtedly her share in their German father's estates in Hanover, beside her child-bearing hips. Charmaine remained an outsider in this particular contest.

The seventeen-year-old daughter of the English Lord Ranleigh, however, provided a much more desirable option, except that her upbringing, despite being under the great influence of the British aristocracy, was somewhat stunted by lack of society.

Although the girl was confident and forthcoming, she simply lacked the experience and worldliness she may have acquired had she been able to attend court or, say, a Belgian or French conservatoire, or a Swiss finishing school.

It was going to be an uphill task to utilise her strengths for a number of years, which, in truth, the Count feared would be too much of a transition. Not for the lady, but for his own comfort.

He needed a wife, to attend, to watch, to listen, to participate. He needed someone who could be an asset to him in his dealings, someone like Kirsten.

Now there was a prize, indeed. He firmly believed that Kirsten could pick up the reins of the Don Bosco 'empire' and run with it, should the occasion ever demand.

He knew Banoldino had suffered ill health. Taking *his* position had to be considered an option, although playing an integral role in the development of the colonies did not appeal in itself.

He had considered the eventuality that Banoldino should meet an early demise, and what the outcome might be in a power struggle. He had decided, in fact, that, in such an event, he would certainly gain an improved position, but that he would need allies to work with him.

He believed Kirsten might see the sense in allying herself to him and vice versa, if it came to a point where a change of 'figurehead' in society would be within his compass.

He believed Ranleigh a spent force, though still influential. He considered the alliance of his house and theirs a desirable option, but as to the consistency of their strength in trading and completing deals, would a teen-aged bride be of any value to him?

This question was distracting him night and day, although in pursuing his options he had already hinted to Lady Eve, and to Ranleigh, that he would wish to be considered as suitable for the hand of their daughter.

Ranleigh had initially insisted on her reaching eighteen before anything was progressed, but frequent opportunity brought them together in a way that the dashing Count could barely resist the precocious attentions of the Lady Anabelle.

The best way he could deal with the situation was to be openly overt to her demands for attention and to treat her as a playful niece may be treated. Always with the slight hint of a promise of what might be, when the 'subject' came of age.

Carstein was careful, but not lacking in the skills necessary to keep the girl dreaming.

Demands were made upon the growing communities south of the St Lawrence. New England, concentrated around the developing towns: Boston, Philadelphia, and Maine, along with New York, formed the strongest and wealthiest communities.

Britain relied heavily upon these regions for support in manpower, resources and a constant supply of hardware through the ports and harbours along the coast.

Both Carstein and Don Bosco provided every response to these demands at the outset. Their enterprises were geared to provide importation and mobilisation, transport and storage. Everything the military might require could be found between the two. Competition was not on the agenda, both were in such demand.

As time progressed, unfortunately, this became more and more of a problem. The British were slow payers. Not only that, but the Crown levied a tax upon many of the commodities that were provided by not only these two, but on all the commercial interests of the region.

Britain was a partner with a huge appetite, but its favours came at a high cost.

It soon became more of a burden to be favoured by the British Crown. Loyalty came at a high price at the outset. Many of those providing actual support and high-quality goods to the British cause were not British, and, among those of Dutch, German, Austrian, Spanish and even Swedish origin, many found it a battle of conscience even when the rewards were great. Now the rewards were becoming thin, the quality and even the commitment provided by these communities deteriorated and came at a premium.

Tensions were high: a significant swell of protest was experienced as each new demand took effect.

For the moment, many of the established families continued to trade and to gain from the relationship. But the better of the commercial leaders spread their business so that they were not totally in the grip of the British Crown.

Diversification and new trading partners became a priority, and forming alliances, welcoming new arrivals and winning over their support was an undercurrent to all trading relationships.

Not all of the effects of the strengthening British grip on the Americas proved negative. A new wave of settlers and a new class in the social order was established — the 'Officer Class'. Many of the Expeditionary and subsequent postings brought with them young gentlemen of good breeding, many of whom settled or were bent on settling in the new territories and making a life for themselves in the developing world.

There was a level of swagger and over-confidence among these men, but there was also the courage in the face of adversity, experience and achievement in the 'field' and the support network of the British upper classes.

These men became a force to be reckoned with, when attached to the military or when they had reached amicable arrangements and handed back their uniforms.

There was also a hard core who caused more upheaval than they were worth. The gambling houses thrived on the lost fortunes of the young cavalry officer. Relationships developed and turned disastrously. Ventures were undertaken which ended in tragedy.

A ball, thrown by the Governor to celebrate the first anniversary of the formation of the Colonial boundaries, brought out the whole of society and a phalanx of hopeful young officers.

They were toasted by the leading lights and over-stuffed with approbation. Many of them became intoxicated by the atmosphere and the libation. The young women of the community were in high demand. Dance cards were filled up and a six-piece orchestra provided lively cavalry tunes for the ladies to prance around the floor on willing red-coated arms.

Anabelle was among those in great demand, and for once she threw off the chains of family responsibility, and even the presence of Carstein, splendidly matching the British military finery with his own family regalia, consisting of a high-ranking officer's uniform, including Hapsburg stars among his bright work.

He was happy to see Annabelle, reaching her prime, matching the spirit and adventure of the growing throng on the dance floor. He also considered it highly appropriate that he was seen by the community as still unattached and without any specific design on the young of those available.

Instead, he provided an able partner to both Harriet, the Governor's wife; Kirsten, when a gap in her own well-marked card allowed; and, of course, Charmaine, the sister of his friend and cohort, Von Rickenbach.

Carstein was taking a breather whilst exchanging a few well-considered comments for the benefit of British Major Willingham, who was in deep conversation with Don Bosco.

'You have nothing to fear for the moment, Major. There is a substantial reserve of horses for your immediate needs. Don Bosco and I have signed up deals with the best of all providers, the Native Americans. They are among the finest horsemen I have ever seen, and they breed wonderful animals. They capture them in the wilderness and bring them under discipline quickly and without breaking their spirits. Meanwhile, we have been breeding our own good stock by blending the plains horses with strong European blood. The outcome is the perfect cavalry mount: swift, nimble, tall and powerful. I am confident we can meet your needs.'

Don Bosco continued, 'There you are, Major, I could not have been more convincing myself. Carstein has summed up our position; now can you lean on your paymasters to release some of the money owing and you will find our stock ready and available by the time you take your next review?'

Just then, a commotion broke out as two officers began swinging at one another, although neither had landed a blow of any consequence up to this point. There was a little blood sprayed around from the nose of one and the eyebrow region of the other.

Major Willingham excused himself and moved into the proximity of the brawl. Barking an order, he brought the two to attention and regaled them for the 'appalling spectacle' they had made of themselves.

Blowing hard, a young Lieutenant, tall, with floppy, brown hair, and a bloody nose, made an immediate response, 'Permission to speak, sirrah.'

'Denied,' called Willingham.

'The Captain insulted the young lady, sir. I was just defending her honour!'

'Permission *denied*, Lieutenant! Remove yourself from this gathering at once and report to me in the morning.'

The Lieutenant saluted and turned away, quick-marching himself from the room.

All around, the guests had hushed and appeared to be scrutinising the proceedings with intense interest.

Turning to the other, a Scot, rugged and pock-marked, with a square jaw, the Major appeared more vehement. 'McLean — you again! I have lost count of the number of occasions…! You will report to me also, in the morning!'

'Sir, in my defence, the young Lieutenant attacked me. What was I supposed to do? I am a soldier, not a dancing fop!'

'And you are suggesting that Lieutenant Sherrington *is* a dancing fop? Captain, you are responsible for the men in your squadron. I expect you to lead by example, on social occasions as well as when you are on duty.'

'I was minding my own business and the young fool took advantage of me. Attacked me from behind while I was wheeling the little skivvy around the floor.'

At that moment, Anabelle let out a stifled cry, whilst whirling away and making for the door.

Carstein noticed her sudden movement from across the floor and moved to find out what was troubling her.

He caught her arm just as she was half through the door.

'What is wrong, my lady? Are you quite well?' Anabelle sobbed and fell into his arms. 'There now, what is wrong? Tell me.'

Just then, McLean was making a stand against his Senior Officer. 'I could see Sherrington was making a play for the skivvy, and I decided I would give him some competition. I offered her the next dance and he attacked me.'

'Liar!' Anabelle was suddenly moving towards the centre of the room. 'I was dancing with the Lieutenant! You pushed your way in between us… and… you!' She wiped the back of her hand across her mouth as if in disgust. 'You put your face into mine and began attacking me… you pushed your lips against mine and crushed me against the wall. If it hadn't been for the young Lieutenant…'

McLean suddenly realised he may have misjudged the lady upon whom he chose to impose his attention.

Major Willingham closed on McLean. 'Is this true, McLean?'

Carstein intervened. 'Sir, if the lady says it… it is true, I assure you.'

Willingham responded immediately. 'Of course, sir. It was not my intention to doubt the lady's word; I merely intended that this man accept the accusation as fair and take the opportunity to show some level of remorse, which may yet be solicited from a man about to find himself in serious trouble.'

'I made a play for her. Yes. What do yea want me to say?'

Major Willingham interrupted. 'McLean, you stand accused of insulting and attacking the Lady Anabelle, daughter of a Peer of the Realm, in such a way as to cause great offence not only to our hosts, but the whole of New England society. I am going to have you flogged at first light. Consider yourself under arrest.'

'Flogging? A Captain? You are joking, of course?'

'Guard, call out the night watch to take this man into custody.'

In a swift and athletic movement, McLean had pulled a ceremonial dagger from his belt and thrust it towards the throat of the Lady Anabelle, holding her around the neck and positioning her between himself and the gathering. He had his back towards the French doors at the side entrance to the Hall.

A number of the officers in close attendance moved towards her defence, including Major Willingham and Lord Ranleigh. But he was fiercely determined, and in this enraged state he was going to put up a fight.

'Back... all of you! I have had enough of this man's army! I am finished anyway! There is no chance of me surviving a whipping and living to tell the tale, so I may as well go in a way that someone will remember!'

Anabelle's head was locked into a dangerous position, her slender neck scraped and raw where her necklace had been roughly dislodged, her ball gown hanging askew, exposing her shoulder, the look of horror clear for all to see.

Carstein was the first to respond. 'Wait! Release Lady Anabelle! Release her right now... and I will personally guarantee you a fighting chance of survival. Should any more harm come to her, I can make another promise. You will never see another dawn.'

McLean shifted position again, dragging his captive closer to the doors. As he dragged her, her heels scraped along the polished flooring and one of her slippers dislodged. Her stockinged foot now slipped from under her and she began to swoon as the powerful arm of her captor squeezed the life from her.

Some of the ladies in the crowd gasped and again several of the gallants moved towards them. Carstein again held up a hand to quell any rash challenge.

McLean spoke again. 'Now, let's all be calm, shall we? I am intending to leave this place and I am intending to take along the lady as my assurance. If anyone attempts to stop me, I'll slit her throat!'

More gasps from the gathering fuelled the atmosphere.

Banoldino was on his feet, albeit a little unsteadily. 'Everyone! Remain calm! Please! Allow Carstein to handle it.'

The gathering settled a little, following Don Bosco's example.

'Mr McLean, you will not pass across that threshold unless you release the lady. I personally guarantee you will have a fighting chance. Please, I beg you.' Carstein moved a little closer so that about six feet separated him from Anabelle's grasping hand.

'Oh, no you don't — stay back! No! Not on your terms. Not any more' I've 'ad my fill of your type. Not one of yea ever kept a promise to me. I put myself on the line. Time after time. I got the scars to prove it. An' wot did I get for it? Floggin'! That's what I got. Now it's my…'

McLean was edging away slowly as he spoke. He was twisting his head to make sure of his position in relation to the doors.

As he half turned, Carstein had drawn his sword, flicked away the blade and thrust McLean clean through the neck, burying the tip of his rapier into McLean's skull.

The soldier sprung back in surprise, dropping Lady Anabelle at his feet. As he staggered backwards, he crashed through the French doors onto the lawn.

Anabelle had not suffered further injury from her fall and was quickly up, burying her head into Carstein's heavily braided shoulder, resting safely in the protection of his arms.

The crowd gathered around them. Willingham, having pursued McLean into the garden, returned to declare him dead.

There was great appreciation shown to Carstein. He was heartily slapped across the back by the entire gathering. Ranleigh approached him with a firm handshake. 'I have never quite seen anything so well executed, if I my say so, old fellow. Ask anything, anything you desire in this world, and I am honour-bound to meet your request.'

Banoldino clapped his friend on the back, puffing out his cheeks to indicate that he appreciated how fine a margin was required for the manoeuvre to succeed and that he also fully appreciated the way it had been executed.

Anabelle was taken into her mother's arms. With Lady Eve and Kirsten in close attendance, they managed to restore some colour to her cheeks.

Carstein was thanked by Willingham, who then said, 'Gregor McLean was a villain, but a true soldier. There was no one you would rather have alongside you, going into the fray. He was a man married to soldiering and sadly lacked all of the social graces.'

Carstein also had a few words. 'I took no pleasure in my actions, Major. I simply did what was required for the lady's safety. I do not think any other outcome would have achieved this. I also believe a man like that would have met such an end sooner or later. He was, as you say, at his best in a conflict.'

'I am not sorry he has gone. I hope no one, most of all the young lady, will suffer as a consequence of these events.' Willingham saluted and, in taking his leave, rounded up the remaining members of his garrison. It was clear that there had been enough for one night. He begged indulgence of his host and promised to have 'the mess' cleared immediately.

The Redcoats streamed away and activity outside on the lawn was obvious by the arrival of a wagon. Driven through the courtyard, it confirmed that there would be little evidence of the disturbance come the morning.

Anabelle was soon 'presented', recovering and beginning to force a smile, despite some bruising to her neck. She was greeted by the establishment.

The Governor held out his hand to Carstein. In turn, Banoldino, standing just to his left, and Ranleigh to his right, made up a group intent upon demonstrating that all was well.

Anabelle put out a tentative hand, expecting that Carstein would brush his lips against it and make his departure for the evening.

'Count… I just don't have the words. I don't know how I should ever be able to thank you. You saved my life! I can't think of anything more a person could do for another person than to offer them a chance to live.'

Ranleigh agreed. 'Hear, hear!'

Lady Evelyn was tearful and simply hugged the Count; with a gloved hand on either shoulder, she thanked him from the bottom of her heart. Then she added, 'I can't think of a man more capable of protecting a young lady's honour.'

Carstein saw his moment. He was equally as decisive as he had been earlier in the evening.

He realised that there were nine or ten of those in immediate proximity who represented the cream of New

York society and that in one, well-judged moment, he would be able to crush any opposition to the match.

'I would always be first to take up that challenge, Lady Evelyn. I would like to pledge my life to your daughter's protection and well-being. Indeed, I would like to ask her for her hand in marriage.'

Anabelle's hand was still resting on his arm, despite the close attendance of her mother. At this moment, when the others all around immediately fell into silence, Annabelle was the first to respond.

Gathering herself, she managed to steady her voice sufficiently to be able to reach for him, and, looking into his eyes, she said, 'Yes, I would be proud to be your wife.'

There was a sustained round of applause throughout the gathering and lots more back-slapping.

Suddenly, Carstein felt his age, but the young girl clinging to his arm, accepting the love, receiving the approval of a community, turned his mood around and made him a proud man again.

Their wedding was equal to that of a minor royal in central Europe, the most dazzling event that could be staged in a developing community. Carstein spared no expense to ensure it would match every expectation.

A grand affair, it brought representatives of neighbouring counties to the doorstep of the New York elite. Banoldino and Kirsten played a prominent part, Banolo as best man and Kirsten as lady-in-waiting. This was an event which would go down in the annals of North Colonial America.

Even dignitaries from Europe arrived and, despite observing events through monocles and at as much distance as they could manage, they appeared to approve of the proceedings.

Ranleigh was in his element playing the 'Grand Lord'... greeting everyone as though the developing county was his own kingdom. His personal ambitions were modest, in truth, but the occasion was more than could be resisted by himself and Lady Evelyn — the entire event was one of the last in an era where class was observed in all its waning glory.

Who knew what tomorrow might bring? Who could speculate about statehood? Who could imagine that a state would be a republic and require elected representatives? Who could predict the British Crown's influence would diminish?

Chapter 21
Destination Trinidad

Captain Daemon Quirk relayed his orders to Baptiste and the *Durham* leaned into the wind to continue making twelve knots towards the setting sun.

Since leaving Barbados, they had seen no sign of man nor beast, unless the tall, menacing fin of a hammerhead shark could be counted. Baptiste had such a complete understanding of their schedule that Daemon found himself more and more at ease in leaving things under his control.

He wondered if Standing had had that same confidence when leaving Daemon or charging him with a task. His mind drifted across the days they spent together, the laughs and the trials and tribulations. He could see John at the wheel, at the prow. Eager and full of anticipation, a friend and companion.

Daemon swallowed hard. The train of thought could not be turned, and the next moment he was holding a large sheet for Lady Daphne, radiant in the Mediterranean sunlight. He imagined her flirting with him. He imagined her embracing him. He could almost feel her warm body.

Then his thoughts turned to Margaret. When he first saw her, in chains, in rags, her long dark hair a matted, oily cowl, she was cowering in a corner on a meagre gathering of damp straw. He saw her proudly holding her head high and waving, both to John, and then to himself. She reserved a special smile, something of gratitude and something perhaps a little 'in confidence' just between them, as the ship pulled away.

His head snapped on the pillow, bringing him back to stark reality. He was charged with sailing this ship to Trinidad, selling off two hundred slaves and returning with a cargo of sugar and tobacco to Europe, turning a sum of profit or goods over to Standing's Arab partners, finding Lady Margaret, breaking the news of John's demise and making over a fair proportion of the remaining profit.

The commitment almost overwhelmed him. His head spun and at that moment he could have been offered almost any alternative, and he would have taken it.

This immediately brought thoughts of Gertrude van Eyck. Her charms, abundant, her wealth equally substantial, the life of a country squire, a farm the size of County Mayo, with employees, slaves, a team of people at his beck and call. What was he thinking? His decision to abandon that now seemed incredible even to himself. He found his hand rubbing at his temples. Then both hands, massaging his own head through his thick wavy hair.

He noticed the sweat making his pillow damp, as he tossed and turned. He was not getting the rest he had hoped for. He was not resting at all.

This went on for several hours. Eventually, Daemon found himself on deck, the breeze making his sweat-soaked shirt cool on his skin. He placed himself beside Baptiste and opened a conversation.

'All quiet? How is our cargo?'

'They are as well as they can be. Do not worry, monsieur, all will be well. Baptiste is 'ere.'

Daemon laughed. 'I do not worry, my friend, when you are alongside me! You are right to chide me.'

'You 'ave a disturbed night, monsieur. I can tell!'

'I have many things to deal with, and without…'

'Oui. Without John Standing, you 'ave to make theez decisions all alone. But a man can only do so much. Per'aps he can make one desire, the important one, and if this is achieved…'

'You have a good point there. I would first have to decide what is the 'one'. What must I do, above all? I think I can answer my own question. I must get these negroes off the ship. I want them to survive this grotesque situation. To live, at least half a life. Then, I think, my conscience will tell me what I must do.'

'This is good, non? I think you 'ave made a good decision. It is our first, 'ow you say? Priority? Now go! 'Ave some sleep! You need it.'

'But what about you…? It is almost my watch.'

'Go! Avante!'

Daemon smiled and left Baptiste at the helm.

The *Durham*, having been gliding through the calm seas three hours earlier, had changed dramatically, wakening Daemon to another challenge. His cabin door swung on its hinges and its thudding against the bulkhead eventually brought him to his feet.

Daemon gathered himself, heading up the seven steps in two strides.

Arriving on deck, he found himself submerged as a wave crashed onto the deck. Baptiste had pulled on a greatcoat and was struggling with the wheel. Erik, alongside him, was soaked to the skin, although still lightly clad. Daemon raised his voice to be heard.

'What's happening, Baptiste? Where did this come from?'

'Very sudden, monsieur! About fifteen minutes ago, the clouds seemed to roll down on to the surface of the water and boil up the sea!'

'What? You mean like a fog, a mist?'

'Non, it just descended like a large black ball and the sea whipped up. We could not go around it — we are now in the centre, I think!'

Daemon turned to Erik. 'Get every able man on deck. Go! Hold her steady, my friend. That's all we can do for now!'

Another great wave crashed over the rail, swamping the deck. From below came the first signs of unrest from the Africans. A murmur became a babble, then there were hands appearing on the grating.

The first of the crew appeared, racing towards the poop for instructions.

'Secure all the hatches. Make damn sure nothing is left loose. Then cover the gratings; we must try to contain the swell from flooding the hold.' Daemon was yelling at the top of his voice. This alone told him of the ferocity of the conditions.

All around, the sky was a deep shade of grey. Lightning flashed inside the clouds, causing an angry glow rather than a bolt. The sea roared up and swamped the deck at every third wave. Now the bow of the ship plunged deep into the swell, before emerging bow first, almost vertically.

Daemon found his hands on the rail were white-knuckled as he held on to steady himself, although he knew that fear also gripped him.

Baptiste was yelling at his side. 'We must turn and ride the storm. This is our only hope.'

Hearing those words found Daemon swallowing hard and for a moment he was not able to respond. He realised only too well that this was the first crisis he had to face alone.

'Monsieur, monsieur?'

'Yes, turn and ride the storm. Make ready.' He called out to those within hearing. The crew darted away in different directions and began lashing sail. Daemon joined Baptiste at the wheel, pulling on the rudder, easing her around. A huge wave smashed into her sides as she came broadside on to the next.

The ship leaned so heavily to one side, the transom on the second tier traced a foaming, white slash against the base of another wave. Mercifully, the next wave straightened her up. Completing the turn, the *Durham* suddenly swung violently to the opposite side.

Now she was helpless, caught in a maelstrom which took hold of her and spun her around, completely at the mercy of the ocean.

Below deck, the natives screamed for deliverance. They wailed and cursed and brought down the gods on their captors. They were thrown into piles, dragged this way and that and throttled by chains, many of them violently retching up everything consumed in the past hours.

They pulled against the hard steel of their shackles. Blood was spilled from a hundred open wounds. Salt water sent them delirious, yelping in pain. Man, woman, child, every last one of them suffered. A seething mass of humanity, helpless and bewildered and unable to do anything except survive.

Daemon stayed on the wheel with Baptiste while the remaining crew lashed themselves to every available timber around the deck. Waves swamped them every few seconds, with hardly sufficient respite between to draw breath.

A moment on and the situation changed again. This time the worst imaginable horror. The ship appeared to be picked up on a spout of water, violently twisting, swirling around. The world seemed to be spinning. Everything loose simply flew away into the abyss.

Daemon and Baptiste held on to one another. For a moment they managed to keep in contact, but the violence of the spinning motion wrenched them apart.

Daemon grappled with a rope, trying to tie himself and to cast a loop towards Baptiste, but each had to fend for himself with pure instinct to survive.

The ship swirled again, almost lifted out of the seas and began to fly. Daemon had virtually begged for forgiveness, with no thought beyond that of meeting his maker. The *Durham* was lost!

Suddenly, the ship bucked and fell, until it seemed to be resting, in calm water; the noise and fury all seemed to be rushing away from them.

The decks were awash but began to drain. The swell dimmed to nothing more than a gentle roll. Away across the water, two hundred yards, three hundred yards, half a mile, a swirling column moved away, pulling up a water spout with each full turn.

Daemon scrambled to his feet, peering through a heavy shower of rain which danced on the decking in a thousand bright, sparkling explosions. Across the deck he could make out the colour of Baptiste's heavy medieval cloak.

'Quickly, my friend, help me!'

Members of the crew began to emerge from the shadows where they had taken refuge. A bewildered Rinaldi appeared on deck.

All looking gaunt, bemused and exhausted, Daemon gathered them, knowing the task ahead would prove a severe test of each one of them.

'We have to get the Africans up on deck, tend to them! Release their shackles — it will get them out more quickly. Doctori, please! If you can, muster enough linen...'

Rinaldi shrugged his shoulders, returning to his quarters, resigned to making use of his own bedding.

'Men, we must break out the guns! The Africans will come up in an aggressive mood. Please do all you can to restrain them. Nobody fire a shot unless I signal. Now make ready. Bring up all the fresh water you can find.'

Immediately, a barrel was rolled out and split open.

The hatches were raised, and the men set about unlocking shackles. The Africans began to emerge. A hand grazed and bleeding. An arm, bruised. A head, weeping and bedraggled. Slowly, they climbed on to the deck, dirty, soaking wet and battered.

Ten armed sailors stood forming a corridor, allowing a procession to make for the water. One broke away from the others; he held aloft his bloodied arms and looked pleadingly towards Daemon and Rinaldi. The native fell on his knees, begging, pleading. Neither Daemon nor the

Doctori could respond. Daemon guided him towards the water barrel.

Taking a rag, Rinaldi dipped it and bathed the man's wounds. He demonstrated how they should wash and rub vigorously. He then organised them into two groups: those needing patching up and those merely exhausted and desperate for a drink of clean water and a dousing.

Those who cleaned up and drank were allowed to slump to the deck, glad of clean air and calm, and, with the sun on their faces, they began to ease gratefully into a slumber.

Rinaldi and Erik began tearing at strips of linen and dabbing alcohol onto open wounds, then wrapped or sutured where needed.

Eventually, those emerging from the hatches were the less able. A female grappled her way up and managed to stand, but the child strapped to her with old rags hung limp and waxen, the life squeezed out of it when thrown about in the storm.

Rinaldi attempted to take the dead child, though its mother fought like a tiger, until only exhaustion made her give up.

Next came a boy whose arm had been torn off. A girl minus one foot. A male carrying a youngster whose head had been badly gashed; blood smeared his chest and ran down his legs.

A pregnant woman emerged, blood-soaked and ashen. She had lost the baby. Somewhere in the slops down below, a foetus would swirl about until the scouring got underway.

A tall, strong male dropped to his knees in front of Daemon. 'Massah, massah!' Holding up his bleeding palms, blood clotted where his fingernails had been.

'Free! Free! Free!'

Daemon picked him up and brought him to his full height. He pointed to the horizon.

Holding up one finger, Daemon pointed to the sun. He tried to make the native understand: two, three more sunrises. The man merely looked, pleadingly. Then he launched himself at the line in an attempt to grab a weapon. Slipping on the blood and slops on the deck, he stumbled as the carpenter brought him down with a blow to the temple with his musket barrel.

Other natives rallied and began to protest the only way they were able: they jumped up and down menacingly, threatening, balling their fists and howling.

Daemon stepped forward. 'No good! This must cease! No good!' He raised his arms to calm them, but pain and desperation simply made them care less for their own safety. They jostled and pushed and spat at their captors.

Determined to bring them to order, Daemon backed off. 'Please! No good! We are here to help! We are doing all we can. No good!'

Erik rose and began pushing them back. Baptiste and another sailor were roused to support him, as they began pushing and forcing the throng back against the rail.

As a result of allowing too much latitude, an attempt to compensate for all the hardship, the rebellion surfaced. Forced into the most inhumane situation, the ferocious change of conditions at sea had brought them to the limits of their endurance.

Rinaldi, strapping up the damaged arm of one female, was suddenly attacked and fell to the deck heavily.

Daemon spotted the incident and quickly realised it was almost at the point where they could lose control. Without Vasteron's marines, his meagre resources were always going to struggle.

He quickly snatched a musket from the hands of a crewman and fired point blank into the crowd.

Immediately, they fell back, squashing against the bulkhead, some of them running towards the steps of the bridge. Daemon grabbed another musket and brought one of them crashing down on to the deck, blood spattering in every direction.

The shock worked. They had looked on him as a 'leader'; to them he was a 'God'. The hand that fed them, kept them safe, cleaned and watered them. Now he was an angry, punishing God. Some of them began to pull back. They now knew there was nothing to be gained. The natural leaders among them began to quell the others.

Daemon gave them a moment to restore order. But now he was angry. Angry with himself for giving too much. He had cost the Doctori a severe beating. They had brought out the worst in him.

He ordered that the natives be immediately tethered again.

Their faces dropped immediately into sombre acceptance as the clink of chain brought reality back to them.

Backing off again, forming into smaller groups at the centre, they stumbled backwards as they retreated, tripping over the prone figure of the tall male, who was clutching his stomach in a bid to hold in his intestines.

Blood flowed from him and the deck was slick where the scrambling feet of his countrymen had stumbled and shuffled past him. There was no longer any movement from the man himself.

'You men — pass me your muskets!' Four passed their loaded forearms to him, then quickly fell to the task of collecting the two dead bodies, dragging them away and covering them in sailcloth.

Suddenly, Daemon yelled at them. 'Wait. No! We will not do this with ceremony. Throw them over the side! Now! Do it!'

This was Daemon desperate to show the Africans that he would be ruthless to any further attempt at insurrection. He quietly prayed that they understood his meaning, as it had cost two men their lives.

They stood watching the two bodies as they were flung over the side, while Daemon waved a weapon at the others now cowering to one side of the deck.

Their actions in bowing and groaning seemed to show their compliance. Only one or two could be seen looking into the vast ocean, saying their own private farewells to their lost companions.

Daemon thrust out his jaw. With musket cocked, he organised the remaining procession into a line to the fresh water and to the Doctori, where Erik had picked up Rinaldi and set him back on his feet.

When the hatches were battened down, and relative peace restored, Daemon reflected that he had never felt so lonely. Despair engulfed him, and for a time his drive and ambition faltered. This was a feeling he had not known since captivity. He felt lost and alone, and there was no familiar face to appeal to, no waiting hand to hold him up.

Most of all he mourned the dead Africans.

Chapter 22
The End of the Line

Three days later, land was spotted. Instead of the thrill and expectation of the first landing, when they had spotted Barbados Daemon felt unsure; a tide of foreboding was all that he felt when he considered the task ahead.

The crew performed, their own enthusiasm undaunted, the thought of drinking and womanising on shore filling them with renewed vigour, and they set about their tasks with admirable spirit.

Consulting Rinaldi, he determined that they had indeed made Trinidad, and, across on the northern horizon it's 'twin' Tobago.

There was no port of any significance on the easterly side, but Rinaldi, returning for the third time to a familiar island, steered Daemon past an infinitely long strip of golden sand, around the southern tip, and north to Port of Spain. This was a sparsely populated island at the beginning of its development, hungry for immigrant workers.

'By some miracle,' Daemon said, almost to himself. Rinaldi, however, insisted that Daemon's seamanship had been fully responsible and that he had achieved an extraordinary feat.

Anchoring just off the harbour, Daemon and Rinaldi took the boat into the port, where three other vessels, two of similar size to the *Durham* and a galleon much larger, were also anchored. Along the jetty, another dozen vessels, ranging in shape and size, implied the growing importance of the island.

Rinaldi was of great assistance, his familiarity with the township enabling him to navigate a way through the crowded streets. Daemon was immediately steered towards the Governor's residence, where Rinaldi was able to affect an introduction.

There was a slave auction the following day, so Daemon was advised that his own auction must be withheld until the Saturday following. A wait of three days. However, the 'official' assured him Saturday would be by far the more profitable, when the major landowners would be in town. Governor Palletta had 'many duties' and would not be able to entertain him, but wished the Master of the *Durham* every success with his business.

Meanwhile, posters could be placed in all the usual public places, and Rinaldi went in search of an apothecary whilst Daemon was to see Garcia, the local printer, and arrange for an itinerary to be drawn up.

All this was achieved in the first afternoon, leaving Daemon to take a moment of free time to visit a local hostelry. Two large rums later, Daemon was able to reflect on the epic events of the last months, feel the solid earth beneath his feet again and respond to conversation with the townsfolk.

Daemon realised that Trinidad and Tobago were not as commercially advanced as Barbados and that he would not expect to receive the same considered attentions as he had done at the smaller island, particularly given the fact that the island's current authority owed allegiance to the King of Spain.

He again reflected on how well he had been received in Barbados, and again, on the charms of Gertrude van Eyck! A wry smile crept over his face as he watched the purple liquid swirl around the bottom of his glass.

'May I offer you a replacement, sir? It would be my honour to stand for your next drink.'

'Well, I wasn't thinking... Er... well, why not? go ahead. Daemon Quirk, at your service. I should say Captain Daemon...'

'Indeed, sir, it is myself needing an introduction and I beg your pardon that there is no one in attendance to make the formalities. Therefore, I shall assume responsibility... Henry Ridaker, retired Captain Henry Ridaker, as I no longer have a ship. However, I am a man in my prime and I still have time. I understand you have brought in a cargo of Africans for the salerooms? If I may offer my services, I have some experience of this sort of thing, and would gladly act as your agent, should you require my services.'

'Ah, well, I don't think I do, at this moment. But I will keep it in mind should the need arise.'

'The need, sir? I do say the need has arisen! You are here and you have to unload a seething mass of African humanity onto these shores. Ergo, there is a need.'

'Do I detect a little blarney in your accent there, boyo?'

'Ah, sir! You have uncloaked me! You may have detected something of the Emerald Isle in my distant past, but I assure you I have long ago become a man of the world. May I enquire as to your very own origins, my friend?'

'Aye, well, I began this life in Donegal, had a brief stay in the 'South', and since then I have hardly been on dry land!'

'Donegal, is it! I'm a Galway man myself! Couldn't wait to leave the place, but as long as I have blood in me, a Galway man I am! Either way, I'm delighted to make your acquaintance, Captain Quirk. Indeed, 'tis a long way from Donegal you have come to be captain of as fine a ship as the *Durham*.' May I enquire as to the state of the cargo? Would you be expecting premium rates for these detached souls?'

'I do believe they will pass any inspection. They have been through the toughest of times; indeed, only three days ago we were swept up in the most freakish storm: there was this rampant twisting cloud and it sucked up everything. It nearly pulled us off the face of the earth. I confess I do not know to whom we should offer a prayer of thanks, but the gods must have been with us!'

'Ahh! There was a twisting spiral sweeping past the island. Missed, by a mile or two. We said that anything that gets in its way might disappear for good. But you survived, you say? Amazing! Seamanship of the highest order.'

'Believe me, sir, seamanship had nothing to do with it. Divine providence may have everything to do with it!'

'Nonsense — I will tell everyone that you flew into the eye of a maelstrom and navigated your way out the other side! Be sure, this will swell our coffers very nicely on the day!'

'Er, did you say "our" coffers?'

'Indeed! Did you not just appoint me as your spokesperson, your Agent? I am at your service, Captain.'

Daemon looked askance at the figure in front of him. Well-dressed, except for a little wear and tear. Impressive in some ways, wearing the attire of perhaps an attorney-at-law, or a jaded aristocrat. Either way, the face was likeable and the eloquence a thing that was turned on and off easily without detection.

'What was the name again? Mr…?'

'Call me Ridaker. Henry Ridaker if you wish, but I will answer to the former.'

'What exactly is it you would do in your role as my Agent?'

'Well, sir, I know people. I know what appeals to them. I know what they are capable of… what money they have, in truth! I know if they are worth the, shall we say, "courting", or whether a lot of time may be wasted in dialogue with a blown-up single-handed farmer who may only afford one little pequininny, whilst you may miss the genuine buyer of ten full-grown field hands who just passed you by because you were too busy talking to John Smudge!'

'John Smudge?'

'Yeah. Well, you'll know John Smudge when you meet him! Beware. There is more than one John Smudge on these islands!'

'And how do I pay you for this vital, noteworthy information?'

'Fifteen percent of all sales value.' I promise, you will make all of that and more in the deals I do for you.'

'So, whilst I am talking to "John Smudge", you will be talking the talk with the real buyers and selling off our stock wholesale?'

'Precisely! You have it in one!'

'Ten percent and not a penny more.'

'Sir, you injure me… Do you not think I am worth the greater consideration? Let me show you how I work.'

'I have brought these people from the bowels of Africa, nurtured and cared for them for three solid months. I have lost the finest friend a man could ever have. I have seen death, destruction and emaciation. I offer you again — ten percent — for a few mornings' work — let's say — you may earn every penny, but every penny I give you will be washed clean with tears.'

'Ten percent — and I do believe we have a deal, Captain Quirk. I will drop by in the morning with my terms…'

'Er, Henry, if you are working for me, you start right now. Posters, when they are ready — well, they need posting! I am sure, with your great experience and knowledge of this business, you will know the best posts to put them on!' With that, Daemon stood. 'I tell you what, next time we meet in a bar I will definitely take that drink with you. But for now — we have work to do.'

As Daemon left, Ridaker watched him go, then suddenly grabbed his jacket and followed out of the door. Briefly, he held Daemon up, agreed that he would personally arrange for the posters and, having extracted the exact itinerary, he tipped his hat and made off for Garcia's to scrutinise the run off.

By arrangement at the Governor's office, the cargo could be brought ashore at the earliest convenient moment.

Daemon chose the morning following to charge the crew with preparation for clearing the ship; with the promise of an advance on their dues and free time in the town, they set about their task with great enthusiasm.

The Africans were brought on deck one final time and washed down, wounds re-bandaged. A rub-down with tallow to make their skin glow again, however briefly, was organised by Rinaldi.

Daemon watched the entire proceedings. Some of the faces had become familiar. In each he saw pain, fear of the unknown and dumb acquiescence. He wanted to take away their pain. He would have preferred to free them!

What he wanted was not his priority. He was managing John Standing's affairs. Even so, he knew in his heart any other fate for these Africans was impossible. They could not be just dumped into a New World. They would perish. They knew nothing about survival in such a place. They would end up homeless, friendless, helpless.

As he watched, an occasionally pleading eye would catch his own. He did not know what it was they would plead for or whether they simply knew he was giving them up to something else. The terror was that they did not know what it meant.

They were draped as best as could be arranged with the remaining calico. The women were afforded a square to wrap across the bosom and another to wrap around the waist and hang towards their knees. The men, a loincloth!

Daemon noticed that many of the females had braided hair — they had found ways of achieving this, in the dark, in the cramped conditions, without the help of any tools. He shook his head in wonderment.

As soon as they were readied, Daemon issued arms to ten of his men, issuing Erik a musket and the lead position in the column.

Another five with pistols, Daemon figured, to prevent the natives from bolting, but equally in order to protect them.

They were lined up around the internal perimeter of the ship, and to Daemon's eyes they were as presentable and well prepared as was possible.

Some of the children began to cry as if their mothers' anxiety was being passed on to them. The men were sharp-eyed, watching for any threat.

Ridaker arrived with perfect timing, having just placed a poster on the wall of a cantina adjacent to the harbour.

'A fine morning, sir! I trust all is well?'

'Morning, Ridaker. As well as it might be for such an undertaking.'

'Captain, I sense that you have no appetite for the task in hand. And yet I look about me and see a job very well done.'

'Excuse my sour constitution, my friend. I admit I have no stomach for the business of slavery and my greatest desire is to be rid of it.'

'Allow me. As arranged, I have posted a dozen fine notices of sale of the prime "Nigra" stock you have brought to our shores.'

'Nigra?'

'Of course! They have been brought from the river Niger, have they not?'

Daemon raised his eyebrows in recognition of the name. 'More or less,' he responded.

'Therefore "Nigras" — that's what they are called in these parts.'

'It sounds like a curse to me, rather than a name, but I suppose if that's the way of it. What is your opinion of our prime "Nigra" stock?'

'Very fine indeed! A little battered and bruised, but the best fruit may still be edible even after falling from the tree!'

'You certainly have a way with words, Ridaker. I hope others see with the same eyes.'

'Don't worry. The most shocking and bedraggled *Nigras* have landed here and still been snapped up. This climate has a way of restoring them. Believe me! You have brought them to a better life. Once they get in the fields, they thrive. They sit around their cooking pots every night, singing and laughing at every opportunity!'

Daemon himself laughed at that. 'I would like to think your description justified. Forgive me if I retain some suspicion that the *life* they are bound for is not all that you say.'

'My friend, believe me, they are not shackled. They roam freely as long as they do their job, and they are well fed. They are allowed to breed. Even marry! Some are even given responsibilities, and others even make house slaves, cooking and cleaning for the masters. Why, they live better than you or I!'

'Well, 'tis a fine picture you paint, Mr Ridaker! If it is half the way you predict, then let's get on with it!'

Daemon rose from his position astride the rail of the poop. 'Erik, Baptiste, let's away.'

It was a fine morning, with uninterrupted blue sky as far as the eye could see.

The sun's warmth could be felt penetrating clothing, even though it was still quite early.

They affected a marching column as best as could be achieved and followed Rinaldi's directions up from the harbour and beyond the main commercial buildings, passing some hostels and cantinas along the way.

The route was lined with townspeople of every description. Children flocked to the street corners. Whores hung from balconies, housewives held off beating rugs and some of the shiftless drifters leaned against railings, mocking and deriding. As always, the most handsome women drew attention, the whores reserving their remarks for the athletic form of the bucks.

The Governor had provided an escort in the form of a phalanx of a dozen perfectly turned out Guards, under the guidance of a ranking officer. They formed up at the head of the procession when they neared the warehouses at the far end of the harbour.

On arrival, a sweating, shabbily dressed official brought out a clipboard arranged with documents and was introduced as 'Bertrand'. Rinaldi looked over the documents and agreed that a full account of the numbers, names and ages of the 'stock' would be raised.

This meant that the natives were required to stand in the broiling sunlight for more than an hour and a half whilst the schedule was compiled.

Rinaldi again provided most of the necessary information. The inevitable difficulty with names and ages meant that most of it was guesswork and invention. Where no name could be extracted, the height and some form of identifying feature, such as large nose, or broad shoulder, long ear or 'scar', was noted.

It was an arduous task, but Daemon argued that there was no other means by which it might have been achieved.

Had they been provided with a name when they descended into the hold each day, how would the same name be applied the following day? The thought of 'branding' had crossed his mind, but was rapidly dismissed from his thoughts.

Now the line was diminishing, however slowly it seemed, and at last the remaining few approached the table which Bertrand had set up near the warehouse doors.

Daemon decided to wander into the warehouse. Hot and humid, the natives slumped against the walls and supporting timbers. He walked among them for one last look at them. He wanted to remember their faces, but he could see the distress being caused by the heat.

Outside, he sought a pail and advanced on a standpipe, filling the pail and taking it into the warehouse.

He began to issue a cupful of water to each of them and looked for a response. They were distant, avoiding his gaze, and downcast. He didn't know what he had expected. Some 'thanks', a look of recognition, a smile? He got none of those.

Outside, he passed the pail on to Erik and instructed him to get the men to fill and refill until all of the Africans had all been refreshed. He told Erik to leave the bucket inside when he had done.

A full count was completed, the business done for the day.

Daemon turned to Ridaker. 'Am I to trust our stock to the Governor's men? Do I need to provide food for them?'

'I would organise your own men. Ones with their wits about them. They can remain outside the warehouse. Change them over at intervals, of course! Send a wagon up to feed them tonight and another tomorrow. That should be enough. The sale will take place in the corral over there. A canopy is usually arranged by the Governor's office. I'm afraid the Governor will want a cut — a fee; call it "tax" — he may take up to ten percent, depending on whether he likes you. I suggest you get up there and make yourself known to the man. I will tell you everything you need to know about him over some libation!'

'That would be appreciated, my friend.' Turning to Rinaldi, Daemon said, 'Well, Doctori, what do you think?'

Rinaldi reached out a hand and grasped Daemon's shoulder. 'Capitain, I think you have achieved everything possible. The stock will fetch good price.'

Daemon smiled. 'It would be a good thing to see the local merchants and make a deal or two for the returning voyage. I am sure Ridaker will be of use in this. He will have negotiated his fees already.'

Rinaldi reminded him, 'We can talk with the Governor's office about any shipments he may intend for Europe on your journey east whilst there is still an alliance between the Dutch and Spain. If they trust you, there may be some handsome commissions for you.'

'*Our* journey! You are returning to Europe with us. I have always assumed it?'

Rinaldi looked at him with a half-smile, hiding his embarrassment. 'I have been meaning to mention... I have no stomach for another voyage. I think I may find myself somewhere comfortable, with a splendid view of the sunset and settle down!'

Daemon shrugged: he had no great enthusiasm for undertaking the return voyage himself. He looked closely at Rinaldi, perhaps for the first time. He saw a middle-aged man, with a kindly face, wrinkles at the corners of his eyes and greying at the temples, in what remained of his hair.

Daemon nodded towards him, then took Rinaldi in his arms and held him for a long moment. 'I thank you for all you have done, and wish you all the luck in the world, wherever you decide to settle.' He patted his comrade on the shoulders and turned towards his new friend. 'Well, Ridaker, about your business. I would assume certain individuals would wish to take a sneaky look at the stock?'

'Leave all to me. I have made an assignation or two. I know a certain plantation owner who would be very interested in doing some business. The news will be spread, have no fear.'

Daemon retreated to the safe haven of his cabin aboard the *Durham*.

He knew there were several days before business could be concluded, and, he thought, time to consider his future.

The following day Ridaker brought three merchants to meet with Daemon and deals were struck for sugar, coffee and cotton to be loaded-up
On the assurance of payment in full upon the completion of the slave auction.

There was a huge undertaking for the crew, when sobered-up sufficiently, in removing the racking, chains and shackles from the hold and storing them deep in the bowels of the ship with the ballast. All were pressed to the limit to make 'below decks' ready for receiving a very different form of cargo.

The auction completed and the rewards plentiful, Daemon settled all accounts and rewarded Ridaker. Making a journey to the Residence, he negotiated a fair compensation for the Governor's purse. With all the business done Daemon returned to the ship to contemplate the journey ahead.

He had not been at rest for long when Rinaldi came scampering across the deck.

'Capitain, Capitain, are you awake? Quickly, come up, I must speak with you!'

Daemon swung off his bunk and unsheathed his sword from where it hung from the coat-stand. Leading with the point extended, he made his way through the galley doors onto the deck, where he anticipated an exhausted Doctori would be breathlessly waiting with his news.

'Speak man, what is the matter?'

Taking a lungful of air, the doctor managed to outline the news. 'From Barbados... they have arrived... looking for *you*!'

'Who, in God's name? What are you talking about?'

'Van Eyck, and the Lady... they are asking for you!'

'Ahaa! I see. Where are they?'

'I think they assumed you would be in the town, probably at some place of libation! They will no doubt find their way to the Residence.'

'So, I have a few minutes... but to do what? I can't escape with the crew scattered all over the harbour, I can't run — the island is not that big! I suppose I have no option but to confront them! What do *you* think?'

'Well... I'm afraid I have no idea. What is it that you have done? Why have they followed you on such an arduous journey? It must be...'

'Well, I won't go into detail, Doctori, but the lady and I... well, let's say we had a bit of an encounter...! I, er... had to leave in rather a hurry.'

'Why...? Did you force yourself upon her...? Did you...?'

'No... nothing like that, Doctori. You are a man of the world. The lady and I, well, I have to admit, it was a wonderful encounter! The problem is, she wanted to prolong... well... she wanted to hold me "captive", shall we say! I had no alternative but to flee. Shall we just say I left in rather a hurry and was unable to observe the proper, er, decorum.'

'So that's it! That is why we set sail in such an 'urry! They were already in pursuit!'

'I suppose they must have been. I never imagined they would follow me. Well, it's ridiculous — they have sailed three hundred miles! At what cost...? I have no idea what they intend.'

'Well, from the information I was able to gather... they have not come to kiss and make-up! What will you do? It's time for a bold decision, my friend. If you wish to set sail, then you can rely upon myself to look after your financial affairs.'

Daemon clapped Rinaldi on the back and thanked him. 'But... no... I feel I have to face my — er, "friend" and find out how I may make recompense.'

Striding up the gangplank and hopping into the boat, Daemon turned and fired last-minute instructions at the doctor and the watch, a skeleton crew, who had drawn short straws in the matter of who would be given a final *assault* upon Port of Spain.

Making quickly for the Governor's residence, Daemon had to pass through the sprawl of quayside buildings, many of which were simple timber sheds with trestle-tables and benches out front. Ale and bowls of fruit sat on shelves and bar tops and a mêlée of vagabonds, sailors and thieves lurched in various stages of stupor between establishments.

The smell of rotting fruit, sweat and excrement pervaded , and a bawdy swell of laughter and chatter filled the air.

Daemon suddenly became entangled in the arms of a raven-haired prostitute. She pressed her firm body against him and whispered her intentions with equal force into his ear. Trying to untangle his neck from her arms, he used more force than needed in his haste to engage with the Van Eycks. The girl tumbled over a bench and knocked over a pail of slops.

Her head was instantly drenched, water and waste-matter dripping around her shoulders and running into the valley between her breasts, rendering her out of commission for at least the remainder of the day.

She screamed retribution upon Daemon and began throwing stale bread and empty goblets in his direction.

Torn between pressing on with his journey and the instinct to recompense the girl for her loss and discomfort, he dodged one way then the other.

Eventually deciding upon a solution, he threw her a small pouch bulging with coin, and waved his farewell, promising to return at the earliest opportunity to make good his apology.

Weaving in and out of the crowded lanes, he was soon at the Residence, pulling anxiously at the bell which hung from the outer gate.

Attendants arrived and flanked him as he followed the lighted pathway to where he believed the Governor and his surprise visitors might be waiting.

Chapter 23
Baptiste

At the rear entrance to a rambling chateau, a puny, dark-haired boy sat on the cold stone steps.

His ill-fitting shirt hung loosely from stooped shoulders as he spat small blobs of saliva onto the stone paving and shaped them into childish animal images.

A bird, a pony, a rabbit!

The figures became distorted and shrunken, as the globs dried and soaked into the ground.

Sniffing, as he had done since birth, and wiping his grubby sleeve across a runny, permanently cold nose, he presented a most unwholesome figure.

'Francois! Francois, will you go and fetch a fresh pail? I need water for the Master! I will never be finished. This day will never end! Please, I am exhausted!'

'Sorry, Maman! I'll go in a minute.'

'Go *now*, Francois! Go now please. I may collapse in a moment.'

Francois stood, looked around for the pail, before finally picking up the rope handle and dragging it along the ground in the direction of the well.

The thunder of hooves brought him sharply to attention. He ran across to the wall and leapt up the five steps onto the timber scaffolding.

Peering between two buttresses, he could see a group of riders, heavily armed, hunched over their saddles, cloaks flapping wildly in the wind.

'Maman! Maman!'

Madame Baptiste appeared in the kitchen doorway, drying her hands as she called to him. 'Francois, what is it? What's happening?'

'Soldiers, Maman! Soldiers!'

'Come, child! This way, quickly! Run! Tell the Master, tell him to come quickly!'

Running through the kitchen, despite banging into the bench at the side of the table, he made his way into the corridor. Madame Baptiste began hiding food and equipment. She grabbed everything that could be moved and rammed it into a cupboard or drawer.

She pulled two candlesticks towards her and grabbed them to her bosom, before making her way as best she could, with her skirts flapping around her considerable girth.

Making her way through to the Main Hall, she rushed to the front window.

The Master, Hugo la Broche, a former courtier and petty minister at Louis XVth's Court, was now stooped and aged, hardly able to haul himself up the wooden steps.

Ten or twelve villagers, a mixture of young and old, formed up behind him, holding what arms could be gathered from the haylofts and dungeons. They stood out of sight in the courtyard, as he announced himself to the soldiers from the rampart.

'La Broche, at your service, monsieurs. Can I offer you some sustenance?'

'Hugo la Broche, in the name of Madame de Pompadour, I have a Warrant for your arrest! You will surrender yourself to me and prepare for the journey to Paris, where a salon at les Bastille awaits your attendance!'

'There must be some mistake, gentlemen! I am not your prisoner! I have committed no crime!'

'Sir, you will face trial for *treason*; therefore, as of this moment, you are my prisoner. Please do not resist. I do not believe you have the resources to repel my extremely irate Guardsmen! We have ridden through the night and I assure you, we are in no humour to be detained any longer than necessary.'

'I do not understand. What treason? What are you talking about?'

'Madame de Pompadour has brought charges, monsieur. You spoke out against her and attempted to raise a delegation to challenge her authority.'

'When was this so-called offence committed? I am innocent of such actions. I have never met Madame and have no desire to!'

'There! From your own mouth! You show your treachery in every utterance! You fail to accept the authority of Madame, the strength behind our Government. The King's most able ally. You sent your Audit to the Crown one month ago, declining to pay the tax for the equipping of a personal bodyguard for Madame.'

'Absolutely! I decline to impoverish the sixty men, women and children of my estate. Yes, I did, and would do so again! I refuse to pay the Tax. Yes! I have nothing against Madame de Pompadour — but if she has enemies, and I am perfectly at liberty to believe that she has provoked many, she is welcome to gather all the protection she needs. But *I* refuse to subsidise her personal protection! The King may feel obliged to provide her with a small private army, but I'm damned if I will see my people starve for the privilege!'

'You need say no more! Hugo la Broche — you are hereby under arrest and will accompany me immediately. If you care so much for this bunch of peasants, then you will want to make your arrest as peaceful and painless as possible, for their sake.'

'But who will provide for them when I am gone? What will become of my Estate?'

'I am sure a new benefactor will soon arrive.'

'Who? For instance, you? I know how the affairs of State operate, monsieur! I know you are carrying out these orders for your own personal gain!'

The leader noisily pulled his sword from its scabbard. 'Count de Rochefort at your service, sir. I have quite enough to concern me in my own Estate, to show any interest in this place, Sir. No, I believe Madame will have in mind a member of her own household to come down to this "small-holding", where an income may be produced with an application of hard work.'

'Sir, I beg of you. My people — they have been loyal, dependable. They do not deserve to be flung out of their homes.'

'You should have thought of that before you slighted Madame and brought her wrath down upon them as well as yourself.' You were once a Statesman — I know of your reputation. You must know that one show of dissent, one chink of resistance going unpunished can cause an avalanche of insurrection. A huge upheaval! You may not have realised at the time, but a movement began with your refusal; fifteen houses, so far, have been razed to the ground. You have survived because your property has potential. I will not mince words. Your day is done. Let us be gone — there is nothing more to be said.'

La Broche turned towards his people. My friends, you have been good and faithful people during all my years here... Please carry on with your duties. Perform them well for the new Master. I am sure you will be looked after.'

He turned, making his way down the steps, and removed the crossbar from its anchors, allowing the large oak door to swing on its own weight until the gap was sufficient for him to pass through.

His clothing hanging loose around his stooped shoulders, and his black fur trimmed, woollen cap sitting askew on his head, he emerged into the light.

Rochefort sat upright on his bay mare. She wheeled around in a complete circle, before pounding the dry earth with her right hoof.

La Broche held out his hands, a sort of evangelical gesture, although there was little appreciation from the waiting troops.

'Monsieur, we must arrange for a carriage.'

'No. I will leave my coach and horses on the Estate. My people will need them.'

'Monsieur! I insist, no fuss! We require a carriage to return to Paris. You are not able to sit astride a horse for half a day. You cannot walk. Therefore, it is carriage or hay-cart. It is your choice.'

'Bring my carriage — one horse only will be required.' La Broche slumped even further as his spirit broke, leaving him helpless to manage himself for such a journey.

When the carriage pulled up, Rochefort signalled to one of his men to dismount and take the reins. 'Make sure the Count has a smooth ride.'

With that, he turned and led the entourage away.

The Estate gathered to watch, until the column disappeared. Now they began looking to each other for leadership.

'What can we do?'

'Should we fight them? Should we try to rescue the Master?'

'There will be another Master along soon!'

'How can you say such a thing! He always treated us well. Made sure we had enough to eat.'

Madame Baptiste spoke up. 'Stop! Do not argue among yourselves! Let us go to the chapel. The Monseigneur will know what to do.'

There was a general agreement and the gathering moved slowly through the courtyard; hens and goats swarmed about their feet, but made enough room for them to pick a way forward. The sounds of normality returned. A cow in a distant field. The cat and a mongrel hissing in a corner of the barn. Pigs squealing as though they had been skewered.

It became surreal. They were in shock, not able to account for their actions, or lack of them. They simply had no leader. Their leader was taken. Without him, they were uncertain whether to continue their duties.

The Monseigneur stumbled out of the chapel and down the four stone steps between them. 'What is it…? What has happened?'

Again, Madame Baptiste. 'The Count has been taken — did you not hear? Did no one call you when the force arrived?'

'It was terrible! They accused Monsieur la Broche of treason!' the blacksmith offered.

Monseigneur Rappaport stumbled on his words. He was acting nervously and was not his usual easy mannered self.

'Er, how did this happen? What was said — what evidence?'

Madame Baptiste's anger surfaced. 'They said he had spoken out against the Pompadour! They accused him of causing insurrection! He only meant to feed the poor, to keep the Estate alive, when he refused to pay their tax.'

'Madame Baptiste, you are getting too excited. Tell us slowly... what did they intend to do with the Count?'

'They are taking him to the Bastille! They said the Estate would have a new Master!'

'Well, we shall have to... I must go to Paris and speak for the Master.'

The gathering murmured approval, although there was uneasiness in the atmosphere.

'Will you go alone, Monseigneur? Do you need companions for the journey?'

'I believe I am safe. I will travel in my formal attire. I believe there is still respect for the Church, even in Paris.'

'We will prepare some food for the journey. You must take great care. Will you take a horse or carriage?'

'Er, a horse should be sufficient. I am sure I can manage. If I may borrow a decent mare from the Estate, I will set off immediately.'

The smith, stock-keepers, shepherds and maids all gathered, while some of the wood-cutters and stone masons came out to give the Monseigneur a send-off.

He mounted the mare and managed to set himself in the saddle, although he may have been the least experienced horseman in the county. A little cajoling found the mare breaking into a steady trot and the black-hatted priest bobbed along on its back.

The villagers turned to one another and there was a general willingness to stay together in time of trouble, which resulted in a hog being mounted on a spit. Wine flagons were readied, until a fire roared in the great hearth in the old courtyard and fifty or more peasants sat and drank, until the hog sizzled and the wine flowed. Their spirits were raised in unison.

Two days passed before there was word, carried by poste chase, that Monseigneur Rappaport had crossed the bridge at Rheims and was making tortuous progress towards the capital.

Weeks went by before, quite dramatically, word reached the villagers that the Monseigneur was 'en route' and would arrive the following day.

There was almost a carnival atmosphere about the Manor as the villagers, and the Estate's people, gathered again in anticipation of a great day, marking a new beginning.

Madame Baptiste had gathered together three capable helpers and prepared a welcoming feast. The aroma of fresh bread filled the air; olives, cheese and garlic were spread around the edges and fresh-cooked ham was carved into horse-shoe slices and laid out in crescent-shaped rows.

There was music drifting across the courtyard as four minstrels plucked on lutes, whilst a padded drum was caressed with pompoms on sticks.

La Broche's carriage finally pulled into the courtyard and the door swung open. A footman placed a stool on the ground adjacent to the door and a buckled shoe emerged, before planting itself onto the stool. A fine set of pantaloons in green velvet followed, and the gold braid decorating the matching tunic came into view.

The crowd almost gasped audibly when Rappaport's head followed as it became clear that La Broche was not to be returned to them, but something had happened to Rappaport! They fell silent as he finally stepped on to the hardened earth of the courtyard and stretched his arms into the air.

'Ah. Good people, I am so delighted that you have gathered here to greet me! It is with great sadness that I must report the demise of our former Guardian, Count la Broche. He did not survive the journey. His heart gave out.' Rappaport hung his head in deep sorrow at his memory. The villagers murmured their sympathies with deep sadness and looked to one another to share the moment.

'However, I have an announcement. I have a charter here, in my hand, that means we can resume our lives in the village without fear of hindrance from afar. We may resume our existence, secure and happy in a prosperous future. The King bestowed upon myself the honour of succeeding Count la Broche. I have been blessed with good fortune — I am now "Lord of the *Manor*", and I have you, my dear friends, to work with me to make this parish proud again.'

Almost carried away in the euphoria, Rappaport's voice rose to a high pitch, making the ensuing silence all the more noticeable.

The villagers stood for a while without a word being uttered. Madame Baptiste was first to find her voice.

'Monseigneur — it is, of course, wonderful news that... a man... of the village is to take over the, er, "mantle", so to speak... I... Well, begging your pardon, but you have been in our community less than two years. You are — something of a stranger to us. Yet the King has seen fit to... give you... the village and the income of the Estate?'

'Madame, er... Baptiste? Yes? I trust I may count on you for your support — and the Estate workers, collectively? I trust all will be well. You are all to be of great assistance to me whilst I am finding my way, so to speak. You will be my allies. The villagers will know they can continue to trade with us as before. Indeed, I hope the numbers attending chapel may grow into a congregation to put other parishes to shame. I will be obliged if every one of you attends to receive a blessing and to hear of our plans for the future.'

The level of comment stirred in the courtyard until it became a loud audible gaggle, the noise drowning out a valid response.

Rappaport stood up on the stool still vacant next to the carriage.

'Please. Please! Let us be calm! Allow me! I have some words for you. For all of you. Heavenly Father...' The roar of disapproval rose from the crowd. Some began to surge forward. They grew hostile, fists waving towards the priest.

Rappaport became pinned back against the carriage. A tomato burst over the top of his head and another missed his ear by a fraction. His hat became dislodged and a desperate hand managed to grasp it as it slipped from his head towards his knees.

The angry crowd shook the carriage and the swell of noise increased even further.

A pistol crack broke the momentum and finally the crowd began to regain some composure.

Two horsemen held cocked muskets at their shoulders and glared down at the faces now turned towards them.

Now Rappaport was aloft the carriage. In his fine new attire, he looked like a peacock, and he thrust out his chest in similar fashion.

'People of St Raquel — enough, I say! Silence!'

A hush descended upon the crowd.

'I pray your attention, because I will say this only once! I did not wish to bring an armed force into the village and had hoped you would greet my elevation with approval and kindness. Now I see I must behave in a way I did not wish. I will make this village grow. I will make it strong. I will inspire you all to better yourselves.

'We will not remain a quiet back-water! This parish, this region, will grow around St Raquel — I will grow, and you will grow with me. This will be our time. Forget the old regime, it is dead and gone. You will work with me. You will help me make this a place to be proud of.

'Now — I want you to go about your work. Come to me for guidance on any issues outstanding at the end of the day. Report to me on Sunday after Mass. The chapel will always be open.

'I hope to win your respect — but if I do not, I will win your fear. You will come on this journey with me, whether you like it or not.

'Now, depart! Madame Baptiste — you will prepare supper for me and my men.'

'Er, y-yes, Your Lordship! And how many men would that be?'

'Fourteen. Now go!'

Serving fourteen men was not a new experience for Madame Baptiste; however, the torment she endured at their hands was!

'More wine, you, fat slag!'

'Come here, let's see what you've got under your skirts…!'

'Come — a little respect for your priest… bow down, kiss… take his hand…!'

'Go on — pull off my boots — more wood on the fire, you, old sow!'

After a continuous tirade lasting over an hour, Rappaport finally intervened. 'Gentlemen, a little decorum, if you please! Madame has served you up a decent platter and deserves your respect; at least you could show her a little gratitude.'

At the conclusion of his speech, a bearded, lank-haired soldier rose and grabbed Madame by the arm, pulling her down across his platter and onto the table. He threw his leg over her and buried his head into her ample bosom. 'I'll show my appreciation, all right! Come on, let me show you…!'

'Leave me, off with you… you animal! Get away! *Help*! Monsieur, monsieur, please… let me go!'

'Why, you, ungrateful old witch! This, is how much I appreciate your cooking…!'

Just then, her young son slapped the soldier across the back with the handle of a broom. The other soldiers cackled and roared with laughter, and the offender climbed slowly off his victim, turning to see who had dared to 'whip' him.

A half-smile slit his scarred face and his eyes lit up. He picked up young Francois by the throat, flinging him across the room.

Rappaport leapt from his chair and brought his shooting stick down hard on the back of the soldier's head, sufficiently to bring the man to his knees.

Turning to the others, at that stage still laughing at the other… he growled at them, 'Get him out of here! Tie him up in the stables until I think fit to release him.' Two others rose and dragged the man to his feet, before manhandling him out of the kitchen door.

Lifting Madame Baptiste from the struggle she was too obviously having, and returning her to an upright position, he bowed and begged her apologies.

'My boy… What have you done to my boy?'

'Nothing more than a scrape, Madame… nothing a growing boy will not shrug off, I am sure! Come, let's gather him up and see him off to bed for a night full of sweet dreams.'

Approaching the boy, who lay in a heap in the corner, Rappaport feigned concern that he had not yet come to his feet. 'Come, little fellow, let's have you up. Come along.'

But, instead, the boy lost balance and slumped back to the hearth again.

'Maman! Maman, please! Ahh!'

He was unable to stand. Kneeling to feel down his leg, she discovered that it appeared to be bent in an unnatural way.

'Ahh, Maman, no! Please don't touch!'

'My God, what have you done to my boy…? What is it, child? Show me.'

Sitting him on the table, his mother pulled at his leg, but failed to straighten it.

'Madame, I am sure it will heal. Now get the boy off to bed; these weary guardsmen need their fill! You must see that your work is not done here. Come… I will have one of my men help you!'

At a signal, one of them stood, dribbling wine from his beard, and he hauled the boy up into his arms, bringing a fresh yelp of agony from his lips, tears left trailing down his grubby little face.

Madame Baptiste could do nothing but scurry along in his wake, guiding him eventually to the room where the boy's cot lay vacant in the corner, draped with a single blanket.

'Please, put him down gently. Here, just here, that's it! Your pig of a friend could have crippled him! An innocent boy — he could be ruined for life. He did not deserve this. Have you no shame?'

She lay her head down on the boy's belly and cried out.

'Madame, I will make sure Lavache pays for his crime — no child should be treated that way. I will make him sorry for his actions, you mark my words.'

'I blame *him*! The Monseigneur! How could he sit there and allow such behaviour — a Man of God!'

'Bah! "Man of God"? I doubt it, Madame! He is no more than a land-grabber! He has taken down your old Master in a greed-driven sham! He has been crowing about his intentions and his plans! He is a viper! You would do well to take care — you and your boy. Nothing I have heard so far about this Rappaport would make me believe him a *Man of God*!'

'Monsieur, I thank you for your kindness. If you could give me a moment, I will return to provide further sustenance for you and your men, but I am now aware of the dangers, even more than I feared when he showed himself in the courtyard this afternoon. I am prepared for what may come, and I thank you.'

Turning, she proceeded to make the boy more comfortable, placing a cushion under his twisted leg. She bathed his face with a damp rag and kissed him on the forehead.

'Rest now, my son. I will not be long in joining you. Do not worry about these men — I believe we have a protector among them. Good night, my sweet boy.'

The events of that evening were quickly forgotten, and Madame Baptiste discovered that there was no protector among the soldiers. When the boy was at least well enough to manage a makeshift crutch, she made her escape.

In Marseille, the streets ran with sewage. Animals and humans alike crowded public places from dawn until dusk. The bars never closed. The bordellos overflowed onto balconies and porches. It was all Madame Baptiste could do to pull the boy close to her skirts and block out some of the sights.

The rotting fish, effluence of every kind, a dead goat, festering on the quayside, the noise, the fetid smells, the heinous laughter and shrieks of pain and pleasure in unison. The stench made both mother and son quite nauseous.

Head down, holding tightly onto her valise and to the arm of her son, she cut through the gangs and clusters of sailors like a barge under full sail.

Breathless and dropping to her knees, she finally slumped at the door of an old stone chapel, which jutted out from the bent and broken timber hovels that surrounded it.

Moments passed, allowing her to regain some composure. She pulled herself up and looked about her. A priest in a dust-covered black gown rounded the corner and walked briskly towards them.

'What can I do for you?'

'Er, Papa, I, er... Nothing! I was just resting for a while.'

'You have not come about the position?'

'The position?'

'I am looking for a housekeeper — I have recently disposed of the old one.'

'I have only arrived in the city moments ago. I am sorry, I have not come to you for a position.'

'Do you want the job?'

'I need a job, and a place to stay. For myself and my child.'

'Yes. Well, providing he makes no noise! I will not live in a kinder-garden.'

'No! He is very quiet. Silent. He will not make a sound. I guarantee it.'

'We will try it for one week.'

'Oh, Monsieur, Papa! I am so grateful! I am so, so grateful! I owe you my life.'

'I would be happy to see you give thanks! You will attend Mass every week, without fail. Your boy will attend school, here, in the chapel conservatoire. That, and exceptional *oeufs* for breakfast, is all I ask.'

Life turned around so quickly following their escape from St Raquel! Madame Baptiste found the priest easy enough to please. He made few demands on her, other than over-indulgence at meal-times.

The boy attended school for a few months, but his leg was buckled. It did not mend, so he continued using a stick under his arm, like a crutch.

His mother tried to keep him clean, but he spent more and more time squatting outside the church and watching people come and go. He would run errands, fetching and carrying, but he communicated less and less.

He withdrew into himself — no doubt his infirmity was the cause. He could not keep up when other young people scurried around.

As his mother became irreplaceable to the priest, and the church, the boy drifted into the background, eventually into the night.

He preferred the shadows. He avoided going about during the day and blended with the other creatures of the night. By the time he reached his teens, he had become known along the waterfront. Those who bothered, called him 'peg-leg', even though it was clear to all that he had two legs, albeit one of them badly twisted.

His gait was a matter of bobbing up, then down, and lurching forward, before coming up to his full height —

although his full height never became much above five feet.

'Peg-leg, get over here, you imbecile!' Henry-Jacques, the landlord of the Fleur de Lys bar and bath-house, called across the room to where Baptiste was crouched over two coins, amid a group of shabby street urchins. The coins flipped against the wall and rolled to a halt on the dirt-ingrained, wooden floorboards.

'Yeah, yeah. Encore, encore!' a cry went up, and there was much movement among the group, grabbing one another and dancing around, before the crestfallen Baptiste rose and left them. He lurched away, his small heap of coins on the ground where it lay.

As he reached the landlord, Henry-Jacques' hand swung through the air and caught him a glancing blow, dislodging the flaxen-grey hat from the back of the boy's head, until it flounced down behind a vacant chair.

Baptiste's head came up as he ruffled his hair until it fell back down around his ears.

He leaned over and grabbed his cap, before swinging it up, onto his head, like a gnome's head gear, a sleeping cap, making his appearance most un-promising to the stranger.

Hopping from his good leg to the bad, then back again, he sniffed. 'Yes, Master, what is your pleasure?'

'My pleasure? Watching you clown about the place, of course! Fetch me another pitcher from under the counter… and be quick!'

Baptiste shuffled away, to return moments later with an earthen jug of cloudy white wine. In placing it down before the landlord, he slopped some of it down the front of an already soiled blouse.

The back of Henry-Jacques' hand landed squarely in Baptiste's face, sending him backward across the room to land at the foot of the stone hearth. Blood spurted into the air, before Baptiste could grasp a towel to stem the flow.

A roar of laughter echoed around the room. Baptiste rose, hearing the laughter as though from the end of a long tunnel. Staggering left, then right, he felt the need to breath fresh air and turned towards the open end of the bar room.

Turning into an alley behind, he slid to the ground with his back to the plastered wall and coiled up, holding the cloth to his face. He knew his nose was broken, probably in more than one place. He could hardly open one eye, and the blood continued to spill out of the towel into the dry earth. He sobbed quietly for many minutes, before managing to rise and limp away towards the chapel.

Nearing the chapel, he realised the distress it would cause his Maman if he lurched through the door in that state.

Instead, he turned towards the well at the far end of the graveyard and reached in for a pail. Cleaning himself up as best he could, he pushed the broken cartilage of his nose one way, then the other, allowing it to come to rest at the position it least pained him.

That night, the landlord awakened to a scratching sound emanating from the long wardrobe in his bedchamber. Expecting to find rats in his shoes, Henry-Jacques lit his night candle from a burning ember in the grate and stood erect, turning towards the wardrobe. He coughed. A rasping, growling noise filled the room as he released phlegm from his chest and spat it into the fire, causing a minor explosion in the ashes.

He felt something cold, but the impact of the razor-sharp kitchen knife did not have an immediate effect as it entered his body just above his kidneys. It travelled through other vital organs until the hilt, and the hand that held it, prevented further ingress. He felt a stinging, then the first real pain in his lower abdomen as the blade was twisted.

Turning, he looked down, sensing a smaller body adjacent to his own. The candle came up to give him a better view of the visitor: the sandy hair, the frown across the bushy eyebrows, intense blue eyes, peaking through the dark rings that had appeared on his face some hours after the assault.

As Baptiste's battered face stared up at him, a smile broke out.

The landlord felt a rush of cool air as the blade slid out. He looked down to watch a dark pool on the floorboards expand rapidly as his blood drained from the gaping wound, running down his leg.

His nightshirt quickly became soaked. Searing pain engulfed him. His heart stopped, his mouth fell open. He was in catatonic shock. His heavy body lunged forward, the head crashing into the open wardrobe, as his body suddenly went rigid.

Baptiste hopped nimbly away, avoiding contact. He left the premises by the same window through which he had arrived, the one he had left ajar that evening, when, having cleaned up his face and changed his old woollen jerkin for a faded grey blouse, and britches, he had returned briefly to flesh out his plan.

He had hidden his puffy, reddening face from the crowd, as if some of the drunken debauched drinkers would ever have noticed. Tipping his forelock to those who had idly observed him, he drifted away, without making contact with any of the other flunkies.

Baptiste considered his options. His mother had called him and offered him bread and porridge, which, in truth, looked very inviting, but he did not want the bother of answering questions just yet. His nose would never be the same. Just like his leg, though he knew the black rings would fade; one was yellowing even at this stage.

He left the house and found a place on the flat roof adjacent to the priest's house, where he would often, unseen, lay out in the morning sun, absorbing energy from its life-giving rays.

Today, he contemplated the uninterrupted blueness of the sky, the distant noises of the Township coming awake, even happiness spilling from some of the windows of the shacks nearby.

Then alarm! Shouting! Dogs began to bark. A horse and carriage rattled along the cobbled streets as the Magistrate and a physician arrived. Then a frantic visitor at the Sacristy, and the swinging of doors as the priest was summoned.

A babble of noise arose as the crowd gathered. Baptiste began to cry. As vile and vicious as the old landlord had been, he was regarded as an important citizen in his own little world. A cornerstone of the community. Such was the community that a creature of his standing could be respected so!

Baptiste had to decide upon his course of action. He could drift over, show concern and join the crowd as it would swell throughout the day, simply hoping that no one would ever consider for one second that he, 'Baptiste the simpleton', the young flunky, could ever perpetrate such a brutal crime.

Or he could slip away, now, before anyone raised the alarm, putting as much distance as possible between himself and the scene of the crime, and thereby condemn himself as the guilty party.

He thought of his dear mother: he couldn't bear the idea of her being victimised in his stead. He must brave it out and assume innocence!

He clambered down from his secret lair and made towards the Fleur de Lys.

He had only turned one corner and he could see the crowd already swarming around the square. Waves lapped at the harbour wall on a high tide. The harbour was busy, with small boats criss-crossing to the bigger ships, weighing heavily in the water, with their loads of provisions precariously bobbing in the wash of other boats.

But the focus was in the near corner, where the jetty encouraged the small boats to moor, bringing a never-ending throng towards the inns and taverns.

Now there was no room for any to moor alongside. Boats were tethered to other boats and their incumbents hopped from one to the other, then onto the jetty.

Baptiste made his way through the crowd, his size and insignificance enabling him to eventually arrive at the kitchen doorway, where two soldiers had taken up guard.

They each chatted merrily with the crowd as a carnival atmosphere developed.

Suddenly, there was movement from within and the two stood to attention.

Four men appeared bearing a body on a flat table top.

The body was lightly covered, but the outline of a large and imposing profile was visible as the sheet flapped lightly in the breeze.

A hush settled across the gathering. Heads were bowed, the sign of the cross was made a hundred times. There was still a significant babble from the rear of the crowd, where word had not filtered through that Henry-Jacques had emerged.

Room was made around the Commissioner's cart and the body was placed ceremoniously onto the backboard.

The crowd turned into a procession as the cart drew away. There were tears. Some of the old women began wailing.

Baptiste stayed close to the kitchen. One of the flunkies emerged and put a protective arm around him. His surprise at this gesture made him suddenly aware of his position. He was regarded almost as a member of the bereaved family.

The hangers-on, and the kitchen staff, the regular drinkers and game players, all suddenly had status. They were 'his' family: they belonged, and they had lost their figurehead. Been deprived of a living. They were to be pitied.

Respect was openly shown as people filed away, passing the open doorways of the inn as they followed the carriage up towards the chapel.

'Don't know what's to become of us!' said a voice, friendly and in confidence. Baptiste turned to look into the eye of the speaker. One of the regular bar girls pulled her scarf tight around her, covering her tarnished silk dress as well as she could. Her undergarment still flowed over that, and the milky bosom in turn flowed over that.

Her frizzy red hair was bushed out by a thousand proddings, and her ruddy, freckled skin did not completely hide the prettiness of her mouth and piercing blue eyes.

'Don't know, Miss. I... I dunno what will 'appen! What about 'im?' Baptiste shook his head in the direction of the disappearing crowd. 'The Master. What 'appened?'

'Someone carved 'im up! Blood everywhere. He was done in! 'Ere, what's 'appened to your face, dearie? You look terrible!'

Baptiste dropped his head. 'Er, nuffink. I had a little run-in with an 'orse. I was s'posed to keep 'im calm while 'is Master was imbibing of a few drinks, an', well, it's 'ead and mine sort of come togevver!'

'Oh, really? You ought to be more careful. Look at your poor nose; you never used to look so bad before... but...'

'I never knew you even saw me before!'

'Don't be silly, you been 'ere all the time! I see you every day! Good little worker. That's what we all say!'

'M... Miss? I didn't know you even saw me! I never looked at your face before today!'

'I'm Dolly — you don't 'ave to call me Miss. What a funny fing to say! Course we look at you! You are one of us! Look, you don't need to worry, neiver. You stick wiv that story about the 'orse! No need to mention ol' Henry-Jacques smashed you in the face! Don't want any one pointin' a finger at *you*! 'As if!' she chuckled.

'Er — you mean... some will fink it was me that done for the ol' man?'

'Course not! Well, it's just better not to draw attention. They'll soon sort it out. The guilty — some sailor 'e wronged. Or someone he owed money to. It's always the way.'

'Well, what 'appens to this place...? Will you be workin'? Y'know, will you be workin' tonight?

'Don't know, dearie. Why? You interested?'

Baptiste blushed. His head bowed, he pulled his hat about his ears.

'Come on, don't be shy!'

He caught her eye again, before turning and shuffling away.

There was little more about the day that proved unusual. Baptiste hung around the bar mostly watching in case anything developed, but nobody even spoke to him or looked in his direction.

A carriage arrived late afternoon and a young dignitary emerged, pulling off his tricorn before entering the premises.

He was inside for some time before another carriage pulled up, from which alighted a heavy-set, jolly-looking man, also in skirted-coat and tricorn hat.

He was a tall man, who stooped to enter the tavern. Some half an hour passed before the two re-appeared. The first climbed into his carriage and the other shook his hand, but turned and re-entered the Fleur de Lys. It was obvious that the new landlord had arrived and that it would be business-as-usual that night, and every other night for such a vital facility on the Marseille waterfront.

That night, the salon was bursting at the seams. Not only the regular crowd, swelled by the arrival of another merchantman, but the curious, the morbid and fascinated from all around the town.

Everyone wanted to see the blood-stained floorboards. Everyone wanted to stand and even lie where the body had been indelibly traced in blood.

There was a carnival. There was never a night like this in the long history of the Fleur de Lys. The party continued late into the night, and morning broke before the throng dispersed.

Baptiste had blended in where he would normally have been seen. He did not work this out, it was not tactical. He simply fell in with the routine and could not have been more comfortable in his surroundings. He knew no other way; and yet, even in those times, he had enjoyed his freedom to roam and to mingle the way he did. Suddenly, he found new confidence, and others were talking to him, even asking him how he was doing.

He had never known this. He felt his broken nose, tender, to say the least! His upper lip was swollen as a consequence, and he resembled a panda, with the two black rings around his eyes. But somehow, these were the badges of 'courage' or survival that improved your standing in such surroundings, and he was suddenly enjoying his status!

No one connected him with the 'shocking' demise of old Henry-Jacques. It must have taken a mean, evil and powerful man to have taken out old Henry. So, attention was completely diverted away from his close circle. Baptiste had found himself, somehow, amidst all the uncertainty and threat of imminent danger, someone who could 'cope'.

Time passed, and Baptiste grew into something of a novelty in the harbour region. He was recognised by the big players as someone who could carry a message, deliver a package or 'get a result' when given a task.

To others, he was a friend — someone who could talk you up when you were down. Someone who would go out of their way to make your life a little brighter.

He worked. The new landlord got him collecting flagons, clearing out rubbish and making sure things went smoothly. Baptiste had grown a powerful upper body, compensating for his poor gait, and occasional lack of balance.

He could pick up a chair, single-handed, by one leg, even with a normal-sized man sitting in it!

This was a feat people would pay money to see, and it became an attraction that visitors would seek out.

He was considered a celebrity as time passed and his world became a tolerable place. He even gathered up enough courage to visit Dolly one balmy afternoon, when the bar was fairly quiet and the heat of the day made everyone lethargic.

Dolly had drifted through, her corset loosened, allowing a little air to circulate around her pinched hips and torso.

Her bosom hung heavy and full at a tantalising angle, the outline of her legs clearly visible as she passed by a window, with the fullness of the sun shafting onto the floor.

Dolly had never looked younger, fresher, fuller. Baptiste followed her. He watched her lean against the door post. She knew he was watching and turned just enough for him to see the corner of her mouth turn up in a smile.

Two years after Henry-Jacques had been dispatched, the skipper of a Barque, a known privateer, ambled into the Fleur de Lys. He ordered red wine and asked for Henry-Jacques.

He soon established the fate of his old comrade and showed his displeasure that the perpetrator was never found.

Finishing several goblets in quick succession, he set off for the Governor's residence in a determined fashion. He meant to find out what had happened to his 'brother'.

There was little general acceptance that the man was actually the brother of Henry- Jacques. He had been seen some years previously, but the most he was credited with was that he and Henry-Jacques had some unfinished business.

Two days passed before he returned. He made all aware that he was not a happy man. Henry-Jacques must have owed him money, or at least a favour; if not, some information which was intended to be of advantage to the man. So, finding Henry-Jacques gone to his grave was far from what this man expected.

He was introduced and became known as Captain Gavrille, an experienced and successful merchantman, a privateer, who had taken on the English in many a tight corner and still emerged with his ship and his reputation.

Returning from the New Territories, he had run guns and supplies into the French forces in Canada and South Maryland and had a reputation as a fierce combatant.

Within a couple of days of his arrival, Baptiste knew enough about the man to realise his best course of action was to avoid his presence at all costs. Nothing would entice Baptiste into his circle, and, as days wore on, it became clear that Baptiste was taking up every possible option, any job, any task that ensured that he and Captain Gavrille would never cross paths.

A week went by and the plan had proven successful. Baptiste had fulfilled some errands and taken some visitors on a two-day jaunt to a nearby monastery. He had lingered long in the shadows and had no cause to meet or greet the newcomer.

He spent much of the evening at the rear of a nearby tavern, where some of his old friends, the street urchins, the great unwashed, would gather and toss coins late into the night. Sitting aside from the action, he watched and observed, making certain he had an escape route if any approached him.

The moment came when he was least expecting it. He had taken some bread and cheese from the landlady and just turned to resume his spot at the bottom of a flight of five stone steps, when a tall, stringy sailor appeared at the foot of the steps.

'Monsieur Baptiste? A friend would like a word with you.'

Baptiste saw the cocked pistol in his hand, the two high, stone walls to the side of the stairway, and behind him the closed door to the kitchen.

The street gang had retreated into the shadows. There seemed no option but to proceed ahead of the pistol. The direction pointed for him and his own instinct knew he was being guided to the Fleur, into the hands of Captain Gavrille.

The Captain sat behind one of the long tables. A flagon stood nearby and a half-filled glass, an empty platter and an embedded dagger showed that the Captain had recently dined.

He waved to Baptiste to sit opposite and the area was cleared, leaving them facing one another.

'My little friend, I have been looking for you. I wonder you have not called in today, to the place where you have served, as I understand, for some time.'

Baptiste sat, head bowed, not daring to look into the eyes of his inquisitor at that moment.

'I have been attempting to find out what happened to my brother. Your old friend Henry-Jacques. I have been told you were one of the last people ever to speak to my brother. Is this so?'

Baptiste raised his head a little and was able to nod twice in response.

'The day my brother died, he had cause to punish you for a misdemeanour, so I hear. He made a mess of your pretty face, so I hear.'

Again, Baptiste nodded affirmation.

'You saw Henry-Jacques late that day. I have been told you returned to the inn. Is that so?'

Baptiste raised his eyes. There was no way he could lie to this man. Such was the conclusive way he pronounced facts that made what he said absolute and final.

'I have to ask you, my friend: did Henry-Jacques... say anything? Did he give you anything? I must know. I am searching for something. A map, a small message containing some instruction. I have to find what I came for. Can you help me in any way?'

Baptiste, almost unable to breathe, realised that the man had nothing. He realised that he did not suspect, for one second, that it had been Baptiste that sent Henry-Jacques on his way. He knew for certain in that moment that he was safe.

'Monsieur, may I speak?'

'Please, my friend, speak. Tell me everything you know!'

'That is just it, monsieur — sadly, I know nothing. Henry-Jacques did not confide in me. He treated me well. He made sure I did not starve, and I did some little tasks each day to repay his kindness. But he would never confide in me. It could not have happened, monsieur! I... I cannot think...'

'Perhaps you were confused — after your unfortunate beating. Perhaps he did say something...?'

'No, monsieur; no, nothing! I would like to help you.'

'And I you. I would that you had the information I am looking for... that we could become friends!'

'I, too, I wish...'

'I sail tomorrow at high tide. I would like you to come with me. Perhaps, in time, you may recall something, however small — anything that might help me. If I am half way around the Caribbean when that moment comes, and you are here, then there will be no benefit, no help for my cause. But if you were with me, by my side... you may remember, something might come back to you... and there I will be! What do you say...? Would you join me on my adventure?'

Suddenly, Baptiste was sure the game was up. He believed this was a ruse. He would be enticed on board, carved up and fed to the seagulls! His fate had been sealed.

He knew there was no point in protesting. He could not say 'no' to this man. He knew at that moment he was going to sea! That was his fate. He found himself nodding agreement. He looked at Gavrille, who's eyes were wide with expectation. He agreed verbally. 'I will go with you, sir. Who knows, something might return to my head. I could be of value to you in so many ways... May I say farewell to my mother?'

Gavrille stood to his full height. He waved a hand towards the entrance. 'Go, bid your Maman farewell; you will be at sea tomorrow. We will have an adventure together, my little friend. I feel it in my bones!'

Baptiste shivered all the way from the base of his spine to the top of his head. He simply took his leave.

He kissed his mother goodbye an hour later, taking a rolled-up woollen jacket in a bundle which contained some other bits of clothing.

Making his way back to the harbour, as if compelled by a force outside his own body, he spotted Gavrille's rangy matelot at the harbour wall, holding the ropes to a dinghy.

Four seamen were sprawled out in stages of recovery after a night of debauchery. Upon seeing Baptiste, the sailor called to him. 'Come on, my friend, jump!' The matelot grabbed an elbow to hold him steady as he landed in the boat. He cast-off and yelled at the drunkards to pull on an oar.

Two of the sailors responded, and the tall one steered the boat towards the harbour mouth, where an imposing three-master sat gently rolling on the tide.

If he were on his way to the executioner, Baptiste did not feel the condemned man. He felt a strange excitement. He simply watched as the day took its course. He would soon be aboard a sailing ship and heading out to sea. This was an adventure, and he would make the most of today. If it proved to be his last, then so be it.

His life had been one round of misery followed by another. He had survived by the skin of his teeth, for what? He could not answer the question, but it began to dawn on him that perhaps the adventure was not over. Perhaps it really was just beginning!

Standing behind the wheel on board the *Durham*, Baptiste pulled his cap from his head and began twisting it between his hands. He made ridiculous shapes, folding it and turning it inside out until it resembled a rabbit.

He had achieved many shapes with this soft, woollen cap, which had a long tail and bobble on the end. It hung limply on one side of his head like some old sock most of the time. But he had had it so long now, he could make it come alive!

It was not a gift of which he was particularly proud, and he never performed that act for anyone; but when he was troubled, he would do it incessantly for himself as some sort of therapeutic occupation.

Now he was truly troubled. He had been at Daemon's side for the past three months. But before that he had stood with John Standing at the wheel, or the helm, of one ship after another, foraging in the Mediterranean and the Indian Ocean for that life-changing encounter.

Many times, it had come close over a period of eleven years. Many times, he had been in danger of losing his life. Many times, he had escaped by the merest coincidence, or chance occurrence.

Before that, he had served Captain Gavrille through tumultuous battles, mountainous seas, drought, starvation, near-drowning a dozen times. Adventures which would have to be told of another time, but when John Standing put a bullet through Gavrille's head, Baptiste had knelt in gratitude, as Gavrille would surely have been the cause of his own death sooner or later.

Chapter 24
The Tide Turns

Watching John Standing die had been a blow from which he could barely recover. He had hidden most of his feelings as Daemon took charge and stepped up to the mark in so many ways. He had watched Daemon grow in confidence, grow in stature. He knew the lad's heart was in the right place, he knew his sworn oath was to make good to John's family and all that John had lost, yet he felt in his own heart that somehow this would never happen.

He held a mighty respect and even love for the young Master, but deep down inside, he, Baptiste, believed there was only one person who should take over John's Estate, return John's ship to its port of origin, deliver the profit and gains to John's widow and his legacy to his family in England.

Baptiste believed this was his responsibility, his task, his right.

Now, Daemon was the problem. The lad meant well. But he was only a lad! He had a lot to learn. He had risked everything in frivolous encounters, and may even now be having to pay the penalty.

What would become of John's ship? What of the return cargo, tonnes and tonnes of sugar and coffee stacking out the hold?

The ship may be seized with all its contents. Daemon might be wiped out! He may never have another opportunity of riches and social acceptance. It could be that Daemon Quirk might never be heard of again, and with his demise, the fortune that was due to John Standings partners and his wife would be forfeit.

All this crossed the mind of Baptiste, the faithful right-hand man. The loyal, unswerving follower. Now he was plotting treachery — but in the name of a man whom he had cherished and respected beyond all.

The ship stood at the ready. High tide had been reached and was on the turn.

Baptiste leapt on to the rigging, waving a paper in one hand as he clutched at the lanyard with the other.

'Attention! Attention! Approchez-moi! Répondez. Vite!'

He reverted to his native tongue when at his most nervous and desperate.

'I have a message! The Master — he has been imprisoned! He may face a trial. He urges us to take to the high seas, without delay. We must, before they come to seize the vessel!'

The crew gathered, and immediately began to mutter and call disapproval.

'Men, comrades, we must respond to the Master's wishes. We have to stand by his orders. This paper is his word. He knows we must make this our pilgrimage. Our Destiny! Return the ship to Europe. To the Old Master — to John Standing's family.

'We will be rewarded for our courage; we have to take charge of our own destiny! You know me, my shipmates. I will not fail you. I can take you across the ocean. I, Baptiste, will see you home safe. I have made such perilous journeys many times, my friends. Those of you who know me, those who served with me under John Standing and even under Gavrille, you know my loyalty — you know my reliability! I will take you home!'

'What of the Master? What if he escapes? What if, this minute, he is making his way to the quayside?' Treadwell shouted from his position at the rigging.

'He has a strong ally in Captain Vasteron. He has told me that Vasteron will soon return with other British ships. He has told me not to wait, but to *fly*, mon ami. Will you fly with me?'

Such was the power of the words, almost irrespective of from who's mouth they spilled, the men were stirred.

'Come! The tide will soon turn, and we will lose the ship. Come — full sail, let us be gone!'

In the Governor's apartments, Van Eyck and Gertrude sat, drinking tea from fine china, in a group of six, which included Jorge Gardinier, the Governor's personal aide, and Lt-Colonel Dejan Capaldi, in charge of the Squadron assigned to maintain the *status quo* on the island.

The Governor's Lady, Pedrella, dressed in turquoise, accompanied by all the ornate finery seen at the Spanish Court, sat comforting Gertrude by joining hands across the low table.

The doors to the salon flew open and Daemon marched in.

Upon his arrival, Gertrude stood and put out a hand, as if to stop him where he stood. That was precisely what she achieved, with Daemon not sure whether to advance or retreat. He had no choice but to remain at a distance.

Van Eyck rose and stood, squarely facing Daemon, with his hands on his hips, whilst Lady Pedrella rushed to Gertrude's side and remained there as if to prop her up.

The Governor, Fernando Palletta, arrived himself by this time, entering behind Daemon and passing him without a glance. Palletta was clearly in the throes of dressing for the evening, pulling a long, flared jacket of gold and purple over his flowing blouse and tight silken britches.

Daemon had the feeling he was fulfilling a part in a play, possibly a charade! None of this seemed real, and he almost laughed, looking around for the clowns to enter the scene.

Palletta took his seat at the head of the dining table, which was set for dinner. He waved to a seat a few places away from where he was seated. 'Capitain, please!'

Daemon looked around him, before realising he had been addressed. Palletta watched as Daemon took faltering steps towards the designated chair.

'Come, my friends, let us sit like civilised people and dine on this good food. We should not let it spoil.'

The others looked towards one another. Van Eyck was rendered speechless, and Gertrude raised her handkerchief to her eyes, but nonetheless moved towards her seat, where she sat at Palletta's right hand, his lovely wife at his left.

Instructing the attendant staff to proceed, he turned to his guests and raised a glass. 'His Majesty!' He smiled benignly as the others followed suit.

'His Majesty,' echoed Daemon, only vaguely aware as to whom he had raised his glass, and let it rest at his side.

A fine dinner was served, and polite conversation followed, although two in particular played little part. Van Eyck and his daughter's roles were 'indignation' and 'tragedy' in turn, as they awaited the Court's verdict upon the young 'villain'.

When, eventually, Palletta had dined to his satisfaction and become mellow on good wine, he addressed the two sides.

'I have before me a gathering of intruders; in each I recognise a potential friend, a companion, a vivacious addition to my wife's household. Instead, I fear, we have two sides, protagonists, determined to go to war!

'The fine English playwright has it all encapsulated so that we may feast upon it from time to time:

'*I, the Duke of Verona, these the Montagues and here the Capulets, two rich but opposing families. Is there a plague upon both your houses, or, could we find a way to marry the two sides and bring peace to our fair Dominion?*'

All those around the table looked towards the Governor in surprise; Daemon, in truth, because he knew nothing of the Montagues or Capulets, and Gertrude because she recognised herself in the description. Her father in disgust because he knew the outcome of the tryst.

'Now, what are we to do? For myself I would wish to skip to the epilogue of the story and find a happier ending. Senor, what have you to say for yourself?'

'Sir, I... Governor, your honour, I know nothing of what I am accused. I do not know what to answer for.'

'Come, come. We know you have taken advantage of this innocent young lady, and that her father demands satisfaction. It is a simple enough matter — propose to the girl and have done with it! Peace is restored, and the story of the star-crossed lovers may yet end happily.'

Daemon rallied for a moment. 'But, sir...' Suddenly, he looked at Gertude, her face a picture of dashed innocence. He knew it would be ungentlemanly to expose her as having played more than a willing partner in this folly.

'I... er, would like to ask the lady if she is sure it is myself by whom she has been offended.'

Van Eyck stood and raised both arms to the heavens. 'Shame on you! Shame! Is this the actions of a gentleman? To accuse an innocent lady of improper behaviour with others — of more than one indiscretion!'

'No, sir, please. I accuse no one, not the least your daughter. I am merely asking to... well, I need to know... er... I would...! Please! Allow me to speak with her alone for a moment.'

Van Eyck looked towards Palletta and nodded agreement. Daemon rose and moved towards the adjoining doorway, hoping it would lead into an empty chamber where he could talk some sense into her!

Very slowly, feigning reluctance, Gertrude rose and followed him through the door. Closing it behind them, they found a small salon with a lounge seat and a stool. Daemon chose the stool and sat opposite her.

'Gertrude, look me in the eye. Now, tell me what it is you want of me. Why, in God's name, have you suffered a week at sea, risking everything, to follow me to these islands?'

'It is simple. I am in love with you!'

Daemon smiled. 'This is not a story, it's a fairy tale! But you are a.... an experienced, worldly lady, not some innocent young princess! What on earth do you want with me?'

'You know I love you! I showed it, didn't I? And you loved it!'

'I, look, I have things to do. I have to make my own way in the world. I... even if I loved you in return, I could not think of returning with you. I have much to achieve before I think of settling in one place.'

'But you love me! I know you do. No one could have shown me everything that you did, if you did not love me!'

'Gertrude, what are you talking about? Have you lost your mind? You and I had a beautiful encounter, we indulged ourselves in a fit of, well, intoxication. It was glorious! But not... life-changing. I thought you were willing to make the most of the mood, the moment. But not take it to heart.'

'I am with child!'

'Now, let's not be ridiculous! Even I know that it is impossible for you to know that. It is impossible that our union has had any physical effect upon you... yet! If you are with child...'

'I am, I know it! I feel it inside me...!'

'Then it has bugger-all to do with me! If you feel something inside you, it was planted there when I was still on the high seas!'

She rose and smacked him full across the face. Daemon bit his lip and contained his anger.

'How could you say such a thing? How could you treat me this way?'

'My dear Gertrude, you have grown up on a plantation. You know how to put a stallion to a mare. You have administered it yourself. Do not try to suggest that anything produced by our encounter could have provided you with a child. It is too soon, too... impossible!'

Gertrude cried into her hand-kerchief. 'Swine! What will you do with me?'

'My dear, I have no intention of doing anything with you. I think you intend to use me. You want a father for your child. You imagine I can give you respectability and keep quiet about the impossible conception of that child.'

'Please, let us talk, let us be sensible! I have to go to Europe. You have to return to Barbados. If in one year we both feel the need to re-unite, it will happen. All you have to do is send word. And I promise to write back.'

'If I am capable — I will return to your island and we can talk again... we may even decide to spend some time together and maybe even marry eventually!'

'You shame me! Do you think I could marry a man who tosses me aside in my time of need?'

'Lady, you must not! Please, do not make me the enemy. As it stands, I actually *like* you, admire you. Please don't spoil my good opinion.'

'Oh, so, good opinion, is it? You have ravaged my body! You have treated me like some stud mare! I have been used, and now you wish to toss me aside!'

Daemon had run out of words and, in similar vein to their previous encounter, he could think of nothing but putting distance between himself and the lovely Gertrude van Eyck.

He looked towards the window, assessing the potential for a break-out. He knew the ship was at the ready. As with Barbados, they could be under-sail within the hour.

'My dear, I would speak with your father.'

'What... what lies would you tell him?'

'I promise you, no lies. I would like to seek his advice.'

'Very well. Call him.'

'Please, return to the Governor and his wife — for a few moments.'

Gertrude left him, and her father arrived a moment later. Daemon stood wringing his hands.

'Sir. Thank you for... I mean to say... I have to speak with you man-to-man. Your daughter is a very, very... f-fine, lady. I am a humble seaman.'

'Young man, my daughter has taken a liking to you — I do not approve. Yet she was convincing of your intentions sufficiently to drag me across the Caribbean. I have only two things in life I value: a good smoke on my pipe, and.... my daughter. I will do anything to secure her happiness.'

'I... I do understand, sir. However, I must return to Europe. It is a promise to my dying friend and mentor. I have to return and place his ship and his fortune in the hands of his wife and family. Beyond that I have no other desire in life that... well, would keep me from... er... becoming a friend, and... who knows? One day, a companion for Gertrude.'

'This is a serious matter. If you leave these shores... then God knows when, *if*, you may ever return! I believe, in fact, it is most unlikely, for I do not believe you are a slaver. I do not believe you have the stomach for it.'

'No, sir, I would be first to own up to that! I am only glad it is over. I am bound for Europe with a cargo of goods, and this is closer to my liking.'

'But you agree that you are unlikely to return?'

'It is difficult for me...'

'I have a proposal for you. Marry my daughter before you depart. Then you have reason to return. I believe you are honourable enough to return to fulfil a vow before God.'

Daemon shook his head, but words did not flow. He was struck dumb by the suggestion.

'I am not a fool! I will give you even more reason to return. I will sign over to you, one third of my holdings in Barbados. You would instantly become a man of substance.'

'Sir, you overwhelm me. However, I may become a man of substance, but not a man of honour. I do not... that is to say... I am not in love with Gertrude. She is a lovely, if I may say, lusty girl... and I... But to marry her — especially since you have put such a huge price on her... I would feel like a...'

Van Eyck let out a long sigh. His head dropped, and he appeared to be studying the design on the rug.

'I am getting old. I have worked hard all my life and made a fortune. But I want peace. I need to know everything I have worked for is in good hands before... well — as I said, I am getting old!

'I am asking you to compromise. I believe you could make my daughter happy. I believe you could continue to grow my business. I have met other visitors from time to time, but you, Sir — you struck me as a decent young man, a man of determination and not a little intelligence. Consider my situation. It may be ten years before another man such as yourself lands on our shores.'

'Aye, and it might be ten days! Gertrude... Look, Mr van Eyck, I... Give me time. Please, let me reach my own decision. Should you press your complaint, whatever that may be, should the Governor be forced to restrain me... then nothing in the world would make me endear your daughter less. I have found freedom. I would never look kindly on the man or woman who denied me that.'

Van Eyck again stared at the floor, appearing downcast. It struck Daemon that he was a man used to getting his own way. Daemon also saw an older man, somewhat weary. His daughter, and his significant holdings, all drew upon him, and Daemon believed him to have been sincere when he made the offer.

Van Eyck rose and called Gertrude.

She had been at the looking glass with Lady Pedrilla, combing out her hair, which had been rolled and plaited tight for the journey. Now it fell in flaxen, shimmering gold around her shoulders and reflected light on her neck and bosom. She looked at her best, and Daemon found himself having to swallow hard.

'My dear, come to your father. I would take your arm. I like your young man. He and I have spoken. We will stay with Governor Palletta for two more days. Captain Quirk will return to his ship and consider his options. He is a young man with commitments and a desire to do the right thing. I will not stand in his way.'

Gertrude turned towards Daemon and looked for a moment as if she might fly into an attack. She balled her fists, but left them hanging at her sides! 'Father, I understand. I will await the Captain's pleasure. I would ask him to visit one more time before the two days are over, and let us discuss once more, like two civilised people, whether we have a future.'

Daemon breathed a sigh of relief. Stepping towards her, he took her gloved hands in his own.

'I thank you, Lady. I will indeed return. For the moment, I have to look to the security of the ship and consult with my comrades. If... well, whatever comes between us… I have to know that the *Durham* is in good hands.' He bowed his head and kissed each hand in turn.

Then, turning to Van Eyck, he bowed once and walked from the room.

The Governor shook his hand as they passed one another. He appeared fully at ease with the situation, even though he had not been witness to what transpired. Daemon smiled to himself that, almost certainly, Palletta had the means to have been watching, or, at least, listening, to every word.

Daemon almost ran the whole way to the harbour, once out of sight of the residence.

He felt exhilarated and, of course, free again! His steps were light and rhythmic as he rounded the last timber structure onto the moorings.

The red-headed girl called out to him from an upper window. 'Senor, Hi, Senor…what about Lola?" Daemon could only wave his farewell without breaking stride.

His boat rocked gently on the water, still tethered where he had last seen it. But there were no crew in attendance. Daemon looked out. There were two ships anchored in the bay: one of them had brought Van Eyck and Gertrude. The other was not the *Durham*!

Daemon ran along the mooring, hopping over baskets and netting. There were sailors and fishermen chatting away as if nothing had happened. But Daemon, frantic now, leapt over everything as he made towards the harbour wall. Bounding up the steps, he mounted the narrow harbour wall and raced to the end without taking his eyes from the vacated space where he had left his ship.

There was not a sign of the *Durham*, her crew or anything familiar. He could not bring himself to accept the possibility that she had sailed. Suddenly, he replayed the picture in his mind, of the *African Xebek* gliding out of the natural harbour of Baltimore, Ireland, leaving in its wake that ransacked village of so long ago! He felt the same desolation and bile rising in his throat.

He eventually turned towards the township, where life continued in its own bustling way. Just then, he spotted Ridaker emerging from a tavern.

'Hoi, my friend! Hey! Wait! Did you...?'

'Captain Quirk, my dear chap! What on earth are you doing here? First of all, I see you racing towards the Governor's residence, then I return to see the mighty *Durham* pulling out of the harbour! And there was I thinking you had forgotten to say *farewell* to your dear old friend and partner...!'

'When, how long ago? Who was at the helm?'

'Well, no more than two or three hours since... you can check the tide if you need... I suppose she got under sail nicely, nothing holding her back, as the anchor came up. I watched her go. I scanned the deck for you, but concluded that you must be at your charts or whatever.'

'Damn, damn me! We have been hijacked! Hijacked, I say! Someone has taken over the ship!'

'Well, that may be the case, my dear fellow, but there was no sign of a struggle. All was calm and I just assumed you were aboard and in control of things.'

'No struggle, you say. Then what in God's name has happened?'

Chapter 25
The Promise Abandoned

Aboard the *Durham*, Baptiste poured himself a large glass of brandy and brushed aside charts and implements from the table. He occupied the captain's seat, in the captain's cabin, but he felt anything but a *Captain*.

His chin came to rest on his chest and he closed his eyes for a few moments.

He could not shake the image he conjured up, of Daemon returning to find the *Durham* gone! He could see the bewildered face. He imagined the hands reaching for a pistol. He imagined the pistol being trained upon himself.

Since those very early days when he found himself at sea, totally unprepared, and yet, suddenly feeling at home, he had never faltered in his loyalty to his Captain, whoever that had proven to be over the years. He had served each and every one of them unquestioningly. Now he sat alone.

The *Durham* plunged on through a minor squall, which served to provide an exhilarating spray across the deck with such regularity that it had formed a 'rainbow' in the sharp rays of the dipping sun. He watched it for almost an hour from his place at the wheel, whilst the crew performed their routine tasks.

Their numbers had increased since finding, during the loading, seven willing hands wishing to escape the confinement of the islands. A decent set of lads they appeared to be. But there was a quiet, unfamiliar atmosphere pervading the ship. Baptiste knew there would be a time for confrontation. He knew the men would grow restless once the tasks had been completed.

They had 'taken' a ship! They had stolen a cargo and all the possessions of the owners and its captain. That is not what they had signed up for!

Daemon was popular. To a man, they had been impressed by the way he had taken things in his stride since the death of Captain Standing. They respected him. After all, was he not one of the straightest men they had ever sailed with? Honest and dedicated. Didn't he lead them when things became difficult?

Yes, Baptiste would have to face up. He knew it hung in the balance. He had never commanded a ship before, but some of these men had sailed with him ten or twelve times and they knew his worth. He was a capable seaman. Very capable. Now he had to get over his physical imperfections and use all his skill and experience in order to provide a swift and trouble-free passage back to Europe, where no one knew from one week to the next under which flag they would sail, let alone who were the appointed custodians of every vessel.

Many were privateers. Those not attached to a particular Royal household would be fiercely independent and doubly dangerous.

He would have to invent a 'demise' for Daemon Quirk! After all, wasn't John Standing dead? Couldn't it just as easily happen to his replacement?

Baptiste loaded two duelling pistols and tucked them into his broad, silver-buckled waist-band. He limped to the stairway and rose briskly to the deck.

A group of four or five had gathered near the beam of the ship, where hushed conversation continued for some moments after he emerged.

He marched towards them and accepted the courtesies offered.

'Friends... what is going on?'

'All is well, monsieur; we are making good time, no?'

'Yes, but I do not like it when men gather and talk idly. You know it would never be accepted by the Capitain. I beg you... take no liberty with Baptiste, hey?'

Erik spoke up first, as expected by Baptiste, he had been less committed to fleeing with the ship than the others.

'If we knew your intentions, monsieur. You have to be reasonable — we are now mutineers... What are our chances of seeing this thing through?'

Baptiste answered impatiently, 'What is it you want?'

Treadwell, a plain-speaking Englishman, responded next. 'Another day of freedom, at least!'

The others all rallied. 'Yeah... freedom!'

'Quiet, fools! There will be more than a day! More than a month, a year! I have taken the ship so that we may return to Europe with a prize, and live as men of wealth and power, not as pig farmers, or sailcloth menders.'

'That is what we all want,' echoed Treadwell. 'But we had a fair shout with the Irishman. He showed he was a reasonable man!'

'But he is now in captivity. Did you want to sit around while the authorities impounded the ship?'

Erik interrupted. 'But we could have rescued him! We could have, we still could, have gone back for him!'

'We have no chance. The residence is well guarded. I saw it with my own eyes. It was hopeless; they might string him up after what he did to that girl in Barbados!'

'What are you saying? What *did* he do to that girl?' Treadwell was showing some defiance.

'To the best of my knowledge... but it is not for me to say.'

'Come on, you can't just leave it there; you are accusing Mr Quirk of... what, exactly?'

'Well, I can only assume... the night he returned to the ship and we made sail within minutes! It was a desperate escape! I met him... as he re-joined the ship: he was... well... 'ow you say... like a ghost. He was afraid. Then, two days ago, a ship arrives in Trinidad. They have followed him a long way to pass common courtesies.'

'Captain Quirk *was* greatly disturbed', offered Erik.

Baptiste needed to take command and twisted the truth. 'Men, listen to me. I 'ave been wrongly accused myself... there was a time when I had to flee my own country! Believe me... I 'ave looked over my shoulder every day since! If the Capitain is innocent, it will be better for 'im if 'e stands up for himself! Running is not the answer.

'Now... let us think of our own freedom! We 'ave committed no crime! We 'ave brought this ship many, many miles, to deliver for masters we do not even know! We 'ave to take what is ours! Nobody in Trinidad and Tobago is there with a prize waiting to reward us for *our* loyalty!'

Treadwell would not be silenced. 'But what about the authorities? They will alert the British Navy, they will hound us to the ends of the earth! What about that Spanish-sounding skipper? Vasteron, or whatever... 'e was Daemon's friend — they drank together!'

'Quirk will be held in captivity! Vasteron will not want to be associated with him.'

'But we don't know that! Lads? Come on... what are we doing?' Treadwell did not have the words to express himself further.

'Men, I am Baptiste! I have it in my power. I will deliver you freedom and riches! I have 'ad enough bowing and scraping to others. Follow me! I'll show you another way. Pirates! Pirates, that is what we are! That is 'ow we go forward. We owe nothing to no man! Let Baptiste show you!'

'We will talk to the men. If they say aye, then we will see... *I* am not going to swear allegiance... not yet!' Treadwell turned away, intent on reporting to the main body of men, who were mainly English or French-speaking Arabs.

He took two steps before Baptiste swung an arm and caught him above his left ear with the butt of a pistol. Treadwell slumped forward, out cold for the moment.

Erik grabbed Baptiste's free arm, but the Frenchman pulled the second pistol and held it under the big Swede's nose.

'Back off, my friend! I know you are mates with the Englishman... but we do not want bloodshed! Let us just calm ourselves.'

'Erik responded, 'I thought we were *all* mates with the Captain!'

Baptiste was beyond listening. 'Back off, all of you! We will talk some more until you all realise this is the only way! It is my way or nothing! Pick up your friend. Lower him into a boat. See if he can *row* himself back to England!'

'You cannot mean to leave him, unconscious, without water — he will be dead in two days.'

Baptiste still had the cocked pistol in his hand. 'Throw him into the boat with a bottle. Do not underestimate a man's survival instinct. I am sure he will see his family again, one day! Now move, quickly! We must make headway.'

The crew watched as the boat drifted away, feeling the impact of their own progress as it quickly became a speck in the distance.

Baptiste was also watching, but his mind raced. What if Treadwell was rescued within a day or two? What if a British warship found him?

A sick feeling built up in the pit of his stomach. He knew pursuit and capture was the most likely outcome.

'I want you to follow me to the cabin. I want to show you the charts. I will ask you one more time to give me your trust.' He had to think quickly. If Treadwell warned the authorities, if he told them of his plans...!

Baptiste had laid the pistol down on the table and was leaning over the charts.

Treadwell knew of his intentions to return to Europe and to secure Standing's interests. What now? With such information, it would be a matter of days before they were run down. He should have put a bullet in Treadwell! Now his plans would have to change.

He needed a new destination.

'This is our goal. He spread his fingers across an area of the chart. The others crowded around him and looked on. They could make out nothing of what they were looking at. Lines on parchment. Long straight lines and short curved lines. Some close together, some parallel.

Baptiste traced a long, vertical line on the chart.

'I have thought again about our options. This is our new destination. We will sail to the North American territories. I hear of free men! I hear of opportunity! Charlestown, New Orleans. Here we will find many Frenchmen established and making a life with the native Americans. We will go there and seek our opportunity. You will be free men. The French will not give a fig for the origins of a ship full of cargo! If they can get their hands on such a prize, they will take it. They might wait many weeks, months, for fresh supplies to arrive from the south.

'Here, we will be welcome! Here, I will do a deal with the French authorities to trade the *Durham*. That is my plan. It will mean freedom for all of you within two or three weeks.'

Erik was first to respond. 'A fine speech, my monsieur. But what about the cargo, what about Captain Standing, his family, his fortune?'

'What about the others with families? I have a wife in Norfolk,' said Dalton, a dour former farm-boy from the Fens.

They all turned to Dalton, a man who rarely opened his mouth to speak.

Baptiste laughed. Some of the others joined in. 'Your wife will be missing you, my friend! After all, how could she live without you for one more day?' They all laughed this time.

'I do not dismiss what you say, my friend! You will 'ave every opportunity to travel a little further and find in

New England many like yourself, making a new life. But also, many ships back and forth to old England! If that is what you want, you will find yourself passage, of that I am certain!'

Baptiste rounded on the others. 'Are you with me?'

Erik shook his head, but most of the others muttered 'Aye' in agreement.

Ledley found the courage to speak. 'Baptiste, you have the pistols, so no one can argue with you! You 'ave brought us 'ere on a lie. We was goin' 'ome, to England. We was goin' to bring John Standin's family their returns from the voyage... Now we're runnin', we are! We ar' gonna be runnin' for the rest of our lives.'

Baptiste drew his pistol. The barrel was aimed at the centre of Ledley's forehead.

Ledley backed off and melted into the crowd.

Without taking an eye off Erik for a split second, Baptiste reached for the rum and poured each a tot. 'To the future! To freedom!'

Another 'Aye', this time with more enthusiasm, and a pact had been made. Erik slumped against a cabinet.

Baptiste looked at him, catching his eye, he raised his glass once more and received a glum acknowledgement.

Baptiste concluded to himself that he may have to kill the Swede.

Chapter 26
Van Gahl's Arrival

A smart three master cut through the choppy waters with a fresh breeze filling her sails. Her skipper, an elegant Dutchman, an experienced captain in the Dutch Royal Navy, stood on the deck, a hand on the rigging ropes, as he scanned the western horizon, expecting to sight land at any moment.

'Pardon, Master.' A neatly dressed matelot tugged at his forelock.

'Speak! What is it?'

'Begging your pardon, Capitain, I believe we have passed a boat. I am almost certain it was not just driftwood.'

'When was this? Why did you not bring this to my attention?'

'It was a moment or two. Perhaps three. On the starb'd bow.'

'You are an idiot!'

'Oui, monsieur, I am!'

'Show me!'

He followed his crewman across the deck and the crooked finger as it pointed into the distance.

'I see nothing.'

'Er, beggin' your pardon, it was there, just there. A moment ago.'

'Tell me again, how long ago?'

'Mayhap ten minutes... all together.'

'Are you certain it was a boat?'

The hapless sailor nodded.

'You did not report it because you did not wish to face my question about your idling at the rail instead of undertaking your duties on the gun deck?'

The sailor nodded again.

'You were correct to assume I might not appreciate that you were neglecting your duties. However, I will tell you something you have undoubtedly heard on another occasion from me. We are at sea! We are dependent upon knowledge. Knowledge of where the next crisis will come from. From which position we may be attacked, or from which direction foul weather may arrive. We are, all at once, the eyes and ears of an early-warning system. You would not be doing your duty if you were not sharp-eyed and diligent every time you step onto the deck of my ship. Now, point once more in the direction that your keen and watchful eye set upon this vessel.'

'Monsieur, it was hardly a vessel, just a boat... It was there.'

'Bring her about, Mr Kruyff, the Captain yelled over his shoulder.

The wheelman, having idly watched the proceedings from a distance, immediately responded and began to turn the rudder for a starboard turn.

Crew appeared from below and took up positions at the ready.

'Van Beek... we will need a little adjustment as we turn into the wind.'

Van Beek, an experienced First Mate, barked orders and the men climbed the rigging to affect the sail. They had been disturbed from the boredom of an idle morning during one of those many periods in life at sea when there was, in fact, little for a crewman to do, other than to lay back and let the well-set ship plunge on through the surf.

Now, some activity. There was much to do in bringing the vessel around when under full sail, when she had enjoyed a following wind and fair weather.

By now, two young seamen had joined the Captain at the starboard rail.

'We are looking for a boat, gentlemen. A sharp eye, if you please.'

Moments passed, during which a nervous member of the gun crew stood wringing his hands and tying bits of rope into knots. A half hour passed, whilst his anxiety had become almost unbearable. He begged permission to take some water and enjoyed a look of disdain from the captain as he caught his eye as he ladled the water between parched lips.

'There, Captain! Three hundred yards!'

All attention diverted to a southern point, where a boat rose and fell on a white-crested sea.

'Well spotted, Roffman! Ease her around Mister Kruyff. We will reel her in and see what cargo she carries.'

Within fifteen minutes, a hook caught the side of the boat and pulled her tight to the bow of the *Kastel de Haar*.

Men handed up the prostrate form of a pale, thin seaman.

'Resume our original course if you please, Mister Kruyff. Captain van Gahl delivered a few more instructions, and Treadwell was laid out on a bunk next to the galley.

'Bring him round, Westbrook. Gently, if you please. Allow the water to permeate, not drown him! Fetch some broth — he looks half-starved!'

Chapter 27
Parting the Waves

In Trinidad, a crowded hallway and clamour of people with the business of the day at hand provided the backdrop to the day's proceedings at Governor Palletta's residence.

Captain van Gahl had arrived from the east and required an audience with the Governor.

Daemon Quirk had spent the last week enjoying the hospitality of his new friends. The Pallettas had taken to this charming Irishman, who's natural exuberance and boyish enthusiasm had brightened up a generally mundane existence at this secure seat in the most civilised of the Spanish dominions.

The Van Eycks had also enjoyed the hospitality extended. Gertrude and Daemon had, in fact, formed a genuine friendship, although he resisted with all his powers of restraint any further physical engagement with the vibrant Ms Eyck.

Returning to the Governor's residence following his discovery, he stood at the mercy of all and told his story plainly to the gathering.

'I appear to have lost everything. My ship has been taken under circumstances completely and utterly beyond my control. I am unable to think up a response. I have no alternative but to ask for your guidance, Senor Palletta.'

Van Eyck spoke for the Governor. 'You say your ship has been taken? What of the cargo, what of your possessions?'

'I have none of it! Everything has disappeared with the ship! Senor Palletta, I do not know what can be done. If you could provide a ship? Would it be possible for me to take some men and pursue the *Durham*?'

Palletta spoke. 'Nothing is quite that simple! I do not have a vessel capable of pursuing a ship of the quality of the *Durham*. I await the arrival of a flotilla from the Spanish Court. I am to provide a base for my countrymen, to re-stock and make good repair, before it commences it's patrol. But, in truth, it is quite possible my intentions and indeed my tenure here may well be curtailed. It is also quite possible I will be replaced by the British at any time.'

Gertrude turned to her father. 'Why, Father, we could set sail with Daemon, and a few soldiers; *we* could chase the *Durham* and bring whoever is responsible to justice!'

Daemon turned in admiration. 'Gertrude, your suggestion might work! I have to assume most of my men are on board and acting against their will. If we could just catch her, we could still turn her.'

'Father — can we?'

'Dearest, I would be first to rally to the cause, but I am not as young as I was, and I cannot agree to let you go on your own. I would never rest at exposing you to such danger. This is work for the Navy, not for a two-masted clipper.'

Daemon intervened. 'But, sir, your ship is swift, and I would be at the helm. I am sure I could find her.'

Van Eyck spoke again, calmly. 'Daemon, I would provide the ship. I would support you, but I beg you, let's settle things between yourself and my daughter...'

Palletta again, 'Gentlemen, please let us think this through. There is overwhelming danger in such a pursuit. We can only guess at which direction the *Durham* is bound! Soon, we will hear further. I am certain of it. You will please accept my hospitality until we have news.'

Now, Van Gahl stood before the Governor, alongside him the ungainly English sailor, having been provided some clothing not of his own size.

'My respects, Governor Palletta, Van Gahl at your service, sir, Master of the *Kastel de Haar* out of Rotterdam.' Van Gahl raised his tricorn and bowed slightly. 'This here is George Treadwell, late of the *Durham*, which I understand had been visiting Trinidad & Tobago recently.'

Palletta stood and paced quickly up to Van Gahl, grabbing his hand. 'Captain, we have awaited news for some days. You are most welcome, but I must ask you to hold your story for a few moments. I have the Captain — he is here with me.'

Van Gahl was taken aback at first at the enthusiasm of the greeting. Palletta was shaking the hand of his companion and called for his attendant.

'Quickly, go and find Mister van Eyck and his daughter, and ask Captain Quirk to join me in the salon immediately.'

Daemon knew immediately there must be news when he was summoned. He entered the room and his eyes immediately alighted on Treadwell, hugging him to his shoulder and patting him on the back.

Treadwell immediately broke into tears and begged forgiveness when Daemon demanded his story.

Intervening to take a little of the attention away from the sailor, Palletta introduced Captain van Gahl to Daemon. 'Captain Quirk of the *Durham*.'

'Did you find my ship? Sir, I beg of you.'

'Non, my friend; if only I *had* found your ship, I would have been the happiest individual. However, I found a boat, and in the boat, I found Mr Treadwell. He has a tale to tell.'

By this time, Van Eyck and Gertrude had arrived. The briefest of introductions were allowed, before Treadwell was ordered to speak.

'Captain, I... I was cast off; they attacked me and threw me into the boat. I had one flagon of water. I awoke from a stupor to find myself alone on the sea.'

'Who cast you off? What happened to the *Durham*?'

'It was 'im! It was... well, a week ago, was it, or longer? I can't say! 'E got us to make ready, we weighed anchor, we set off out of the 'arbour! We were given our orders. Then a few of the lads, Erik, me and Dalton, we turned on 'im to find out what was goin' on.'

'Turned on who?'

'Baptiste! It was 'im. 'E clubbed me round the head with a pistol. Nearly finished me! French bastard!... Pardon me, madam... er, beg your pardon, sir.'

'Baptiste?' Daemon was struck dumb. Incredulous! 'Baptiste? What of Baptiste? Tell me, tell me all you know!'

''E told us of your capture, an' said you was for the gallows! 'E said the *Durham* was to be imp... whatever. 'E said John Standin''s legacy was going to be taken from us, and we would lose our prize and lose our wages.'

'Where could he have come up with such a tale?'

''E said you was taken' We 'ad to take matters in our own 'ands! Return to Europe, give John's wid'er what she was due! I told 'im you was the man for it! 'E said we may never see you again.'

'And you believed him?'

'Ye... well, no! I didn't. I knew we was for it! I knew 'e ...'

'Steady, please, Treadwell... you did right. I understand, it nearly cost you your life. I just cannot believe Baptiste capable... I am lost... He never showed anything but fierce loyalty.'

Van Gahl spoke. 'My friend, I don't know the background, of course, but I 'ave to say that sometimes the fiercest loyalty is the worst kind! Such a man may suddenly have fierce loyalty to another, or to a memory. It may turn on you when you least expect.'

'I accept the point, Captain! You may be right in Baptiste's case. He seemed equally loyal to each Master! But this story has amazed me. I can hardly bare to think of it. Treadwell, my friend, I ask you again to recall all you heard, all you saw. Did he intend to make Europe his destination? Is that what you believe?'

'Aye, sir, that is what I remember! Erik argued with 'im. 'E didn't want us to talk to the men! We was for getting 'em together and talking it over, but 'e didn't want that! He was 'ell bent on the open seas! 'E took up arms, 'e 'ad the pistols drawn and cocked, but the others 'eard 'is reasonin' and accepted it! 'E threw me overboard!'

'You must get some rest... Give me time to think! Please, Senor Palletta?'

Palletta stepped forward and summoned an attendant. 'Take care of Mr Treadwell. Let him eat and drink all he needs.'

Daemon turned to Van Gahl. 'Captain, could you show me, exactly, where you picked up the boat? Could we check your position? I must have some idea of a location.'

'Of course, Captain!'

Palletta summoned both into the library, where they spread out some charts.

'Here is our position when the boat was first sighted, and here, when we rescued it.'

'There was a delay then, in collecting the boat?'

'Yes, sir. One of my men was reluctant to offer information about the first sighting. He had been wandering in an area which did not concern him in his duties. Eventually, he informed me that he thought he had sighted a boat, and a little time later we were able to recover it.'

'Once again, I thank you for your actions and in coming to us without delay.'

'Not at all, Captain. Now, might I enquire as to your intentions?'

'I intend to pursue my ship and return the cargo to its rightful owners. It is a long story, sir, that I will not burden you with at the moment. But the ship has been unlawfully taken, and I intend to put that right.'

'May I be of any assistance?'

'That is a very kind offer, Captain. I have an idea of how I might achieve my aim, but if I may, I will also consider your offer. Now, I must appraise my friends of the situation.'

'Yes, I am sure your fiancée must be most anxious.'

'Er, Miss van Eyck is not my fi... Oh, never mind; for now, let's just say we are friends!'

The captain smiled, but did not pursue the matter further.

Daemon took Gertrude's hand and smiled into her eyes. 'I have come to know you better in these last few days. Indeed, I have come to believe there may be some hope that in the future...' His eloquence ran out at that point and he felt like grabbing her shoulders and planting a kiss on her mouth!

Gertrude became quite demur for a moment, her eyes half-closed, and her lashes fluttered up and down. 'I, too, have realised the folly of my actions after... Please, let us think only of the future. You must reclaim your ship. Nothing is more important than that for the time being. I wish you God speed. I pray for your return.'

It had been agreed that Daemon would take the Van Eyck vessel, *Rebecca*, in pursuit of the *Durham*. Van Gahl had offered additional crewmen. It was therefore implicit that Daemon return to Gertrude, either to Barbados, or to Trinidad and Tobago, so that they would be reunited.

This was resolved when Van Gahl offered to return Gertrude and her father to Barbados and then to return to Trinidad to continue his business interests at Port of Spain.

Daemon turned his attention entirely to the task of pursuit. The boat had been gathered up about four point five degrees east nor'east, albeit after days of aimless drifting, but this provided Daemon with something to go on.

The *Durham*'s direction was declared to be 'east-bound' for Morocco, likely to turn north for Bristol when sighting land. and that was most important.

It would require a three-to four-week pursuit and very good fortune for *Rebecca* to make up the distance, but both captains agreed that other sightings, particularly if Daemon could encounter the British en route, may be vital to the cause. There was always the hope that the British might capture the *Durham* and that Vasteron may be suspicious of any explanation offered by Baptiste.

Daemon had plenty of time to consider what his actions might be upon his own encounter with the traitor!

Chapter 28
The Army in New York

Kirsten held her son. seven years of age, tall, handsome, with a shock of golden curls. She knew, having seen it for the first time. She realised that the father of her son was a long-lost lover from a distant land, who may be alive or long dead.

She closed her arms about him, pulling him into herself, as hard as she could, until John Nathan almost groaned, 'Mother, what's the matter?' He was breathless with the effort of pulling away sufficiently that he could look into her face. He saw that she had been crying. 'Is there something the matter, Mother?'

'No, darling! I just want you to know how much I love you. How special you are to me. I will never let any harm come to you.'

'I know, Mama! You are special, too!'

She caressed his hair and looked again into his eyes. She shook her head, finding it hard that she had not seen it before, or even that she had not thought of it.

The image of Daemon Quirk flickered into her thoughts. The destruction of Baltimore, the village on the southern tip of Ireland, seemed no more than a dream. The painful memories of the attack and the resultant capture, the loss of all her childhood friends, seemed to dim the memory of the brief encounter with the handsome young stranger.

She had wondered over the years if he might have survived. She considered all the possibilities, that he had fought with the Moors, had been cut down.

She blanked any further thought, reminding herself over and over that she had not seen him during the attack. She considered that he may have witnessed everything from afar, dared not to intervene. She gave him excuses, that he was not from the village, that it was not his fight. Then she thought about their passion and the promise of a long-lasting love, and she knew in her heart that he would have put his life on the line for her.

So, what could have become of him? Could he, in any stretch of her imagination, have set off in pursuit of her? Was it he, the 'young man' who travelled so far with Missie O'Connor and the refugees? Where would he start? Would he not know the ship had gone down? Or would he think her lost, drowned? Would he have simply got on with his life?

She released her son, gently teasing him into a seat at the large polished table which sat in the centre of the library, surrounded on all sides, from floor to ceiling, by row upon row of books.

She watched as he opened his book. Diagrams and maps had his eyes flickering in wonder at the Earth and the stars. A rare book brought many miles from Oxford, where such learning was commonplace. But here in the colonies, the fabric of an educated society was only just laying down its early roots.

Kirsten looked over towards the open French window. On the veranda, Banoldino sat back in a rocking chair, with a floppy, wide-brimmed hat pulled down over his eyes as he slept.

He had worn himself out visiting the stables earlier in the day. He had supervised his son's training in horsemanship. 'Equestrian' — the French had a name for it, taken from the Ancient Greeks. John Nathan had a natural talent for riding and managed jumps and mounting and dismounting at speed.

He gave his father much satisfaction in his prowess. Banoldino was proud of the boy. He loved him dearly and took every opportunity to spend time talking and nurturing the boy's interest in the world around him.

John Nathan played endlessly with tin soldiers and set up battlefield strategies. His 'Cabalieros' ranged across the library carpet, fought the crusade wars over and over. Salahadin, the Muslim leader, against King Richard and Philipe's Crusaders. He talked, with fierce enthusiasm, about becoming a cavalry soldier and fighting under the British flag. This was the source of inspiration that filled John Nathan's mind during those formative years. Another time Banoldino would guide him through the European struggles, telling the boy of his grandfather's exploits although Banoldino had to feign affection for the man he hardly knew.

Banoldino stirred. 'My dear, could you bring a glass for a poor old soldier? I must have dozed off for a while. I have such a thirst...'

'Could you take some tea, darling? Surely it would be better for you than Madeira, no matter what the vintage...!'

'A glass for me. You know I find your tea so... well, let me say a warm, odourless and utterly tasteless pastime! I beg of you. A little wine, a man needs a little wine...!'

'I shouldn't, but what can I do, a mere woman...? I could not refuse you, no matter what I believe.'

'And what do you believe, sweetness? Do you believe I am going to die with a sour face as my tea dribbles from my open mouth? I think I deserve to go out with a smile on my face!'

'Enough! I do not wish to talk more about yours or anyone else's passing. Please! I wish to talk about our son's education.'

'Education, is it? I will hear of no such thing. The boy should grow up in ignorant bliss, and when asked an opinion, he may smile happily and say, "I raise a glass to your question and care not a fig for the answer!" There, that's what a boy should strive for... not bookish learning! Where would I be if I had my head filled with bookish learning?'

'Madrid, possibly, or Granada! Those wonderful places you told me of when we lay those long dark nights aboard the *Star*.'

'What times we had! What an adventure! Was it so long ago? It could have been yesterday! But you... look at you!' He made his wife stand in front of him. He pulled her towards him until his head rested on her belly. 'You are as beautiful as the day I first set eyes on you.'

'Oh, I wish it were so... I am not that girl any more.'

'In my eyes, you are! And my eyes are not so dimmed that I do not see it. You are so... There is not a man alive who would not be proud to call you his own.'

She held his head close to her for many moments, feeling a rush of tenderness. She knew only too well his inner turmoil. She knew he was far from the man he wanted to be. She could do little to help him. She cried a little inside, wondering if perhaps he might prefer death to the life to which he had been condemned.

He raised his head and looked into her eyes. 'I am thankful, every day of my life, that I have known you, that I have you beside me and that I can reach out for you. Anything else? Well... a man has no right to demand more of life.'

Kirsten realised that she still had a part to play. That she could give him all that he wished for, and make his life worthwhile. She realised that she must continue to be that person, the 'girl' in his life, however limited the relationship might be. She would be his, for as long as he needed her.

Riders appeared at the turn in the track that wound its way up to the main house.

Both looked, pausing for a moment to consider who it might be.

Carstein's magnificent mount Bavaria, ate up the distance to the inner yard, as two others trailed up alongside him.

'Greetings, my friend. I hope you are well this fine day?'

'Carstein, come on down; we will find refreshment for you and your men. Please, let me arrange for your horses to be watered.'

'I thank you, my friend, but apologies that we arrive here unannounced. I have brought an associate, and trust you would not mind a little discussion about an urgent matter of business?'

'Never let it be said that Don Bosco declined an opportunity! Please come... Kirsten, could you summon...?' Kirsten had already paced forward and grasped Carstein with both hands. They always greeted one another with such genuine delight upon meeting.

She quickly acknowledged the others as they were introduced, then melted into the background to organise the servants in providing refreshment.

Banoldino rose, a little gingerly, and shook the hands of the visitors as they were introduced.

Carstein set the background and brought the situation up to date, before a fresh-faced, eager businessman was introduced as Watson, a successful shipping agent.

'A ship has arrived, possibly of Portuguese origin, in good order and containing sugar and tobacco. A skeleton crew has brought her from the Caribbean, where she had survived a volatile encounter, despite losing many of her crew.

'No ownership papers have been discovered, but a brigand, offering the name "Baptiste", claims that all aboard were offered joint ownership and a share of the reward for the cargo.'

Watson, intoned, 'There is no other claim to ownership. The French in New Orleans had threatened to impound the ship, but Baptiste distrusted the authorities and set sail again. They have landed here in New York, seeking asylum and a share of the profits with value, should the vessel sell at auction. I must say, as fine a ship as ever sailed the high seas.'

'Gentlemen... whoa! Please give me a moment. The question of the ownership document is one of high importance before we go any further. What of her origins, what of her masters, what of the cargo which brought her across the Atlantic in the first place?'

Carstein took the opportunity to express his own interest. 'Banolo, my good friend. I understand your concerns, and I have sent dispatches to the Governor and to England, asking for any history. But as I see it, we have two choices... we can arrest the crew and impound the vessel, just as the New Orleans French might have done. Or, we could give them a fair price for her and welcome a fine addition to our fleet.'

Watson's right-hand man quickly added to the proposal. 'A new name and a fresh crew, and this ship could provide a very 'andsome' profit for all of us!'

'Drummond, I don't think Senor Banoldino requires your guidance on matters of enterprise and profit. Please excuse my young associate, senor... his enthusiasm...' Watson intoned.

'I understand; this is a tempting proposition. We must not curb enthusiasm, however unbridled', concluded Banoldino.

Refreshments arrived, and Kirsten sat aside from the group, but listened intently to the proceedings.

Banoldino posed a question, 'Could she have been a slaver...? What does this Baptiste have to say for himself?'

Watson responded. 'He is a wily old fox; however, there is a certain charm about him. He insists that he has rightful possession and that he offered it to the French initially because he suggests the ship was first commissioned as a Dutch merchantman.

'He insists that he joined the ship in Jamaica, his role as First Lieutenant, and for a promise of reward for enterprise. They traded their prize for a hold full of cargo and again the promise of a share when returning to Europe.

'An encounter with a privateer — the name Amerigo de Ville was mentioned — there were losses and the ship's Master, John Standing, killed. The crew did their best to gather what they might and complete the voyage; but, without the Master, their efforts were constantly thwarted. They confess to having fled Jamaica with their cargo, which had been temporarily stored in a dockside warehouse, whilst, they claim, the authorities refused their rite of passage.'

'Whilst this is all very interesting,' offered Banoldino, 'we have no more claim to the vessel than any other, even if we pay a sum of money for her. How can we ever prove ownership? I am inclined to seize her and deal with the crew.'

'Sir, if I may.' Watson this time. 'The right to ownership of an abandoned vessel may fall to "salvage", should the vessel be rescued from the open sea.

'Could we not consider that is precisely what the crew did? They rescued the vessel, and the lack of proof of ownership, the lack of a Master, concludes in the law that those whom rescued the vessel may claim ownership.'

'I am mindful of the law on these matters and would consider such a proposal in a Court of Law as tentative, and easily countered.'

'Ah, yes, but only if there is any counter-claim or defence provided.'

Banoldino was becoming impatient. 'We could not act upon this matter until we have thoroughly explored all such possibilities. Is there an owner in Europe awaiting the return of his vessel and cargo? Or is there an Arab potentate awaiting the return of his slaver with the profit in gold which a valuable slave cargo would have produced? Where is the gold?'

Carstein intervened. 'Payment in part, or payment in full for the handsome cargo aboard the ship, no doubt. This Baptiste insists that the cargo was rightfully claimed and was to be loaded aboard the *Durham* imminently. They merely took it upon themselves to alleviate the Jamaican authorities, which we believe are currently Spanish, of making a decision.' Baptiste had twisted the truth in parts — Jamaica instead of Trinidad — to blur the lines of accountability.

'Well, Britain is not at war with Spain. Not for the moment, at least!'

'True, my friend, but when the vessel was disentangled, I believe a state of war did exist between the two sovereign nations.'

'When was this action?'

'In December, last. If this Baptiste is to be believed.'

'Banoldino, what is your instinct in this matter? I personally see an opportunity. However, I am quite prepared to follow your guidance. I have no great desire to flaunt international authority, and I certainly would not pursue this without the consent and co-operation of my trading partners.'

'Hah! My friend, you inadvertently cast all responsibility into my hands. You have expressed your own opinion, but in claiming that you would only act with my collaboration, you make the decision *mine*! Nonetheless, I will take responsibility. Incarcerate these pirates and await the ownership documents. The ship should be impounded — we must verify that the cargo is secure or place it in a warehouse, under lock and key.'

'Senor, your words disappoint me.' Watson stood. 'I brought this opportunity to your good auspices and you have slapped me in the face.'

Carstein chimed in quickly. 'Mr Watson, I also had risen to the idea of instant profit from this situation. Yet I truly accept Senor Don Bosco's guidance on the matter. There are those among us who need to take profitable gains at every opportunity. Take advantage of every situation. Senor Don Bosco and I are not among them. I agree with him that international law must be the resolution. We must take time.'

'As you say, sir, there are those who need to make our fortunes and those who have already made their own. I am among the former, and I thought, learning of your reputation as a man of accomplishment, that I would bring this to you. However, I see I was mistaken. I bow to your experience, but will follow my own instinct on this matter. I will call in to the Governor's office and make my case for custody of this vessel, and I suggest that you and the senor' — bowing in Don Bosco's direction — 'have declared your disinterest in the outcome. I bid you good day, sir.'

Banoldino raised one finger. 'A moment, Mr Watson. I understand your desire to make the most of this opportunity, but I must warn you, I may have to oppose any action, through the courts, should I think the common interest is likely to be disregarded. Think carefully, before you take any further action.'

'Is that a threat, sir? I do not wish to antagonise a man such as yourself, but if that is the only way, then so be it.'

Carstein intervened. 'Gentlemen, please. I feel responsible for having brought you together, and now I have created a schism. Please let us all take a deep breath and consider our positions. I fully accept that such matters may have to be dealt with in the court, but let us remain friends... We have to live together, after all!'

Watson clicked his heels, bowing in the general direction of Carstein, took a furtive look towards Banoldino, and bade his associate follow him across the yard.

Just before stepping from the veranda, he swiftly turned towards Kirsten. 'Excuse my manners, Mrs Don Bosco. I hope we meet again.' Kirsten bowed her head slightly, but did not rise from her seat.

Banoldino whispered aside to Charles, his attendant, and Charles hastily set off for the stables to issue instructions enabling the visitors to make a hasty departure.

Carstein spoke first. 'Banolo, my apologies. I brought these gentlemen on the premise that we might do business. I regret my judgement was not as sound as that to which I would normally aspire.' He bowed and lightly brought his heels together.

'Not at all, my friend... I initially saw an opportunity just as you did. Only after sensing the desperation — well, perhaps desperation may be too strong a word — but I thought perhaps our visitors would do almost anything to achieve their aims. We must not underestimate the force of a hungry animal.'

Kirsten spoke. 'Banolo, I hope you have not stirred the hornets' nest, my love! I did not like that man, not at all.'

Carstein again, 'My dear Kirsten, I believe I also owe you an apology. I will make certain that any dealings with Mr Watson and his companion will be kept at a safe distance from all our acquaintance in future. Please forgive me.'

'Carstein, please, take a glass with me; indeed, my dear, would you bring a bottle, the one with the black label? Carstein and I must discuss our next move.'

A week later, Banoldino attended a meeting of the Council, where he and Carstein had both been approached to run for office.

Carstein met him in the hallway and drew him to one side.

'Banoldino, my friend, I understand the fate of the *Durham* may have been taken out of our hands. It has been reported that she has set sail under cover of darkness and is unlikely to re-appear, at least to our shores.'

Banoldino's expression twisted as he took the news on board. 'Surely, McCarthy, the harbourmaster, could have placed better watch upon her? I must say I am disappointed. I would not put it past our friend Watson to have had a hand in this! Ahem... If I am elected, I shall certainly take steps to ensure that our borders and ports are more secure.' His laugh was tinged with irony.

Carstein agreed with a shrug of the shoulders. 'By the way, I will not run against you, my friend. I would like to serve the community as much as any man, but I hope to sit on a Council which includes my friend.' He patted Banoldino on the back and the two men strode into the Council chambers.

Several days passed before a spectacle was provided in the harbour!

A two-masted brig was seen to be towing a larger ship into the harbour. A gathering numbering six or seven hundred crowded the moorings and harbour walls.

As the manoeuvrings came to a halt, Watson, the Shipping Agent, an unfamiliar Sea Captain and a limping old sea-dog alighted a boat and, clambering up the steps, approached the Harbourmaster at the end of the quay.

'I would like to declare the *Durham* a Salvage Ship. I have taken possession of her under Maritime Law and wish to claim my reward.'

McCarthy smiled at him, shook his hand and, acting with minimum formality, led the way to his office. The crowd, in carnival humour, cheered as the small procession disappeared through the doorway. Many lingered in anticipation of something developing, and the atmosphere was maintained throughout the hot afternoon.

The explanation was that the ship had been hijacked by a malicious itinerant, the skeleton crew forced to get her under sail. The ship had made the high seas and would be lost and gone forever, had it not been for the great good fortune that Watson had commissioned a clipper and was carrying out a survey along the coast, when he spotted the familiar sight of the *Durham*.

After a short pursuit, the *Durham* was overtaken and boarded. Monsieur Baptiste had been released from captivity and with co-operation they vanquished the abductors into a small boat and returned both vessels safely into harbour.

Upon hearing this, Banoldino turned to Carstein. 'Watson sued that the *Durham* should be considered "salvage". There may, of course, be a difficulty in accepting such a ruling, as the origin of the ship remains unknown.'

Carstein agreed. 'Watson has pulled a master stroke. Although I agree, it remains to be seen how the courts will rule. We may have missed an opportunity.'

'There was no course of action we could have taken legally and end up with the prize.'

'Perhaps, but Watson is slippery character! We will have to watch him if he remains in New York.'

Watson proposed to McCarthy that the cargo be removed to a dockside warehouse, and a number of enquiries were immediately received for the purchase of the stock. However, no party offered to cover the cost of bonding the goods.

A court hearing convened to consider the issue and the courthouse was packed to witness the proceedings. Among the gathering were Don Bosco and Carstein, watching with interest as the events unfolded.

A judge was brought from Boston: J T Whittaker was proposed because of his experience of similar cases. His heavy beard and weather-beaten face suggested that he had been a sea captain himself.

He started the proceedings with a short speech intent on assuring the protagonists that there would be no need of histrionics and that he would hear what they had to say without frills or distraction.

The first to speak was the Deputy Governor, James Fortune, on behalf of the Crown. 'Gentlemen, we have a straightforward case which hinges upon the version of events provided by law-abiding and educated men. Please listen carefully to the witnesses we will provide, who will tell you that this ship arrived here after being rejected by New Orleans authorities.

'There is no known origin. No documents and no one claiming ownership; except, of course, the plaintive. Mr Watson, and his cohorts, will tell you they rescued a drifting vessel and brought her safely into harbour.

'Let me tell you, without hesitation, that this ship was never in danger, never abandoned by its owners and never should be called "salvage".'

Whittaker intervened by addressing Fortune, 'Thank you, Deputy Governor, you have presented your case. May I hear from the plaintive?'

Before there was a moment for Watson to make his case, the Dutch Commissar rose and waved a paper in the air. Whittaker was obliged to listen as Wortens summoned a naval attaché, who stepped forward to take a place alongside him.

'Your Honour, I would request that you accept a third suit on the designation of this vessel. The origin of the ship has now been established as Dutch West Africa, a slave ship owned by an Arab business consortium. There will be evidence supporting this claim and until such time as the evidence is produced, I plea that the ship come under the protection of my colleague here.'

Whittaker, in a resigned, almost laconic manner, bade the Commissar forward with his sheaf of papers. Examining the documents, he shrugged his shoulders and dismissed the gentleman.

'I record the intervention of the Dutch attaché, but cannot for the life of me find anything in this simple plea which might persuade me to find in favour.'

The Dutchman threw his arms in the air in protest, but was herded back into line.

'Please, Mr Watson, I sincerely hope you have a stronger claim on this property?'

Watson stood and walked into the centre of the room. 'I speak for myself in this matter. I have claim to this ship as she was found, at sea, with a small, frightened and inadequate crew, following an unprovoked and devastating attack. The vessel was sailed into perilous waters. *She* had to be rescued. I was on hand in my own vessel and able to intervene. The pirates that had taken her were vanquished, escaping into the night.

'I brought the vessel home. No ownership papers have been produced. The crew has explained that they are afraid and desperate to seek asylum on our shores and have no desire to set to sea again.

'I will call Monsieur Baptiste, the loyal crewman who attempted to save the ship from capture, and who sailed her through difficult waters and through heavy weather to try to reach a safe and sympathetic port.

'Monsieur Baptiste will explain that the ship was attacked on the high seas by privateers, and only narrowly managed to avoid capture. That, during the defence, the Captain and the senior officers were killed or are missing at sea.

'Monsieur Baptiste will attest that he believes the privateers pursued the vessel across the Caribbean to New Orleans, and then to New York, where attempt was again made to capture the ship which had escaped them earlier.

'We have a duty to see that Baptiste and his remaining crew are rewarded proportionately and that we attempt to put the ship into service, where she may be of great value to the Colony of New York and our sovereign masters.'

There was a significant swell of comment and reaction from the gallery, where the public had gathered in numbers.

Whittaker beat the block with his gavel and asked all present for silence and respect for the hearing.

'Thank you, er... Mr Watson. I understand the issues of this case and would like to hear from a couple of witnesses, for both sides of the issue, so that we may understand whose interests are at stake. I have no doubt that the matter may rest upon the word of the crew, as they have been the only ones involved throughout. If they tell the truth and we have to be satisfied that there are no parties involved or making a counter-claim, then there is a genuine case for establishing the situation as it has been presented. Now, let us have Monsieur Baptiste sworn in and get on with the proceedings.'

Banoldino arose and attracted the attention of the judge with a raised hand.

Whittaker looked in his direction and signalled his permission to speak.

'Senor Banoldino Don Bosco, at your service, Your Worship. I would like to put a further option forward which may inevitably hinder a swift conclusion to the hearing.'

'Very well, senor. I recognise your name, sir, and understand you have the respect of the New York establishment... so please continue.'

'I would like to suggest that the owners of this vessel may yet be established. I was approached myself some days ago with the proposal that I assist the crew and its agents in their attempt to gain official status. I considered the matter of interest from a purely business point of view, but declared that until the question of ownership had been thoroughly investigated, I did not believe we had the right to act or take any controlling interest in the ship or in its cargo.

'My associate took the liberty of sending to Lloyds of England for the origins of the vessel, and to see if something of her history could be established. We have not yet had word and would respectfully suggest the proceedings be suspended until such time as we have received a response.'

Whittaker responded, 'I accept that you have presented another point of view and I respect your actions. I am prepared to consider any evidence which may emerge and would ask you to make your position formal by entering a plea.'

Looking around the room, Whittaker saw the expression change on some of those present, and fully realised that this was not going to be the formality he had expected when being asked to preside.

'I would like to call today's proceedings to an end and suggest that we return to the hearing tomorrow at 9.00am to continue. At which time I will admit Senor Don Bosco's alternative plea and declare the interest of all parties.'

Showing a slight degree of irritation, Whittaker then continued, 'Meanwhile, should any *further party*, wishing to declare interest in this matter, please let themselves be known at the earliest possible opportunity.' With that, he banged his gavel and bade them all a 'Good afternoon!'

Chapter 29
Baptiste's Folly

Baptiste turned to the others. 'What would you 'ave me do? I cannot turn back the clock! We chose our path and I have done my best to achieve it.'

There was a growl of disdain for his response. '*You* chose the path! You promised we would sell our prize and live like gentlemen! Ain't that right, lads?'

Baptiste stood, leaning toward his antagonist. 'I offered you a chance! I gave you the means to end your lives in a decent way after all these years of toil and danger. I offered you a chance! Now you condemn me!'

'You made us steal the *Durham*! You made us turn traitor on Daemon Quirk. We ought to string you up! Come on, lads!'

Erik stood in their way. 'Wait. Stop! Think what you are doing! Getting rid of Baptiste now is a mistake. We will show ourselves as a bunch of cut-throats. They will not heed our explanation. They will never believe we were led against our will. We have to stick to our story. There was no mutiny. There was a bloody battle. We lost our skipper. We had to survive. That is a language the authorities will understand.'

The others pushed forward, but he spread his arms wide and put a shield in front of Baptiste, who now retreated towards the back of the room.

'Let's get 'im, lads!'

'Erik, don't get in our way.'

'Come on. All of you!'

Erik pushed back and the pack gave way, breaking up the centre, spreading the grappling maul across the width of the room. Now it was impossible for him to defend Baptiste as they outflanked him.

Suddenly, the bolt on the door turned and was loudly dislodged, allowing the large oak door to swing open on its hinges.

The attention of the mob was suddenly quietened, and they attempted to appear orderly as Watson and his followers filed through the doorway.

'Baptiste? Where are you, man? Let us sit down. We need to discuss the situation.'

Baptiste emerged from beyond the gathering and eased his way forward.

'I see that there is unease. Is there something I should know?'

The crew surged forward.

'Talk to us! Not 'im!'

'I see there has been a shift in the *status quo*. Monsieur Baptiste, please sit down. At least for the moment, I must speak through you.'

Following Watson's direction, he sat opposite as the lawyer slid some documents across the table.

There was a swell of comment from the crew.

'What is going on? I assume you are still in command... of the situation? And of your men?'

'We have had a difference of opinion, monsieur — I 'ave to explain to my men the position we are in. They feel like prisoners. I cannot 'elp this! I told them, we are simply awaiting the outcome of a hearing. Not a trial.'

'Yes, yes! You are not under arrest. The authorities simply wish to establish on what basis you are entering the colony. Nothing to concern yourselves with.' Watson glanced around the room so as to catch the eye of the majority.

'We have a good claim. I am certain of it. There is one man standing in our way unfortunately. Senor Don Bosco. He opposes our every move, and I am expecting more trouble from him on the morrow.'

'Why don't you deal with 'im? It is simple! If one man is all that stands in our way, then let us see to it that he can oppose us no more.' There was a babble of agreement from the crew.

Watson calmed the situation. 'Now look, we are not barbarians; we must deal with Senor Don Bosco — but he is well connected. The richest man in New York! I think we have to tread carefully. We misjudged the man once. Let us not make the same mistake again.'

Baptiste responded, 'If you will not deal with 'im, then I shall!' He turned to the men. 'I owe it to you to make sure we get an end to this resistance to our claim. I will deal with the problem. Men, trust me! I promise you I will deliver.'

Dalton raised a hand. 'I wants nuffing to do with murder.'

'Dalton, you again! I told you I would deal with it. I did not say I was going to murder the richest man in New York. Do you take me for an imbecile? No one would get away with such an act. Non! I will make the senor change his position on this matter. I believe he will see our point of view.'

Watson turned to the men and saw the desperation in their eyes. To Baptiste he said, 'I will return in forty-eight hours; somehow, we will apply pressure to Senor Don Bosco. I do not want to know what you are thinking. I will delay the proceedings to give you the chance to come up with a solution.' With that, he stood and clicked his heels, departing the gathering and heading for the street.

Once outside, he turned to Drummond. 'We have lit the fuse! I wonder in who's face the cask will explode?'

Baptiste had control of the situation once again. 'I beg of you, men! Trust me! I will deliver what you all want.'

The proceedings were once again delayed when Don Bosco delivered his own complaint on behalf of the Port Authority of New York, that the vessel be impounded until such time as its rightful owner be established.

The judge entered the plea and adjourned the proceedings for a further forty-eight hours at the behest of the claimant, allowing a period of time for research into the legality of the Council of New York's intrusion.

Watson acknowledged that he had not foreseen the complaint being lodged on behalf of the Port Authority and realised that Don Bosco was merely the instigator. Removing him from the dispute would have no bearing on the situation. It would merely expose their party to a risk of being complicit in any attempt to pervert the course of the hearing, and to personal damages, whatever they might amount to.

Watson immediately left for the Harbourmaster's premises, where Baptiste and his crew were temporarily detained.

Pushing through the door, Watson called for Baptiste to join him. A murmur arose from the gathering, before Erik broke out and addressed them. 'Monsieur Baptiste has left the building. He took advantage of some lapse in the attendant's concentration. He left under cover of darkness and we believe he was intent on approaching this Senor Don Bosco... He did not confide in the men... I understand you agreed with him that he should attempt an approach.'

Watson suddenly appeared anxious. 'Er... well... yes, we discussed an approach. Please, when did he leave? Last evening? About what time? Ten of the clock?'

'He has not returned; we must assume he has been detained. I will find him and return him to you.'

Watson turned on his heels and went swiftly for the door.

Finding Drummond, he told him of his worst fears and suggested that Baptiste be found immediately. 'He must be stopped!'

Banoldino stretched his legs and raised them on to a footstool. The house-boy moved quickly into position, easing the polished thigh-length boots from his master's feet.

Reaching for a glass which had been part-filled and left for him, he sipped on a full-bodied red wine.

'I must confess, my dear, I am feeling my age! This has been quite a day. I need the rest.'

'Not possible, my love! You know Lady Eve and Ranleigh are expected at seven, and I took the liberty of asking George to join us for dinner. Since he made Major, he has been keen to share his latest exploits with you and seek your counsel on one or two matters. I thought he and Allison will enliven the evening.'

'Dearest, I am certain the evening would be enlivened sufficiently in the company of our oldest friends, and, of course, Ranleigh, and I would like to take a few moments over a cigar to talk a little business.'

'Darling, you would still be free to talk. George is a trusted friend. I and... well, Allison, is so anxious for him to be brought in from the frontier. I wondered if you might...?'

'You have asked so many times. I am beginning to wonder if it is you that wishes the 'gallant' Major Smith to be brought in from the cold! Not your friend.'

'Banolo, darling, don't! You are making fun of me! I am concerned for my friend. He is a loyal and decent man and he deserves your patronage.'

'Aha! See! He deserves my patronage! Those are not Allison's words... they are yours!'

'Nonsense. I have put her feelings into words, that is all. Will you talk with him?'

'My dear, I will do more than that. I owe my life to that young man and I will never forget it. I am keeping an eye on him. When the moment arrives, he will know that he has a friend.'

'Oh, Banolo, I knew you were teasing me! Come, let's make ready for our little soiree...' Leaning forward, she kissed him tenderly and draped her arm about him.

He kissed her forehead as it rested against him. 'My dear, if you do not allow me a few moments to close my eyes, there will be no soiree.'

He watched as she nimbly gathered up her skirts and swept through the doors.

278

As Banoldino dozed, he did not stir when a gentle click gave away that the French window was being eased back. A furtive character slipped inside the hanging drapes just as they began to billow upward with the influx of air from the garden.

The intruder grabbed hold of the heavy drape to ensure that it did not disturb anything within the room. The sun slanted from the window, reaching across the floor to light up a bright section of heavily infused Indian carpet and a square of polished flooring beyond.

The ornate clock ticked steadily, its timing chain swinging gently to and fro'.

A shadow moved across the floor until it reached Don Bosco and held, motionless, for a full moment.

Banoldino's nostrils twitched and a lazy eye opened. He jerked upright in a movement which startled the intruder. Baptiste backed off, but held the pistol steadily in his hand, pointing it directly to a position at the centre of the Spaniard's forehead.

'Senor... who are you? What are you doing in my home?' The latter question rose to a commanding level, which again saw the Frenchman flinch.

'I would like you to come with me. For a short walk.'

'But who are you? What in God's name do you think you...?'

Baptiste positioned the barrel of the pistol between Don Bosco's lips.

'I assure you, sir, I am not able to walk very far. My boots...'

The pressing of the pistol and the motion of Baptiste's free hand signalling that he intended for him to rise, which meant Banoldino had no choice but to obey whilst the pistol scraped his front teeth.

'After you, monsieur. Outside, and please, keep on walking across the grass until you reach the tree line. We are going to inspect your property.'

Banoldino turned and led the way, managing to walk at a steady pace, his one thought to get this villain away from the house, away from his wife and his son.

Within a minute, Baptiste called a halt and placed himself in front of Banoldino.

'If you intend to execute me... may I at least ask how I have offended you, or your masters?'

'Non, monsieur. You may not!'

Baptiste drew the pistol up to the level of his own eyes and pushed it out at arm's length. His finger gingerly moved to a firing position. A deafening, sharp retort broke the silence as a flurry of birds flew into the air.

Baptiste's head flicked sideways and then jerked away to his left. A fountain of blood spurted from his mouth, spraying the bluebells and the surrounding grasses.

Banoldino crouched low, his instinct for survival telling him there may be a follow-up.

George Smith strode towards him across the lawn, his musket cradled across his chest. He held out a hand so that Banoldino could rise to his feet, then crouched over Baptiste and felt his neck for a pulse.

Banoldino let out a breath in a long slow hiss. 'George, I don't know what to say! By some miracle you have saved my life once again! I...' Suddenly, Banoldino reached out a hand as if he needed to prop himself up. 'I'm sorry, George. Could you please...? I think I need some medication...!'

Smith tossed the musket into deep grass and caught his friend under the arm, supporting him sufficiently to prevent him toppling forward.

Together they were able to make the house, where, in pushing the door wide enough for two to pass through, they disturbed a tall stand on which a fine porcelain vase had stood for some years.

The noise and general commotion brought the servants rushing to assist, and Kirsten flew into the room, where she found an ashen-faced Banoldino, with George Smith holding a large brandy to his lips.

The chime on the outer door brought fresh alarm, as Kirsten imagined Ranleigh and Lady Eve may find them in a distressed situation.

Kirsten opened the door herself and was taken aback to find Mr Watson standing there and bowing deeply before her. 'Madam, please excuse my lack of manners, but I must speak with your husband immediately.'

'I beg your pardon, sir, but my husband is indisposed I am afraid...'

'He is not harmed? Please tell me he has come to no harm!'

'Sir, why would you assume...? Perhaps you had better follow me.' Kirsten led the way into the drawing room, where a gathering tended to Banoldino, making him comfortable with cushions at his back.

'Enough!' he was insisting. 'I am perfectly well! I had a scare, and I am feeling a little tired. Could you please let me be...?'

The servants backed off, but George Smith persisted in making his friend more comfortable, and holding his brandy in close attendance in case of sudden need.

Both men turned in surprise to find Watson striding towards them and Kirsten attempting to lever herself into the small space in between.

'Senor Don Bosco, you are... not harmed I trust? I am very much relieved to find you, sir. I have news of a most threatening situation and wish to alert you to possible danger. For a moment I thought perhaps I was too late!'

Banoldino gathered himself, clearing his throat before speaking. 'Mr Watson, I am very anxious that you tell me your news, although I have the feeling, I have already had wind of it.'

'I trust that is not the case, sir. Without further delay, your life is in danger! A turn of events beyond anyone's control has occurred, and I offer my services in any capacity that it may prove of assistance.'

'Please, Mr Watson, tell me — in what particular danger am I?'

'Sir, when the court announced a delay in the proceedings, word reached the harbour, where the crew of the salvage ship were retained. I understand that one of the crew broke out and went missing last night. There is great concern that he holds yourself responsible for his great misfortune and was intent on challenging your authority.'

'Would this individual be a short, limping, unwholesome creature? Wearing some ancient, military silk and bandana?'

'Why yes, sir, I believe that would be the man.'

'Well, you will find him lying in the bushes on the perimeter of my property, where he was prevented from putting a pistol ball into my head by my very good friend Major Smith.'

Watson visibly wilted, lowering himself carefully into the chair opposite Banoldino. 'I am speechless, sir. I can only thank the good Lord that the attempt failed! Are you certain he would have tried to...?'

'Believe me, Mr Watson, the attempt was a split second from succeeding — Major Smith's was a most timely intervention.'

Watson rose from his seat. 'I am truly gratified that no harm has come to yourself or your family. We may have different expectations in the outcome of this dispute, but I would walk away this instant from any further involvement should the dispute escalate into violence. Please, senor, madam, Major, I would take my leave and discuss the entire proceedings with those who's interest I represent. There may be a swift conclusion to the matter, as I do not believe there is an issue worth the long-term depletion of this community. Sir, please, I will see myself out. I assure you I will play no part whatsoever in a protracted dog-fight over a mere vessel.' Turning quickly, he made for the door.

Banoldino held his gaze on the door as it closed behind Watson, then turned to George, who's countenance mirrored his own. Both men held a furrowed brow as they considered the actions of the departed visitor and his speech.

He had shown no interest in the body of his former associate.

Smith spoke first. 'Colonel — I would be very wary of that gentleman if I were you. I think he knows a lot more about what was behind the attack.'

'I am almost of the same mind myself; his protestations — or what would you call... attempt to disassociate himself with the intruder — were all too anxious for my liking. Yet he put himself in considerable danger in coming here at all.'

'Seems to me you have opened a can of worms here, senor... I will do my best to find out what's happening in town. Meanwhile, you get some rest... or call your doctor! If you'll pardon me, ma'am.' He turned to Kirsten. 'I will skip your kind invitation to dine with you folk tonight... I will remove the body from the yard and take it to the morgue. The Governor will need an explanation, so I can also deal with that while I am away.'

Tipping his hat, he smiled apologetically and Kirsten for a moment looked longingly into his eyes.

Banoldino noticed none of this as he shifted his position and made to raise himself.

Kirsten ran to his side, all attention now on her husband.

He insisted on standing and taking Smith's hand once again and thanking him for his actions and his aim.

The soldier departed, leaving Kirsten tending her husband.

Chapter 30
A Needle in Ten Haystacks

Daemon Quirk was left with a huge dilemma.

He stood at the rail, gazing out at the endless ocean, and considered what fate might have in store for him.

If by some chance he encountered the *Durham*, there would be a fight, but he felt certain that, with the support and fighting men afforded by Captain van Gahl, he could overcome whatever resistance Baptiste may put up. Besides, he felt certain that he could turn the men, if he had a moment to address them.

Then, he considered the possibility that he may not overtake her: she was swift with a following wind. He would then be bound to return to Barbados, where Gertrude was waiting. There was a life there to be had; whether they were to marry or not, Van Eyck needed someone to manage his estates.

Something was lacking. He knew in his heart he did not love Gertrude, and yet...! That was not the point. It was his unfulfilled promises, the undertakings he gave himself in bringing the right and proper return to John Standing's wife and his family back in England.

He felt the burden of those promises. Yet what could he do? Without the *Durham*, it was a completely hopeless undertaking. He could fulfil none of his obligations.

He picked up a glass and scanned the horizon afresh, determination set in his face. Finding the *Durham* was the key.

His eye caught something, so he retraced his path back and again from left to right. Had he spotted something south-easterly? He shook his head and stared at his boots for a moment to clear his vision. Now back again through the glass. There: not one, two, more, now three! He saw the flotilla of ships through the mist, ranging across a line of fifteen hundred yards.

It must be Vasteron! He knew in his own mind it could not be anyone else.

The British had come to the West Indies to clean-up the Caribbean and sweep away the privateer threat from the region, all the way up to New England, where they would then join up with the Northern Fleet, completing Britain's claims along the whole length of the Eastern Seaboard.

Daemon barked instructions to the crew and had the *Rebecca* swinging south-easterly, towards the breathtaking sight that now filled the horizon. A total of seven ships, flying the Red Ensign, regally cutting through the choppy, blue-black ocean.

Daemon ordered his helmsman to head straight into their path. He reasoned that the Flagship would fully understand that no single foe would dare approach an entire flotilla, and that there would be no risk of attack from this lone vessel.

Within half an hour there were signals being exchanged. Although Daemon was blissfully unaware of the appropriate responses, he did his best to reassure the

Flagship that his intentions were entirely peaceful by flying a white flag at the prow of the *Rebecca*.

On board, Captain Vasteron advised his First Lieutenant that they should engage the approaching vessel and ascertain any information about other traffic in the immediate region, and an update on the *status quo* between the islands.

He directed his attendant ships to tack forward with reduced sail.

Cutting free, he swooped around the *Rebecca* and hauled her in to a safe distance, before intercepting her with a long-boat.

Climbing aboard, he was astonished to find his old friend Daemon Quirk standing squarely on the deck as he landed.

Following a brief salute, the two men hugged and vigorously slapped one another on the back. Both the crew of the *Rebecca* and Vasteron's two attendants looked on in surprise at the show of friendship.

Arm in arm, they made for the cabin, where rich ruby wine was poured and a toast to King George started off the proceedings.

Sitting at ease in one another's company, they both told of their recent trials and tribulations, holding nothing back.

Vasteron shook his head after intently listening to Daemon's tale.

'I am utterly amazed at Baptiste's behaviour! I could not account for his treachery, had I witnessed his actions with my own eyes. He appeared loyal, nay dedicated, to your cause! Is it possible he was misinformed of your status with the Governor? Could someone else have persuaded him you were a lost cause, so to speak?'

'No other person, no name, or incident of any consequence has ever been mentioned during the whole affair. Baptiste had no connections on the islands, although I assumed, he had never sailed in the Caribbean... He may have met someone, but surely the crew, Erik at least, could have resisted... but who knows?'

'So, what will you do?'

'I ask you again, perhaps, to seek information from your other ships? Has anything been sighted that could possibly have been the *Durham*?'

'I assure you, Daemon, I wish it were not so. We convene every two days. We exchange information and remain in communication at all times. Had so much as a canoe passed within ten nautical miles since I linked-up with our flotilla, I would know about it! We are on constant watch for the privateer. A ship as substantial as the *Durham* would have been seen.'

'I know, my friend, I am desperate! I had to ask... but I already knew the answer. My only motivation in life has been to recover the *Durham* and its cargo and deliver it to its rightful owners.'

'Daemon, I am afraid you may have to give up your quest. The ship will be long gone. You may have no alternative but to write to the family, explain what has happened, and hope they understand and accept your version of events. Having said that, I am happy to support your proclamation with assurances of my own, bearing witness to the truth. If that would help, my friend, you have my promise.'

'I appreciate your offer, Captain. Your support would be of great value.'

'Do not think of it. I would stand up in a Court of Law and attest to your honesty! Please accept my proposal; it is the least I would do. Now, about the future. What course of action have you decided upon?'

'I only wish I could demonstrate a positive course of action. However, I am in a dilemma. If I am unable to fulfil my quest, I must return to Barbados, where an opportunity awaits me. I do not know if this is where my heart belongs, or if it is simply an easier choice. Almost too easy an option for me to take.'

'You must decide between two fundamental things first. Do you desire a life at sea? Or would you be content with a life on a 'farm'? That is the question. All the rest is just incidental. From what you have told me, the farm holds very great promise: a wife, children, substantial holdings and everything a man could wish for!'

'You have summed up my situation very well. I would also wish to find myself, along the way! Who am I? Where do I belong?'

'Everything in life comes down to circumstance and opportunity. You may have been born to the life of a gentleman! You may have inherited huge estates! Pure circumstance, nothing whatever to do with you or your capabilities. You now have an opportunity, which has been brought about by your own endeavours. Yes, there is an element of fate or destiny, but *you* made the decisions, you took the knocks, you continued to strive for what you believed in! You are as entitled to the trappings of wealth as much as any man! All you have to decide is whether you would be content.'

Daemon smiled ironically at his friend's words. 'You provide me with much to consider. Your counsel is of great help to me. I thank you for your friendship and for your support. Now I suppose I must make a decision. I believe I should give up my quest. Perhaps I have been driven by some form of pride or vanity. That I should achieve the impossible. I do believe I could love the life in Barbados — and yet, I could also use my opportunity to work for something else. It may be merely a stepping stone. That is how I must look at it. If I can learn the ways of trading, doing business... then perhaps this is only a beginning.'

'You have youth on your side! Anything is possible, my friend.'

The two men refilled their glasses, drank down one last toast and shook hands.

'I assume you have the legs to keep up with us?'

'Just you watch me!'

'In that case, it's a race to Barbados! Whoever sights land first is the victor!'

'Don't worry, I'll wait for you!'

Vasteron disappeared over the rail and took his place in the craft. Minutes later, he was clambering aboard *Elsinore* and, with a wave of a hand, he turned back to his own task and got the flotilla under full sail again.

Daemon issued orders to his crew to hold hard onto the tail of the flotilla until further orders. He settled back and swung in a hammock for an hour, creating a scene in which he went down on one knee to propose to Gertrude and shook hands with her father on the inheritance of his vast holdings. Life promised to be sweet, very sweet indeed.

Chapter 31
Van Gahl

Captain van Gahl had been at sea since he was twelve years of age. Approaching twenty long years earlier, his father, a second son of a Dutch Baronet, who had earned his own commission in the Dutch Royal Navy during the early eighteenth century, drove him to the harbour, kissed both cheeks and waved goodbye to his own fourth child.

Dieter van Gahl bore the early years heavily, and for a time it seemed that he would buy himself out of the service at the very earliest opportunity. At twenty years of age, having reached Second Lieutenant, he was poised to make the break. He had sailed into New York, which had been known as 'New Amsterdam', and found a small township, bustling with activity and with a determined, eager populace, which welcomed new energy and appeared to be keen to reward enthusiasm. There was much about New York which suggested Dutch influence making him feel 'at home'.

He met a girl, Angharad, ironically, of British origin, whose parents had both died on the voyage from Bristol to the New World. Angharad was serving light meals in a coffee house on 'de Waalstraat', *Wall Street*, where traders met and exchanged pleasantries during the daytime.

Having engaged her in conversation one quiet afternoon, he established that she was part-owner of the cafe and worked all the hours available, with her friend and mentor, a Dutch matron, who had provided her a place to stay on settling in the township. Between them, the two provided a service, from early morning, six days a week, until the bars and gambling halls claimed the attention of all those remaining on the streets after dark.

Angharad explained to Dieter that they ran a 'respectable establishment', where it was perfectly normal for a lady to enter and to pass some time at leisure, without the company of a gentleman.

Van Gahl found he would make time every single day, whilst the ship was being refreshed for her next voyage, to partake of the rich ground coffee and small pastries which Angharad prepared herself each morning before opening up shop.

To say he was smitten by his new friend would be to underestimate the power of attraction a man may feel after seven months on the high seas. But not for him the bordellos which lined the streets to the north of the harbour. He privately sought the gentle conversation and the nearness of a young, eloquent woman who smelled of fresh flowers and warm bread.

After six days of her intoxicating freshness, he sought out his commander and made his approach. He would ask for his release!

He had begun his request by retrieving his memories relating to the circumstance of his induction into the navy, having progressed to a stage where he reminded his captain of the small part he played in the capture of an English man-of-war off the coast, near Le Havre, some four years earlier.

The captain appeared preoccupied, but occasionally nodded and grunted agreement to the account, sufficiently for Van Gahl to proceed with his speech.

'If you will allow, Captain, I was at this point considering no other course of...'

'Yes, yes, dammit, I'm very glad to hear... but, Mr van Gahl, *you* may not consider that you have achieved the recognition some might associate with such gallant deeds... but I do! Now, I have to intervene, because I wish you to call the officers to my quarters without another moment's delay. I have news.'

Van Gahl accepted the true intentions of the intervention, and stood, clicking his heels as he turned to make a swift exit, He cursed himself for the coward he had undoubtedly become in such matters. Nonetheless, he made contact with the other officers in double-quick time, bringing them to the captain.

Van der Mer rose and placed his hands behind his back. His head sank to his chest momentarily as he struggled with his opening address.

'Gentlemen, we are at war with Britain! I have just received my orders and there is no alternative but to quietly slip out of the harbour. We are required in Rotterdam at the earliest opportunity. We set sail as soon as we have a full complement of men.'

Van Gahl and his fellow officers immediately set off in given directions, to collect up as many of the crew as was possible, and to take on a few additional members from the periphery of the 'Salon' district.

Dieter knew he had to reach Angharad to explain and to make his promises to her. It was in his mind to go missing and hide away until the ship was at sea, but such an action would only have led to the ruin of the girl's life by asking her to give up everything for a life on the run. All he could offer her was to flee to the west, towards danger and the unknown.

Besides, he had not even kissed her, and had no idea whether she would even consider him as a suitor.

Although they had the task of extracting the crew from the myriad of entanglements which a week onshore had provided, it had to be done in such a way that no hint was given to the people of New York that there was to be a rapid departure. To alert all to the urgency of their actions would be treachery, and all knew the punishment for such indiscretions.

Dieter had the difficult task of explaining his feelings, providing assurances and at the same time establishing whether any of it held the slightest degree of significance to the lady in question.

He took a place near the window, away from the other three diners currently occupying seats. 'Miss, er, I would like to take coffee, but, miss, I know your name... Angharad! But you have not given me permission to... may I call on you?'

'What exactly do you mean, sir? You may call me, if you wish... Miss, or Miss Angharad... It is only reasonable; after all, you come here every day!'

'I am glad you have noticed that! I do come here every day. I come to see you!'

'Oh! I see! You do not like our little tea-cakes?'

'I adore your tea-cakes...! Yet it is not just the tea-cakes... Look, may I speak?'

'Sir, you are speaking!'

'I am very... fond... of you! I would like to explain...'

'Sir, am I not mistaken, is that not the uniform of an officer... a navy officer?'

'Yes... that's it, that is exactly what I wanted to tell you.'

'But that is something I already knew!'

'I wanted to tell you that I would not always be a navy officer, as you put it. I have been contemplating my, er... future. A time when I am not a navy officer!'

'Well, that is interesting. But how does it concern me?'

'That is just it! *You* are my future! You are the reason for me having a future!'

'Oh! I see!'

'I wish to ask you to... wait for me!'

'I take it you were thinking of marriage?'

'Er... yes, exactly, I was thinking of marriage!'

'How long were you thinking of...?'

'For ever, of course... Oh, I see! This morning I was thinking of... two days. But now...'

'But now...?'

'I am thinking of two... years!'

'Two years indeed? May I enquire as to why this has changed, suddenly, since this morning...?'

'Non. I am not at liberty... Non! I am sorry!'

'This is very strange!'

'You must think me...'

'Sir, may I know your name?'

He stood to attention. 'I am Dieter Johann van Gahl, of Haigh de la Salle, Lieutenant of the Royal Dutch Navy.'

'That's a very fine... er… I am Angharad David from Welshpool.'

He bowed low. 'Delighted to make your acquaintance! May I enquire as to your status?'

'My, er... Do you mean if I am wedded, or betrothed?'

'Exactly!'

'I am neither.' She blushed slightly. Her golden curls framed a fresh, white complexion, which was now adorned by a patch of rosiness, either side of her lightly freckled nose.

'I would like to declare my intentions. Is there someone I should...?'

'My father and mother have died. The lady I... er, my Mistress, well, she is a friend and we have this...' She waved a hand around. As her eyes diverted to the kitchen area, he took a pace forward and was close enough to plant a kiss on the side of her mouth. As she turned full on to him, she stood on tip-toes, and engaged him fully with a long, meaningful kiss in return.

He pulled away, suddenly aware that the other three pairs of eyes in the room were on him.

Momentarily, he slumped into his seat. She came near to him so that they could continue in hushed tones.

She could sense his despair. 'What is it, Mr... er, Van Gahl?'

He looked up into her eyes — his own were tearful.

'It is hopeless. I... I must leave... I have to go away! There is war...!'

'War?'

'Yes, Angharad... war! I am called away immediately. I have to return. We are at... I can't say anything more. I would be court-marshalled for saying this much!'

'How long...?'

'I don't know. I was about to leave the service. I was going to settle... here... with you!'

'Now you must go. You mentioned, earlier, you said "two years".'

'Yes.'

'This is a long time... a lot can happen in two years... two years of war!'

'I know. I would ask you to wait. I have no right.'

'I think you have a right! You have declared yourself. You have given me... I will wait. Whatever happens, I will wait... There, you have my word!'

He rose, kissed her again and walked out onto the street. He had gone only seconds and she had not moved from where she was standing, watching his shadow disappear from the doorway.

He suddenly returned, striding towards her. He unbuttoned his tunic and reached into his collar, producing a small gold medallion. Quickly he undid the clasp and hung it about her neck.

He took one last, long look at her and turned away again, leaving this time for good.

Angharad pressed the medallion to her chest and held it there for a long moment. She turned to the table, where a white linen cloth held an empty coffee jug and a single cup. Collecting them, she slowly walked across to the kitchen, her head still and fixed, and her eyes staring ahead.

She turned, taking one last look at the open door as a half-smile turned up the corners of her mouth.

Dieter van Gahl's sense of duty had overwhelmed him when war had been declared, and he made his choice to devote himself to the navy until hostilities died down.

It was two long years before he returned to New York, assigned to conduct a flotilla of trading ships on the trans-Atlantic crossing. When the ship finally anchored in the harbour, he was free to pursue his destiny.

Dieter's legs could hardly carry him quickly enough as he made his way uphill from the harbour.

He found the familiar row of trading houses along Wall Street and stopped at the door to straighten his tunic. He dodged his way through the light timber doorway to an area just as he remembered, partly occupied by tables and chairs. He eased himself into a seat facing the swinging gate which led into the kitchen.

His mouth went dry in anticipation of the figure of his heart's desire coming through that gate.

Instead, the matronly owner appeared, carrying two jugs, which she laid in front of an elderly couple seated just to the right of him. She turned and asked him, 'Can I fetch you a drink, monsieur?'

'Er... I was hoping I may... er... That is to say... is Mistress... is she coming?' He glanced toward the kitchen.

'I assume you mean Angharad. Well, I don't know how to tell you... Angharad has left the establishment.'

'You mean... she has left...your little cafe?'

'Well, I hope she has reached the frontier and perhaps beyond by now. Her husband... well, he was posted to...'

He stood with such suddenness that his chair was knocked over backwards.

All the diners turned towards them.

'Monsieur, I am sorry, I did not mean to upset...'

'No matter... No... I apologise, I had no right. Did she not... leave a message, or... any word...?'

'I am afraid she departed in some haste... She did not say anything that I might convey to others... About twelve months past... She became entangled with a British officer, a dragoon. They were stationed outside the town for several months, you know. Eventually...'

'Thank you, madam. I think I have heard enough... I expected her to wait... but...'

'Monsieur, please... She left this...' She quickly turned away and went to the dresser, reaching for a jug on the next to highest shelf. She produced the gold medallion. 'She told me, "If — he ever returns", I was to give you this.'

He lifted his hat and turned away. 'You keep it, madam.' He disappeared, never to return to that quarter again.

Some turbulent months ensued when his ship was engaged by a British warship and he suffered some severe damage to a leg. Nonetheless, he returned to action and fulfilled all his duties finding the Dutch now allied to the British. Hostilities came to an end some five years later by which time he had become devoted to the navy

Chapter 32
Daemon Has a Rival

Captain Dieter Van Gahl never did attach himself to a woman again. He satisfied himself in the bordellos of the harbours and townships he visited over the years. His opportunity of meeting a suitable life-partner was very limited, and he became indifferent to women in general, tending to treat harshly any whom attempted to get too close.

Now, risen through the ranks and achieving the respectability of his position, he had begun to consider his future. He envisaged perhaps two or three more years at sea; then, well, who knows? He had heard of much opportunity on the west coast of America, where California was opening up, whilst the salons and ballrooms of Paris held a certain attraction. At this point in his life, he had not resolved any plan or objective which concerned a wife and family.

Here he was, suddenly in a position which he had neither envisaged nor sought, yet it held enough intriguing possibilities to fill his head with the kind of dreams and contemplations that had not occupied him these last fifteen years.

He was in the company of a vivacious, exciting and impossibly wealthy young woman upon a voyage of seven or eight days' duration.

The opportunity to engage with her, to talk, to tease and to seduce, were endless. Yet he stood off for a time, not really trusting himself with the task of conducting a courtship.

Gertrude also stood off. She was still excited at the possibilities of her life ahead with Daemon Quirk as her partner and lover.

She had genuinely felt a tug in her heart strings as the *Rebecca* disappeared over the horizon, but this time she knew he was bound to return. She knew he would see things her way and that he must give up on his folly rather than pursue a distant dream.

For the second time in three months, Daemon guided a ship into the harbour at Barbados. The familiar sight of the Dutch warship of Dieter van Gahl swung very slowly on her anchor, as the *Rebecca* passed along her larb'd side.

The smaller vessel was able to enter all the way into the moorings on the quayside, and half an hour saw the ship securely tied to her berth.

Vasteron and the flotilla had signalled 'farewell' as they pressed on to their main objective off the coast of Curacao, leaving the Rebecca alone for the last few nautical miles.

A group, including beggars and a trader or two, as always, gathered to meet her occupants, but nothing like the clamour of when a new ship arrived in port.

Daemon passed through the gathering without interference and found a stable, where he was able to negotiate the use of a horse.

An hour passed before he drew up at the Van Eyck estate, where the servants greeted him and bade him wait for the master.

When Van Eyck appeared, he greeted Daemon with a genuine friendliness and unbound pleasure, congratulating him on his return and asking with genuine interest as to the fate of the *Durham*.

'Unfortunately, nothing was seen nor heard of the ship. Captain Vasteron, with a large flotilla, intercepted our passage, assuring me there had been no sighting of a ship of the stature of the *Durham* and that, they believed, the pursuit was hopeless.'

'I am so sorry to hear of it. I am sure Gertrude would echo my sentiments; she certainly prayed for your safety and swift return, fearing that had you caught up with the ship, there would be a terrible fight!'

'Alas, the opportunity has now gone for good. There will be no fight over the *Durham*... Nor perhaps for any ship, as far as I am concerned.'

Van Eyck nodded his head, briefly. 'Enough of this. You must tell all over dinner — in the meantime, I am sure you would wish to refresh and maybe even take some rest... Come with me.' Van Eyck led off, summoning Daemon to follow.

'I thought, perhaps, Gertrude might...'

'Er, all in good time, my boy. All in good time...'

'If I may just pay my respects...'

'It will wait... I am certain she will run to you once she returns.'

'Ah, she is not at home?'

'Er, no. She has taken a carriage with er, Captain van Gahl... They have set off to a small village on the north of the island, where a friend has reared a pair of Staffordshire cart horses. You may have encountered the breed yourself...? Fine workhorses, many years of good service on a farm...'

'She has gone with Captain van Gahl?'

'Yes, yes! I had no stomach for the journey, and Van Gahl kindly offered to ensure the safety of my daughter on the journey.'

'The captain has stayed on during my absence, I see.'

'Yes, well, we have much in common... We are like family!'

'Has Gertrude... well, has she spent a lot of time...?'

'My boy, I can see what you are thinking. You need have no fear. She talks of nothing else than your life together. Van Gahl has been a gentleman, patiently attentive, but always with good spirit.'

'I was just surprised that he did not have more, er... pressing matters to attend to. His stay of — what is it, more than three weeks? — must have been a surprise to yourself and... Gertrude.'

'We will rest before dinner... Come!'

Daemon allowed the old man to lead him by the arm. He was shown to a guest room on the third floor, nothing like the comfort of the other rooms in the house! 'You understand... we have more house guests than normal. But I am sure you will find the room comfortable.'

Daemon proceeded to remove his boots and shirt. Sluicing his face in fresh water from the bowl brought in for him by one of the servants, he opened the small window and lay back on the bed.

To his surprise, he awoke from a deep sleep, the room notably cooler and the light not quite as brilliant as it had been.

He sat up and looked about him to get his bearings.

In the distance he could hear a hum of noise and activity, then laughter. He realised there was a gathering in the grounds to the rear of the house. He leaned out of the window as far as it would allow, but could not gain a significant enough view to be able to take in the cause of the fuss.

He freshened up once again with clean water and pulled on his shirt, taking the steps down to the ground floor in a matter of a few moments.

Following the raised voices and laughter, he found himself outside the doors on the veranda, looking at two magnificent, powerful horses, seeming to meld together and move as one. Although tethered by a light bridle and long leads, they moved freely back and forth and around in tight circles, in unison, each showing total commitment to the other, as two lion cubs might play.

The gathering watched in admiration, Van Gahl standing just to the side, a goblet of white wine in hand and looking quite imperious. Gertrude, in full-length gown and shawl, her hat thrown carelessly back and held just by ribbon around her neck, looked radiant and happy, playfully calling and cooing to the two magnificent beasts.

The old man observed the spectacle from the comfort of an armchair. Two gentlemen stood admiringly to his right, where another chaise found two ladies, presumably their wives.

Daemon had to make a sound with his throat to attract attention.

Hearing Van Eyck proclaim his arrival at the scene, Gertrude turned and flung her arms about him, lifting her feet off the ground as she swung from his neck.

She gave him the fiercest hug and held him tightly for some moments. 'My darling... I am so pleased to see you back safely! I cannot express my delight at seeing you...' She kissed him and turned to the gathering. 'This is my fiancé, returned from a perilous voyage!'

Daemon felt uncomfortably hot and excused himself from her embrace, shaking the hands of the islanders and bowing politely to their ladies. One of the gentlemen engaged him for a moment to mention the quality of the 'Nigras' he had purchased, 'when you first dropped in on us'.

Daemon assured him of his pleasure at the news and wished them a long and happy 'association', which the land owner appeared to find odd.

He turned to greet Van Gahl, at Gertrude's prompting, 'And, of course, you know Captain van Gahl...'

'Captain, I am pleased to see you again. I have to thank you for your part in allowing me to pursue the *Durham*, and, in particular, for returning Gertrude and her father safely home.'

'It has been my pleasure Captain, and may I express my personal disappointment that the Durham was not re-captured.'

Daemon responded, 'Thank you Captain, it was in the end a hopeless pursuit.' Turning to Van Eyck, he said, 'And, sir, may I just re-assure you that your fine ship the *Rebecca* has come to no harm and is standing proudly at the quay awaiting your inspection.'

'Naw, I am sure of it! I don't need to inspect the ship, young man. I have great faith in you. That is why I was able to hand over the *Rebecca* in the first place. It was the least I could do.'

'Nonetheless, I will never forget your generosity, Captain. I trust the passage from Trinidad was trouble-free? You all seem to be in such good disposition.'

Gertrude clung to his arm. 'Why, Captain van Gahl was extremely gallant, and took care of everything! It was not an unpleasant journey, let me assure you. The Captain has grown quite fond of our humble surroundings; I think he likes it here. Am I not right, Captain?'

'Em... indeed, Mistress... I like the island very much and the inhabitants even more so! I only wish I could remain for...'

Gertrude interrupted, 'Well, Captain, the island needs men like yourself. I am sure you could settle here very well.'

'Alas, I have my duties, and they have been neglected of late... It really is time I left to continue with my orders. The British fleet, I understand, is in the region?' He turned towards Daemon.

Daemon hesitated for a moment, considering whether the *status quo* allowed him to admit that the English fleet had arrived. Deciding that it appeared, after all, old news, he felt quite comfortable in acknowledging that 'the British would take over the Dutch interests in the region and police the waters between the Caribbean and the Canadas'.

'I am happy to abide by the treaty and simply assist Dutch trading vessels if in any danger from privateers and pirates. Hostilities are, after all, now of the past!'

'I hope you will meet Captain Vasteron one day, monsieur; a fine man, a very dedicated officer,' Daemon suggested.

'I, also, would like to meet with him, much more now than before the treaty was signed. I am sure he would make a formidable foe!'

'So, when will you set sail, if I may enquire? I ask merely to consider whether you may convey a message for me?'

'Er... I do believe in a day or so we will be at sea.' Suddenly, there was an uncomfortable silence. He looked at Gertrude and she smiled and turned to her father.

Van Eyck suddenly stood. 'We will invite some guests; you must have a good send-off, and we must celebrate the return of Captain Quirk to our home. It will be Saturday, when the work has been done for the week. I will send out invitations. Is that what you would like, my dear?'

Gertrude ran to his side and hugged him. 'Yes, that would be wonderful, and only fair, to... Dieter... for all his kindness.'

For reasons he could not quite explain even to himself, Daemon felt a little displeased that Van Gahl had stayed on more than two weeks longer than necessary. He also looked long and hard at Gertrude to consider her demeanour towards himself. Had it been exactly as he had expected, or would he have had it different?

He had enough problems with his own feelings towards her. He still did not consider it love, or devotion. He liked her, and he desired her. That was fair enough. But why was he jealous? Why did he feel threatened? He could not quite understand his own feelings. Now he was questioning hers.

With Van Gahl her constant companion for nearly four weeks, staying at the house, conducting her around the plantation every day! He knew Gertrude for her appetites and hoped that, in time, he alone would meet all her expectations. Had she been faithful? Had he any right to expect her loyalty? Did she indeed expect his return so soon?

Many questions troubled him, and now there was to be three further days before he would have her to himself, to explore the relationship, to be certain of his feelings and hers.

He began to feel restless. The call of the sea? So soon? He began to imagine pulling anchor, the wind filling sail, the fresh breeze and the smell of the sea! Had he become a sea-farer? Was this the answer to Vasteron's question?

Dinner passed pleasantly, and Gertrude showed that her inclination toward him appeared as it had been before Van Gahl's arrival. She was attentive and possessive at the same time. Van Gahl behaved in an exemplary manner, a gentleman in every way.

The conversation again switched to his options for the future. Would he ever consider a life on the island? Would he ever abandon the sea?

He made suitable denial that there could be any such choice in his immediate future.

Gertrude told of her desire to establish a family and make the Van Eyck holdings the most powerful in the Caribbean.

Daemon, good spirits restored, began to imagine his role and became more comfortable at the prospect the longer the evening went on.

They turned in for the night after much wine had been consumed, plans for the following evening had been fully explored, and they all looked forward with great anticipation to receiving the Governor and the pick of society.

It was another warm night, the breeze becoming gentle as the humidity grew. Daemon undressed and sat in his britches on the edge of his small bed and was about to stretch out when the handle on the door turned.

Gertrude appeared in her nightgown, her feet gently patting the floor as she made her way swiftly towards him.

She flung herself into his arms and he felt her lithe, athletic form wriggle beneath the soft linen. Her kiss was long and urgent, asking questions with her mouth, telling him how much she had missed him.

Breathlessly, Daemon responded. He held her, positioned her, brought her down beside him and reached for her satin-smooth thigh as her shift crumpled and rode up her legs

'Wait! No, wait, we must not... We are to be married. It wouldn't be proper...'

Daemon had her earlobe between his lips as he whispered heavily, 'Darling, it is hardly worth... I mean... we already "know" one another... Surely...?'

'No — we can't; we have to at least show some restraint... The others, my father...? It is only right that they think our wedding night will be...'

Daemon laughed. 'You are a mystery, Gertrude... I don't know what I am to do with you! You told your Father I had 'used' you on our first evening together!'

'Oh, don't scold me, darling! You wouldn't want to make me cry, would you?'

'No, my love, I would not! In fact, I think that might be a task I could not achieve all on my own.'

'What do you mean...? Your poor little Gertrude, I am just a girl, and you, my Captain, my hero... I am under you spell! Do what you want with me!'

'Now, what is it to be? What I want is to devour you, right here, right now! To let you crawl back to your room exhausted!'

'That is exactly why you must not! We have such a day tomorrow. We have to prepare, then we have to entertain. The day will be long... and...'

Daemon planted another long kiss on her lips as his hands explored her body.

Suddenly, she leapt to her feet. 'No, we mustn't! I am leaving you. 'Til the morning!'

With that, she was gone.

Daemon lay back, his hands behind his head, propped up slightly. He blew out the bedside candle and lay back again.

His thoughts raced from one memory to another, tracing the past six months, and before...! He dropped off into a deep, deep sleep.

Chapter 33
A Grand Affair

The gathering bubbled with excitement among the forty or so guests, many of the first families of Barbados: of mixed origin, some Scottish, English and Spanish; also, an Irishman of little breeding.

Although Daemon had learned well the traits of a gentleman during his time of friendship with John Standing, he still had a lot to learn. The longer the evening progressed, the more out-of-place he felt.

Meanwhile, Captain van Gahl was as much at home in the ballroom as the State Room aboard ship.

He effused elegance and charm, danced like a master and bowed and scraped courteously to male and female alike.

Gertrude and Van Gahl were thrown together, as much by circumstance as by any design, but nonetheless he occupied the lady's arm for much of the evening.

Daemon himself was taken aside by a dark-haired Spanish lady who appeared to be in sympathy with his discomfort and determined to ease it.

Daemon established that she was the daughter of Senor Spinosa, widowed due to the untimely fall from a horse suffered by her husband Andrew Ross-Drummond, a son of one of the early migrant families in the aftermath of the English Civil War.

Sadly, alone with the gift of substantial holdings of her own, she had returned to the patronage of her father, a year before, embracing the role of young widow without too much resistance.

Now eligible again, and extremely attractive, she stealthily explored her options, with Daemon a playful distraction.

Once into conversation, Marianna found Daemon far more engaging than she had anticipated. He did hold a certain charm, and he had his own bearing and easy manner. His range of conversation impressed and amused, so each proved to be good company for the other.

'You must come to visit! I will take it as a personal insult if you do not!'

'Why, that would be the last thing in the world I would wish, to insult a lady such as yourself! I will talk with Gertrude to arrange to call on you…'

'Captain Quirk, you misunderstand me. I asked *you* for a visit… Gertrude and I… well, we have little in common!'

Daemon sat upright and his head pulling away a little. 'I… er, I think I understand, senora… but perhaps you forget that Gertrude and I…'

'Well… let me just say that my intuition suggests… well, it is not for me…'

'No, please go on.'

'I spoke out of turn. I should not!'

'You are thinking perhaps Gertrude and I are not a good match.'

'Not at all. I just believe there may be a rival… for her affections. There, you have made me say it! Besides, I am not interested in another's cast-offs, so I do not believe…'

'No, senora, you have only echoed my own fears. I believe my Gertrude may have her head in two places. It is possible I left a door open. Now I have a situation to deal with.'

'I see my instinct was not wrong! You have a rival! What do you intend to do?'

'Nothing, for the moment. Please, senora, it is not very gallant of me to sit and discuss another lady in your presence. You deserve every last bit of my attention.'

'How kind of you, but forgive me, I brought up the subject, and now I fear I have injured you.'

'No, senora, you have not! I had to face the truth at some point. I have been returned just a few days and have not had time to really consider my situation.' Daemon turned to look into Marianna's eyes. 'Senora, I beg you, please keep open your invitation... until I have a clear view of things. I cannot tell you how intrigued I am at the prospect of visiting your estate.'

The evening passed with much frivolity and many pleasantries, before the doors closed on the last guests. Van Gahl wished everyone the best of pleasant dreams and took himself away.

Gertrude clung on to Daemon as they had both bade him a 'good night' and toasted his forthcoming departure. They agreed to meet in the morning to finally wave him off.

Gertrude steered Daemon to her bed, and this time they consummated the evening in an hour of passion equal to that of their very first encounter those long months before.

Chapter 34
Double Departure

They awoke to a bright, fresh morning, sun slanting through the shutters, a gentle breeze flowing through the open window. There was not a single thought between them that did not encompass the future in harmony, as their own family would grow around them.

Refreshing themselves, they dressed in cool linen and walked down to breakfast, arm in arm.

Van Gahl was standing near to the window with Gertrude's father, and they both addressed a scroll of parchment.

They turned in unison as Daemon and Gertrude entered the room.

'News, my dear... Daemon... please, sit... take some coffee.'

Gertrude slid into a chair, but Daemon rounded the table to stand over his shoulder, making an attempt to read the parchment.

Outside, a horse clomped on the cobbled yard as its rider turned the mount's head back towards the road and galloped into the distance.

'Not bad news, father, I hope?'

'Well, my dear, it is certainly a surprise... Captain van Gahl has received this message via the Governor's office, accompanied by some dispatches which had arrived from New York.

'It appears Captain van Gahl is required at once, to accompany the returning flotilla to Rotterdam... much as Dieter himself had predicted. However, there was another message, requesting that Captain van Gahl seek out any information he may, concerning a "vessel and full cargo" seemingly originated in this region, which may have reached New York harbour during the last month!

'Captain van Gahl and I are both of the opinion that the vessel concerned is none other than the *Durham*!'

Daemon snatched the parchment from his hand and scanned over it, before looking up to where Gertrude's eyes were fixed upon his own. He nodded. 'I agree with both of you! The circumstances suggest, in every way, that this is where the *Durham* has turned up. None other than New York! It is the very last place I could have imagined.!'

Daemon sat at the table, his head in his hands for a moment.

Van Gahl spoke first. 'Daemon, it would be my pleasure that you join me on a journey to New York. I will have you there faster than a message could be sent in response. If that is what you want?'

Daemon rubbed his eyes. Looking up, he spoke quietly. 'I have no choice... You realise, I still have a commitment. For as long as that vessel is afloat, she is my responsibility. I have no other option but to accompany you to New York to assess the situation.'

Turning to Gertrude, he said, 'My dear, I hope you understand. I am bound to my ship! I am not free until I have fulfilled my obligation.'

Gertrude responded, wistfully, staring into the distance, 'You have to do your duty... I suppose this means a return to Europe... and beyond.'

Daemon rushed to her side. 'Please, my dearest, please bear with me. I will return. You have my word.'

'When will you return?'

'It is not possible for me to know that, at this moment. But you have my promise.'

Gertrude turned to Van Gahl. 'Captain, my friend, you, too? Both of you leaving? I… will not have it!' She stood, and for a moment looked as if she would take flight. Somehow, she calmed herself sufficiently to say to them, 'This situation is impossible! Go! Both of you! I never want to see you again!'

Dieter knew that a response was required as she turned, raising her skirts, before hastily leaving the room. 'I was not aware there was a "situation". Believe me, monsieur, I have no wish to compete for the lady's hand; indeed, you have full claim over her at this time.'

Daemon almost smiled, his look of bewilderment getting the better of him. 'Captain, I also am not exactly certain of the situation. I *think* I am betrothed to the lady, but, on the other hand, there is nothing… well… binding! I have to confess, I do not even know my own heart.'

'Monsieur! May I suggest that we take a boat, make sail and cast our fates to the wind? For I have no stomach for this and prefer to be facing an enemy on the high seas than to face the inconsistencies of women!'

'Well said, Dieter… well said! Now we must leave for the harbour.'

They departed the scene, each almost glad to have reached the gates and perimeter fence when they passed.

They made good time and were able to set sail before sunset. The tide was favourable and saw them pulling away from the island on a calm sea, a light breeze, a 'wing and a prayer'.

Some fourteen days later, the ship dropped anchor in New York harbour and both Van Gahl and Daemon stood at the rail, gazing at the skyline, which boasted the tallest, most densely arranged and imposing buildings you might see anywhere outside of Europe's capitals.

New York was thriving, spreading; it spanned several rising banks above a wide arrangement of tributaries and islands. Everywhere, bobbing on the tide, was evidence of her enterprise. Boats of every description, shape and size, some emptied, some awaiting unloading at the harbour's edge. There was bustle about the place, a hum of activity, music spilling from the bars and taverns, the aroma of coffee wafting across the bay, candles glowing from a thousand windows.

They marvelled at the scene for some moments before, by intuition, each knew that such a moment, detached from the 'fray', could not last for ever.

They turned to the men, Van Gahl issuing orders, and making fast the gunnels and hatches and organising the night's watch. Almost as they were about ready to take to the boat, responding to their signal, another boat clunked into the bow beams just as voices of Dutch origin reached their ears.

Van Gahl peered over the side to establish what was the cause of this unexpected intrusion and, almost as his eye fell on the small craft, a greeting reached him from one the passengers, bringing Van Gahl immediately to attention.

A Dutch dignitary appeared above the rail, adorned by a tricorn boasting a pale orange and white feather.

'Monsieur, I identified your vessel and immediately set off in my humble dinghy in order to greet you and avail you of some news. I beg of you, allow me to board. I would seek a safe place, a sanctuary if you would. I am most relieved to see you.'

'Monsieur, please introduce yourself.'

'I am Johan van Geesagem, the representative of the House of Holland, in other words the commercial attaché to the Dutch Crown. As you know, the British have assumed control of this territory; indeed, I believe they have designs on the whole continent of America!

'There is great unrest among the Netherlanders. We have, shall we say, no rights in the town, and many of our interests are being consumed by leading Britishers, and an Austrian, Count Carstein.'

'Not good news! I agree! Monsieur van Geesagem, may I introduce my, er, friend, Captain Quirk? We have arrived from the Caribbean. It is my mission to escort two Dutch traders, home to Holland.'

Pulling Van Gahl by the arm, Van Geesagem said, 'Captain, your friend — he is British, no?'

'Er, well, I think "Irish" is what he would prefer, but please feel free to talk in his presence! No harm will come of it!'

'The two Hollander vessels had to flee! There was serious talk about them being impounded! All sorts of unrest has developed since a ship arrived here some months ago under the command of a few roughnecks. A full cargo of sugar and coffee, and this fine ship! Claims of ownership have been pursued and a judge sent from Boston to sort it out!

'An attempt was made on the life of one of the leading dignitaries, and all sorts of recriminations have been fired in all directions like buckshot!

'From information received, the owners of the Dutch vessel maintained that the origin had to be Jamaica. The crew, a mixture of French speaking Arabs, Scandinavian and English, would provide no further explanation. Accusations of further hijacking were cited, and the two sides were drawn — the British, led by this Don Bosco, and the Dutch led until recently by Van Tees, the trader, and myself.

'I am not — how would you say? — completely safe in my own house! I fear some recrimination and the whole thing could escalate.'

'Monsieur — I understand how you must feel facing the establishment. However, I have news for you. Captain Quirk here is the rightful owner of the vessel. I have brought him from Barbados — which is an island of mixed society — British and Hollanders live side-by-side. Captain Quirk's vessel — the *Durham* — is registered in London and was heading to England before returning to North Africa when the *Durham* was, er, I think your word "hijack" is suitable.'

'Captain, this is important news indeed! I imagine it will calm the waters and at least remove the threat of a drawn-out conflict. However, I am disappointed that the British will win the moral high ground again, and we poor Hollanders will lose our place at the table.'

'My sympathies, monsieur,' interrupted Daemon. 'If it is of any consolation, I can remove any attempted

319

aggression towards the Dutch, and indeed offer only praise for their co-operation. Without my friend Van Gahl, I would never have been in a position to pursue the *Durham*, and I am, in fact, betrothed to a lady of Dutch origin, back in Barbados. I will do all I can to appease the situation.'

Van Gahl interjected, 'Monsieur van Geesagem, if you would be good enough to conduct us to the authorities, we will do all in our power to guarantee your safety and the return of your office.'

The three, with a small escort, were rowed into the harbour, where they were greeted by the usual throng, but some abuse was being hurled around and aggressive gestures made towards the former official and the unmistakable uniform of the Dutch navy.

Daemon, although a little uneasy and watchful, with one hand on the butt of his pistol, smiled warmly to all in the vicinity and waved as a returning hero might . This confused the mob sufficiently to enable them to pass through unhindered, as far as the Town House, where British guards held them up.

Daemon explained his own situation and requested a meeting with the Governor at the earliest possible opportunity. He explained that he had arrived 'courtesy of a Dutch naval captain', who had afforded great assistance in his endeavours, which would be explained in full in due course.

After a ten-minute wait at the main doors, they were conducted into a chamber and offered refreshment. Almost two hours later, there was a burst of activity, arrivals and a short conference in the adjacent chamber. Moments later, the doors opened wide to a highly polished oval table, at which eight or nine men of substance were seated.

'Gentlemen, please!' The Governor introduced himself and named the other attendees, a mixture of names, of mixed continental origin, none of which stuck in the minds of the newly arrived.

The Governor, satisfied at the introductions provided by the former Dutch attaché, asked them to proceed.

'Gentlemen, if I may?' Daemon took up the invitation. 'I am Daemon Quirk, more recently Captain Quirk of the *Durham*.

'The *Durham* was constructed in Holland, a fine vessel, coming under the command of John Standing, third son of the Earl of Olney, and partner in commercial enterprises in the region of Morocco.

'I was invited to join John Standing in an undertaking to bring the finest African natives to the Caribbean and to trade in goods and the financial rewards of the enterprise.'

A voice from the Council, 'This was, in effect, the maiden voyage of this fine ship?'

'Yes, to the extent that the original vessel had been modified and re-fitted for purpose, in that respect it was her first voyage. There were two Arab partners in the venture, but John Standing was the one who registered the ship with insurers. I am a little surprised the Titles have not been retrieved from London; as I understand it from Monsieur van Geesagem, this issue has been contested for some months.'

Another member of the Council rose and addressed Daemon, 'Sir, Henry Loughton, attorney. No papers have yet been established to attest the origins of the vessel.' He sat down.

'Gentlemen, if I may proceed. During the maiden voyage we came under the protection of Captain Vasteron

321

of the British Navy. He is currently serving in the Caribbean aboard HMS *Elsinore*. The Captain would attest to the validity of every word I have spoken. The *Durham* supported *Elsinore* in an encounter with privateers. During the encounter, John Standing was mortally wounded.'

Daemon paused for a moment, gathering his thoughts. 'With his dying breath he bade me complete our undertaking and return with the rewards to Europe, where his wife would be the main beneficiary of the estate. His wife Margaret is currently residing with the British Consul in Rabat, in North Africa, a guest of a lifelong friend of John Standing.

'It is my intention to fulfil his request to the full. I was preparing for the voyage when I was detained briefly on the island of Trinidad. Returning to the harbour, I established that the *Durham* had sailed out of the harbour on the morning tide.

'Monsieur van Gahl is a friend, and captain of a ship of the Dutch Navy, ahem... as I am sure you appreciate! Under the Captain's influence, a Dutch plantation owner, Van Eyck, provided me with a ship and means of pursuing the *Durham*. I was given to believe her destination was Easterly — to Europe and eventually Africa.

'However, there was no sign of her. I persisted in the pursuit until I came into contact with the British Fleet, and accepted their assurances that no sighting had been made on their voyage to the Caribbean. I concluded that I would never be able to catch up with her.'

'I believe there has been some unrest, but the Captain here is a very decent man, and has orders to calm the situation.'

'I assume he will remain in attendance should we require assistance?' the Governor interjected.

Daemon continued, 'Certainly. Hindered as I was, by mis-information that the *Durham* would be sailed back across the Atlantic to either Europe or North Africa, I was amazed to find that *'she'* had turned up in New York. Captain van Gahl will support my story.'

A tall, distinguished gentleman rose with the aid of a crested walking stick. 'Senor Don Bosco, Captain. I don't think that will be necessary. I believe your story in every detail. I may speak for my colleagues around the table, whom, like myself, wish to see an honest and swift resolution to this problem. I do believe you may count on my support in your endeavour to re-claim the vessel.'

A few murmurings followed from around the table.

A bewigged gentleman rose at the right hand of the Governor. 'Senor Don Bosco — there is the small matter of the hearing, for which I was obliged to travel from Boston to oversee. We have not exactly concluded the matter formally.' Turning to the other members, he said, 'However, at this point I support Senor Don Bosco's conviction; in fact, after all the nonsense we have been served up over the past two months, it is most refreshing to hear the truth!

'Please attend court tomorrow morning at 10.00am. I will make official the findings and I believe you may be able to seek out your vessel and prepare for a voyage within a matter of days. Gentlemen, I bid you good morning.'

One or two others bade Daemon the best of luck and departed. Senor Don Bosco remained whilst formal introductions were made. Lord Ranleigh, Mr Carstein,

Fitzroy, and an attorney, Mr Smyth, were lined up. They were swift with the offer of refreshments.

Daemon shook hands gratefully, expressed a wish to return to his vessel at the earliest opportunity, but realised that you do not shake off men of this substance without the courtesy expected, and a story or two to brighten up their lives.

Indeed, the matter of the *Durham* had preoccupied them for some time: the intrigue, the guessing game and the determination not to let her fall into the hands of some profiteer or tub-thumping politician, or indeed the Dutch merchant fleet.

'Please, Captain Quirk, if you would be so kind as to sit with us, we may be able to make some sense of this mess.' Carstein motioned towards the more comfortable armchairs arranged around a small table in the salon.

An attendant was soon at their side, holding a tray. 'Sirs, may I offer some refreshment?' It was elegantly put.

'Please, Captain, would you join us in a brandy? A "heart-starter", some of us have been calling it! To be taken early in the day — just after coffee!'

'It sounds like a very bad habit, sir, However, at sea we usually take a glass when we have mastered a difficult situation — whether morning, noon or evening — so if I may?'

Don Bosco enquired after Daemon's origins. 'I am from Donegal, Ireland. I have been at sea these seven years.'

'Ah, Donegal. In the north-westerly part of Ireland, I believe. We have many of your countrymen here in New York. Indeed, my own dear wife is from Ireland.'

'I would be delighted to meet her one day.'

'You will, I have no doubt of it... I gather the cargo of slaves for the Caribbean was the first for the *Durham*. Was it, indeed, your own first voyage?'

'Well, sir, I will say that I am not a "slaver" — by the tone of your voice, you are somewhat surprised that I would have chosen this profession. I served in His Majesty's Navy for several years. I... er... ran into difficulty in North Africa when the ship was badly damaged in an encounter with the French-Spanish alliance. I was incarcerated for some time in Africa, when John Standing came into my life.

'I have never known a finer man! John was... well, he *became* a close friend. I can hardly bear to think about his passing; it was such a terrible waste. I have stated my intention to honour his memory by returning to Europe with the ship. I was horrified that a loyal crew could be turned to such an outrageous act.'

'I understand. It must have been very difficult. You had no warning that the crew may be inclined to mutiny?'

'None whatsoever! I would never have believed Baptiste... I had come to think of him as a friend. How could he allow the others...?'

Carstein interjected, 'Captain, I'm afraid Baptiste was the architect of this mutiny; he *turned*, I'm afraid. It has happened since time immemorial that a good right-hand man can suffer some perceived oversight or disrespect and can sometimes turn traitor.'

'I find that hard to take, sir! Baptiste — he never uttered a word of dissatisfaction; he was an ally!'

'Unfortunately, also a villain — he made an attempt on my friend Don Bosco's life! He was shot and killed in the attempt.' Carstein shook his head in exasperation.

Daemon shook his head, incredulous, 'I am totally shocked, and would like to say, if in any way I brought this to bear, I am truly sorry, senor,'

'No! No! Not at all! I will not allow you to blame yourself. You have been wronged and that is an end to it. Please, do not feel that there is anything to answer for. My friend Carstein merely wished to tell you of the outcome. Now, please, I request that you dine with myself and my wife this evening. Carstein, Ranleigh, I would be happy if you would join us.'

Daemon attempted to decline, again insisting that the ship was his absolute priority.

Don Bosco again came up with an offer too good to refuse! 'None of it! I will arrange for a carriage to take you to the dock. You can inspect your ship, and indeed we have some of the crew incarcerated. If you would like to visit them, perhaps establish the full story? My carriage will be at your disposal right up to the moment you join us for dinner at around six-thirty. My driver will take you wherever you wish to go. How would that suit?'

'How can I refuse? If you will allow me to take up the offer immediately, I would have all the time I need to appraise what needs to be done before I am able to get under sail.'

They all rose and headed for the front of the building, where Don Bosco summoned his driver and gave instructions.

'Sir, how will you be able to go about your business for the rest of the day?'

'Don't think of it. I will have another conveyance brought out from the house. In fact, I believe my wife will be in town and I only have to locate her and send word. Go, and have an enterprising day, Captain!'

Daemon spotted Van Gahl on the terrace, in close discussion with van Geesagem.

With a nod of thanks, Daemon climbed aboard the chaise and sat up close so that the driver could hear his instruction. Pulling to a halt at the bottom of the seven stone steps, Daemon leapt down and met van Gahl half - way. The two shook hands vigorously and bade one another 'farewell', Daemon expressing his deepest gratitude.

Settling again next to the driver, he was able to sit in contemplation as the four well-matched horses turned as one and trotted into the distance.

'A fine young man, Carstein. I hope he may one day return to us. We need honest young men to make this town great. I think we may have discovered one.'

'I hope you are right, my friend! He has a charm about him, that is certain. I hope he has the determination he will need to meet his promises. Meanwhile, I look forward to hearing more of his story.'

'Stories, it seems, is what we live on these days! Our days of stretching our own horizons are somewhat behind us,' offered Banoldino.

'Nonsense, gentlemen! I believe there is a whole new chapter about to be written. There is much to achieve yet, I fear. This Colony is fast becoming ungovernable, and my British friends know it.' Lord Ranleigh was poking his fingers into his vest pockets in resignation.

'Ranleigh, you epitomise the colonialism that your great country thrives upon! I have no doubt you would have us choosing sides within the month! You would be drawing up battle lines — the "Republic" and the "Crown"!'

They all laughed, returning to their inner sanctum to contemplate upon the future of the Americas.

Chapter 35
A Reconciliation

Daemon bade the driver straight for the harbour, where he was glad to receive first-hand information as to the location of the *Durham*.

Upon seeing her, tied-in, stacked, with other vessels barring her path to the open seas, Daemon felt a wave of emotion, a lump rising in his throat. He thought he glimpsed, for a moment, the figure of John Standing, moving in the rigging. A loose flap on the fore-s'l, and the slanting rays of the sun, played tricks with his vision. Drawing nearer, he could see how mistaken he had been.

He shook his head and lowered it, resting upon his chest for a moment, his thoughts swimming through the cloudy 'pond' of the past, of Standing, of the *Durham*, of Sven and Baptiste.

Clearing his head, he asked the driver to pull over.

Daemon swung through the rigging until he dropped noiselessly onto the deck.

He made for the cabin and an eeriness enveloped him. An empty vessel, the ghosts of the past, passing him right and left. A shiver caressed his spine, bringing his shoulders up to his ears.

It took Daemon a few moments to adjust to the light before he allowed the cabin door to swing shut as he entered.

Nothing much had changed. Little was disturbed. He expected at least a few broken bits of furniture. A bloodless coup, he kept thinking. He had heard those words associated with a regime, capitulating without a fight. He wondered that perhaps none had perished in defence of his name, his authority. He felt a wave of disappointment.

In a few minutes, he had checked the cargo. The authorities had decided against removing the cargo as the ship was still strong and dry and more safe than any warehouse. Nothing had perished, the sugar and the cotton baled and dry, the tobacco still moist and fresh.

There were barrels of water, rum and ale. The water would be refreshed but the ship proved almost ready for sea.

How long had he been away — how long had she been in others' hands? He felt anger; he touched the rail and the wheel in turn, felt the lustre in the timber and felt a great affection for this vessel.

He resolved to take charge, to be in control, and to never let things around him ever become out of control again.

Soon, he had reached the compound where the crew had been detained. There was still no official restraint placed upon them. They had stood no trial. Each was blaming the other for their actions. Each maintained that they were forced by 'another', and no charges had formally been drawn.

They had become dispirited by long-term idleness, although, despite having been fed minimal rations, they had not been allowed to fall into ill health. These many weeks were, at worse, inconvenient.

Now Daemon hesitated before grasping the door handle. The lock had been slipped aside by an attendant, so the door was ready to open inwardly.

Stepping out of the shadow of the half-opened door, a few heads turned to see what had disturbed the quietness.

Suddenly, seats ground out raking noises and benches fell over backwards. A cup was spilled, the contents dripping off the table onto the dry boards of the floor.

'Captain! Begging y'r pardon!'

'Captain Quirk! Sir!'

A number of remarks in quick succession, each from a different direction, filled the air. All stood and turned as well as they could, given the cramped conditions, facing up as he stepped further into the room.

Silence descended as he looked the men up and down. He walked from side to side so that he could estimate the numbers and identify those who remained.

'Stand over there, all of you. Pass this way. That's right, single file. I want to get a good look at you.'

Most raised a forelock as they passed, few held his gaze. Only Erik held his head up and looked him squarely in the eye. 'Captain, sir, I am pleased to see you.'

Daemon did not respond. 'Line up, facing me!' They were arranged two-deep the width of an eighteen-foot wall. Daemon figured there were twenty-eight, perhaps thirty in total.

'Is there any reason why I shouldn't see ye all hanged for mutiny? Can anyone give me an answer? What I want is someone to tell me, truthfully, what in God's name you were intending to do with my ship?'

'Beggin' y'r pardon, sir, Captain Quirk, we... er... we was press-ed into it; we were forced, at gunpoint!' Dalton spoke up, but immediately looked as if he wished he had kept his mouth firmly closed.

'Erik? *You* will tell me truthfully. That is all I ask of you.'

'Captain Quirk, sir, apologies. I am distressed to tell the story. I have no right!' His head bowed low and diminished him to normal height for once.

'Tell me, anyone? You are all in danger! The court may yet decide what to do with you, even if I had a mind to saving you! You may as well talk and tell me everything.'

Erik shook his head, too embarrassed to offer his explanation.

Dalton stood, and by the way the others parted for him, the way their heads sank even further into their shoulders, Daemon sensed that this was the only voice to which he could listen.

Dalton moved a stride closer, breaking ranks, separating himself from the others.

'Captain, may I speak...?'

'Please, Dalton — go on! I want to hear what you have to say. Speak up, man!'

'Well, sir, I am as much to blame as the others. I expect no favour.' There were murmurings from the lines beyond him.

'We failed you, Captain. We were a rabble of scurvy, unworthy wretches and we failed you. You had done nothin' but good, by us.'

'Dalton, please, how did it happen?'

'Well, sir, if you please, Baptiste told us you had been taken! He said imprisoned, by the Governor of that-there island. He says as to how we should take the ship, in John Standin's honour, and return it to his family. 'E says we would be rewarded and live like gentemun, and it was the right thing to do.'

'And you believed him?'

'No, sir. I stood up to 'im and told 'im we should wait. Wait for you, sir. I knew you wasn't locked-up. You 'ad'n't done no wrong to be locked up for, I said. So 'e puts a pistol to my 'ead! 'E was goin' to blow my 'ead right off! I 'ad to follow 'is orders.'

'So, who else followed him? Who took what Baptiste said and decided it was right?'

Erik put his hand in the air. Four others followed.

'So, you were the ringleaders? Baptiste and you four-five, whatever? Is that the way of it? Did you lead these others? Were they like sheep, just following, or did you have a gun to their heads?'

'Pretty much like this.' Erik took a pace forward. 'We let him lead us astray from our duty. We thought for a moment it was the right thing to do. Then we were at sea. We knew there was no going back. So we carried on.'

'So why are you not in Morocco? Or England? Why are you in New York?'

'We knew we would be pursued, going back to Europe, to British waters; we knew this was a big mistake. We thought, *he* thought, Baptiste, that we should come north, be rid of the ship at the earliest moment. We tried to make a deal in New Orleans, then with a lawyer, Watson, I think, but he failed to win the argument. Baptiste decided upon himself to persuade the main opposition that we were the rightful owners of the ship and cargo.

'It has been eight-nine weeks since we left the ship and were detained here under guard. We do not know what happened to Baptiste, although some of the guards told us he was dead.'

Daemon spoke after a long moment. 'I am leaving you here. I have not decided what is to become of you. Indeed, as I have said, it may be out of my hands anyway. However, I will see that you are represented and have a fair hearing if it comes to that.'

Daemon walked out and slammed the door behind him.

The driver followed his last command and guided the horses up through the town and out on to the open road towards the Don Bosco ranch.

Chapter 36
Don Bosco's Invitation

Up at the mansion, Don Bosco had explained to Kirsten that they were to entertain an unexpected guest.

'But, dearest, who is it? Could you not have at least one or two evenings when you could rest and recover? Must you go on and on...?'

'Now, my dear, please, no more. I am determined to live my life. I have told you many times, this will not defeat me! I will not become your patient. I am your husband... I am still capable...'

'Of course you are, darling! I have never tried to confine you. Surely you understand, I am only concerned for you. Since that *madman* tried to shoot you...!' She raised a hand to her mouth. 'I have never felt such fear since... since Baltimore!'

Banoldino pushed himself up from his chair. He was at her side in a moment, pulling her head on to his chest and holding her tightly. He brushed the long wavy hair into place and calmed her. She looked up into his eyes, her own eyes moist as tears escaped.

'Darling, I don't want to lose you.' She said, this has been the greatest adventure for us! We came here with the clothes we stood in and a prayer, and now look! Look what we have... you did all this! I don't know what I would do if...'

'Now come, my little angel! You know very well that you would survive. In fact, I think you would take on the business and do it better than I.' God help them in the finance houses and on the political platforms if you ever decide to hitch up your skirts!'

'Well, darling, you will be glad to know that I am quite happy doing what I do. I flit here and flit there and if I do a bit of good along the way, then I am happy for it. But I have no wish to rule your empire. Not at all. I need you. So, please do not push yourself too hard...' She tapped playfully against his chest and pulled away in mock disgust.

'I shall go out to the back porch and sit for a while. I will try very hard not to think about how we came here. Or what happened even before that. But no doubt it will be the very first image I have when I close my eyes.'

'Wait, darling, you cannot go! I have not told you who is coming tonight.' Banoldino did not want their dalliance to end.

'Well, come, tell me what delights you have lined up for us.'

'A young man. A sea captain! No other than the rightful owner of the *Durham*! The ship that lies chained up in the harbour.'

'Oh, indeed! So, someone has emerged to remove that accursed thing that nearly cost you your life?'

'Oh yes, my dear! And a fine man he is. He has arrived here courtesy of the Dutch Navy, another fine fellow at the helm — van *Dah*l, I think. Anyway, this young man has a story to tell. He was bound for Europe on a mission to return the profit of an enterprise set up by his friend and mentor John Standing, Earl of... something... from England.

'Standing was killed in an encounter with pirates; this Quirk... Captain Quirk... he promised at his friend's moment of death that he would return the vessel to his family, with the profits and the cargo earned from the voyage.'

'A very noble undertaking, I am sure, my dear. He must be a man to be admired. Where has he come from?'

'Why, I think Ireland! I don't recall if I ever asked the question. He has charm, and a very honest face. He is no profiteer, I can tell. I want to get to know him. Indeed, if I can persuade him to return to New York when he has completed his obligation... I see great promise.'

'Darling, I know you are a very good judge of a man. I can't wait to meet him. If he is from *home*, I will enjoy quizzing him on the state of the old country! What time do you expect him?'

'I expect he will arrive quite early for dinner. I have given him the use of the chaise for the day. Daniel will bring him back here around five, I think.'

'Very well, I will make arrangements. I assume our other friends will attend? I am sure they can smell the opportunity of a good story and some entertainment value in the situation.'

Kirsten turned for the doorway towards the back porch, but something clicked in her head and, smiling to herself, she decided upon giving some instruction to the staff, heading up to her rooms to put a little extra into her preparation.

She was thinking perhaps she could encourage a dashing young man to return quickly to their shores and grasp the opportunities that her husband would undoubtedly place before him. She realised her job on occasion was to gently apply the sort of pressure that would be required, once she understood Banoldino's intentions.

Daemon sat easily in the carriage up alongside the driver. He preferred to sit up top and have a conversation with the man at the helm, rather than sit and be carried along like some old maid!

'So, your boss, Mr Don Bosco, he is a good employer? He treats you fairly?'

'Eh he, yassuh! He does. No finer man in the county. On my life.'

'I believe you — you don't have to swear to it! I am just curious. You don't owe me an answer or anything. I would just like to know a little bit about the man. He has been here many years? Since the early settlers?'

'Hell, no! He came about eight, nine years since. He and his friend Lord *Ranelly*. Fine man! Very fine indeed! They was in Ireland, where I believe Lord Ranelly had an estate, but they come to New York to settle here.'

'So, in just a few years they have become so important?'

'Why, yassuh! Don Bosco, they say he the richest man in these parts. He got a good head for business. His lady, too. Lady *Kristen*. She the finest lady anywheres! She got such a way about her.' His eyes glistened as he spoke of her. 'She mighty fine, I promise yuh!'

'I look forward to meeting her.'

Daemon found himself muttering to himself. 'I wonder which part of Ireland she has come from? *Kristen* or Kirsten?... If only *my* Kirsten had survived! If only we had a chance, here in the New World. How grand *we* might have been!'

Sitting up suddenly, Daemon realised they had pulled in to the courtyard of a very fine house.

He hopped down from his perch and looked around at the three storeys of white-stucco render and black-stone window frames. Four or five attendants were dealing with the horses, pails of water being offered for them to drink, then thrown over them to cool them off after their exertions.

Daemon himself was offered a cool drink from a goblet, which he downed with relish.

'This way, if I may, sir.' A young black man bowed lightly towards Daemon and held his hand out towards a doorway across the courtyard.

'Please lead the way... er... if you please.' Daemon raised his tricorn hat minutely in acknowledgement, indicating that the youth was to lead him in the direction he was intended to follow.

Daemon turned and looked up at the windows, most of which were blank and still.

Two storeys up, Kirsten was readying herself in the dressing room, before she would return to the long French windows on the front balcony of her room.

She could not resist the temptation to look down into the courtyard as the chaise drew up.

She saw a quite tall figure hop down onto the cobbled yard, and liked his bearing, the spring in his legs and the square jaw she could detect under the brim of his hat as it scanned along the rows of windows. His gaze passed her own window where she stood off centre, behind a muslin drape.

Watching his antics with the servant, in allowing him to lead the way, brought a smile to her face. Her final view of him was his fair hair and the dark ribbon which held it back.

She hurried herself into her garments and allowed her maid to apply the finishing touches with utmost economy.

Daemon was shown to a room, where he discovered a very fine linen blouse awaiting him, a wash basin and everything he might need to prepare for dinner.

He asked the servant to let Senor Don Bosco know he would be available within half of the hour.

A light knock on the door brought Daemon around from where he had been standing in front of a long mirror, attempting to unravel the quite intricate little ties which would draw together the material at the end of his sleeves.

He flung back the door, where a maid servant bade him good afternoon, and would he 'be so kind as to join Senor Don Bosco for light refreshment, if indeed he had completed his preparations'?

'Yes, yes, indeed. One moment and I will, yes, I am ready!' There were two lengths of material hanging either side of his collar and Daemon looked down at them, not knowing quite where they were supposed to go.

The maid looked at him, eased the door shut behind her and stepped forward, taking the two lengths in her hands, whilst looking quite brazenly into his eyes.

She tied them into a beautiful bow, before looking up at him again and stating, 'There now. And don't you just look a picture!'

Smiling, she turned quickly and led him out into the corridor. In moments he was returning her smile as she held open the door to the salon, where Don Bosco and Carstein had already assembled against the large polished sandstone hearth.

Holding out a glass, Don Bosco called to him, 'Ah, my friend, please join us; we will have a leisurely half hour before the ladies arrive. Ranleigh will be here any moment, I am sure.'

'Thank you, sir. May I add again my thanks for the courtesy of your carriage today? And for Daniel: most helpful, in every way.'

Carstein intervened. 'Hah, I am glad you managed to get around the harbour with that old goat at the helm! I trust you have seen enough to help you decide which course to take?'

Daemon nodded in Carstein's direction. 'I have seen... well, enough, as you say, to know my own mind. I will wait, if I may, until tomorrow, and we have stood before the judge, before I make firm my plans.'

'Of course, yes. Let us not debate further on the future until we have the full authority. Instead, you can tell us all about the recent past, and your endeavours to make good your promises, hey, Don Bosco?'

'Yes indeed; there is plenty of time for us to hear your story... First, more refreshment, and, of course, we must await Ranleigh's arrival.'

Just then, the salon doors opened as the voluminous, light blue skirts of Kirsten's dress whirled through the opening. Don Bosco's face lit up in surprise at the early arrival of his wife. He quickly adjusted so he could welcome her.

Just at that moment, another door banged beyond and she quickly turned on her heels. Daemon turned around, expecting to be included in the greeting, but just glimpsed the back of her dress as she disappeared out into the hallway.

Don Bosco had raised a hand and uttered, 'Gentlemen, my lovely wife... Ah! Perhaps a little premature, gentlemen! Forgive me, my dear wife appeared for but the briefest moment!'

Daemon turned to him. 'Ah! Perhaps the lady, setting eyes upon her guest, decided she would rather dine with the horses!' Both Don Bosco and Carstein fell into laughter and maintained their levity for a moment or two longer.

Dialogue was being exchanged out in the hall. Don Bosco's 'good lady' seemed to be drifting further away as she gave orders to the staff.

A youthful servant appeared in the salon and walked towards Don Bosco. 'Madam sends her regrets, but she will not be able to join you immediately. A lady in the town has been taken very ill and Madam must attend to her.'

'What?' Don Bosco bellowed. 'Madam must attend to her! Kirsten is neither sorceress nor a midwife; why must she attend?'

Daemon again had the temerity to utter, 'Well, at least I held sway over the horses...!'

Don Bosco laughed again. 'Captain, please, I hope you are not offended. However, you have the right to be. My wife's behaviour is reprehensible. But that is my Kirsten! She does whatever her instinct tells her — the last thing she does is what her husband expects!'

Carstein joined in the levity 'Nonsense, Banolo — you know she hangs on your every word! Indeed, she follows your guidance without fail; it just takes her a little time to comply — often a month or so!'

'Gentlemen, I will return; please talk... Ah, here is Ranleigh, and Lady Eve; and, of course, your darling wife, Carstein. What a lucky devil you are!'

Don Bosco quickly affected the introductions, before begging permission to leave to find out what had dragged Kirsten away.

Lady Eve intervened. 'Why? Have you not heard? Mistress de Witt has gone into labour, and, the Reverend is so concerned about her health that he has called on a surgeon and so many advisers to attend. Unfortunately, the only persons she would contemplate having in her room during the birth are Mistress Don Bosco and Mrs Allison Smith, who has been her friend.'

Don Bosco uttered in exasperation, 'My wife *is* now a midwife! She has dressed for dinner, but now, when she returns, she will be just like a *farmer's wife* returned from the lambing! I'm afraid she drives me to distraction! However, my greatest apologies go to our guest. Captain, I pray you will forgive my wife, and myself, for this discourtesy.'

'Senor Don Bosco, I am sure the lady in distress has greater need than I! I have only one regret, and that is to have to wait until tomorrow before I meet the extraordinary Madam Don Bosco.'

'Very well put,' allowed Carstein.

'Your servant,' responded Don Bosco.

'How about some dinner?' demanded Ranleigh, at which they all laughed and proceeded to take their places at the table.

Chapter 37
A Near Miss

Many times over dinner, the name of Kirsten was brought into the conversation. Every utterance of her was enriched with heartfelt respect and glowing admiration.

Every time, Daemon winced! It was Kirsten — not *Kristen*, as the coach driver had it, which made the memory stir afresh of that lovely young girl he had found and lost so suddenly. He wondered again how things might have been between them. He wondered what she would have become had she survived.

He could see her in a simple cotton dress. He could imagine her holding a tiny child aloft. He could see her washing in a stream. He even, for one second, imagined her dressed 'up to the nines' in a bonnet, attending church. It was all he could do to dispel her memory for a moment, to attend the conversation.

The evening was bright and cheerful. They hung on his every word of the voyage, of the slaves on board and the trials and tribulations of the crossing. Of the slave market, and of life in the Caribbean. They were most interested in his reference to the Van Eycks and of his own inclination towards Gertrude van Eyck.

Lady Eve was most keen to establish his intentions. 'You will be returning to Barbados then, Captain? I think that you have every intention of making that young lady your wife!'

'Now, Mother, you must leave the Captain alone! I am sure he doesn't need your encouragement. You have made him blush!' Lady Annabelle could not resist teasing him.

The words, and the way she uttered them, did, in fact, make him blush far more than the fact itself that they were speaking of his intentions towards a woman.

'I have my responsibilities to fulfil; but, yes, my intention is to return to Barbados and, well, we shall have to wait and see.'

Banoldino interjected again, 'Captain, your determination in such a cause, it is admirable. A lot can happen upon such an undertaking. I hope you will always consider that here, in New York, there is great opportunity. We have a growing community. Here, with one or two friends to rely upon, a man like yourself could do very well.'

'I am honoured that you should say so. I will remember the kindness you have all shown me. I dearly hope we may all meet again. The very least I might manage is a visit, once things have been settled in Barbados!'

'What a charming name for an island!' Lady Eve was intent on her share of attention from the handsome young man. 'What do you know of the origins of the name?'

'Indeed, ma'am. I have heard that the word was derived from the Portuguese for 'bearded ones'. It seems the original inhabitants had not perfected the means of shaving the face.'

'Ah, I see... the "darkies" are having an influence...'

Lord Ranleigh chided his wife. 'My dear, that is an unflattering reference to these people! You should know better! They were not Africans more like 'American Indians'.

'Well, I see nothing wrong with "darkies". I think that is perfectly appropriate, don't you think, Captain?'

'I see nothing offensive there, ma'am. Nothing at all. Now, if you will forgive me, it has been a long day. I would like to be up and about tomorrow; I have a hearing to attend and I would like to begin preparations aboard my ship...'

Banoldino was on his feet. 'Captain, I implore you, if you could wait a little, I am certain my wife will return soon. It would be such a shame for you to miss each other. She was born in Ireland, I may have mentioned this. I would wager you would have such a lot to talk about.'

'You are very kind, senor. Before I leave, it would give me the greatest pleasure to meet with Lady Don Bosco, but...'

'Forgive me. A selfish inclination. She will make my life a misery if I let you go!'

'I would not dream of departing these shores without the honour of meeting the lady.'

Lady Annabelle interrupted. 'I know she is going to like you, Captain, but I warn you, she makes great fun of me with my "titles". She would have short shrift of any whom addressed her as "Lady Don Bosco"! Indeed, I believe she was an Estate Manager's daughter when...'

Ranleigh interjected, 'Now, my dear, I don't think the Captain is interested in such things, particularly at this time of the evening. As the young man has said, he has a lot to do. He must find a crew to sail his vessel across the sea. Which brings me to a question, Captain. What would you wish to be done with your old crewmen? Please speak freely.'

'I have not made up my mind, in truth. I know these men well from the voyage. They were a strange gathering to begin with. We were under-manned, if the truth be known. When I think of it now, I wonder how we managed, with what we had to deal with. They were hard working, they fought hard and with determination when we were threatened. I came to consider them as comrades, friends even. My confidence in my own judgement has been affected by the turn of events.'

'I do not think you should be hard on yourself, Captain Quirk.' Carstein was quick to defend. 'Things happen when the force of circumstance might drive a man to a course of action he would not have believed in himself. When a gathering of men begins to sway to one opinion, sometimes nothing can stop the inevitable. After all, at some level, we are all followers! How would a politician ever be elected if he could not persuade a crowd that it was in their interest to support him?'

'I appreciate what you say, Mr Carstein. Believe me, I am inclined to forgive their actions. I am partly to blame. And yet, I have seen men under stress, under extreme difficulty. If there were no discipline, things could fall apart. I am afraid of my own humanity, that it would be seen as weakness, and that all this is my own fault.'

'No, I do not believe it. This Baptiste was a man of no morality. I believe he harboured a great hatred inside him and simply awaited his moment.' Don Bosco was also sympathetic.

'That may very well be true. It still weighs heavily on my mind that he is dead. It seems like only yesterday that we stood together in a storm, hanging on to the wheel for all we were worth. Now, you ask me where I will find a crew to sail with me across the sea?

'I am going to follow my inclination and take my men back with me. In the first place, if I left them to their fate, I would always be troubled by what might happen. Secondly, I could take on a new crew and have to learn their ways and work with strangers all over again. It makes sense for me to trust myself to get the best out of these men, and I will live with the consequences.'

'Admirably said!' Ranleigh rose and patted Daemon on the back.

This was a signal to Daemon that this might be a good time to demonstrate his intent on getting a good start upon his undertaking, and he rose respectfully, so his back was not turned to Ranleigh.

As he moved behind his chair, Ranleigh took his hand and shook it vigorously. 'I would like to offer you a bed for the night at *our* place in town. My wife and I are staying there at the moment, and the house is in readiness for visitors.'

Don Bosco and Carstein rose to their feet. 'I also offer the hospitality of my home, but I suggest that Lord Ranleigh and Lady Eve have an offer which would suit you well, it being close to the harbour and to where you would wish to be, come the morning. May I humbly suggest you take their offer? Besides I am a hopeless host without Kirsten, and you would be in far better hands!'

They all laughed, Carstein interjecting that there remained an open invitation to his own residence at any time in the future; but he also added that he could not be in better hands than Lady Eve's.

349

Daemon gratefully accepted and was guided to the hallway, where he collected his hat.

Just as the goodbyes were being exchanged, he glanced up the grand stairway to the first landing, where a huge painting hung of the most stunning and elegantly dressed young woman. The light blue satin of her dress and stiff, white, embroidered collar framed a beautiful face, and it was all topped by a golden halo, swept high up on her head above her long, elegant neck. The fan she held in her hand, half-open, rested upon her knee.

The picture was delightful and the image striking.

Don Bosco caught his eye. 'My lovely wife. As you see, she is far too good for me! I do hope you meet her come the morning.'

Daemon managed to croak his acknowledgement, but his mind was elsewhere. 'My God, she is like...!' he laughed to himself. 'Well, imagine, what a grand lady she must be!' Inwardly, he determined that before he set sail, he could not contemplate missing the opportunity of meeting her.

Chapter 38
A New Arrival

Kirsten rushed from room to room. She knew things were dangerously balanced: Jocelyn de Witt was of a delicate disposition.

Having been born of Spanish immigrant parents and nurtured in the most refined circumstance, her marriage to Rev de Witt seemed a perfect solution.

Hers was destined to be a life of quiet contemplation, of support and comfort. She was never to be exposed to harsh reality.

Unfortunately, this was poor preparation for motherhood. Indeed, that she had carried the child full-term had impressed the entire community. De Witt, a realist and a pragmatic individual of little imagination, brought the local doctor and insisted on Morgenstern, a Professor of Medicine from the Catholic College, in support.

Jocelyn, at once, railed at the idea of a room consisting of only men, and as the day wore on, she became increasingly averse to any male attendance at all.

The doctor was restricted to attempting to assess the remaining time span of the labour through two layers of linen, beneath which the object of his interest remained hidden.

Finally, in a fit of unbridled resistance, Jocelyn banished them from the room and brought Kirsten and Allison to her side.

Seven hours later, Kirsten had rolled up her sleeves, released several skirts from underneath her dress and covered herself as best she might with another linen sheet.

Allison dabbed at Jocelyn's forehead with a damp cloth whilst Kirsten now whispered into, very distressed Jocelyn's ear.

'Look what I've brought you, dear. Look.' She jiggled a small wooden carving of a reindeer up and down on the mound that Jocelyn's right knee had fashioned.

'Look, dear, the stag has been stomping around in the wood. He is waiting a newborn! A beautiful fawn! He will be so proud when she arrives. He will race to the top of the hill and beat the ground with his hooves, his proud head raised towards the sun!

'Come on, dear, let's help him! Let's make him proud! Push! Let's push like we mean it. With all our might. With all our might, darlin', let's push...!'

Jocelyn's face creased, her eyes bulged and the vein on her neck protruded from her delicate skin, thick and blue.

Sweat poured down from her hair-line, and her face reddened. No sound came from her lips, which were drawn back across her clenched teeth.

A long moment passed as her expression became fixed. Kirsten awaited her next breath; waiting, hopeful, for her friend's body to become loose and relaxed.

All at once, her face appeared without pain: pretty, hopeful, pleading. A groan emitted from deep within her throat. Suddenly, as if collapsing from within, she did go limp, all of her body deflating.

Kirsten screamed, 'Doctor, please come! Quickly, sir!'

Allison turned and ran for the door, but it swung open just as she reached for the handle.

Doctor Pratley pushed past her. Quickly, he put a hand to Jocelyn's neck, feeling for a pulse. Suddenly, he smacked her face, once to the right, and again to the left. Jocelyn's eyes sank into her skull and her head hung loose.

Kirsten pulled on a loose arm, begging her to come round, to look up, to open her eyes.

Then she looked to Pratley, pleading, then despairing. 'Oh, no. Please God, no!'

The professor arrived behind Kirsten, easing her out of the way. Leaning over Jocelyn, he called for his bag.

De Witt arrived with the bag and, emitting a deep groan, he immediately fell to his knees, clutching Jocelyn's head tightly to him.

Morgenstern quickly extracted a small, fine blade from its leather binding and sliced through the linen layers covering the stricken figure.

Her swollen belly was exposed to the light, large and rigid, with a sheen to the tightly drawn skin.

Below the distended navel, the professor traced a long curve across her belly. Immediately, a fringe of blood flowed down into the folds of linen remaining around Jocelyn's thighs.

Morgenstern inserted a hand into the pouch he had created, as if seeking something he might take a hold of.

Suddenly, he pulled out a limp, blood-soaked figure by two tiny limbs. Holding up the figure, he slapped twice in quick succession on the tiny rump.

Immediately, the figure began to coil and let out a tiny spluttering cry.

'Quickly, take her! Madam! Be quick!' He sliced through the cord and quickly tied a knot in what remained.

He passed the tiny figure to Kirsten, her own eyes now bulging as she took the baby into her arms.

Laying her down onto the cushioned mound which was to become her first cradle, Kirsten began washing and soothing, and wrapping the child in a warm blanket.

Turning to Allison, she bade her 'fly' down to the Bowery and return as quickly as her legs could carry her with a wet nurse.

Morgenstern set about quickly repairing the rend in the abdomen of the stricken mother. All this was achieved without De Witt loosening the hold on his dear wife's head.

Motioning that they all allow De Witt some privacy, they began to leave the room. The child lay quite still, eyes wide, appearing to take in the sights and sounds of the room.

Kirsten motioned to De Witt; putting both arms about his shoulders, she bade him come to meet his daughter.

His tear-stained face reared momentarily. He sought her eyes and, without speaking, conveyed to Kirsten that his heart was truly broken.

She showed him the child, its angelic face turned, and, she could have sworn, almost smiled in recognition.

Kirsten left them together.

Some moments later, Allison returned with a stout, black woman, whose very aroma confirmed her profession. 'Ma'am, this is Lucretia; she is a wet-nurse, very highly spoken of in the town.'

Kirsten led her into the room. Lucretia's eyes opened wide and her head shook from side to side on her first glimpse of Jocelyn's body.

Allowing her a moment, Kirsten introduced her to De Witt. The Reverend gave her his blessing, allowing her to look over the baby. 'My, what a bootiful chile...!' she uttered, as she hoisted the baby. 'What's 'iss chile's name, Reverun'?'

Turning to Kirsten, De Witt smiled into her eyes. 'You must name her for me. Will you? Will you look to her now?'

'Of course, Reverend, anything I can do, for you and for Joc'... I would be so proud.'

He took both her hands and kissed them in turn.

Slowly, he walked from the room. Kirsten watched him leave, her expression confirming her bewilderment.

Turning to Lucretia, she began to talk through her instructions, although she knew very well the woman was more than capable of managing the next few days entirely left to her own devices.

Nonetheless, she advised Lucretia that she herself would return on the morrow and consider whether a few days out at her own house would be in the child's interests whilst De Witt gathered himself.

Allison returned and began to tidy up the room without touching the bed or the sad, pathetic corpse.

As they completed the task, Allison was beginning to untie the knot which had been holding her apron in place, when a loud bang rang out, echoing throughout the house.

Kirsten looked up and found Allison's eyes. Tentatively, she eased her way towards the door.

Morgenstern and Doctor Pratley had prised open the door to the study. Both men appeared frozen, unable to advance, nor to retreat, from what they had discovered.

Kirsten pushed her way between them, where she could see the figure of Reverend de Witt slumped over his desk, a smoking duelling pistol in his right hand. A dark, thick pool of blood spread out from beneath his temple across the smooth oak surface of his desk.

Kirsten did not return home that night, nor for a further three days and three nights.

She oversaw all the arrangements. Catholic Father Tweedale agreed, under great duress, to preside over the burial of Protestant Reverend de Witt and his wife.

All arrangements were completed before Kirsten returned home to her husband, with a baby in her arms.

Chapter 39
Van Gahl Makes His Move

Dieter van Gahl smiled to himself. His position in life could be on the verge of a major change. Having quickly been recalled to New York, to present dispatches to the Governor, now a trusted ally, he immediately assumed a superiority over the French and Spanish, heavily in favour of Anglo/Dutch interests.

These dispatches were indeed of high importance. Three thousand British in seven heavily armed ships were en-route for the New World to support British interests on the Canadian seaboard.

Such a force would have a major impact on the coastal community, bringing impetus to the local economy in supplying the needs of such a force in everything from ship repairs to cavalry and pack horses.

The Governor would need to make a significant contribution to their entrenchment and almost certainly support the coming campaign with ships armaments and supplies. However, the price would be handsome, and many gains were to be made. The governor would have a matter of three weeks to make his arrangements, so that nothing moved in the region without his involvement.

Van Gahl almost immediately having delivered his dispatches, received fresh orders for himself. Provisions had to be given a boost with the utmost urgency. New supplies of coffee, sugar and Mahogany were urgently needed in preparation for the arrival of the new expeditionary force.

Barbados and Trinidad could provide most of their immediate requirements. Van Gahl was to escort three merchantmen to the islands and return them safely to New York packed to the gunnels with supplies.

Van Gahl could not hide his delight, having learned that Daemon had set off for Europe determined to fulfil his own mission. Van Gahl knew he had several months in hand before any possible interference.

His objective was the winning of Gertrude's hand!

For many dark nights he had harboured thoughts of Gertrude. The more he dwelled on her image, the more exotic, alluring, tempting she became. He chastised himself. He had been far too much the gentleman on his latter meetings with the lovely Gertrude.

He had stood aside whilst his friend captivated her heart, had accepted the situation as inevitable and failed to stake a claim. Yet he knew, somehow, Gertrude herself had been torn between them. Her sensibilities were clearly inclined towards himself, of Dutch background, of the familiar tongue and a history in common.

She had hardly been able to conceal her own feelings as she visibly raged at the fates for removing both of her suitors at one fell swoop.

Van Gahl knew that he had to take his chance. The opportunity had been presented to him. He had not sought it. He would never be able to look himself in the face if, this time, he failed to stake his claim. He determined that, for once, he must consider his own future.

He would have few chances in life better than the one that presented itself. Sure, it was fraught with danger — the lady was difficult at the best of times.

He would never have a better chance to impress her, to get her to forget the dashing Captain Quirk. And, of course, Van Eyck himself presenting even more of a challenge.

Now, as he steered the flotilla towards Barbados, familiar, friendly waters, he reflected, he was hatching his plan. He would have to be sure of his ground before making the first move; then, by his demeanour and behaviour, he would convince first the father, then darling Gertrude that he, Van Gahl, was the one she could invest her future upon.

He was here, he was devoted to her. He would buy himself out of the Dutch Royal Navy and take his place at the head of this pioneering community.

He licked his lips, subconsciously relishing the opportunity that lay ahead.

With the flotilla anchored, and sails trimmed; all preparations for a short-term stay were completed. Twenty-four hours later, Van Gahl readied himself for the task that lay ahead. The three ship's masters departed for their assignations with the traders with a view to securing all the coffee and sugar required. Whilst Mahogany was to be collected from another familiar colony, Trinidad.

Van Gahl convinced the merchantmen that they were indeed in 'safe waters', and his suggestion that they complete the second part of the mission without naval escort was accepted without too much resistance.

He reached the jetty at the head of his launch, standing at the prow, as the four oars were drawn. The boat bumped heavily into the timber decking and, timing to perfection, Van Gahl hopped onto the mooring.

Hardly had his feet touched the ground than the carriage door of the Van Eyck conveyance was flung open, allowing Gertrude to alight without waiting for the steps. She flew into his arms and hugged him for an unseemly long moment.

Quite breathless, he disengaged and made his formal greetings, by which time, Van Eyck had made his own painstaking way to join them on the dock-side.

'Delighted, my boy! I could hardly be more pleased to see you on our shores again.'

Partly in shock and almost completely unprepared, he managed only to utter a muted greeting. He accepted the offer of joining them immediately in their carriage to prepare for an open invitation of hospitality. They hastened to add that the Governor was to arrive at the residence that evening for 'discussions about the state of Europe's political alliances'.

Van Gahl accepted, and, under the perfect pretext, he was fully able to isolate Gertrude and seek out his opportunity.

Polite conversation ensued as duty was satisfied with simple half-truths. Van Gahl passed on Daemon's letter, explaining that he was bound for Europe and North Africa to 'fulfil his mission' and could offer 'no guarantees of his return', despite the promises he made when leaving the island. Gertrude immediately pushed to the back of her mind the implications of Daemon's letter.

Undeterred, she was radiant, her attentions flattering and unerring. Van Eyck treated him like a long-lost nephew, and spoke about the future as though theirs were already intertwined with his own.

From that moment, there was only one inevitable outcome: that Gertrude would cast off her former suitor and marry Van Gahl.

Plans were made, dates were considered for the spring. Gertrude played her part, too, as 'chaste', attentive and a perfect companion.

Van Gahl could hardly believe his good fortune. The plantation, the shares in other enterprises, the shipping, the bank balances: everything was revealed and passed before him as if for his approval. He revelled in the intimacy and the growing confidence in their relationship.

The forthcoming alliance brought great expectation for the island. They would be celebrated as the colony's 'first' couple. Prosperity for all was envisaged, as the new generation would exert influence over the future. The Hollanders on the island were delighted at the prospect of a virtual 'royal' family, a new dynasty, and two young Dutch at the head.

All appeared to be perfectly set up, and Van Eyck even enjoyed better health, revelling in the new confidence that surrounded their enterprises.

Gertrude showed off her new suitor around the island. They met and greeted everyone of prominence. They began to dabble, here and there, in opportunities that only too readily dropped into their laps.

Van Gahl's attachment to the Navy, and indeed to his own ship, was dealt with. Encouraged by Governor Deakin's impassioned correspondence with his superiors,

Van Gahl's future was assured. He could extricate himself from naval service with immediate effect, his reputation intact.

His ship, with a new Master, recently arrived by means of another Dutch Navy vessel, left in convoy with the fully stocked merchantmen, bound for New York.

Van Gahl watched without regret as they sailed into the distance just four months after his return to Barbados.

For them the time flew by until a month before the wedding was due, a ship entered the harbour.

Chapter 40
Daemon's Return

Daemon had enjoyed a swift crossing of the Atlantic virtually without incident. With a substantial breeze at his back almost the entire run, the *Durham* spread her wings and almost flew across the surface of the deep waters.

His only encounter proved to be quite helpful to his cause.

A British Naval vessel, bound for the Northern Territories, crossed their path on the fifteenth day.

Her captain conveyed that he would do very well to make his first port of call to Liverpool, where the Crown was filling its warehouses with supplies for the forthcoming winter and the certainty of continuation of hostilities with the French. Cotton mills in Lancashire were desperate for supplies to re-stock the army with uniforms and blankets.

Daemon steered the *Durham* into harbour on the banks of the Mersey River, in September 1752. Within hours of arriving, he had made a deal with the Agent for the British Army and proceeded to unload the entire cargo at a single berth.

He validated the draft at a bank along Water Street and spoke with Customs House about the possibilities of carrying a new cargo to North Africa.

Trade with the region was managed at that time, but there were few consistent demands other than transportation for the British Army or re-stocking a fortress. For some months during which time Daemon dwelt upon his failure to return either to Barbados or to North Africa, he was able to take on small commissions which paid the crew and gave him time to consider his future.

On one such excursion he was obliged to sample the North Sea at it's worst and land a cargo of wagon wheels at Helsinki. This gave Erik the opportunity to visit his family, a trip from which he never returned.

Upon his return to North West England, Daemon found the key to his return to Africa.

As it happened, a career politician, and former Cabinet Minister, James Routledge, had recently been awarded the Governorship of the Barbary Port Factory at Dakar.

His role would be to improve organisation and well-being of slaves awaiting transportation. Such were the numbers of Africans in the process, that it became essential to establish these 'factories' along the African coast. Initially controlled by the Dutch, but since the 1745, mostly under British authority.

A 'factory', effectively a fortress-camp, provided a temporary rest place, compound and transit shed for thousands of slaves. A garrison was required to maintain security and to confine the slaves, but many would agree, an improvement on the appalling treatment afforded to slaves by their initial captors, presented a demand for greater organisation and efficiency.

So, *Sir* James Routledge had been rewarded for years of service, with a peerage and a potentially miserable and demanding ending to his career, the prospect of which did little for his humour.

He had arranged for all his worldly goods — not inconsiderable — to be wrapped and crated and transported to a warehouse at the pier.

A meeting had been arranged with the Port Commissioner to introduce Routledge to his means of transportation to his new posting.

Daemon greeted him formally, removing his hat out of respect. Routledge showed sufficient decorum to reveal his gentlemanly background, but Daemon instantly detected a deep loathing of the situation within his new acquaintance and resolved to attempt to improve that, at least, during the journey.

Routledge's assets were swiftly loaded up. The block and hoist, and the efficiency with which they were applied, was a tribute to the organisation and compliance of Daemon's new regime.

Nonetheless, Routledge found every possible opportunity to complain, to chastise and protest at the handling of his goods.

'You there, imbecile, do not treat my bureau with such disdain! It is twice your age and far more valuable!

'You, that man! Desist in grappling with my chaise! It is to be handled with *care*! Could no one equip this scoundrel with a pair of gloves?'

And so it went on, hour after hour! Routledge threw his considerable weight about at every opportunity. Daemon eventually intervened.

'Mr Routledge, sir. Would you do me the honour of joining me in the salon. I have a selection of wines, sir, which I am guessing even a man of your refined taste might find agreeable.'

Routledge turned on Daemon. 'What? And leave this rabble to manhandle my belongings? Surely, sir, you will remain to supervise?'

'I will accept every responsibility for even the smallest detectable evidence of damage or harm and compensate you ten-fold should a man under my command be found responsible! Please accompany me; you will find the voyage much to your satisfaction if you would allow us sailors to sail and allow yourself the luxury of a fine ship under a fine crew!

'I am certain that we are capable of delivering your good self and your worldly goods to the furthest outposts — if you would just step back and allow us to do our work.'

Routledge reluctantly acquiesced, led by the arm and constantly looking over his shoulder, and found himself sitting in a comfortable bath-chair, nursing a goblet of fine Madeira with both hands.

Daemon chose his conversation carefully, knowing a man of Routledge's disposition was likely to react at the merest hint of an affront. Eventually, the conversation and Routledge's demeanour improved to such an extent that laughter could be detected from a certain vantage point up on the deck.

Routledge, it evolved, was an intelligent man, a good listener and of resolute character.

As reluctant as Daemon was to share his experiences as a Master of a 'slaver', he eventually trusted Routledge's temperament sufficiently to be able to provide a vivid picture of the disposition of the slaves in captivity and in transportation.

Routledge placed great store in Daemon's information, and took copious notes with quill and parchment, to remind himself of some of the information to which he had been privileged.

He was mightily impressed with Daemon's stance on slave transportation, resolving to do all in his power to unburden the slaves under his own regime.

'I am bidden to provide organisation, a firm rule and discipline among the garrison. There has been an appalling lack of all of those things, and the establishment has descended into chaos.

'I am determined that, under my rule, the fortress will be different! I will establish a true transit station. A place where business can be conducted properly. I am determined that the movement of humanity shall be conducted with Christian principles, and, with God's will, I will make the change.'

'I wish you well, Sir James. May I enquire as to the situation of your family? Will they... anyone, er, accompany you?'

'Indeed yes, Captain. My dear wife will be along very soon. My daughter Ariadne, and my mother-in-law, Dame Margot, will also make the voyage.

Within hours the Routledge family had joined the ship, been settled into their accommodation and prepared for the voyage. Daemon noticed the demure, dark haired girl who fussed about her mother and father making sure of their comfort. She smiled upon introduction but faded into the background when matters of import were discussed.

They had four servants and fourteen volunteers from the East Lancashire Regiment of Foot, to complete the entire passenger list for the voyage.

Daemon had used the crossing of the Atlantic to drill discipline and good habits into the reinstated crewmen and Erik had been replaced by Robert, a statuesque African emerging as his new, dependable 'right-hand'.

With everything stowed away and the departure smoothly achieved Daemon was able to concentrate on the comforts of his passengers acting as host.

He resumed discussion with Sir James at the first opportunity intent on pressing his views about how things might be improved.

Sir James was not enamoured of the regime he was to replace, understanding that discipline and general efficiency had dropped alarmingly in recent years.

"I am also determined that my family will be housed and entertained in royal fashion during our engagement in the colony. Indeed, I would hope to bring "society" to the region.'

'If I may, Sir James, recommend my friend, Gerald Samson, second son of Lord Chelmsford, who has been located in the fort St Louis at Rabat, for some years. He has, like yourself, a taste for the finer things... I am sure you would get along very well in his company, should you have the opportunity to, perhaps, exchange visits with him.'

'Surely, sir, you mean General Burkett's family? His father and I became close friends when assigned to Marlborough's retinue in the campaigns in Holland.

'The whole household, don't you know, were massacred in the Fort by Bedouin tribesmen on the rampage! They objected to British interference in the way they controlled the movement of the African population which, as you know, owes an immense amount to Arab slave-masters. No one survived.' Daemon rose from his seat, leaning over the table to be sure he did not miss a word.

'The king himself was so outraged he sent his Household Cavalry and three regiments of foot to root-out the heathens and put them to the sword! Poor Burkett was found. He had been buried alive on an anthill. Goddamn savages! All his family were abused and put to the sword. Not one survivor, I'm afraid.'

'My God! If that is the case, Sir James, I have lost not one, but five dear friends, and... I am devastated! I was instrumental in bringing a young lady to the Burkett household. I was personally responsible for Margaret's marriage to John Standing, third son of the Earl of Olney. I refuse to believe that Samson, Lyndsay and... Margaret! I just cannot accept...'

'You will be referring to Lady Margaret, who offered herself in place of Gerald's wife, and child, only to find that both were taken anyway. Lady Margaret was also murdered, and her own child was found among the debris in the arms of an Arab woman!'

'Her *own* child?'

'The story could not have been known in the European capitals, had it not been for this woman's actions. She protected the child and delivered her to safety. I believe the child is now resident with the family at Olney.'

Daemon was speechless. He simply hung his head.

Routledge stood, pouring them each another drink.

'I am afraid I have burdened you with the saddest and most shocking news. I truly regret that you had to learn of your friend's fate from my own lips. I wish it were not so, but I knew them, and I also mourned them their terrible ordeal. Come, my friend, drink and let us toast their memory and pray silently for a moment.'

For long hours, Daemon watched as Sir James slept, leaning against the bulkhead, glass at a forty-five-degree angle, upon his considerable paunch.

He rubbed at his own temples, trying desperately to reconcile the fact of his loss. His mind began to meander, to play tricks upon him. He saw himself as some sort of demon, a force for evil. A 'Jonah' to all his friends. Almost everyone he had loved, begun to love, one by one, had met the most tragic, fateful deaths! He was convinced it was his own doing. Somewhere, along his early travels, he had acquired an aura, a shadow, the shadow of death!

He recounted his uncle and cousins in Baltimore, Kirsten, Lady Daphne, John Standing, Margaret, even Baptiste!

Could it be that *he*, Daemon, was the jinx upon their lives? Had his own determination and ambition thrown them into danger? Into a place they would never have been.

He felt a terrible burden. He knew something was wrong. Guilt enveloped him.

All of them had been killed following his acquaintance... Such remorse overwhelmed him. He could not bear to hold up his head. He slumped. He sank to the floor. Darkness engulfed him. A retching sound penetrated his hearing.

He knew he was being violently ill. He realised hands were pulling him upright. He knew he was not in possession of himself.

He cried out long and loud. He wanted someone to take him. To do away with him. He cried for help. To the wrong deities! But not even the *Devil* would come to his aid. He wanted to inflict retribution upon himself, but he had not the means, nor the strength.

He realised he had become feverish. He felt unable to breath, his mouth parched, he believed himself in captivity in the desert again.

A goblet of fresh water was pressed against his lips, but he was unable to take it. He almost preferred to feel pain! He felt more satisfaction in pain.

'God, no!' he heard someone crying out, then realised it was himself. He knew how senseless it was to cry, but his mind gained some relief, some release of pressure. So, he cried again. His whole body shook, his teeth chattering together and a perforated moaning coming from his lips.

A long journey, through the desert, passing skeletal corpses, engrossed his mind. He came upon a temple with many steps; he could not reach the top; each hundred steps found a platform. On each platform stood a block and an executioner's bloody axe.

A pounding in his head, the burning sun on his face, he twisted this way and that but a sweat soaked shirt stopped him turning.

Distant howling became louder, he twitched as the sound grew deafening, he could not escape it, the pain unbearable, he passed out.

Voices could be heard, in the distance, Standing, Baptiste, Don Bosco they were discussing himself. What to do with him? There was laughter, Dieter Van Gahl, Gertrude…!

Now he was vomiting, now passing water. He could not feel his own face although he tried to reach it his hands were numb. He was crying again, but he knew not what his tears were for. Then laughter, the Africans were laughing at him. A child with no hand at the end of a bloody stump reached up to touch him.

He sat bolt upright in terror.

A cool hand pressed a damp cloth to his brow. His eyes blinked open. A delightful smell, was it lemon, filled his nostrils. He made out only a shadow at first. An outline. Then dark and shade, then features. A kindly, friendly face, half-smiling, peered down at him.

He tried to rise. 'Excuse me, madam, I am… am indisposed...'

'Shhh! Lay back! Do not try to struggle. You are going to be well. I can see you are over the worst. Here, take some water. Please, do it for me.'

He found himself responding; he followed her instructions and felt better for it. A solid, thumping pain locked his head in one position for a moment, but, laying back, the pillow felt good beneath him and the cool of the damp linen did its job on his face.

He drifted into a sound and merciful sleep.

Chapter 41
Kirsten and Child

Kirsten rocked gently back and forth, a low murmur coming from her lips and forming a lilting lullaby. Her head slightly to one side and peering down, she looked tenderly upon the tiny figure. Her arms began a series of easy little jerking motions, which found the baby's head almost imperceptibly moving from side to side.

Kirsten had no doubt whatsoever that the movement was sleep-inducing, and the baby's audible exhalation and slightly flaring nostrils told of a deep, comfortable repose.

Looking up, she found Don Bosco's face, and, equally in harmony with her own movements, his head signalled his approval of the treatment and that he was also convinced of its effect.

They jointly supervised the child's descent into deep sleep and utter contentment.

After ten or more minutes, Kirsten signalled to her friend Allison, all this time sitting some ten or twelve feet away on the opposite side of the coffee table on a lavishly upholstered chaise-longue.

Allison left briefly, returning with a cradle, into which the baby was placed.

Allison set the cradle down a short distance away, on the dining table, where a thick blanket protected the polished surface.

Kirsten had insisted that the child slept within 'hearing' of herself or Allison at all times. She was watchful for any sign of discomfort, and though the child had been given a completely clean bill of health by Doctor Pratley, Kirsten was watchful that a minute lack of air could spell the end for this tiny little being.

It became her mission. Nothing was going to happen to this child whilst she herself had breath in her body. To lose both parents in such a way was the most devastating thing that could befall a newborn.

Kirsten resolved *this* child would thrive, would grow and would be compensated for such unfortunate fate. *This* child would be given every chance to not only survive, but to become a very privileged one indeed! Something very special awaited this child. She would see to it.

In hushed tones, they sparked up a conversation. At ease with each other, and with Allison such a valued part of their own family, they talked of relief and delight at the child's recovery and of her christening and formal adoption.

Banoldino shrugged and acquiesced without a moment's hesitation. He could see Kirsten had made up her mind. This child was to be an addition to their own family and she would move heaven and earth to make sure it happened as quickly and as smoothly as it was possible.

'Rebecca' would become Senorita Rebecca Maria don Bosco, and Kirsten considered her a gift from God! A little recompense for the trauma and sadness of their own marriage in the light of Banoldino's injuries.

A month later, the family gathered around the marriage bed. Young John Nathan sat at one corner, too mature, these days, to be cuddled by his parents. He looked intently into a glass ball, which had a miniature inside surrounded by flakes which, when shaken , looked like snow falling.

No matter how many times John Nathan shook the bauble, he was immediately prepared, when the last flake settled, to begin all over again.

Between Banoldino's legs, on a hammock formed by the outer covers, rested the tiny figure of Rebecca, now blessed with a curly shock of blonde hair, and the biggest blue eyes. She chuckled as Banoldino let her rise and fall suddenly, for maximum effect on her tummy.

'Not too much, darling, you don't want her to be sick. She will throw up her breakfast if you do that once more!'

Kirsten lay beside Don Bosco and held one of Rebecca's tiny hands, holding her upright so that she could 'ride' the waves her 'Pa-pa' was creating.

The child had become an essential element of life and the completion of the family, as far as they were concerned.

Everyone accepted the child, everyone admired what they had achieved. Everyone was in love with Rebecca — except John Nathan, who realised in his own way that Rebecca was an intrusion. He was jealous of the attention lavished upon the child. He had been so used to being the entire focus of their attention, that he felt cheated by this pretty little bundle of humanity.

He watched the snowflakes fall and decided — well — he would show his Papa exactly what he was made of. He wasn't going to let this girl child steal his own childhood away!

Chapter 42
Daemon Enslaved Again

Daemon took some weeks to fully recover his strength and vitality, but it proved to be some of the most relaxed and carefree times he had experienced.

Ariadne was a fresh-faced, charming and determined young woman to whom the prospect of being left in England and coming through the various milestones of a society upbringing did not appeal. She simply would not contemplate being arranged into marriage with an old 'fuddy-duddy'.

Her father had insisted at first, put his foot down as only a loving father could do, but failed completely when his darling daughter showed her mettle.

She was determined that she would accompany her family on their great adventure into dangerous waters, and she would find out what destiny might have in store for her.

Now she threw herself into her role as *nurse* to the dashing young sea captain who had succumbed to a spell of 'sickness of the mind', and she determined to provide the cure, whatever it might take.

Quite early on, she had demonstrated to her father how capable she was, and in particular how clear and decisive she could be. She would care for Daemon Quirk until he was well enough to care for himself, and 'that was that!'

As the days turned to weeks and the voyage neared its end, a relationship had been formed. Daemon fell for his 'nurse', head over heels. Ariadne fell deeply in love with her patient.

There were no boundaries between them; mentally and intellectually, they were matched.

He, the more experienced by far, talked of things she could only have conjured up in her nightmares. She told him of her inner thoughts, of her hopes and dreams.

They kissed on his third 'outing': a walk around the deck under the warm semi-tropical breeze. She held his arm, supporting him as she had done several times, but found she tended to snuggle up to him rather than provide a prop.

Daemon leaned a little more heavily into her than his condition merited. They both played out the same game. Intimacy was sought and found in both.

When she admired the night sky, pointing out some star clusters, he leaned down and kissed her upturned face. It was a moment of sublime pleasure for both.

He had emerged from his comatose state to find this delightful creature flitting here and there about his cabin. She had held his head and eased fresh liquids into his mouth on a hundred occasions. The nearness of her presence intoxicated him to the point of a longing to press his lips to hers, in what seemed to him the only possible conclusion of their hour-by-hour encounters.

Now her upturned face was there, waiting, and ready. It filled his heart to an extent that he had hardly ever felt.

He drank in her aroma, she melded to his manliness, his recovering strength. They were matched once again.

Daemon suddenly felt ill at ease. He pulled away, determined not to cause offence, but he gently set her aside, almost demonstrating that he would not be able to offer up a defence for his actions.

Slightly taken off-guard, she accepted his gentle rebuff and took hold of his arm again in both hands, pressing herself into his side once again to continue their stroll.

Daemon began to feel a little uneasy; he knew what was in his own mind and bit his lip as his thoughts began to crystallise. She acknowledged a little edginess but excused it as merely normal for a man recovering from such affliction.

His coma had lasted four days and nights, and he 'lost' those days entirely without realising it. He responded to her ministrations, day by day, for a further week, until he had felt strong enough to rise. All this time she, to him a stranger, trusted her instinct that this was a man to whom she could dedicate herself. Now she excused his latency and decided upon even greater nurturing in the days to come. She would show him what she was made of.

In his mind, he had brought up a shield. There were deep reasons why he would not allow himself to follow the whirlwind of his emotions, and hers! He feared for her! His feverish meanderings returned to him. *Was* he the 'Jonah', the blight on the lives of those he loved, and those who loved him? He remembered Barka the carpenter aboard the *Warrior*. 'Lucky Daemon – or is it *Demon*...!'

He could not contemplate risking her well-being, her very life, by making her his own.

He became almost convinced he could pass on to her his 'curse' and that, instead, he must find a way to protect her.

He chided himself for being over-dramatic, for being sentimental and foolish. He derided his own reasoning and felt like kicking himself; but, no, this precious young woman was not going to become another victim. He would rather die himself than lure her towards a life of misfortune or death.

The following morning found him rising early. He stood at the prow of the *Durham*, looking into the distance and praying for sight of land.

Routledge joined him, startling him out of his melancholia.

'The journey will soon be over. I hope you have recovered enough for what lies ahead?'

'Er... yes. Thank you, sir. I believe I have recovered. I cannot find words... or indeed actions appropriate to thank your daughter sufficiently for her attentions.'

'I believe *I* can! For that matter, if you were to stretch your mind a little, I believe you also could find a suitable response. Or perhaps you should look to your heart.'

'Sir, I think I understand your meaning. However, I am surprised. Your daughter is a fine young lady, the... finest!' He found himself almost choking as the words formed. 'She will make a great match one day with someone who deserves her...'

'Daemon, I think you have to come to know my daughter. "Something of her character, at any rate. You must have seen how independent she is. How capable? She will not accept an "arrangement"; she will not follow procedure! She is intent on making a life for herself. She will not waste her life at her embroidery, surrounded by meaningless chatter. She wants a real life. She will choose her own partner. I believe she would choose you.'

Daemon shook his head, turning away. 'No. It cannot be!'

'Why, man? What is wrong with you? She has all a man could wish for; she...'

'No, sir, please! I have the greatest respect for your daughter, but... the fault is mine.'

'Do you have a wife and family already? Do you have a home to go to?'

'Nothing of the kind, sir, but I believe I would be doing Ariadne the greatest disservice by offering her marriage.'

'I must protest! I have seen you together. I have heard her singing to herself. I have never seen her happier. What is wrong?'

'I... I cannot explain. I have... matters to settle, so much to attend to. Yet, I have nothing! Not even this ship! I have no position. I have no possessions.'

'Captain, please do not insult me! My daughter comes with a substantial dowry. You shall have a living. A good living, unless you turn out to be a wasteful gambler! You will, I know it, find your way, and find a place to settle her restless soul. Please, let us not argue. Think about your situation. Think about Ariadne's needs. We will talk again on the morrow.'

He held out his hand and, although Daemon shook it, he believed himself immune to any acceptance. He remained in turmoil and realised his only course of action was to seem to abandon her. He knew in his heart it was the only way to save her.

The last few days of the voyage played out with cordiality and good manners masking any kind of indifference on his part. Ariadne was playfully overbearing, making sure he took his rest, feeding him good, solid food at proper meal times.

The seas were calm, but the breeze prevailed, allowing them to make excellent progress.

Charting a course with Routledge constantly at his side preoccupied their conversation each day, avoiding further in-depth discussion.

The coastline lay ahead, and they were able to identify coastal configurations and argued about this or that landmark, until satisfied that they had passed the Canary Islands and that Rabat was the next mainland port.

Daemon could hardly contemplate the idea of returning to the residence where he last saw Margaret and Standing's dear friends. His mind was in turmoil. So much had happened. In truth, only Ariadne's presence had made the entire voyage bearable.

He told her his story, how he came to meet Margaret, how John Standing saved them both, and how fortunes changed, for a time, at least.

Ariadne was understanding. She was in awe of his achievements. He merely derided himself. He leaned towards self-pity, and she determined that she would not let him wallow in it.

The more time he spent with her, the better he became both mentally and physically. She salvaged his self-belief and renewed his inner strength.

'What happened when you reached the West Indies? It sounds so exotic.'

'You would be amazed; it is very orderly and civilised. The islands have been cultivated; in Barbados hardly a square yard of land is left. The soil, the nourishment of the sun... makes everything grow big and strong. They cut down whatever grows and it provides something useful.'

'And what about the workers?'

'The slaves, you mean? Well, they seem to adapt... they work long hours every day, but you can hear them singing — or chanting and laughing a lot. They find everything amusing. When they are told about Jesus Christ, everything appears to make perfect sense to them. They grasp this... religious enthusiasm, almost excitement... They find their own ways to worship, even when there is no sign of a priest.'

'Do they long for their homeland?'

'It doesn't seem... well, most of them just settle down. I hear some others chanting, strange, almost sinister chanting. The kind, that if someone from England was doing it, they would be burned for witchcraft.' Daemon laughed, and Ariadne shook her head, amazed.

'There are some, a few, they may be the strongest, or be the tallest in a group, many of them are magnificent creatures, but they have the look of discontentment. They are often the ones at the heart of any trouble. The natural leaders, so to speak.

'They will catch your eye and hold the stare until one of you gives way. Then again, you may catch them looking into the distance, at the time of the setting sun. They seem to understand that they have come far from their own land, but that one day they will return.'

Daemon left it there. For the while, he peered into the distance and was lost in his own thoughts. Ariadne watched him for some moments, then leapt up and grabbed his hand. 'Come, we must talk to father. I want to ask him something...'

'Wait one moment, young lady... what are you planning? I must know you will not pull another idea out of the hat. Your ideas always seem to mean trouble for me.' He playfully held her back. 'Wait, tell me, before we get there.'

'No, I mustn't, it is a surprise! I will only tell you when we're all together.'

Daemon allowed her to lead but made sure she was aware of his resistance every step of the way.

'Father, there you are. I hope you are well this morning?'

'Well, dearest, my back aches, my head throbs, my mouth is permanently parched, and I feel as though my stomach is permanently empty! However, I am feeling surprisingly well.'

'Oh, Father... I have rarely seen you in better health.'

'That merely indicates to you the true extent of my ailments, that I can be so well when under such duress! Everything is relative, my dear.'

'Father, is it possible for a woman to become a priest? A minister?'

'Well... anything is possible in this world, except for a woman to become a priest! This is God's law, passed on with such vigour by the Holy Church in Rome. Priesthood is a man's domain. Indeed, according to doctrine, a woman is too impure to handle the body and blood of our Lord

Jesus Christ. But why do you ask, my dear? What preposterous notion have you come up with this time?'

'Father, don't chide me! I have a genuine feeling that I could do some good in this world. I would like to minister to the poor. Not just food — but the things they lack, the things they need — spiritual help, in understanding the "Word of the Lord".'

'Very noble, my dear! There are women of the cloth... nuns, of course; many do work with the poor and needy, others simply spend all their lives in solitude on their knees! I do not see you in either capacity.'

'No, Father, in truth neither do I. But I would like to find a way — perhaps I could teach them? I could become a teacher... is that not a woman's domain either?'

'It is quite common for a woman to become a governess and teach worldly things to children. As you know very well, Mistress Glendenning was very helpful to your Mama and I, in bringing you up, so to speak.'

'Well, that is how I see my life... I would be Mistress to children, not two, or even four, but hundreds!'

'Daemon, my boy, please help me here — please interject. Will you tell this child that there are far better things for a lady than to stand around in wooden huts, in the broiling heat, to wet-nurse a bunch of natives.'

'No, sir, I beg your pardon. I would not wish to deflect a person's dreams. I believe it a very noble cause and...'

'Nonsense, man! Marry the girl and have done with it! She can bear her own brood and whisper pearls of wisdom into their ears until her heart is content.'

At this suggestion, both began to show discomfort. 'Father, please, you will embarrass Captain Quirk!'

'No, sir, please don't. A woman should be allowed to find her own way. But excuse me, I would not wish to offend. I have things to do.'

Daemon left and set off for the poop deck, and although he had departed the scene, his presence was felt strongly and the exchanges between father and daughter continued for some time on a theme which had become familiar.

'Please, Father, do not push Daemon and me... do not push us together! It is unseemly!'

'Bah! Nonsense, girl. It is a father's duty to see his daughters well married, and I know he is right for you.'

'But, Father, please, he has... his past, you must try to understand. He has had... such tribulations. I do not know whether he will allow himself to think of a wife... or a family.'

'My dear daughter, please speak with your Mother. Please consider my advice. It is for your own good. You need a man in this world. I will not be here forever. I would not be doing my duty if I did not consider your future. As you know, I did not want you to leave the security of England.'

Chapter 43
A Sad Return

In port at Rabat, an opportunity to take on some fresh fruit and a couple of barrels of water was welcomed, whilst the real purpose of the short diversion was for Daemon to visit the resting place of his friends.

In a brief excursion, he was accompanied by two of the crew, to a now-neglected manor house. Vines had begun to climb the walls unabated and the ground had dried up, leaving stalks and rangy, dry grasses where there was once a lawn.

Towards the far wall of the enclosure, a dozen wooden crosses stood, mostly at awry angles. A small ceramic plate was affixed to the centre of each. Among the names vividly clear in blue script, hardened into the glazed, clay ovals, 'Lady Margaret Standing' stood out clearly.

Daemon retched and an audible sob echoed around the flaking plastered walls.

He sank to his knees and held his head for a long moment. Only the loud buzzing of flies and the distraction of a seething mass of red ants brought him to his senses. His mind had followed those ants where they disappeared into the ground. Down endless tunnels, weaving a pattern to where the body of a once fair young lady now lay, decaying and merging into the dry earth around her.

He pictured the red ants weaving in and out of her bones. He imagined her flesh being systematically sucked away from them and transported closer to the surface; he imagined himself kneeling on part of what had been a vibrant human being, now turned to dry, lifeless dust.

He thought of her in spirit. Rising into a bright sky, blue, with fluffy white clouds hovering in the near distance. He saw Margaret, sitting as if side-saddle, on a low stool; he saw Lady Daphne, John Standing. They sat around in a group like Grecian gods on Mount Olympus.

He resolved in his own mind that they were not alone. They had found each other, and they had found contentment, away from the harsh troubles of this bitter, bitter world.

The buzzing increased. He looked down to see a large black insect with two fangs sinking into his forearm. He swept it away and rose to his feet, wiping away perspiration. Before replacing his hat, he turned and strode away.

Under sail again, Daemon stood at the rail for more than an hour, before she approached him.

'I know you must be going through torment. If... if I can help in any way, please...' She put out an arm and rested her hand on his shoulder, which was taut, his hand gripping the rigging so firmly.

He looked down into her face. Her eyes, dark though they were, sparkled as if reflecting a star from overhead, where a clear night sky showed a million more against the black, velvet, heavens above.

'May I help?'

Daemon smiled, perhaps more of a grimace. 'If anyone in this world could help me feel better about things, I think it would be you, Ariadne. You are a wonderful person. You have already helped me, more than you know.'

'Then let me do so again. Please do not think of my father's words. They... well, let me just say, he means well. He does not understand; there is more to life than simply finding someone to... to simply lay your life at someone's doorstep.'

'Why, you are so perceptive. You are so right. For someone of your age, you understand things far better than many I have known. You are a girl who would make any man proud. Make any man strive to achieve...'

'Wait... I don't want to be that person... I think you misunderstand. I do want to do something with my life, but that does not seem important to me right now. I have time, lots of time. I am only just beginning my journey. *Yours* is more important right now. I feel I must put myself in a box until you are well again.'

'But I am well. I have fully recovered, I promise you.'

'I think you have, physically, returned to your best, but there is more. I think you have not recovered in here...' She held a hand to his heart.

Daemon clasped hers in his own hand and held it to his chest. 'I said it already. You are the one person I would allow, but I fear that I should not let you into my world.'

Ariadne withdrew her hand. 'I don't understand. You do not want me to help you? You would not wish to receive the comfort... that I am offering?'

'Please do not be hurt. I am mending myself, bit by bit. You are here. That is enough for now.' His hand brushed her cheek and pushed a wisp of hair back behind her ear.

Reaching up, she pulled herself to his height and held her lips firmly to his. He attempted to pull away for a moment, but her will overcame his resistance and her probing, anxious kiss drew him closer and closer to her.

For a long moment they held each other, kissing feverishly, until Daemon suddenly pulled up and held her at a distance.

She looked at him, puzzled and breathless. He muttered almost to himself, 'I just... wanted... to look at you... I...'

He stepped away and turned to the rail.

The bow of the *Durham* plunged deep into the blackness and the ship hesitated, before coming up and riding the next wave. Onward, onward she plunged, the surf hissing as it swept past the bow and sizzled before dispersing.

His hand held on to the rigging tightly.

'There may be a little weather tonight. The swell is growing.'

'Oh, Daemon, I don't care if there is a hurricane! I can hold on to you.' Her arms wrapped around him and he felt her head nestling into his back.

He wanted to turn and put distance between them, but his courage failed him as he allowed her to remain there, hugging him for a long moment.

'Ariadne. What does your father think of me?'

'Why don't you ask him? If you are truthful and genuine, I believe he would grant anything you wished for.'

Almost two days passed before any conversation was possible. The 'weather' arrived as the ship leaned into the wind, as relentless rain slanted in like spears.

Chapter 44
The Fortress

All hands were needed to stabilise the vessel and keep her from being consumed by the heavy seas. Daemon next found Ariadne in the corner of her cabin, sitting, knees up to her chest and head deeply cowering under a shawl.

'I think the worst is over,' he called out over the thunder of the crashing waves. She managed to raise her head from the folds of the woollen garment.

'I pray to God you are right! I have never been so afraid.'

'What? A girl of your courage...! I am surprised you are not aloft, rigging the loose sail. I could use an extra pair of hands.'

'Please, dearest, don't mock me. I would be Daniel in the lion's den before I would face another hour of this... terror!'

Daemon found himself staggering towards her bunk and trying vainly to remain on his feet. He crashed into her and they sprawled beside each other on the soft straw mattress. He held her tightly as the ship bucked in the other direction.

Then he found her holding onto him to prevent him slipping out of her grasp onto the deck.

They began to laugh at their incongruity as the seas gave them a strong buffeting.

Holding her felt so good to Daemon, so he exaggerated every movement. He clung on to her when the sway threatened to part them, he pressed her hard when it threw them together.

Now his lips found hers and again they could not be separated.

The longing he could sense in her profoundly moved him and his own passions would not be denied. They pulled at one another's clothing and found each other. They rose and fell with the rhythm of the seas and her passionate pleadings could only just be covered by the noise of the storm above them.

By the time their own passions were subsiding, the seas were becoming calmer and much quieter. They could talk, intimately and gently, to one another. He told her of his feelings for her. That he had loved her almost since the beginning, when he awoke to find her ministering the life-preserving potions and liquids which brought him through the fever.

She told him of her undying devotion, of her utter commitment. She would be by his side 'forever!'.

A long day followed in bright, fresh conditions, where a south-westerly wind drove them ferociously onward. They regained sight of land, which had disappeared among heavy cloud and the storm it brought. Now they could re-establish their bearings and predict the time of reaching their destination.

Only a day, maybe two, were left in the close, intimate proximity into which fate had thrown them.

Another 'accidental' encounter had turned into the deepest and most passionate afternoon Daemon had ever enjoyed. How they were not discovered was something of a miracle, but they rolled in each other's arms and stifled the audible sounds of delight they both experienced for a sustained period.

When they returned to the galley, joining the family for the evening meal with the seven other passengers and two senior crew, they both told an undeniable story through messages given out by the sheer colour of their faces and awkwardness of their demeanour! No one present could be in any doubt that here were two lovers each of who revelled in the physical presence of the other.

Routledge assumed a gruff displeasure over the proceedings, as though to admonish the two young lovers for... well, simply being in that state, although the 'state' itself remained unmentioned, and unmentionable.

'I hope you have been more comfortable this afternoon? I know the past few days have been something of a trial for you, sir,' Daemon ventured.

'So much for your enquiry, sir. You are damned right if you think I have suffered discomfort! I have indeed, sir! I have never been less comfortable in my living memory! If that is what passes for "seamanship" these days, then God help us all!'

'Sir, I do hope you appreciate that in such a storm there is...' Daemon felt a sharp knock against his ankle and immediately appreciated that Ariadne was trying to convey a message.

Catching her eye, he knew exactly what that message conveyed.

'Er, my apologies, sir. I appreciate your views. I only hope, as I say, that you are more at ease today.'

'At ease? I am damned if I am...!'

'Father, please, must you curse so frequently?'

'Excuse me, young lady... I will damned-well curse as much as I see fit. I do not appreciate your inference that a man may only curse when he is in prayer!'

'Father, you know well my meaning. I merely expressed that the other people around the table may not wish to share your expressions at such regular intervals.'

'Well, well, it is a fine thing to be admonished by one's own daughter when one's own daughter may, in fact, be due a good deal of admonishment herself!'

Daemon felt obliged to interfere. 'Sir, I beg you. Should there be any need for admonishment, then please choose myself upon whom you may pour forth at your will. I am entirely responsible for your daughter's behaviour, and I would ask that you re-direct your displeasure towards me.'

'Well, sir, I will! In fact, I may decide upon a course of action, most reluctantly, which both of us might regret.'

Those gathered for the evening meal at this point collectively took a deep breath. Some great indiscretion had taken place, which involved the Captain and Mr Routledge's daughter, and they were all agog that the indiscretion may soon be the cause of an accusation and a challenge.

'Sir, I would only say this: my love and deep devotion to your daughter cannot be denied. I would ask you to consider myself as a suitable prospect for your daughter's hand.'

'Well, that, sir, is an entirely different kettle of fish! I am completely at ease. For a brief moment I thought that perhaps you were about to take advantage of my daughter's kindness in nursing you back to health, but I now realise that my pistol has completely misfired, and that your intentions are honest. I offer my apology.

'As for your request... I accept you as a suitor and I encourage my daughter to consider your proposal. I never liked her idea of becoming a nun!'

The gathering appeared most relieved at the turn of events and expressed their satisfaction with a spontaneous round of applause.

For the next few days, as they prepared for landing, Daemon watched Ariadne as she went about her duties with efficiency and determination in the care and consideration for her father and the completion of her every task, undertaken with a smile upon her face.

She conducted herself with assurance and dedication. Daemon was filled with admiration for her.

She demonstrated her self-confidence, her delight in the simple things and simple tasks to which she applied herself. Nothing was just 'gathered-up'.

She was orderly, she arranged everything to perfection. She tied beautiful knots in string. She pulled garments together with precision. Daemon had never observed the activities of a woman at such close quarters, and he found her every movement a source of pleasure.

She never pushed her hair back indiscriminately. Seemingly without any effort, it always fell into place to perfection. She would arrange it behind her head in a high top-knot when the climate became sticky, and her top-knot always sat perfectly upon her head.

Her neck was always displayed long and elegant. Even her eyebrows sat so comfortably on her face. There was never a single expression or a 'look' on that face, which was not the most perfect and profoundly appealing that he had ever encountered.

Daemon was in love. He enjoyed the reality of this condition for almost forty-eight hours.

It was then, as the furniture was being unloaded, and the personal belongings were being manhandled, as the travellers were saying their final *au revoirs* with the crew that something changed.

Daemon felt it in the pit of his stomach first. Then he became distracted and lost concentration. The preparations were so well planned and orchestrated that the change in him went unnoticed, everything proceeding so well and all objectives achieved.

Then he came to realise what was at the heart of the change. He began to fear the future. He began to fear for Ariadne! He realised his trauma had returned. He became terrified for her.

He truly believed her destiny would take a fatal turn for the worse if she became part of his life! He came to believe the last thing in the world he would attempt was to become permanently attached to that most wondrous young lady. He would rather throw himself overboard than risk placing her in such danger.

His firm belief returned that he, Daemon, *was* the 'Jonah' — the threat to everyone to whom he had ever become endeared. He believed he would bring down upon her an awful fate. He could not do that! He *would* not do that!

Something must be done. He had to give her back her *future*.

Chapter 45
Kirsten's Dilemma

Carstein doted on his new daughter. Born in October 1753, Helena was his first child to Lady Annabelle Ranleigh, and, had careful attention to detail been established, the two hundred and seventh in line to the British throne through the house of Hapsburg.

The 'royal' families of New York grew ever closer as their wealth and interaction brought them together.

Kirsten and Banoldino now had their own daughter to raise, alongside the ever-demanding John Nathan, now nine years old.

The two young ladies Rebecca and Helena would grow together, become firm friends, inseparable and devoted. For the time being, however, they were sat opposite one another in a play-pen, passing dollies and rattles from one to the other at the encouragement of their respective nurses.

Their parents sat around a long bench, under parasols, as cool drinks were passed to them by the servants.

The table was bedecked with an arrangement of flowers framing place-settings for a form of outdoor dining which the endless sunshine demanded.

The ladies wore white and pink loose-fitting dresses which were influenced by Parisienne fashion and hung just above the shoulder-line, revealing plenty of bosom.

Having recently given birth, Lady Annabelle's bosom was proudly presented and could not quite be matched by Kirsten, who was not in the bloom of motherhood. Nonetheless, Rebecca sat as comfortably in the family as if she had indeed been the natural child of the Don Boscos. Both Carstein and Ranleigh thought the situation could not have worked out better.

Only Banoldino had misgivings. He knew the effect upon his son had been profound.

He had become moody and disconnected, shunning attention and avoiding outings. He had withdrawn since the arrival of baby Rebecca.

Carstein became a supporting influence, providing every opportunity for John Nathan to ride his string of horses and to indulge in fencing and pistol shooting. Another had equally as profound an influence on Kirsten's boy, her long-time lover, George Smith. A frequent visitor and firm friend of the family, Major George Smith also played a significant part in shaping the young Don Bosco.

Despite his tender years, he was becoming a formidable exponent of military practices, and was destined for the Army. The age of qualification could not come soon enough for young John Nathan. All about him, the rumours of unrest were openly spoken of at every social and formal gathering.

The British were constantly at odds with France, the Northern Territories the battleground, and a constant flow of ordnance and supplies had been arriving along the docks of New Jersey.

Soldiers were billeted in the garrison at Albany, in readiness to support the Northern armies against the French, but most significantly in readiness to impose the rule of British law over the American colonies. The cost of policing the colonies had to be borne, and imposing taxes on tea, sugar and coffee were obvious and easy targets.

The New Englanders were incensed; suffering poor crops and uncertain futures, they looked for leniency from their British overlords, but found none forthcoming.

Meetings were held in secret at first, then in open opposition. Some areas, in particular Boston, a community which often resisted Parliamentary law, complained more vehemently than other more liberal areas.

There were signs of dissidence in the colonies and the British were prepared to master those protests and continue to increase their domination over the civilised world.

Kirsten dreaded the thought of John Nathan following a military career. Hadn't her own husband been cut down in his prime, leaving their relationship in tatters?

Kirsten lay awake long hours consumed by regret and remorse. The close affection of her husband was snatched from her, and an older, damaged hero returned. Their longing for each other died with his inability to respond to her. He loved and cherished every bone in her body, but he showed it less and less. His attentions had diminished to a loving caress, a calming hand, the brush against her cheek of a coarse knuckle.

As much as he had tried to show her passion, eagerness, the more he demonstrably failed. They became as 'father and daughter'.

He admired her, lovingly, from a distance.

He indulged her every whim, and felt proud for her when she excelled, or achieved or was complimented, as she always was, by another male. He loved her dearly, but he knew their relationship was changed forever.

For Kirsten, her fear for her son went deep. It cut her like a knife when she was alone in her bed. She had tried to reason things out with George. When laying, after a breathless encounter upon his heaving chest, she would suddenly question him about life 'on the march', or of life digging-in defences. She was eager to know what may befall her son.

Smith indulged her; he told her calmly about life in the military. About the preparation, the endless waiting, the brief flashes of activity, followed by more waiting. He told her the unglamorous side of things. Then he told her of the joy of victory and the euphoria of survival.

Nothing satisfied her need for comfort. Would he always be there for John Nathan? Would he be close enough during the campaign to see to his needs? Would they be in the same theatre of battle?

Smith told her what she wanted, what she needed to hear. He told her lies.

She would never be prepared for her son's departure; no matter how futuristic the reality might be, she lived with the inevitability as though it was in the moment.

She held George close, one evening towards the winter solstice, when the house was quiet, awaiting a full day of preparation before the arranged gathering brought the usual forty or so guests to the household. Banoldino was in town and John Nathan out, riding with the hostler's son.

Smith had been away for three weeks at Albany, fortifying the inner defences and creating a new range of gun-ports along the redoubt.

He had arrived just after night-fall, eased his way into her room and quickly washed the dust from his tired upper body. He stood in the room with a towel clinging to his waist, his lank hair dripping droplets of water on to his shoulders.

She quickly slipped out of her dress and, free of the under-layers, in just pantaloons and a lace-trimmed bodice, she wrapped herself around him. It was a deep and lasting embrace which had them both hungrily pressing each other, caressing and needing.

They were almost intimate, before moving towards the bed. Everything was tossed aside with indecent haste and the ferocity of their love-making found them writhing from one side of the bed and over the edge at the other.

It was a panting, sweating affair, leaving them both in a trance of exhilaration and wonder for many moments after.

When the throbbing in her temple eventually subsided, Kirsten reached up and grasped a tall fluted glass, filled it with amber liquid, and swallowed a long hard draught of fortified wine. She teased George first, before allowing him to finish off the remainder. As he satiated himself, she eased herself up onto her dishevelled bedding and found a corner of the quilt to cover her torso.

Smith remained beside the bed, on the floor, with just his head resting upon her arm. He was content to remain just in touching distance whilst they recovered sufficiently for conversation.

'George, I have been worried lately that we have tempted the fates too much.'

'In what way? I would tempt the devil himself if it meant one more night with you.'

'No, I'm serious, George! We have indulged ourselves long... too long... I am afraid it will all come to an end.'

'You mean... between us? Parting?'

'No! I mean... being found out. Letting them... know how we betrayed them. I could hardly bare to hurt Allie — let alone my own husband... and my son.'

'But how, how will we ever be found out? How could we ever be caught?'

'One wrong word, one hasty, thoughtless action, one tiny moment of forgetfulness. It is a miracle it has gone on so long. Has no one suspected? Or are we under an illusion? An illusion of security? Maybe we have already been exposed.'

'Darling, what has changed? What has made you so fearful? Things could not be more suited to our... needs. It is almost as if we have been granted a window in which to enjoy this freedom, before we move indoors again, inside the windows and doors around our ordinary lives.'

'There is something else. I have a child, a little *girl* now. She is as much mine as if I had carried her nine months, and I intend to make her life wonderful.'

'And so it will be! She will be the most privileged, the most indulged child in the Americas! She will want for nothing the rest of her life.'

'But she needs love. More than anything, I owe her love. I owe her my time. I fear that if we were exposed, it would ruin her chances... It might ruin everything.'

Kirsten held her hand to her eyes, a sob escaping from her taut lips. George reached for her. 'Please, George, allow me, for a moment... I need to think. I am afraid I will mess it all up. You can't imagine how far we have come. You can't imagine where it all began. I would not want any child to experience such horrors, such hardships. I could have never taken responsibility for Rebecca, had I for one minute imagined not being able to provide for her.'

'Such fears are unfounded!'

'Oh, you think? Such indulgence as we have enjoyed cannot last forever. You know what I believe... "live by the sword, die by the sword". I remember little from my days attending the village church, but this one phrase haunts me. I do believe it, George. No one escapes wrong-doing forever. Our Lord will judge in the end.'

'And what would he judge? That two people who love each other, spend some time together to hold and to cherish? Is it so wrong?'

'The only way you, or I, will ever know how wrong it is, is if we are found out! I do not want that, ever! So, help me... never!'

'Darling, I must dress and be gone. I have duties. As you so rightly point out! I will return to my family and make sure their needs are truly nourished.'

'Even Allie? What of her needs? George, it is a subject I have avoided so much that it never troubled me for a long time. But what of Allie's needs? Have we not just deprived her? Have we not just cheated her? I am fearful for John Nathan. What we do is wrong! I don't want to... contaminate my beautiful child's future in the same way.'

'You think I am some form of contamination? A disease? Or a parasite?' He grabbed her bare shoulder. 'Kirsten, is this how you think of me when I slither away, along the corridor, and out into the night, before I knock on the front door, like some ill wind, contaminating your perfect life?'

'Please, George, do not make matters worse than they are. I already feel something has changed. It may never be the same, just bringing these feelings to the surface. Please, leave me now. We will meet next week when I come into town. I have work to do on Friday and Saturday. Will you be there? Can you manage to meet me? I think we need to talk, but not here. Not now.'

Smith had almost reached the door, but he turned now and lunged for her, holding her to his chest, her warmth piercing the buckskin jacket he had just pulled into place.

'Kirsten, darling, please let us not leave like this. I can't bear to go on if we can't have each other.'

'Please, John, you must! Let me go!' She wrenched free from his arms, her hair swept from side to side as she attempted to right herself as she struggled free.

She looked up into his eyes. The hurt was visible in the intensity of his gaze, his eyes glazing over. Her own, angry, flashing like a tigress. She wanted him gone now. Her lips drew together as she swallowed, about to burst forth her anger.

Smith turned on his heels and left the room, the door swinging shut behind him.

Banoldino Don Bosco conducted the meeting in time-honoured fashion.

He allowed the gathering to relax, provided coffee, passed around cigars.

Just when the atmosphere filled with conviviality, he brought them to attention.

'Gentlemen, we are gathered here today because I have great concerns about the future, and because I feel there is great change coming.'

There was a short burst of coughing, a murmur or two, and two of the attendees shifted their chairs. Complete silence ensued.

Among the gathering were Carstein, Ranleigh, Fitzroy, George Bertrand, General Dean Gardiner, Paul Spiers, Jans Johannson, Peter van der Mere, Patrick McConnaghie, Dr Silas Devereaux, Nathan Goldstein, Fr Kevin Mulcaghie, Ronin Dietrich, Sir Peter Campbell and Eli Rabinovski.

The leading lights of New York State, a gathering of the wealthiest and most prominent men on the continent of North America. Brought together upon the solicitations of Don Bosco and Lord Ranleigh to discuss the political future of the colony.

Kirsten walked the perimeter of the garden with Rebecca, watching as the little girl stooped to pick up flowers. In her heart she knew her relationship with George Smith was at an end. She was sure it was the only way.

He had shown himself to be an honourable man and she believed he would, like herself, sacrifice what they had for the sake of others. She knew he would never betray her. The completeness, the finality of the break was, therefore, justified.

She allowed a tear to drop from her eyelid onto her cheek.

It was over. All that mattered now was this little darling girl on one hand and her tempestuous, over-ambitious son on the other. She would have to learn to manage both.

Chapter 46
The Perilous Outpost

The Hon James Routledge entered the fortress aboard a chaise, drawn by two strong, Arabian mares. The entourage filed in behind, in a series of carts, with four camels and natives with bundles balanced on their heads.

Through the dust, the fourteen red-coated soldiers marched gamely along, sweating profusely beneath their tall pointed headgear, dust and grime sullying their whitened straps and their formerly sharply white collars and cuffs.

The caravan dispersed upon commands and gathered in clusters where fresh water and shade could be found.

The searing heat oppressed the entire procession so much that the outgoing Governor, Sir Robert McGilvrait, sent his aide to greet Sir James, which was indicative of the depths to which the old regime had slumped. Farthinghoe, possibly a decent adjutant in his prime, appeared tarnished and unwholesome in appearance and his skin pale, as sweat glistened between the grubby folds of his tattered collar.

He bowed formally to Sir James and extended a limp-wristed hand, which Sir James duly ignored. 'Arthur Farthinghoe at your service, sir! Sir Robert has asked me to convey his warmest greetings to yourself and your family. Er, please, sir, if you would allow me...'

Sir James did not move, leaving Farthinghoe in his 'After you' position for some moments.

'As Sir Robert has not taken the trouble to extend his welcome in person,' blurted Routledge, 'we shall dispense with formalities.'

A second carriage arrived, with Daemon in attendance on horse-back. Jumping down, he leaned into the carriage to assure himself of the readiness of the three ladies within.

The ladies busied themselves in straightening their attire and readying their parasols. When quite satisfied that all was well, Daemon opened the door, allowing the footman to roll out the steps and guide the ladies on to the stony, sanded ground.

Making as if to present the ladies, Daemon fell in next to Routledge.

'There will be no formalities, Captain. Please, Mr... er, Farthinway, would you conduct my ladies to their quarters?' The four servants joined them in time to follow the gathering. 'Captain, would you accompany me to Sir Robert's quarters?'

Sir James followed his instincts to make his way into the inner courtyard and through the main doors. Crossing the mosaic flooring and pushing through a large carved and highly polished door, he caught Sir Robert in a slightly compromising position, lavishing attention upon a young black female.

'Sir? Er, Sir James, I presume? Er, please allow me a moment. I was not prepared...! It was my intention that you join me for supper after resting your travel-weary bones. Alas, here you are...' The bewigged gentleman, in very casual attire, raised his head.

Routledge crossed the floor in a few strides, with Daemon in close attendance.

McGilvrait half rose from his lavishly cushioned chaise-longue and playfully slapped the rump of the scantily clad maid, shooing her along. Her tiny bare feet padded rapidly on contact with the marble floor as she hastened towards the rear and disappeared behind a decorous screen. She slipped through the archway, beyond which marked the exit into the garden.

'Please, Sir James, and er...? Would you care for a glass of Madeira?'

'I will decline, for the moment, sir. Out of respect for my companion, Captain Quirk, I will refrain from expressing my disappointment at the lack of propriety in our greeting, sir. I would ask you to advise me of your intentions in completing your departure from the colony and relinquishing authority to myself.'

'All in good time, sir... Please rest awhile. Captain Quirk... a glass... I implore you.' Daemon raised a hand, declining the offer without speaking.

'Sir Robert,' Routledge continued, 'I am not a very patient man. I have made a long and arduous journey and you are right in one respect, that I would prefer to be in repose than to be standing here at your pleasure. I find the arrangements here far from my liking. I had heard of your sloppy regime, but I imagined this to be only in the way you treated the natives. I hardly expected you to be running this Colonial outpost like a Moroccan bordello!'

Sir James began to pace the floor, attempting to contain his anger.

'Oh, dear me, we are in a state, aren't we, sir? I have inhabited this fly-festooned backwater for the better part of six years. I am heartily sick of the very air that one is supposed to breathe. I care not for propriety, sir! I care less for your wish to be pampered and cossetted or for your opinions! I will leave here in a few days and my only prevailing memory of the place will be the look of distraction I currently witness upon your face, whilst enjoying first sight of this, our cherished 'possession'.

'Now, if you will excuse me, I have a little unfinished business to attend before supper.'

He made to turn away in the direction of the garden when the sound of Sir James' sword scraping the insides of its sheath stopped him in his tracks.

Daemon stepped forward and grabbed the arm of his friend, holding him in a position where the sword stopped half in and half out of its sheath. 'Sir James, no...!'

Addressing McGilvrait, Routledge spat with an element of venom, 'Why, if I had any regard for you, I would call you out and make a carcase of you by morning! However, I do believe you are even less worthy than that! I should just run you through and have done with you and your disgraceful regime!'

Sir Robert, realising that his adversary was duly restrained, half-turned and said over his shoulder, 'Sir James, when you have spent half a dozen years in this hell-hole, you will not think me such a disgrace. You will come to learn very quickly that civilisation can be torn from a man's behaviour as a festering limb might be severed.

'You will witness the inhumanity of this "regime", as you poetically refer to it. There is no worse blight on humanity than slavery, and here you will become the perpetrator of this foul and evil practice! You become lord and master of all that is vile in human behaviour, and, I say — good luck to you!'

McGilvrait padded away, glass in hand, in search of his chosen form of redemption, or, perhaps something to ease his pain. Daemon watched until he was out of sight before releasing Routledge.

'Captain, I am ashamed of my class! This is no gentleman, yet I thank you for preventing me making a fool of myself. It would solve nothing, and I would have had blood on my hands.'

'Not at all, sir. I would run him through myself rather than see you having to answer for your actions. I do believe you will be rid of him very soon! From his utterings just now, I think nothing would detain him from a swift departure. Will you attend supper this evening? It would appear he will at least make an effort at some hospitality.'

'I am very reluctant to expose my wife and her mother, let alone my daughter to this viper's company.'

'I would not be too concerned, Sir James. Your ladies have the breeding to withstand the hardships and tribulations of a difficult voyage, and the barely tolerable conditions here. I am sure they will not find an encounter with our errant gentleman too much to bear!'

'I thank you for your support, and I would only ask that you attend the occasion yourself and be on hand to remove the ladies at the earliest sign of offence.'

'I will, sir; you have my word that I would not wish them to endure a moment of vulgarity or ill-mannered behaviour. However, you may need to put up with Sir Robert a little longer than you would wish, in order to draw out everything you need to know. I fear he will have left little in order or accountability that you might rely upon.'

'I do agree, except that I have some hope that this 'Farthingham' may prove to be a bookish sort and that he may have kept records and accounts.'

'Indeed, you may be right. I think it may be worth cultivating that gentleman in the hope of some co-operation in return, if you catch my drift.'

'Yes, I think you make a good point. Come, let us find the ladies and establish the condition of the living quarters.'

The two strode off into the interior buildings, seeking some assurance that at least the ladies were settling in to the accommodation.

The salon where they had discovered Sir Robert was by far the better of the rooms in terms of airiness and cleanliness. Much of the property had been given over to accommodation for the garrison, and the remaining rooms were plain and scantily furnished. Drapes like Persian rugs hung from rails above the windows, but there was no glass in the frames, nor shutters to be pulled over at night.

Fireplaces displayed charred wood and evidence of recent use, indicating that the evenings would be cold.

Pursuing a cacophony of noise, they soon discovered the ladies engaged in a flurry of activity attempting to use what they had brought from Liverpool to make the accommodation liveable.

Daemon joined in, lending a hand to move furniture and hang drapes. Working with Ariadne, they applied themselves with gusto, along with Mama and Grandmama, the servants and two attendants brought from the ship. All were swept along by their enthusiasm.

Candles were lit towards the end of the afternoon and they were all ready for rest as darkness fell.

Outside, there was also a flurry of activity as the new arrivals bedded-in to the garrison. Some of the old guard were relieved to be returning to the British Isles, and much ribaldry was stirred by the opposing factions, light-hearted at first, but breaking out into skirmishes as ale was consumed and the cooking fires were abandoned.

Loud voices were heard echoing around the fort well into the night. The customary chanting broke out among the Muslims and the familiar sounds of chirping insects mingled with the wailing of whipped dogs.

Strong smells of rotten fruit and spicy food emanated throughout, and then Daemon detected the haunting hum of distressed voices in the distance: the slave compounds which would be the object of their attentions come morning.

Daemon sat staring into the dying embers in the grate, poking with a cane among the ashes. Ariadne slipped down beside him and, blind-side to her father, who dozed in his chair, she rested her head against his upper arm.

Daemon's head turned to look down on her as her eyes closed, and her breathing suggested she might sleep, even in this position.

She knew his attention was upon her, even through closed eyes. 'What is it, my darling? I know you have been troubled these last few days. Now you are very quiet...' Her eyes flicked open, so she could look into his.

He quickly turned back towards the fire and began poking more earnestly.

'Nothing, love... there is n-nothing...'

'You don't convince me with your words, nor your demeanour! I wish I could read your thoughts at this moment. Won't you confide in me? Won't you tell me of your plans... for... us? For the future, I mean?'

'I have much to consider, my love. Much that I can tell you and much that I can't! I hope you understand.'

Just then, Sir James snored deeply and drew their attention.

The two ladies arrived having made their way to one of the chambers, where cushions had provided a place which at least looked luxuriously comfortable and seemed to draw them to the conclusion of a long and tiring day.

Sir James now stirred again, almost certainly awakened by his own deep-throated snoring.

'Dear me, bless my soul! What a to do!'

'Father, are you quite well?'

'I am, my dear. Quite well! I have seen one or two demons in my sleep, don't you know! Quite took my breath, they did. Quite!'

'Well, I am sure you would appreciate a goblet of wine to help rouse you. I wonder that our host has not provided supper...'

Just at that moment, a lavishly attired, heavily bearded Arab swept in through the archway and bowed deeply, with hands spread theatrically to each side.

'Your servant, sir! Ladies! Sir Robert would appreciate your company at supper; he awaits you in the long hall. If you please...'

Routledge rose and turned to the messenger. 'Sir, may I know to whom I am speaking?'

Daemon and Ariadne also rose and began straightening their clothing, Daemon buttoning his waistcoat as he came upright.

'Sir, I am your servant — at least, I am at your service. I am Pacha Al Damas. I have certain connections, shall we say, with the arrangement of shipments from the port. I have had the great pleasure of intimacy with Sir Robert of some four years and would claim to be more than an acquaintance; let me say a friend.'

'I am grateful for your explanation, sir. I would wonder that you have taken the task upon yourself to bring us to supper, when surely a servant could have adequately performed the task.'

'Allow me, this is not a task for myself, it is a pleasure, I was most anxious to make the acquaintance of yourself and your family. Please consider that we may also become friends!'

Routledge responded, 'I hope we shall! After you, Al Damas! Daemon, would you bring the ladies?'

Entering the hall, Daemon found the three sitting at the head of a long table. Lavish arrangements sat invitingly along the centre. Fine goblets, platters of very high quality, glass-ware with gilt edges shone back a reflection of the candles glowing in the chandelier.

McGilvrait had dressed elaborately in princely Arab clothing, while a silken, bejewelled turban sat impressively on his head.

He waved a hand towards the vacant chairs, allowing Daemon to usher the ladies into position.

Mama and Grandmama sat facing one another next to Al Damas and Routledge, with Ariadne and Daemon taking the next places.

Wine was poured for each of the new arrivals and a toast to their health was raised by McGilvrait. His manner and his entire humour were of an entirely different quality to that of the earlier encounter.

He was charm personified as he addressed the ladies, weaving a silken spell over the proceedings with eloquent dialogue. This was a man so different to that which they had encountered earlier that they jointly considered whether McGilvrait may have a twin brother of far higher breeding.

However, he chose to allow their incredulity to abound whilst he led the proceedings to his own satisfaction.

The food laid before them was both exotic and delicious and had them in raptures. Wine of the finest quality and the atmosphere were supported by a gentle Middle Eastern pipe ensemble which enhanced the sense of occasion, providing intricate renderings.

'Sir James, you will forgive my disposition of earlier in the day. I was, shall we say, attempting to lift my melancholia with some distracting company. It is an indulgence I normally would have deferred had I not been suddenly aware that my departure was an imminent reality, and no longer a fanciful possibility.

'I have, shall we say, become accustomed to a certain liberation whilst in this posting. I found it extremely demanding at first, and I was unable to deal with the conditions.

'Many months passed before I was able to come to terms with my situation. I had no support, nobody 'close' , unlike yourself, Sir James, with your charming family.'

Routledge interrupted, 'I am sorry to hear you have had to deal with such inhospitable conditions alone. I can understand very well the harshness and loneliness of a posting which takes away all good society; after all, I was at sea myself for many years! Perhaps there were some similarities.'

'In part, Sir James, in other ways, not! I found myself despising every moment of my existence. Hot, fetid, uncomfortable, plagued by vermin...! Ladies, forgive me! May I say, the conditions have been improved! We have made changes. It may not be too evident that there are ways of dealing with the harshness of these sweltering conditions which you will come to appreciate!

'Free-flowing air, instead of enclosed rooms, living much as the Arabs themselves do. Long flowing gowns, avoiding tight-fitting costumes and, forgive me, undergarments!

'Bathing frequently — lounging for long spells in cooling, scented water — let me assure you, these are the ways of the Middle Eastern hierarchy which we Europeans must embrace, rather than shun! I myself had to learn their ways. Please allow me to lead you quickly through the stages of acclimatisation more rapidly than you would have expected. Learn from my mistakes, if you will!

'Live as they do or *perish*! That is the direction I leave for you to follow.'

Daemon was next to express his appreciation for the knowledge and the manner in which it was given, but he was intent on bringing the conversation down to earth. 'May we perhaps learn a little of the day-to-day life at the Fort, Sir Robert? Why do we hear of such... unrest?'

'Ah, my young friend, I see you are anxious to make an impact on our little world. You are a man of action, I can see that...! Would you not wish to defer our discourse until the morrow? I assure you there will be plenty of which you will wish you had never heard.'

'My apologies, Sir Robert. I thought you may wish to just describe the current climate in which Sir James may have to become so instantly familiar. I did not wish to spoil the evening. I do believe we would all like to discover the true nature of this unique place.'

'All in good time, sir! Slavery is an unwholesome business, let me assure you.'

Sir James interjected. 'Why, Sir Robert, my friend has conducted a full contingent of slaves to the West Indies. I assure you he is no stranger to the ways of the world. *Your* world!'

'A slaver? Well, I am surprised, Captain! I had thought your experience was confined to that of destinations closer to home. May I enquire as to the nature and outcome of your venture, as you are... most clearly, here to tell the tale?'

'Sir, I owed my Master at the time a deep debt of gratitude. He offered me an opportunity to pay that debt, to accompany him to the West Indies. I came to realise the adventure was in taking a ship-load of humanity on a long sea voyage.

'I did not think it an adventure, not in the least! It was a duty to my friend. I performed it to the best of my ability. However, I am not a slaver. I abhor slavery. I know it is a fact of life; I even understand the economic demands which make it necessary. That is all I can say.'

'Come, come! We none of us actually take pleasure from slavery. We may enjoy some of the economic benefits, but may I also say that, if you were to remain here

— at the very point of embarkation — you would soon see the true horror of this process.

'I have seen slaves shot down, sliced up, drowned, for simply resisting being shackled. I have seen full-grown bucks whimper like children in a heap on the ground, out of indignation, the horror of humiliation. No animal feels humiliation! Do what you will with a dog, a horse, or a pig, but that animal will not colour up, or bite into his own lip until blood flows down his face, out of pure indignation! Vacating the bowels in sheer terror is common. No, sir, this is the kind of unpleasant spectacle one becomes only too familiar with.'

Daemon was beginning to show his distaste once again for McGilvrait. 'You surprise me, sir. I thought exposure to this barbaric process for so long may have hardened up your attitude, or the attitude of any man. You must surely get used to it.'

'Sir Robert, Captain…' Routledge intervened, 'my daughter… please! I apologise, but we must turn the conversation.'

'We must indeed. Dignity forbids me from further troubling you, and I understand the ladies may feel a little offended. The truth is, I cannot wait to board my ship to return to England. The lowest rat in the lowest sewer is treated with more care and humanity than these here "slave" humans! One tribe despises another so much!'

Routledge had the last word. 'Sir, if I feel the slightest sense of regret at hearing these things, you must not misunderstand. I am here to do my job, to serve my country.'

'I know you will acquit yourself well, Sir James. However, please forgive me. I have had my fill!'

Routledge turned to Pasha Al Damas, sitting quietly at the far end of the table, the stately Arab appearing to be more interested in the generous fare which had been set before him.

Licking his lips and wringing his fingers, he suddenly belched loudly and nodded his head, showing much satisfaction.

'May I ask, er... Monsieur Al Damas, what is your own opinion of the traffic of human beings?'

Looking a little surprised at the question, the Pasha continued to clean off the last greasy remnants of his hearty meal, and, sucking his teeth, merely said, 'A necessary evil, I suggest.' At which he burped once more to express his gratitude to Sir Robert.

'Yes, I am sure we would all agree with that sentiment; but are you, how shall I put it, in any way involved in this trade?'

'I! Well, yes, I have to say I have been involved. Perhaps young Captain Quirk here might attest to my experience in these matters?'

Daemon immediately turned in his seat so that he could take in the full countenance presented by the Pasha.

'Er... sir? I do not think we have met. I would not venture to guess at where our paths may have crossed.'

'Ah... such is the passing of time and the fullness of experience which makes such significant encounters diminish to nothing in the mind of the young.

'However, perhaps you will recall a singular evening in the dim and distant past when you were wined and dined royally by certain associates of Sir John Standing. I do believe you and my two sons were among the party. I myself took something of a distant interest in the proceedings, excusing myself on grounds of ill humour from the frivolities of the occasion.'

'Sir, your two sons? Er, Ashti and Amoeba? Ah! I see. I do recall being introduced to a man such as yourself. A gentleman I assumed a member of the household. I do beg your pardon that I may not have recognised your position or importance. I beg ignorance as my only defence. I was very young and inexperienced back...'

'Quite! I am sure you now appreciate that perhaps we have things to discuss and that it is not mere coincidence that finds us once again under the same roof.'

'Er... yes! I do believe we have things to discuss. You will, no doubt, be aware of the fate of Sir John, and, I trust, will appreciate my intentions in bringing the *Durham* safely across the Atlantic.'

'Indeed! Perhaps you and I may find a quiet place in which to engage? We should not trouble the other guests with the small matter of business which exists between you and I.'

Routledge looked on, somewhat surprised. 'If I may be of any assistance to you in your affairs, then please allow me, as a man of law, to offer my services.'

'Oh, I think, Sir James, that there is nothing about which two old friends may not find a solution. Please, Captain, may I suggest we find our way into the rose-garden, where we may find a comfortable seat for our discussion.'

Daemon stood immediately, following the direction of the gesture in the knowledge that the Pasha knew the layout of the grounds better than himself.

Ariadne immediately rose to move to her father's side, with much concern showing in her demeanour. 'Father?'

'It's all right, my sweet, I am certain there is just a private matter between our esteemed guest and the Captain. Hey, Sir Robert, what do you say?'

'Oh, I do not think you should over-trouble yourself. Al Damas is a very civilised prince — not at all like his two hot-headed sons!'

Ariadne again appeared to be alarmed.

'The two sons, they are not here then?'

'Er... no! Indeed, they prefer the encampment. They are not, shall we say, as civilised as their father the prince!'

'The prince, you say...?'

'Er, yes, I do believe the Prince, or Pacha, as we will call him, has a prosperous domain of his own, which may one day become a kingdom as such.'

'What business do you think might concern Captain Quirk?'

'Slave business, I would vouch. I am sure we will soon all become acquainted with the issues which currently appear to be at the heart of the matter.'

Routledge stood, with Ariadne clinging to his arm.

'Sir Robert, may I enquire as to whether or not you were aware of there being a matter of business between our Captain and the Prince?'

'Sir James, please be calm. I merely welcomed an old acquaintance in my final days of duty here in Africa. I soon discovered that there is an incredible system of communication existing in the Arab world, which enables information, "news", shall we say, to travel much more quickly than a human being may traverse these oceans! It has long mystified me how such information may transmit at such speed, sometimes before the incident has yet to occur!

'It was the Prince who advised me of the name of the ship under who's sail you were being spirited to my shores. Also, the name of her Captain. A mystery, a thing of wonder, no less!'

'This must be of great value to a people which spends it's time in the nomadic state. So, Al Damas made his way here, with his sons, in order to encounter Daemon Quirk! How fascinating!'

'But, Father,' Ariadne interjected with some passion, 'you must please find out what is the matter and help the Captain! Please, Father, I beg of you.'

'Now then, dearest, I will not let any harm come to your young man! Do not worry, my dear; after all, this is Crown property. He is under our protection.'

'May I just mention, Sir James, there are occasions when I do feel we are here simply on sufferance of the local potentates and not by any means of power or authority,' McGilvrait spoke mischievously. 'We are a long way from home. I am sure Captain Quirk is capable of handling his own affairs, but it must be stressed that should there be an historic, shall we say, *disagreement* between the two, there is not an awful lot one can do! We are not equipped to wage war against the natives, I am afraid!'

'Sir Robert, I would bid you take a care of my friend. We are the "Crown", and as my friend in Rabat was avenged, then so would my family and myself should things turn out badly. The wrath of the British nation would be turned upon these dominions.'

'And yet they lie in shallow graves, your friends in Rabat! The perpetrators themselves may have escaped all attention and dissolved into the hinterland. Certainly, some punishment was inflicted, but did it deter resistance or revolt? I think we may know the answer very soon!'

'Come, my dear, Ladies please! I trust you have not been too distressed, my dear. Please go along with Ariadne, settle down for the night. I wish to seek out the garrison commander and have a few words with him about our defences.

'Sir Robert, may I thank you for a surprisingly fine dinner, and an evening of great stimulation? I trust we may have one or two further opportunities to debate the future of the British abroad? The "British Empire", might I suggest, is beginning to express itself around the world! We will not fail in our part to carry out the wishes of the Crown to the greater good.'

Routledge ushered his womenfolk off to their chambers, anxious to remove himself from the company of McGilvrait. He made stealthily towards the terrace, where the Pasha and Daemon Quirk were now in deep conversation.

Routledge was able to observe from a distance through the heavy foliage of a series of palm trees and over-flowing terrace planters.

The Prince stood leaning across the table, his fist balled and waving generally towards Daemon at eye level.

Routledge could not make out what was being said, but he knew by all expressions that an intense discussion was being held by two protagonists in full flow.

Routledge made his decision to intervene and attempt to impose his own influence on the proceedings.

Walking forward, he alerted them to his arrival with a growling in his throat that resonated across the terrace.

Daemon rose, and both men then turned towards Routledge.

'Gentlemen, perhaps a glass of port and some fine tobacco might help in determining a solution to your dilemma? May I be of assistance?'

'Sir James, please, this matter must be settled between myself and our friend.' The Pasha spoke, extending due courtesy.

'Surely you will allow me to lend my learned ear. I may be of some use in arbitration.'

'Your servant, Sir James. I find that our friend the Captain is not as co-operative as he might be, given the circumstances.'

'In what way, Pasha? How may he be able to assist?'

'Tell him, Captain. I ask you! Please enlighten our learned friend as to the circumstance.'

'Sir James, Pasha Al Damas owns a three-quarter share of the *Durham*. He funded the voyage to the West Indies and awaits his profit, and the return of his ship. I maintain...'

'If I may interrupt the Captain with his forgiveness! My arrangements were made with Sir John Standing, a man of repute. He was equipped with a fine ship, a cargo of the finest African flesh, and a fair wind. He was to return via Europe, with a handsome profit, to be equally divided between myself, my half-brother in Agadir, and Sir John himself.'

Daemon responded, 'This is what I have been trying to explain... John is dead! I had to take charge of the ship! He passed on his interests to myself with his dying breath. There were problems. Problems which required *gold* to resolve! The profit that was anticipated could not be achieved.

'We are fortunate that the *Durham* survived. That we lived to tell the tale! That any cargo was returned on the homeward leg of our journey.

'I am absolutely happy to turn over the ship and what is left of the profit of the voyage. I can provide very precise documents as evidence of what occurred in the Slave Auctions of Barbados and Trinidad and Tobago. Then, when the ship was purloined by the actions of mutineers, how I have made every effort to recover the ship and complete my mission.'

'There is only one problem, Sir James,' Al Damas interjected. 'The profit appears to be less worth than a camel with a punctured belly! A lot of time and anticipation has been expended by myself and my family! We have the comfort of knowing that our assets are spread about in a number of lucrative ventures; however, the purchase of a fine ship and the cost of filling that vessel with prime African stock is not an insignificant commitment! We demand our reward! We demand retribution!'

'Pasha, please let us be rational. What form would this retribution take if financial matters were not to be abridged?'

'I'm afraid Captain Quirk would make good his debt in kind! He must forfeit his freedom; and, subject to a tribunal, even forfeit his life.'

'May I interrupt those thoughts and dismiss them at once? There will be no such retribution brought down upon the Captain, a subject of his Majesty King George II, I assure you, Pasha! A dead man is in no position to pay

425

his debts! I am sure you would agree. Captain Quirk now has a benefactor, who may make good his deficit, or even subsidise his recovery.'

'How would such a recovery be possible? The Captain is of slender means; he has admitted as much to myself this very evening.'

'There are many ways of achieving satisfaction, Pasha. Please, let us show some compassion. Captain Quirk is a young man. A fine young man, of good moral fibre! I would trust him to undertake any task, with every sinew of his body stretched in order to achieve his objectives! *I* would subsidise Captain Quirk!'

Daemon rose to his feet, having absorbed what had been said. 'Sir James, I cannot let you stand for my indebtedness. It is morally wrong. I have to face whatever fate has chosen for me. I was fully intent on seeking out John Standing's partners and giving an account of how their investment had all but foundered — how I managed, only by the grace of God, to have returned with the vessel.'

The Pasha spoke again, 'Captain, I will have great difficulty in restraining my sons in the event that our reward is not forthcoming. I am sure you understand my predicament. We have waited many months for your return. Although I have no evidence to suggest you would not have honoured the agreement, I have nothing to show for my patience.'

'What would you suggest? I have little to offer and will not accept Sir James' proposal to finance me. Such an obligation would be a burden upon my relationship with... Sir James' family.'

'I fear you have but two choices. You return the *Durham* to my own keeping and place yourself at the calling of my family. I cannot guarantee the outcome, but the least you can expect is to work-off your indebtedness over a period of years. *Or* you could undertake a new enterprise. I have three hundred and sixty Africans ready for transportation. The *Durham* is equipped and appears to be seaworthy. Your experience, gained on your last voyage, will enable you to maximise our profits.'

'Sir, may I interrupt by saying that the last thing on this earth I would wish to do is transport another cargo of human beings, against their will, to a new world. I could barely contain my revulsion at the process and would never have considered repeating the experience.'

'You have little choice, my friend. You take this cargo to Jamaica, or someone else will! I admire your humanity more than you would imagine. I believe my cargo will be in much better hands if you captain the ship. I regret that losses are almost too much to bear with some of the less scrupulous Masters!'

'I dare not contemplate another voyage; my sanity would be at stake.'

Sir Robert felt he had to intervene. 'Pasha, please, Captain Quirk is a capable seaman — he may choose to spend his life on the high seas, but you can see that his conscience makes it an extremely difficult choice... Perhaps we would do better to sleep on this issue and return to it in the cold light of morning. You have my word that Daemon will be the beneficiary of my advice overnight.'

'I agree, Sir James. I will take my leave. Whilst I have the offer of accommodation within the fort, I prefer to return to my encampment and advise my sons of the situation. I will return on the morrow and our discussion will resume. I bid you goodnight.'

Pasha Al Damas left the courtyard aboard a fine golden stallion, accompanied by two outriders on jet-black mounts. In a cloud of dust, they disappeared, the sound of their departure absorbed by the echoes of night.

'Daemon, my boy, you appear to have little choice but to undertake another voyage. I could offer you some most able and trustworthy soldiers to support you on the voyage. You may also supplement your own crew with any number of seafarers you may find here in the compound...'

'Sir James, I thank you for your support. I am not afraid to face my adversary. I would take my chances. But I could not live with the threat that would hang over you and your family should I decide to challenge the Prince and his two sons. It may bring retribution down upon the Fort. For the sake of Ariadne, of whom, you may have come to realise, I am very fond, I am not prepared to put her at risk.'

'Do not concern yourself too much about our position. We are well fortified, and the garrison is strengthened by our arrival.'

'Yes, but look what happened at Rabat. It took a flotilla from England containing almost two thousand troops to take charge of that situation. The loss of the lives of my friends will weigh heavily upon me until my dying day. Whilst I have one request, I would make of you. I believe the son of my friend John Standing has survived and as you mentioned, resides in England, with his family. The sale of the cargo in England *did* make some profit, which I did not declare to the Prince. I would place a sum into your hands in the knowledge that whatever happens, it will one day reach the child'

'You will go, then? If it has to be, you may rely upon me to see the bequest completed'

'Yes, I will go. I thank you with all my heart. So, as the Pasha implied, the slaves will be transported one way or another. I will give them better treatment than most of the slave captains. God forgive me, but I must go. You will take care of Ariadne? I know it is a stupid thing to ask, but let us be certain of one thing, I do hope...!'

'She will be heartbroken.'

'I do believe she may, but this is the only way I can guarantee her safety, your safety.'

The two men shook hands and Routledge pulled Daemon towards him, embracing him like a father.

Preparations were made, the ship re-stocked, the human cargo loaded up; and, despite Daemon's running battle with the Arabs, the numbers packed into the bowels of the *Durham* were too great, ensuring that the voyage would be a difficult one to say the least.

The Pasha's sons arrived, getting involved with the preparations and showing unrestricted levels of cruelty. Daemon had in mind to get this process over with as quickly as possible and get under way. Resisting the inclination to strike down Amoeba almost upon sight, the morning of their departure could not come soon enough.

Sadly, fate had one more twist in store for Daemon.

The ship stood off-shore and hung heavily, loaded to the gunnels with cargo and supplies, and the tide turned, indicating that the moment had come.

Daemon had only one thought on his mind. To make a good parting with Ariadne and leave nothing left unsaid. The two embraced at the water's edge. Sir James strode towards Daemon and again embraced him in a sincere farewell.

Suddenly, a cloud of dust on the horizon indicated a flurry of activity and four fine stallions, decorated with bells and ribbons and over-slung with bright strips of whitened calf skin appeared.

The Pasha and his sons, accompanied by a fine, muscled henchman, turbaned and glistening in the morning sun, dismounted and approached the group on the mooring.

'Captain, I have come to wish you God-speed and to present your two lieutenants for the voyage. My son Amoeba and his bodyguard and cousin, Sofiane.'

Daemon's heart sank at this announcement. All his worst imaginings materialised in a moment. He despised Amoeba, and now he would suffer his ways for a period of time when conscience and humanity would be tested, even in the best of conditions.

Pasha Al Damas had the last word before all three leapt from the jetty into the waiting boat. 'My son, come home to your father, who will be waiting for you as a man deprived of water in the desert.

'Captain Quirk, I urge you to make good time, return my ship and the rewards of this voyage and your tablet will be wiped clean. And if my son returns safe to these shores, you will have my debt of gratitude and much personal reward, perhaps with which to prepare for a life with your first wife!'

'My only wife I trust, and yes, Pasha, I will return, though your son's fate is in his own hands!'

Daemon turned once more to Ariadne, but all the words had been said.

The boat pushed off with Daemon standing at the prow and looking out to sea.

The weather held fair, and the ship lurched into the breeze. And so,
another epic voyage awaited Daemon, destination the *Caribbean*.

Baltimore Book 3

Dieter Van Gahl lined up his aim and released an explosive discharge from his musket. Forty-five yards away two crows tossed about in the air and fell unceremoniously to the ground, each with the lightest of thuds. A ten years old boy in britches and braces, bright red in colour contrasting with his chocolate brown skin, raced barefoot into the cane fields to retrieve the dead birds.

Van Eyck, called out toward his companion 'Damned fine shot Dieter!' That should be enough for the time being — we must have cleared two dozen of the damn creatures. I hope the others are suitably impressed and defer from attacking our crops at least for a short while.'

'Thank you, Father! I am only too pleased to help — and of course it keeps my 'eye' sharp. At least I will not be found wanting in the event of an invasion.'

'Well Dieter — you know we have enjoyed the peace here for a long time. Although — I will say that one day it may not be an invasion we fear. But these Africans — they are growing smarter. Too damned smart for their own good, some of them. We have to keep them in line. I have never intended cruelty — but you cannot trust them. Sooner or later they will turn on us. Like an ungrateful dog might one day bite it's master.'

'I am sure we will manage if there is any attempt at insurrection.''

'Let us hope so, my son. Let us return to the house. I am sure your betrothed is eager for our company — well at the very least for yours.'

Baltimore. Book 3 will be published in 2020.